The Lost Gospel of Barabbas
The Thirteenth Apostle

PART III
"REVELATION"

THE LOST GOSPEL OF BARABBAS:
THE THIRTEENTH APOSTLE
PART III (Revelation)
Copyright 2019 by Kevin L. Brooks
All rights reserved

Cover Art by Jason Bell
Formatting by Polgarus Studio

ISBN: 978-0-9960112-2-8

This book was written, edited, published and produced in the United States of America
Made in the USA

Letter to my Readers

In your hands, you hold the third installment of the Lost Gospel of Barabbas Series. If you have not read Part I or Part II, I highly encourage you to do so before continuing with this book. This novel represents the third part of the story of the notorious insurrectionist found in the pages of the Bible. Faced with numerous distractions and in-depth research, it took me years to spin this tale. I sought to be as accurate as possible in telling my story. This book is a work of fiction. However, the time, the culture, the places and many of the people you meet are very real. The story is told from the lips of Barabbas himself. As a real historical figure, he gives us an eye witness account of the world in which he lived, a world ruled by the cruelty of the Roman Empire. On this journey, you will learn what drove him and what haunted him. We will follow Barabbas throughout this series as he travels all the way to his ultimate fate and his destiny as described in the Gospels.

Enjoy!
Kevin

INTRODUCTION

Professor Hershel D. Moussaieff slammed the car door. His heart pounded as he gripped the steering wheel. His knuckles turned white. Frustration swirled around him. He watched as Deborah and her attorney crossed the parking lot. The attorney placed his hand on her back as he helped her into his car, a black Aston Martin DB11. *God,* he thought to himself, *I hate him. That arrogant little bastard. He was so full of himself, so condescending.* Hershel fantasized about killing him. He could start his car and plow him over right here, right now. Of course, he would go to prison, but it would be worth it. What else did he have to live for? She had taken everything from him. After 25 years, she just up and walked out. She said he had changed. Of course, he had changed. She too had changed. Everyone had changed. They weren't the young idealistic youth who had met in America all those years ago.

Hershel removed his glasses. He rubbed his red eyes. *How had we arrived here? What had brought us to this place?* He thought they were happy, or at least content. Till she started complaining about his work. "Those scrolls are your mistress," she said. It became constant, the bickering. He grew tired, too tired to argue.

I give up, he thought. Hershel exhaled. The sound of escaping breath resounded. His life was complicated. He rubbed his temples. A raging headache was coming on. He could feel it. His pulse throbbed in his head along with his resentment. It clung to him, like a spider. He couldn't help it. Disappointment filled his soul. After all, he still loved her. Twisting the rearview mirror, he stared into bloodshot eyes. They burned. He looked like hell. He ran his fingers through his hair. It was grayer now than just a few years ago, the years before the scrolls. Five years ago, Hershel and his team of archaeologists from the Hebrew University of Jerusalem had uncovered the greatest archaeological find in 70 years. In a cave near Khirbet Qumran by the Dead Sea, they found several clay pots filled with the scrolls. At first, Deborah was so proud. She was the supportive wife, his greatest champion.

Hershel took it upon himself to personally translate the Aramaic and Greek text. He dared not trust anyone else. He became obsessed with his findings – the personal memoirs of a man claiming to be the notorious insurrectionist, Barabbas. He found the story to be beyond belief. History had left little evidence as to this man's identity outside the Bible. If these scrolls proved to be true, it would change history forever. Skeptical at first, Hershel immersed himself into his work. It had consumed him, devouring everything in his life. He became obsessed. The scrolls occupied all of his time to the point of neglect, neglect of his family, and neglect of his wife.

Gaining worldwide recognition, he became a celebrity. Professor Hershel D. Moussaieff became a household name. Hershel was invited to speak around the globe. He appeared on every major cable news channel from Fox News, CNN, Discovery and the National Geographic Channel. He was quoted and interviewed in newspapers around the planet. During Hershel's rise to fame, Deborah was slowly left behind in his shadow. Like two ships in the night, they drifted apart. Deborah fell into a state of depression. Hershel was oblivious as the current carried her downstream. When his eyes were opened and he realized her plight, he knew it was a dark and lonely place. How unloved and unwanted one could feel. He watched the resentment grow in her like a cancer.

Likewise, Hershel felt unappreciated. His obsession with the scrolls had left him with little to no sleep. His discoveries were heavily scrutinized by his academic peers. Some criticism was warranted; some rose out of sheer jealousy. He had a growing sense of anxiety. Suspicion raised its ugly head. Paranoia crawled through his veins. He began to see things, things that didn't belong, things that weren't there. Now the Professor was questioning his own sanity. He feared that his own mind had been poisoned. And of course, there were those ravens, the ravens. At first Hershel thought his mind was playing tricks. Maybe it was simply the reading of the scrolls, but now he noticed them all of the time, large black birds. They plagued him daily. Deborah's anger didn't help either. It manifested itself through her words. They were bitter and laced with venom. An irrational and unreasonable feeling of suspicion and distrust poisoned their marriage. It had all begun with those scrolls.

Hershel's phone vibrated. He glanced down and saw the smiling face of Deborah. He had not changed his screensaver. She remained there, smiling, waiting for him to unlock his phone. It vibrated again. Another text. He ignored it. Slowly he swiped his finger across the face. He touched the icon revealing his photo gallery. He was greeted with the smiling face of his 5-year-old grandson. *Oh my God*, he thought, how he loved that little boy so much. He was the love of his life. He couldn't even express it in words. With a swipe, another picture opened. It was his whole family, both of his sons and their wives. The boys wore tuxedos. They were seated at a dinner table covered with a white linen table cloth. A crystal bowl overflowing with white lilies sat in the middle of the table. Their dessert plates sat empty before them. Deborah stood between the boys who were seated. She leaned forward in a revealing low-cut evening gown. She was still a striking woman for her age. Hershel touched the screen tenderly. He recalled that night. He had received the most prestigious award, "Archeologist of the Year," from the world-renowned International Archeology Institute. He had been honored, but the greatest honor had been having his family with him. Tears filled his eyes as he drifted back to happier times.

A strange thought occurred to Hershel. Barabbas' wife had been taken from him. She had been ripped away leaving a gaping hole in his heart. Now Deborah had been taken away from him. *Of course, it was different*, he thought, *she left of her own will. She had abandoned him.* Yet, he was left with an overwhelming feeling of guilt, a feeling that he should have done something different. Over the last several years, Hershel had developed a strange kinship with the man in the scrolls. He had come to admire the man.

He felt what he felt. An empathy grew within his heart with each passing day. Although separated by thousands of years he felt they were kindred spirits. They were of the same mind, of the same blood and of the same tribe. He yearned to know the man more.

The phone vibrated again. Another text. It was from his office at the University. Quickly, he swiped the pictures away. He must get back to his office. He must resume his work of translating the ancient texts and the words of Barabbas. He must get back to the scrolls. As he drove away, a single black raven watched from his perch.

PROLOGUE

How had I arrived here? What had brought me to this place? I found myself perched in a cleft in the rocks set above a small village. The quarter moon lit the Eastern sky and the stars burned against a dark curtain. Next to me sat a massive black raven. It was perched on a large rock and was fixated on the village. We both stared into the village below us. I watched helplessly from the shadows as Roman soldiers ravaged the poor people of this country village. Women screamed and wailed as their men were savagely beaten. The cries of the little children rose up the canyon walls and echoed throughout the hill country of Ephraim. Standing outside of a burning home, a commanding officer was silhouetted before the flames. Facing the surrounding ridges, he screamed out a single word. "Barabbas!"

CHAPTER 1

I was living in Capernaum with my father-in-law, Jarviss, and his family. Although content, my heart was anxious and a deep longing filled my soul. Last night, I found myself standing in my empty chuppah, a sad and lonely place. Within the walls of our little house, I was visited by my beloved wife, as I had been before. A dazzling blue light danced across the water jar that was our wedding gift. I'd heard the voice of Melessa. *You have a purpose, Barabbas. Go fulfill your purpose.* Following the ghostly encounter with my dead wife, I had made up my mind. I would leave Capernaum. I would obey God's will. I would pursue my destiny, my mysterious purpose. Whatever it might be, it still eluded me and filled me with fear.

This morning, I announced my departure to the whole family. Jarviss teared up. He placed a small leather pouch in my hand. It felt heavy with coins. I tried to refuse, but he insisted that I take it with me. Graciously, I gave them my thanks as I gathered my belongings. Many tears were shed as we said our goodbyes. Yet, peace had settled in my bones. I had a purpose, although it still eluded me, I felt its calling.

Leaving Capernaum, I headed north. I followed the rocky shoreline as waves washed ashore. A cool breeze blew across the water. A strong fishy smell was carried on the wind that morning, the smell of the Galilee. Leaving the great lake, I followed the river into the upper Galilee valley toward the ancient hills and mountains of Naphtali. Crossing several creeks swollen and running from the recent rains, I traveled north along the river to the Hula valley and

Lake Semechonitis, called the Waters of Merom. The entire marshland was flooded, more so than I had ever seen it. There, thousands and thousands of birds were gathered. The joining of their songs deafened like the roar of a rushing waterfall. Wildlife of all kinds abounded in great quantities. The waters were teeming with life. On the far distant horizon, my old friend Mount Hermon loomed. It was a hazy silhouette set against a bruised purple sky. Even a good twenty miles away, it dominated the horizon.

I decided to stay at Lake Semechonitis for several more days and hunt the prevalent game. I found an overhanging rock formation that formed a natural hollow in the mountain and built a shelter. Next, I built small fish and bird traps along the edge of the river. I would check these each morning.

Over the following days, I managed to catch several fish but not a single bird. During the day, especially during the early mornings, I would stalk prey that came to the water's edge to drink. I managed to ambush and kill two antelope and deer. After building a crude drying rack, I gutted and cleaned the game. I salted the meat with a small amount of salt that I had brought with me. Because the days were quite cool, I let each slab hang in the shade for a few days before boning out the meat. I cut the meat into small strips and hung it on the rack to dry. For several more days, I constantly had to feed the fire to aid in the drying process. It was a tedious chore, but it was worth the effort. The meat had a sweet delicious smoky flavor. I intended to carry the dried meats into the towns and villages to sell on my way to see Samuel and Ruth. Deer and antelope all bring a good price.

It was on one of those days, while I was tending to the fire when two young men approached. They stopped at my camp. They were from Capernaum and on their way to Caesarea Philippi. They were no more than boys, both of them quite young. This was their first trip alone without their parents. They said that they were from fishing families. I inquired, discovering that they both knew Jarviss and his entire family, I did not share with them my true identity, feeling that it was better to keep that information to myself. I invited the boys to stay with me for the evening and I offered them some venison straps. Neither of them had ever eaten deer meat before and it was quite a treat for them. In turn, they shared their bread and wine and stories of their families. Their fathers were partners in a fishing business and they owned several boats together. I discovered that they, like their fathers, were zealots for the Lord. That evening we enjoyed each other's company. It was very pleasant. It was odd for me having guests, as I prefer being alone in the wilderness. But I enjoyed their company very much.

The following morning, we shared breakfast and the boys departed. Afterward, I ran my traps to see if I had caught anything. I had not. The rest of the day was spent tending to the meat and the drying process. All that day I watched the sky as huge white billowing clouds formed to the south and west. A cold breeze filled the air in the valley. The meat was almost finished so I began to gather it into cloth bundles just in case it rained. By nightfall, I had completed my task. Next, I set to prepare my shelter for rain, just as Samuel had taught me all those years ago. I recall seeing lightning illuminate the clouds with a burst of orange light. The clouds burned for the briefest moment and were soon extinguished. The thunder rumbled off in the distance that evening, as the sun began to set.

When the darkness fell across the land, a gentle and soft rain began to fall. I stood in the rain enjoying the sweet smell and let the drops splash across my face. Opening my mouth, I tried to catch falling raindrops on my tongue. A memory from my childhood washed through my mind. A memory of Mother and I walking along the shore of the Galilee during a spring shower. She would open her mouth skyward, catching raindrops on her tongue. "Try it," she said with a playful laugh as she smiled and looked toward Heaven.

Without warning, the peaceful night was shattered. Ripping through the night's cool air were the sounds of horrified screams. Startled, I gathered my sword and bow. I was on guard for danger. But none came. I heard it again, a bloodcurdling scream off in the distance. This time it was followed by a rumble of thunder. Without thinking, I was on my feet and running through the short brush and tall grasses that met the foot of the mountains.

CHAPTER 2

I ran for a long way. The rain fell on me as my lungs burned, struggling for air. Fighting the brush, I finally spotted a fire off in the distance. Cautiously, I approached and saw a very large fire and camp, unquenched by the rain. Several figures surrounded the bonfire. This was the origin of the horrible screams; they filled the air. As I approached, I fell to my belly and tried to control my breathing. Each breath was very labored. I tried to calm it, controlling each inhalation. Another scream arose into the night air. Crawling across drenched ground for a better look, the figures began to take shape.

Roman soldiers were gathered at this camp. At least fifteen to twenty of them were visible to me. They were drunk, so drunk they could hardly stand. One tripped and stumbled. He almost fell into the fire once.

Another agonizing scream pierced the night. In the glowing corona of fire, a gruesome scene unfolded. The two boys from Capernaum, who had stopped at my camp the night before, were there. They had been stripped naked. Soldiers surrounded them, laughing. The two young men had been captured. Now, they were being tortured by these Roman monsters. *Why?* I thought to myself, *What had these two gentle boys done?* One of them hung by his neck from a rope tied to the upper branches of a tree. His neck must have been broken;it stretched in a sickening and unnatural position. His body was a bloody mess. He must have been beaten before he was hung. On his face, a terrified expression froze in time. In the eerie light of the fire, his body swung back and forth in a macabre dance. "God damn you, bastards." I whispered under my breath.

Lightning flashed. A bolt of fire split the night's sky. The world was momentarily lit. It was bright as day, but only for a brief instant, temporarily blinding me, stealing my night vision. My eyes slowly adjusted. Yellow light danced before the fire casting wicked shadows. Suddenly, I noticed a large raven sitting high atop the branches of the hanging tree. It's head swiveled from the hanged boy beneath him towards me. He stared at me. Ice filled my veins. As my eyes continued to adjust to the darkness, several more of the hideous and wicked bat-like raven creatures appeared. Harbingers. Creatures that I have come to associate with evil.

Grandmother Ala's words swept through my mind, *Barabbas, never look at them! Never look directly at them. Never! Do you understand?* Memories of that day washed over me, memories of that day long ago when I learned of my cursed gift. Memories of my grandmother filled my heart. A worried look had filled her face. *What do you mean? What are they?* I had asked.

Barabbas, Yakiri, you have a gift. You have a gift that no one else has. It is a gift from the Lord.

What does that mean? I had questioned her further.

You are special, Barabbas, you have the sight. You can see things that other people can't.

She had explained that my Grandfather Barechiah had the same sight. She had told of his visions and his gift, *Your grandfather knew things. Sometimes he would see demons or evil spirits. I saw the fear in him. He claimed the spirits ignore us and they did not realize he could see them. He did not want them to know that he could see them either. He thought it was best that way. Never look at them, Barabbas, never. Look away. Do you understand?*

Another flash of lightning ripped across the sky. Its violence brought me back to the present.

Ravens were perched high on the upper limbs. Others dangled from the same branches as the hanged boy. One even perched atop the boy's shoulder. Their ragged leathery wings flapped ungracefully. Their wicked eyes glowed red in the black night. I watched this horde of hellish phantoms. Their blackened silhouettes clung to the dark night. I glared at them with contempt and hatred in my heart. I could feel their demonic stares watching back at me from the darkness. I knew of their presence. They knew of mine and they welcomed me.

Another scream shattered the night. It was the other boy. Although it was hard to see, firelight reflected in the glisten of sweat and blood on his brutally beaten form. The night was illuminated by another bolt of lightning. It shattered the black clouds across the sky. As bright as day, I could see the poor boy was tied spread eagle to a large dead stump. His appearance was nothing like something human, but more like a grotesque and hideous monster. Several of the Roman soldiers gathered around him. They were cutting something. His fingers one at a time, then his manhood. My stomach turned. I could hear the boy screaming from my hiding place, well over 100 steps away. My blood boiled. He was just a child. The soldiers laughed, jovial and fun. It brought back more memories. A coppery taste filled my throat and mouth. I wretched and emptied the contents of my stomach.

The laughter of the Roman soldiers echoed in my memory. They had killed my Mother and Papa. I had stood in the doorway, paralyzed with fear. I remembered everything, every detail. What I remember the most was the laughter. All four of the soldiers had laughed, louder, and louder, and louder until I felt my head would explode. As a child, I had placed my hands over my ears and screamed, *Get off of her! Get off of her!* I had screamed as loud as my lungs would allow. I'll never forget the look on my mother's face. She had turned and looked straight at me; the expression on her face had been one of sheer terror. *Barabbas, run! Please, Barabbas, run!* That was the last thing she'd said before she had swung the sword, slicing the soldier's face from ear to ear. I had watched his rage, plunging his sword into my mother's chest, pinning her to the table.

Another thunderclap brought me to the present. My anger escalated and I was filled with hatred, red hot hatred. Hatred for these men before me. Hatred for these animals who had murdered my parents. Hatred for the ones who had killed my wife and child. Hatred for all of Rome. Hatred for this world. Hatred.

This was my purpose. It had been revealed to me. I was God's messenger. I was God's Avenging Angel.

More screams filled the night as the boy begged for mercy. The night rocked with a rumbling thunderclap. It rolled across the night's sky and shook the Earth. Reaching into my quiver, I removed an arrow. Running the feathers through my lips, I licked the fletching. Taking careful aim, I raised my bow, pointing high into the air. *Aim high,* I thought to myself. My bowstring felt heavier than it ever had before. When I released the arrow, a quiet whistle cut through the night's sky, a thousand tiny orbs of water sprayed from my string. I watched as the shaft of death arched long with perfect gracefulness. However, I missed my intended target. My arrow found one of the soldiers instead. It pierced him through his back, probably through his liver. His screams mixed with the boys as he fell to his knees in burning agony. He frantically attempted to remove the shaft but to no avail. *Good. May God damn you to Hell, you bastard.*

Quickly, I nocked another arrow. Taking aim, I let it fly. It found its mark in another soldier. The soldier jumped backwards and stumbled, screaming as he flailed his arms above his head. In his hand, he held some part of the boy's body. A huge spray of red hot embers exploded upward into the night's sky as the soldier fell backwards into the fire. The fiery embers erupted like a volcano twenty feet upward into the black sky. As that son of a bitch tossed in pain and tried to gain his feet, his clothing burst in flames. A sadistic sense of satisfaction jolted through me. I smiled.

I nocked another arrow and was preparing to release it when something else caught my eye. I saw dozens of the raven creatures circling the fire. Strangely, they were more illuminated by the darkness rather than by the flames. They darted between each of the soldiers. They moved with incredible speed. The group of soldiers panicked. They were filled with confusion, a mass hysteria. I watched as several began to scramble out of sight, pushing and knocking each other down, while others stood motionless and dumbfounded. I actually heard several continue to laugh as if this was great fun. *Drunken fools!* I thought, *go straight to Hell.*

I couldn't let the boy suffer. I aimed the arrow high. This was a perfect aim, as graceful and swift as a falcon in flight. It found its mark perfectly. His screaming stopped immediately. His pain ended, my arrow buried into his heart. I brought him mercy. I brought him peace.

I jumped from my rock hiding place and raced for the cover of the thicker trees. Within moments, armed soldiers were searching through the thick underbrush in a wide arch. Quickly, they regrouped and fanned out. I was strangely impressed that two had already reached my former hiding place. Hunching as low as I could, I ran from one tree or bush to another trying to make my way back toward my camp. The cover of darkness was my ally. One thing Samuel had not forgotten to teach me – know when you are outnumbered and know when to run.

Pausing at the edge of thick brush, I released several more arrows into the oncoming Romans. I hit two, wounding if not killing them. With another assault of arrows, I moved to another spot retreating from the last. It forced the soldiers to seek cover and delay their attack. Moving into the thicker brush behind me, they quickly spread out. I managed to shoot another arrow into one more of these filthy gentiles as I fled for the trees. I hit him high in the thigh. Blood spurted as he tried to pull the arrow free. He stumbled and fell. He managed to get back to his feet once more before he fell. I feared his screams would draw the others my direction. I ran. My only thought was, *I hope I cut your femoral artery, you bastard.*

The rain began to fall harder, bringing with it a darker night sky. The heavy drops stung like pellets of lead as they beat down upon me, but thankfully, this provided me with good cover as I retreated. Pushing my way through the thicker trees, a dark silhouette suddenly appeared and stood in front of me. I stopped short as the black outline of a man blocked my way. His outstretched arms reached toward me. Instinctively, I withdrew my sword. Its weight felt good. The sword came to life in my hands. The man stood at least a head taller than me, maybe more. He did not move at first. He just stood there blocking my way. As I prepared to strike, a strange feeling came over me. The temperature plummeted to a blistering cold. The acrid smell of death filled my nostrils, like the scent of a decaying corpse. In a long, slow methodical movement, the hooded figure grew taller right before my eyes. A pale white featureless face peered from the shadow of his hood. Wicked dark eyes stared into mine. Eyes that were dead. They were empty and as black as burned coal. Small glowing embers began to burn in the very centers. They flickered. It was the burning fires of Hell. Other than his eyes, the pale face was featureless, no mouth or nose. Just those wicked black eyes against taut pale dead flesh.

His neck swiveled in a grotesque manner, struggling as his skin stretched and a slit tore open for a mouth. Working his jaw bone back and forth, he opened his mouth impossibly wide. Rows and rows of wicked sharp teeth lined his black gums, like thousands of tiny fish hooks lined in rows. Long gray strings of a thick saliva dripped from his lips and chin. A horrible blackish gray tongue escaped his mouth, forked like a serpent's. The tongue itself reminded me of a writhing snake. It licked at his torn lips before returning back down his throat. A wicked grin formed across his distorted face. Throwing his head back, he howled with the booming thunder. The phantom began to quiver violently. His cloak opened, spread and tore apart as huge tattered leathery wings rose and spread wide. They reached high into the treetops.

I stood paralyzed. "Great God save me!" I called out.

Without warning, a blinding bolt of lightning tore across the sky. The thunder was immediate and shook the very pillars of the Earth. Without warning, this creature of Hell shattered like breaking glass. A loud tinkling sound with almost musical qualities could be heard, even above the beating rain. The phantom exploded into hundreds of the smaller raven creatures. A wild flurry of beating wings surrounded me, like a swarm of giant bats. They each scattered, disappearing into the night leaving nothing behind. Tongues of fire ripped through the heavens and illuminated the night. Immediately behind this demonic apparition, appeared a Roman soldier. He charged me with his sword held high above his head. He was already upon me. He attacked viciously, his sword already swinging downward. *Damn,* I cursed myself. He was fast and fell upon me, as I had not seen his approach for the devilish distraction. Without thinking, I reacted. It was primal instinct. Samuel's teachings flowed through me. I dropped to the ground and rolled through the mud toward him rather than away. His blade narrowly missed me. I swung my own sword with all of my might, but not upward as he would expect. Rather, I swung horizontal to the ground, catching him unprotected. I cut him off at the ankles. He toppled forward screaming in agony as he fell face first into the black water and mud. He fell, footless, one foot still stuck in the thick sticky muck, his toes on the other twitching as blood mingled with the water and mud.

Wasting no time, I ran. I ran as fast as my legs would carry me. My heart was a hammer beating within my chest and my lungs burned. But I still ran. I ran for my life. Behind me, I could hear the screams and shouting as I fled. Thunder rolled across the heavens. Following the thickest corridor of trees, I managed to escape back to my camp along the rocky hills. And I encountered no other soldiers.

Without regard for the night, I gathered my belongings, including as much biltong as I could carry. I stuffed it all into my pack and roll. Wasting no time, I headed west into the mountains. The pouring rain cleansed the land and washed my tracks away, making it impossible to follow me. It also washed the blood of my enemies and the two Jewish boys down swirling streams of water. Their blood was swallowed into the bowels of the Earth.

It continued to rain for a week. The rains were both a hindrance and a blessing, as I was forced to travel much slower. It was incredibly slow. I was wet, cold, and miserable. It was almost impossible to build a fire. Two nights I went without. They were frigid miserable nights. The weather deteriorated, and wild game was rare. Despite the rain, I pressed on. I travelled for a couple of more days before coming to the small village that I called home.

CHAPTER 3

There, I found Samuel and Ruth, both well and in good spirits. It was a joyous reunion, filled with tears and laughter along with hugs and kisses. It was good to see these two strong souls. They were strong mentally as well as physically. Both of them looked great, appearing many years younger than their true ages. In fact, both looked better than they had the last time I saw them. My stepmother appeared thin, as if she had lost some weight. However, Samuel might have picked it up, appearing a bit thicker. But, Samuel was still as strong as an ox.

Even with the rain, the entire village all came out to greet me. That very night we had a great celebration. It was such a contradiction to the hellish encounter that I had recently experienced. This was a tight-knit community, like a family. It was wonderful seeing everyone. They were anxious to hear the stories of my travels. I shared some that very evening, but many other nights were filled with those stories.

I only shared the story of the Jewish boys and my attack on the Roman camp with Samuel and Ruth. The images of the poor boys haunted my mind. Their screams filled my dreams. I could still see the one boy swinging from the tree. The twisted and mangled branches lifted him skyward. His neck stretched grotesquely upward. These images were a permanent scar that I could not erase. Yet a small sense of gratification clung to it for the Roman blood that I had spilled. However, I did not speak of the ravens or the demonic presence to anyone, even to Samuel. I had a strange fear of being chastised, of being dismissed for such an unbelievable tale. Guilt hung over me for some strange reason. I could not put my finger on it, but I believed it was my lack of trust. I should have known better, for Samuel was the most righteous and trustworthy man that I had ever known.

Something strange dawned on me that night, something that I had never thought of before. I had no friends my own age from our home town. I never had. They were all either much older than me or they were much younger than me. Samuel had been not only a father to me but also my best friend. I had never actually thought about it. Either way, for the first time ever, this was revealed to me that night.

For several months I stayed with Samuel and Ruth. I helped them with the chores as well as repairs around the house. Samuel and I also helped several of the other people in town with repairs around their homes, especially the widows and elderly. I also helped Samuel around the Synagogue and I took up my old occupation as a scribe. The other men were happy to have me back, as I was as devoted to our work as they were.

On many occasions, Samuel and I ventured into the hills and the woods in search of game. The woods were green and beautiful this year due to the heavy rains. The grasses were unusually lush and thick. New growth abounded everywhere. Samuel pointed out the different varieties of plant life. The years had not slowed Samuel down one bit. He moved through the woods like a ghost. His woodcraft was amazing. Even at his age, his skill with a bow was unmatched. Together, we hunted deer or antelope. Each time, Ruth prepared and shared our quarries with our neighbors, as we did when I was a child; but Ruth always held back the hearts for our family. Samuel and I both loved deer heart.

Samuel always said, "From the heart, you receive the courage and strength of the animal. It also shows respect for the animal that gave his life for us to live."

On one such hunt, Samuel and I found ourselves sitting on top of our old familiar rock outcropping, surrounded by the black forest. Since we had approached in the early morning, it was still dark. A wonderful sense of remembrance came over me. Quietly I turned and admired this amazing man, this man who had made me who I am today. Deep lines formed crow's feet at the corners of each eye. His eyes themselves sparkled with a strength and wisdom rarely found. A strong feeling of respect and love filled my heart.

Something moved in the darkness. The quiet moment was disturbed. Low guttural growling and grunting could be heard. This was a sound that I had never experienced in the wilderness before. A fierce growl. It became even louder and more ferocious. It sounded terrifying and intimidating as the deep growls filled the dark woods. *What kind of beast was this? Was it a bear? Was it a lion? Was it some sort of monster?* I thought to myself. *Maybe it's a phantom from the spiritual realm.* Images of the demonic being standing in the dark woods filled my mind. His featureless face stared at me as the flesh ripped apart revealing his vicious mouth. He quivered violently as his cloak tore apart and leathery wings spread into the high branches. He shattered as hundreds of ravens burst forth. Anxiety rushed through me. My hands were slick with sweat. Gripping my bow, I braced myself.

It sounded like several more creatures were coming through the brush. I looked at Samuel with wide-eyed curiosity and concern. Ever so slowly, touching his nose with his index finger and raising his head slightly toward the wind, he indicated a scent. As a light breeze carried the scent our way, I noticed it – a strong urine scent mixed with vinegar and honey. The musky scent grew in intensity.

We listened to the beasts while they crunched and stomped through the woods, their scent growing stronger. Growls and grunts grew ever louder as the beasts grew closer. Soon the sun began its ascent into the morning sky. Beams of light pierced the black woods below us and a glow illuminated the forest floor. I was astonished at what I saw. At least two dozen shadowy creatures moved through the undergrowth. At first, I believed these might be some of the hellish spirit creatures or apparitions from my vision world. A sudden cold chill ran down my spine and I shivered. I noticed that Samuel was intently watching these beasts; he could see them too.

Samuel turned toward me. He uncovered his camouflaged face to reveal a huge grin. "Wild hogs!" he whispered.

I mouthed the words, "Wild hogs? Where'd they come from?"

"Probably Samaria," he whispered, "nothing good ever came from Samaria."

The light continued to spill through the canopy of trees. I could see better with each passing moment. On the forest floor below me was a herd of wild swine. A lot of them. It was hard to count as they were constantly moving. Between twenty and thirty, at least. Several bared their huge teeth and snapped at each other. Others jumped and squealed.

I had seen pigs before, back in Egypt, especially in the Greek territories, but they were lighter colored, some even white and pink. Those in Egypt also seemed fat and docile. These were not that way at all. Some of these wild hogs were massive, twice the size of a man. Ferocious and almost wicked in appearance, resembling some of the strange spirit creatures that I had seen in my visions. These however, were all covered in a thick black coarse hair. Short stocky legs supported large muscular shoulders and bodies. Several had large humps above their front shoulders that tapered toward their smaller back ends. Small beady eyes were set far back on their heads and appeared vigilant and alert to any danger, intelligent in a strange way. Their heads all seemed far too big for their own bodies. Their snouts were long and several yielded huge curved teeth that extended beyond their curled lips. These were grisly creatures.

Samuel bumped me with his elbow and motioned for me to raise my bow. I hesitated. Samuel motioned to me. I slowly rose to one knee, raised my bow, arrow at the ready. "You take the big one on the far right," he whispered. Obeying his command, I drew my string taut. I took aim at the largest sow. When I released my string, the pent-up energy all focused and transferred into my arrow. A soft thud launched it at an incredible speed. A quiet *whiiissshhhhh* was heard as the arrow sliced through the cool morning air. It buried itself deep into the hog's shoulder. She let out a loud squeal as she darted away into the dark undergrowth. At the same exact time, Samuel had also stuck an arrow into another large hog off to my left. It too let out a great squeal as it leapt and raced into the thickest brush. All of the hogs quickly scattered into the shadows of the forest floor. With incredible speed, Samuel nocked another arrow and sent it on its way. It found its mark on a smaller pig quartering away from us as it retreated into the brush. That pig fell dead in its tracks, kicking violently. I thought to myself how amazing this elder was, a weapons master. I had killed one hog and he had shot two.

These hogs were different from deer or antelope. Most of the time when a deer was shot at or even spooked, it would instantly drop several inches in its tracks as if ducking in place before dashing away to safety. Too often, my arrow had passed harmlessly over a deer's back. Samuel had always taught me to aim a little low on my target. Sometimes the deer would even hesitate and wait several seconds, out of curiosity, as if to get a better look at what had threatened them. The same was true of antelope. However, not with these hogs. At our disturbance, each one bolted straight ahead and with impressive speed. As they left, they crashed loudly through the brush, and then they were silent. Other than the squealing of the arrowed pigs, this large herd of swine disappeared silently into the thick underbrush. *How odd*, I thought to myself.

My heart beat wildly in my chest. Samuel was grinning from ear to ear. "That's my boy!" He said as he slapped me on the back.

"Are we going to track them?" I questioned with a puzzled look.

"Those nasty unclean beasts? Are you kidding?" he responded, still smiling.

"Well, I didn't know. You always said that we always eat our kills, but these are unclean."

Still grinning, Samuel leaned toward me, in a very serious voice he said, "Let the unclean eat the unclean." With that, he hopped down from the rock on which we were perched, with the agility of a cat.

After I climbed down, we walked over to the younger hog, lying dead before us. Bright crimson blood covered the intense green leaves and grasses where it had fallen. I poked the young boar with a large stick. It did not move. He stank terribly, the strong musky odor and urine scented on the wind earlier. Solid black, he was covered with a thick shaggy hair that was matted with dried mud. It had very sharp teeth, appearing like ivory. I opened and closed his jaws, noticing four prominent teeth sharpened themselves as they grinded against each other, like sharpening knives.. The two largest were set on his bottom row of teeth and extended beyond his lips even when his mouth was closed. He was a solid creature, very dense, as if made completely of muscle. "Samuel, if we were not going to eat these, then why did we kill them?"

A funny and surprised look came over his face as Samuel turned toward me. "Barabbas, I thought you would know."

I shrugged.

"These beasts are unclean. They are destructive animals. They root and plow up everything in sight. And now the rains have brought more of them." As he said this, he pointed to several places along the trails where it looked like someone had taken a shovel or a plow and dug up the earth and all the plants. These spots were large and deep with freshly upturned soil.

Samuel continued, "They destroy the crops and gardens at night. They destroy the woods. They chase off game. These beasts are aggressive and mean. I myself have seen a big boar hog attacking and killing deer, especially fawns. I have even heard of them killing young sheep and goats. Some say they will even attack humans, although I have not seen it myself."

I stared at him with disbelief.

"It's true, last year a man from Thelia was attacked. He never saw the charge coming. He was gathering water at a stream when something attacked him from the tall grass. It was a large hog. The beast knocked him to the ground and mauled him. Kicking and punching the hog, the man managed to fight off the attack. He survived but he was badly cut up. The man stumbled back to town where he told of his story. Although he survived the initial attack, within days a terrible infection set in. Fever and poison surged through his bloodstream. The poor man died a couple of weeks later."

I was astonished to learn this.

Samuel picked up his bow, "Let the unclean eat the unclean."

CHAPTER 4

During this time, I took up my position as a scribe. The older men were pleased with my return, and I was introduced to the younger men who had joined us. We scribed and recorded several scrolls, including the Books of Enoch. I was reminded of my stay on Mount Hermon and of the fallen Watchers. My mind took me back to that fateful day standing on the summit of the great mountain. Nearly frozen to death, I stood in the blowing snow as I examined the icy ruins of the ancient high place and temple, Qasr Antar. There I read the words written on the venerable stele, *According to the command of the greatest and Holy God, those who take an oath proceed from here.* I was reminded of the Grigori and the oath they swore together binding themselves by a curse. I too had sworn an oath on that sacred mountain; an oath to serve the Lord and His mysterious purpose, a purpose that I had come to believe was vengeance.

We scribed other scrolls, the books of the Torah and the Tanakh, and the book of the prophet Isaiah. This time I had a far deeper understanding of the prophet than I had experienced before. My eyes were open, and I was enlightened.

One day we began with the denouncement of the idolatry and the wickedness of the Jews, both of Israel and of Judah. I settled into my robes as we worked, reading how Isaiah had foretold punishment and destruction for my people's failure to follow God's ways. He had described the judgment upon the land, as his people were scattered and repressed. But Isaiah provided us with one saving hope.

In the writings, he had foretold of the coming Messiah, the Holy One of God. He will redeem His people, destroy our enemies, and bring peace. As Samuel read the text aloud, the words of the first poem flowed off his tongue like a sweet rhythmic song. We scribes meticulously recorded every single phrase, every single word, and every single letter. We were careful to not dare make a single mistake.

> *Then a shoot will spring from the stem of Jesse,*
> *And a branch from his roots will bear fruit.*
> *The Spirit of the Lord will rest on Him,*
> *The spirit of wisdom and understanding,*
> *The spirit of counsel and strength,*
> *The spirit of knowledge and the fear of the Lord.*
> *And He will delight in the fear of the Lord*

Samuel continued to read from Isaiah's poem as he described how the Chosen One of God will bring peace upon the earth. He continued with the promised restoration of God's people.

> *Then it will happen on that day that the Lord*
> *Will again recover the second time with His hand*
> *The remnant of His people, who will remain*

As we finished scribing that day an impassioned feeling came over me. It was a sense of justice, a sense of restoration, and retribution; it was felt by us all. We ardently discussed the coming Chosen One as we walked to our homes that day, about His coming mighty hand of destruction over Roman rule. Coincidentally that very week, the visiting rabbi, a zealot, preached from this very scroll of Isaiah. His impassioned message burned in the entire village, who had gathered to hear the zealot's words, for we all anxiously anticipated the coming of God's Chosen One and the fall of Rome.

Samuel, Ruth and I discussed the coming Messiah in great detail over our meals together. One particular night was no different as I shared with them the story of the wild preacher at the Jordan River, John the Baptizer. I told them what he said to the people, "I baptize you with water. But one who is more powerful than I will come. He is the one who comes after me. The straps of his sandals I am not worthy to untie. He will baptize you with the Holy Spirit and with fire. His winnowing fork is in his hand to clear the threshing floor and to gather the wheat into his barn, but he will burn up the chaff with unquenchable fire."

Over the next several weeks, I worked alongside the other scribes as we gave our attention to the scrolls of Isaiah. We recorded the Lord's pleadings with His people and His promised impending judgment. Again and again, the Lord rebuked the children of Israel, but then He comforted them. God promised restoration and salvation. I was filled with encouragement. God promises to send us his Holy One, a mighty warrior, a mighty king to deliver His people and destroy His enemies. I recognized the words of John the Baptizer coming forth from the mouth of the prophet Isaiah. Memories filled my head of the wild charismatic preacher man standing almost naked in the clear waters of the tributary called Bethany beyond the Jordan.

John the Baptizer had lifted his hands up toward Heaven as if he were Elijah calling upon the Lord. I could envision lightning falling to Earth in a whirlwind of fire and consuming the sacrifice with the stones of the altar itself.

This man, John, personified the great prophet in so many ways. And like Elijah taunting the prophets of Baal, the Baptizer spoke harshly to the pompous Pharisees. He had quoted the words of Isaiah, *The voice of one crying in the wilderness…*

> *A voice is calling,*
> *Clear the way for the Lord in the wilderness;*
> *Make smooth in the desert a highway for our God.*
> *Let every valley be lifted up,*
> *And every mountain and hill be made low;*
> *And let the rough ground become a plain,*
> *And the rugged terrain a broad valley;*
> *Then the glory of the Lord will be revealed,*

And all flesh will see it together;
For the mouth of the Lord has spoken."

I smiled at the thought of the baptist as we continued to work diligently. We continued to record the words as Samuel read them aloud. Working through the next several chapters of Isaiah, the Lord continued to reveal the promised messiah.

Behold, My Servant, whom I uphold;
My chosen one in whom My soul delights.
I have put My Spirit upon Him;
He will bring forth justice to the nations.
He will not cry out or raise His voice,
Nor make His voice heard in the street.
A bruised reed He will not break
And a dimly burning wick He will not extinguish;
He will faithfully bring forth justice.
He will not be disheartened or crushed
Until He has established justice in the earth.

The prophecies of Isaiah revealed God's Holy One, line after line, over and over, the scrolls were filled with the inspired foretelling of His coming. He will usher in the *Olam Haba*, the world to come. The scrolls described in prophetic manner His coming and what we should expect. The room full of scribes fervently recorded every single letter. Our hearts all burned with anticipation as we recorded the divine words. In the fourth of the Servant Poems more encouragement filled my soul.

More than any time in my past, I now understood the blessed words of the prophet. When I was younger, I had merely recorded the words. But now, they came to life. The words had true meaning. They were a precious jewel, a treasure revealed. Isaiah's words burned in my heart and rolled off Samuel's tongue like sweet dripping honey.

For He grew up before Him like a tender shoot,
And like a root out of parched ground;
He has no stately form or majesty
That we should look upon Him,
Nor appearance that we should be attracted to Him.
He was despised and forsaken of men,
A man of sorrows and acquainted with grief;
And like one from whom men hide their face
He was despised, and we did not esteem Him.

A gentle rumble of thunder was heard off in the distance. I glanced out a window and saw the sky darkening to the South. The clouds were the color of steel. They consumed the sky. A dark curtain formed as rain fell to earth beyond the mountains. It was coming, and I looked forward to it. It was somehow comforting. Samuel's words filled my ears.

Surely our griefs He Himself bore,
And our sorrows He carried;
Yet we ourselves esteemed Him stricken,
Smitten of God, and afflicted.
But He was pierced through for our transgressions,
He was crushed for our iniquities;
The chastening for our well-being fell upon Him,
And by His scourging we are healed.
All of us like sheep have gone astray,
Each of us has turned to his own way;
But the Lord has caused the iniquity of us all
To fall on Him.

Lifting my eyes, I found the room a sanctuary. It was a holy place, a preserve for the very word of God. The sound of Samuel's voice reverberated through the hall, where cool columns held up the roof like sentinels. How often had they heard these words, these walls? The heads of my fellow scribes were bowed as if in prayer. Only their pens moved, like soldiers marching across the scrolls. A conviction of righteousness filled the room. Their dedication was a sign of sanctity for their chosen task, a sign of obedience to their God. Samuel continued. These words had been read to them as a child, to their fathers and grandfathers before them. How often had anyone truly pondered what they meant?

He was oppressed and He was afflicted,
Yet He did not open His mouth;
Like a lamb that is led to slaughter,
And like a sheep that is silent before its shearers,
So He did not open His mouth.
By oppression and judgment He was taken away;
And as for His generation, who considered
That He was cut off out of the land of the living
For the transgression of my people, to whom the stroke was due?
His grave was assigned with wicked men,
Yet He was with a rich man in His death,
Because He had done no violence,
Nor was there any deceit in His mouth.
But the Lord was pleased
To crush Him, putting Him to grief;
If He would render Himself as a guilt offering,

The quiet sound of rain began to beat upon the roof, a muffled drumming, musical. Water fell from the roof's edge outside. Ribbons of water cascaded from the eaves. Large drops splashed across the open window sills, bursting into tiny orbs, some splashing against my skin as I worked. I felt their cool kisses against my face. The sweet aroma of rain filled the room. It was a clean fresh scent, the smell of wet earth. It was a faint musty metallic smell mixed with fresh grass and flowers. It was a cleansing of nature. I loved that smell. It reminded me of the wilderness. It reminded me of the mountains. I closed my eyes to relish the moment. A childhood memory flashed through my mind. I held my Mother's hand as we caught falling raindrops on our tongues. She was smiling as she had before. Her laughter reverberated through my heart. Her memories permeated my soul. I inhaled deeply. The sweet scent filled my lungs. I inhaled again as Samuel's words filled my spirit.

> *He will see His seed,*
> *He will prolong His days,*
> *And the good pleasure of the Lord will prosper in His hand.*
> *As a result of the anguish of His soul,*
> *He will see it and be satisfied;*
> *By His knowledge the Righteous One,*
> *My Servant, will justify the many,*
> *As He will bear their iniquities.*
> *Therefore, I will allot Him a portion with the great,*
> *And He will divide the booty with the strong;*
> *Because He poured out Himself to death,*
> *And was numbered with the transgressors;*
> *Yet He Himself bore the sin of many,*
> *And interceded for the transgressors.*

One of the fellow scribes, a young man named Philo, laid down his pen and then spoke up, "Rabbi."

Samuel stopped his reading. He looked up at the young man, somewhat annoyed. It was unprecedented, a young scribe breaking the silence. Samuel ran his fingers through his graying beard. He scratched his neck and chin. The young scribe continued, "Rabbi, the word says, *'He was stricken, and they made His grave with the wicked, and He poured out His soul unto death.'* How can this be?"

A strange expression came across Samuel's face. Deep lines of crow's feet accentuated his intense eyes, then strengthened against the deep lines that ran across his forehead. He ran his fingers through his beard and stroked it while he contemplated an answer. He paused. "Well, we all must die in time. Surely this is speaking of the end of the messiah's life."

"I thought he would reign forever?" Philo persisted.

Samuel tugged on his beard. "No, He shall come to redeem His chosen people. He shall gather all of His children and establish justice and peace on the earth. Then He too shall pass."

The young scribe disputed Samuel's answer and argued, "I thought He was coming to conquer, crush, and destroy the Roman scourge that plagues us?"

"No," Samuel firmly stated, "It does not say that."

"But other rabbis and the experts in the law say..."

Samuel scoffed at this, laughing out loud. "Experts in the law?" he sneered. Samuel kissed the scroll before laying it down on the small wooden table. With great admiration and respect, he gently touched the scroll with the tips of his fingers. Sweeping aside the long silver strands of hair that hung in his face, he spoke, "Young man, where exactly does it say that? Can you show me where it says the Holy One of God is coming to destroy the Romans?"

Philo was quiet for several minutes. The entire synagogue fell dead silent. His eyes searched the room for someone to come to his aid, but none did. Very quietly he spoke a single word, "No."

All eyes were fixed on that young man as Samuel's reading continued,

"The Lord's servant is coming to recover His lost people and to demonstrate His might and power to the world. For the Lord has comforted His people, He has redeemed Jerusalem. The Lord has bared His holy arm in the sight of all the nations, that all the ends of the earth may see the salvation of our God."

Another of the young scribes raised his hand and stood, "Rabbi, why does it say that He will suffer?"

Several others all agreed adding to the conversation. "If He is God's chosen One, why does He suffer?"

Samuel responded with the words of Isaiah, *"He was wounded for our transgressions, and He was bruised for our iniquities."* Samuel was a patient man. He did not raise his voice in frustration. He looked out over the scribes and continued, "The prophet wrote *'when You make His soul an offering for sin.'"*

With those words, great grumbling arose. A divisive argument ensued over exactly what those words meant and who He is. It became heated as several of the men expressed their differing opinions. Someone shouted out, "There is to be two messiahs!" Another shouted, "mighty warrior king, like a lion!"

Another said, "A gentle lamb." Most rejected this idea, although it is taught in some synagogues.

One man expressed that the Chosen One of God must suffer before He becomes the messiah, and then he will lead his people. He opined, "He is the strong arm of the Lord and therefore He cannot die. He will live forever." At first, I agreed with this sentiment.

However, an older man stood and argued with that point quoting scripture, "It says, '*He was oppressed, and He was afflicted; Like a lamb that is led to slaughter. By oppression and judgment, He was taken away and He was cut off from the land of the living for the transgression of my people. His grave was assigned with wicked men, yet He was with a rich man in His death.*' So, it plainly says He is to suffer and to be killed."

Samuel agreed, "Yes, it plainly states He is to suffer and to be killed."

"How can He be the messiah if He is dead?" a combative and angry voice shouted.

"The messiah cannot die," another man shouted from the back.

"But the scriptures say, He will suffer and be killed."

More angry voices rose as several of the men began shouting at each other. Tempers flared. The disagreement deepened like a great fissure.

"How can He be the messiah if He is dead, I say?" one angry scribe shouted.

An older scribe, who I had known for many years, lifted his voice above the arguing. He stated that some Rabbis believed that after the first Messiah is killed then His seed shall succeed Him. He quoted from the prophet's words, "*He will see His seed, He will prolong His days, and the good pleasure of the Lord will prosper in His hand. As a result of the anguish of His soul, He will see it and be satisfied.*"

More mumbling rose into the rafters of the ceiling. Samuel raised his hands in an effort to quieten the boisterous group of passionate scribes. They obeyed.

Samuel spoke into the quiet, "Some rabbis teach that the messiah is the

Jewish people. After all, they are the seed and the chosen of God Almighty. The word says '*He is despised and rejected by men. A man of sorrows and acquainted with grief.*' I ask you, brothers, who are more acquainted with grief than the children of Israel?"

Another man agreed with this theory adding, "The Jewish people shall bring peace and the salvation of God to all the ends of the earth."

This comment brought more dissension and angry shouting with claims that *the messiah shall destroy all the ends of the earth.*

The fissure deepened. Samuel himself rejected this idea. Some claimed that the messiah had already come and fulfilled the prophecy.

The young scribe, Philo, stood in the back of the room and shouted, "What about Simon of Peraea? Some people claim he was the messiah. He was the slave of Herod the Great. They claim that the angel Gabriel spoke to him. Herod trusted him before he led a rebellion burning down the king's royal palace at Jericho. Simon's followers declared him to be a king. They continued their acts of terror against King Herod, burning and plundering several of the king's other houses. The people called him messiah."

Another scribe rebutted his claim. "King Herod's own commander, Gratus took a party of Roman soldiers and caught Simon. After a long fight, they destroyed his followers and he cut off Simon's head. Simon's rebellion failed."

With triumph in his voice, Philo inserted, "Yes, but it plainly states He is to suffer and to be killed."

I watched Samuel grind his teeth in frustration. "According to the legends, Simon was commanded by the angel Gabriel to rise from the dead within three days." Samuel paused for a dramatic effect. It became silent in the room. "He did not. He did not rise. It has been years, Simon of Peraea is not the messiah."

The argumentative scribe introduced another theory, "What about Athronges?" After a moment of silence, he continued. "After Herod the Great died, revolts rose against his sons' rule. One rebellion was against Herod Archelaus. That rebellion was led by Athronges. He was a shepherd, just like King David. Some claim that he is the messiah."

Samuel replied, "Athronges rebellion lasted for two years before it was crushed. His followers were defeated, and his four brothers were either executed or imprisoned. Athronges' rebellion failed miserably. He is not the messiah."

"Ah, but wait," exclaimed Philo, "Athronges was never captured. He disappeared into the Judean hillside. He has not been seen since. Some believe he will return one day."

Samuel dismissed this idea with a sweep of his arm, "That was over 25 years ago. Athronges is not the messiah. In fact, he is probably dead by now."

A couple of the scribes agreed with the idea that the messiah has already come and is awaiting His time. Someone else mentioned stories of a wild man from Galilee. "They claim he is filled with the spirit of Elijah. Great crowds are following him to the river Jordan. There, he is baptizing the people and forgiving their sins."

With that single comment, several furious voices rang out in unison, "No one can forgive sins except God himself!"

One lone voice called out, "Unless, he is the messiah."

A spark of recognition caught fire in my mind. They were referring to John the Baptizer. The wild impassioned preacher I had encountered standing half-naked in the Jordan River. The fiery teacher whose message so inspired the crowds of people, like nothing ever preached in Judea before. I was swept back in time. I found myself camped on the bank of the Jordan River with my Sicarii brothers.

Several gathered around a fire sharing a skin of wine. My fellow Sicarii brother, Ozias, and our friend, Bartholomew, spoke of the day's events. John the Baptist had been witnessed rebuking and humiliating the leaders from the temple. So, several had come to interrogate John. "Rabbi!" they had called out smugly.

John had stopped what he was doing and had fixed them with a hard stare. "What is it that you want, oh, teachers of the Law?"

"Who are you? Are you the one who is to come?" one priest had asked.

John had been bold. He had answered them, "I am not the Messiah, if that is your question."

They continued to question him. One of the Levites had pointedly asked,

"Who are you? Are you Elijah? Are you the prophet returned from the dead?"

John had smirked at them, "I am not."

"You are not the Prophet?" they had asked.

"No," he had said. John's contempt for these men had been apparent.

"You are not the Christ?"

"No."

"Then who are you?" The frustrated group of priests had pressed, "Give us an answer to take back to those who sent us. What do you say about yourself?"

According to Ozias and Bartholomew, John had climbed up the muddy banks of the river. He had stood on a high spot and looked down on these men. He was a giant. For a moment he had been silent, almost as if he held pity for them. A strange expression had crossed his face. The crowd had stirred and grown as quiet as a dead man. Every eye had focused on him. Every ear had listened. John had lifted his hands up toward Heaven and he quoted from the prophet Isaiah, "I am the voice of one calling in the wilderness… make straight the way for the Lord."

The Pharisees who were with them had pompously asked, "Why do you baptize if you are not the Messiah, nor Elijah, nor the prophet?"

John's smile had disappeared. He had become subdued in his manner. Ozias had seen his eyes burn with a furious devotion. The wild man had turned his back on the leaders and had turned toward the people, "I baptize you with water. But one who is more powerful than I will come. He is the one who comes after me. The straps of his sandals I am not worthy to untie. He will baptize you with the Holy Spirit and with fire." John turned back toward the leaders from Jerusalem. His tone darkened, "His winnowing fork is in his hand to clear the threshing floor and to gather the wheat into his barn, but he will burn up the chaff with unquenchable fire."

The sounds of men shouting brought me back to the synagogue. The memory of that campfire was quenched by the rain and their clamoring. More virulent arguing ensued over the identity of John the Baptist and his ability to forgive sins. Several men were convinced that this was the promised one. But some became irate over the idea that he was forgiving the sins of the people.

I spoke up for the very first time, "No, I have seen this man. I heard him deny it myself. He is not the messiah."

A silence fell over the crowd. Only the sound of the rain could be heard.

Micaiah stood, bristling at me. He was apoplectic. It was out of character for him. He screamed. Spittle flew from his lips. Venom was in his voice. "If he is not the messiah, he is a blasphemer. Only God can forgive sins."

I had never seen this man or any of these men act in such a way. Taken aback, I was surprised at their behavior. Their impassioned and emotional views were like hot smoldering coals. I waited for the raging fire to ignite. My antagonist continued to shout at me, "Blasphemy! Blasphemy!"

I found myself on my feet. My pen was still in my hand. I wielded it like a weapon. I squeezed until the reed shaft cracked and split down the middle. Black ink dripped down the shaft staining my fingers. I raised my voice shouting back in the Baptizer's defense, "He never claimed to forgive sins. It was repentance. He preached for the repentance of sins and baptized the people for the remission of their sins."

Micaiah sneered, "Why do people call him the messiah?"

I responded, "The people are wrong. I heard him say it myself. He claimed he was getting people ready for the messiah. Preparing the way for the Lord."

"Who is the messiah?"

I took a deep breath and exhaled. In a much calmer voice, I responded, "The Baptist said he was preparing the way for the Lord. He said to turn from your sins and repent. You must be holy, for without holiness, no man shall see the Lord."

My antagonist glared at me with contempt in his eyes. I could see frustration written all over his face. Micaiah asked, "Who then, Barabbas, is the messiah?"

I answered, "He never said who. All he said was repent and be prepared, for He is coming."

"And who is He?"

"I don't know!" I shouted back.

Thunder boomed overhead. The older man seemed unashamed. He looked at me. He stared long and hard into my eyes before breaking eye contact. He lowered his head and looked at the floor. He spoke, "Barabbas, please forgive an old fool. My apologies."

I simply nodded as I sat back down. Rain continued to fall as thunder rolled in the distance.

Samuel, breaking the heavy tension that hung in the air, quoted from the Word, "*And by His scourging we are healed. All of us like sheep have gone astray, each of us has turned to his own way. But the Lord has caused the iniquity of us all to fall on Him.*"

CHAPTER 5

During the days I worked as a scribe, I stayed with Samuel and Ruth and helped repair things that needed attention. Samuel and I worked on the house, the synagogue, and several of the elderly and widows' houses. We talked for hours.

When we weren't doing repairs or scribing, Samuel and I hunted the wild game that was plentiful in the forested mountainsides. We did not see the wild hogs again. But we did see plenty of their signs.

One day while walking home from one of our hunting trips, we came across a large hog root, where the earth had been plowed and churned up. Samuel turned to me. With the wisdom of a philosopher, he asked me a confusing question, "God himself forbid us from eating pork. Barabbas, give me one hundred reasons why the hog should be eaten."

Shocked at his question, I protested, "Father, that is blasphemous. It is unlawful. Hogs are unclean. The Law of Moses forbids it."

"Ah, but does it?"

"Yes, Samuel. The Law forbids eating unclean animals." I immediately recited the Torah, "*And the pig, for though it divides the hoof, thus making a split hoof, it does not chew cud, it is unclean to you. You shall not eat of their flesh nor touch their carcasses; they are unclean to you.*"

Samuel smiled a mischievous grin and continued, "But the Torah exists only on Earth in the hearts of men. The Torah is what we say it is."

I was shocked at his comments. They stood on the edge of blasphemy, a dangerous cliff. "The Torah is God's word. It is what saves us."

He stroked his gray beard, "Again and again, the ancient rabbi's warned us to take heed. Consider this Barabbas, when God gave Moses the sacred Law, he placed it in the hands of man. He did this so that it exists on Earth and not in Heaven. It is to be interpreted by men. It is to be interpreted by you and me, in all our frailty. The Torah is what we say it is."

I listened to his words as we strolled through the trees. Samuel spoke with enthusiasm about the joy he found in God's Law. "We are the children of Abraham. We are God's chosen people. He gave us the Law to save us, to make us holy, and make us one with God. By understanding the Torah, we will understand the ultimate nature of God."

Through the wooded hillside, we came across a small stream. Its crystal-clear waters cascaded down the moss-covered rocks. Green vegetation sprang up along the bank. Samuel stopped and knelt down beside the water. He drank by cupping his hands together and bringing the water up to his lips. He never knelt down and drank from the stream. In this way, he never took his eyes off of the encircling forest, always aware of his surroundings, as this was the way of the warrior. Samuel continued, "God's Torah is like this stream. It nourishes our souls. It quenches our thirst. It saves us. Yet in this life, sometimes the clouds produced by man obscure God's truth and His light. But when the will of man and the Law of God clash, the latter must always prevail. Therefore, it is our mission and responsibility to ascertain the Lord's wishes. And you cannot discern it, unless you sharpen your mind. I have found that when one is driven to construct one hundred sophistical reasons for denying Leviticus, one must discover the ultimate character of God."

He stood and wiped the water from his hands on his cloak. Glistening orbs of water clung to his wiry beard. Samuel placed his strong hands upon my shoulders and said, "Barabbas, give me one hundred reasons why the hog should be eaten."

Over several days, I contemplated this enigma. I consulted with several of the other scribes, including Micaiah. We studied the Torah and struggled with Samuel's question. It was a difficult task, shared by several opinions. The annoying young scribe, Philo, came up with one solution. "It's based on a blessing," he said. He advanced his argument, "We often have to choose between two precepts of God that appear contradictory to each other. In the commandments, God tells us *'thou shalt not steal,'* but He himself stole Adam's rib. He did that in order to give mankind its greatest blessing, woman. Now God tells us not to eat pork. But, if we did, we might find it a blessing, also." Most of the other scribes found his answer amusing. Samuel did not.

Finally, I returned to Samuel with my conclusion. "In Genesis, the word says, *'in the beginning God created the heavens and the Earth. At first the Earth was formless and void. And darkness was over the surface of the deep.'* Nothing existed except the Spirit of God, which was moving over the surface of the waters. God began to create. He created the seas and filled them with life. He created the dry land and all the living creatures. After God had created all of the animals, but before he had created man, He reviewed his work. As it is written, *'He saw that it was good.'* Therefore, we find that God made this judgement after the creation of the hog, but before he created man. Consequently, the hog must have been good, also. God spoke his approval without reference to man. So the hog must still be good and, therefore, still can be eaten."

Day after day, Samuel encouraged me to pursue my reasoning. When the last had proved auspicious, he surprised me by saying, "Barabbas, in the Torah, there are 613 laws. 365 prohibitive laws, one for each day of the year. There are 248 affirmative laws, one for each bone of the body. You are bound by this ancient law. I am bound by it. And God Himself is bound by it, for it establishes order throughout the entire universe. It is not within our power to understand the mind of God. Now go, Barabbas, and bring me 100 reasons why the pig cannot be eaten."

I enjoyed living with Samuel and Ruth. I thought to myself that I could stay here and scribe for the rest of my days. It was an honorable profession. I had nothing else. My beloved was gone, murdered by the treacherous Romans along with my unborn child. As each day came and went, their memory became less sharp, like the unkempt edge of a blade slowly rusting away. Guilt crawled through me with this realization.

Samuel and Ruth were my family. I enjoyed being with them. I also enjoyed my time alone in the wild. But something was missing.

A nagging sense of apathy set in. I loved the mountains and the wilderness, but it was not enough. I spent many days there hunting deer and antelope, along with the smaller game. As in my younger days, I would sell the wild game to the small villages that surrounded us. It was quite lucrative. I enjoyed it, but something was still missing. A tantalizing emptiness stirred in my soul. In fact, I had become complacent. And I hated it.

Early the following morning I headed into the woods alone; I was in search of the elusive stag. It was a dark morning with barely a sliver of moon, so the stars shone brightly, magnificent gemstones set against a rich black curtain. But for some reason, it was different this day. I could not quite put my finger on it, but a strange feeling lingered in the air, an uncomfortable feeling.

As I moved through the thick underbrush, a movement stirred in the darkness. Something ominous, unexplainable but felt. I stopped, my senses on alert. I gazed into the darkness. But nothing happened. I knew something was there, hiding in the black night. In my mind, I could hear it breathing but saw nothing. Following a deer trail, I moved deeper into the woods. Something moved through the thickets. *Was it an animal? Some ferocious beast?* I could not tell. *Maybe a lion or a bear? Maybe one of the ferocious wild hogs Samuel had told me about.* All I could see was the subtle movement beyond the thick branches. Whatever it was, it seemed to be stalking me as it moved parallel to my movements, maneuvering only when I did.

Keeping just beyond my sight, this ominous presence seemed to mock me. Each time I stopped, so did the strange movement. Remarkably quiet, it kept cadence with me. Much quieter than any animal I know. A strange fear came over me. I fought back a rising panic. My mind told me to turn and run, but I refused. I had never before felt this way in the woods, but on this particular morning, fear gripped me.

I picked up my pace, so did it. I began running, trying to navigate the obstacles on the dark trail. Limbs and fallen debris made the darkness treacherous. Something hit me. A sharp branch scratched across my face, stinging as it cut. I tripped and fell. My hands and knees screamed out in pain as sharp thorns embedded into them. I cursed. Rising to my feet, I stared angrily into the black woods. I sensed it, the strange invisible presence stared back menacingly. A momentary twitching in the limbs and branches and without warning, a blast of icy cold air blew past me with the force of a rushing river. The cold stung like tiny needles. Then it was gone. The burden seemed lifted. Somehow, I knew I was alone. Solace came at last.

Turning away from this unexplainable occurrence, I continued deeper into the familiar woods. Soon I came to one of my favorite hunting trees. It was an old oak tree that had probably been there since the days of Alexander the Great. Fortunately, since it was far enough from any village or town, it had escaped the ax and the fires. I'm sure if it were closer, it would have been cut down many years ago. I had developed a deep admiration for that old giant. In a way, it reminded me of myself. It was rusted and weathered. The old rugged bark was rough and peeled in places, like a skin that peels and just won't heal. It had stood through many storms and been damaged, yet it still stood strong. This old tree reached toward the heavens standing taller than all its brethren, yet its roots sank unimaginably deep into the Earth.

The tree stood where several game trails all converged providing an excellent ambush spot. I began to climb to the highest branches. I reached for the strongest limbs and swung my legs upward pulling hard. I continued this until I came to rest on a long flat branch ideally placed at the highest fork of the tree. It made a perfect resting spot, creating a seat and a place for my feet. It was well camouflaged. The surrounding branches and foliage provided excellent cover. From the ground, I was invisible. In the past I had cleared out shooting lanes, allowing me clear shot opportunities. A small creek ran directly behind me. Thick brush provided plenty of forage for browsing. Wildlife abound here. This was a good spot. In the past, I've had very good success here.

On this day, the cool morning breeze blew through the leaves and I settled in and began the wait for the warm morning sun. After such a strange experience earlier that morning, I was glad to finally be sitting in my tree. It felt safe. With my bow in hand, now I waited for the first light and my unsuspecting prey. I gathered my wool scarf around my head. I made two quick wraps covering all but my eyes. I pulled my outer tunic tight around my shoulders, providing warmth. Soon, I was comfortable and relaxed. I fell into a deep sleep.

I found myself standing knee-deep in a gentle river. The current lazily flowed past me, pulling at my bare legs. The sound of the churning waters and passing current was calming. It was nature's music. It brought solace to my soul. This was a beautiful river, a life-giving river. Upstream the water was a brilliant blue. A magnificent waterfall cascaded down a rocky cliff before spilling into the stream. It was covered on both sides by lush green trees and plants. The stream was surrounded by massive mountains that glowed purple in the sunshine. Snow capped their summits as their jagged peaks reached high into the heavens. An incredibly blue sky hung in the firmament. Sunlight spilled over the mountain tops and danced off the sparkling surface of the rippling waves. The water was cool and crystal clear. I could see the smooth river stones below the current. They were smooth, polished by time and painted with every color imaginable. Although artful to the eye, they pained my bare feet.

I stood and admired the scenery before me. Rainbows danced in the spray from the cascading water falling over the rocks. Every color imaginable decorated the magical mist. The fragrance of cedar and pine mixed with the smell of fresh water. It was a sweet and pleasant aroma, an incense burned in this most magnificent temple. I inhaled and smelled the sweet pleasant scent of the mountains. The ambrosia stirred my soul. As I stood admiring nature, a large flock of birds swooped across the river. Their shadows danced across the surface of the water. They moved in unison, hundreds of wings moving as one, a swirling cloud of feathers. At first, they appeared black; but as the sunlight reflected off of them, it was clear that they were a deep rich navy blue. Clear attentive eyes were painted yellow. The flock swirled as one and then dove, skimming the surface of the water. Like a wisp of smoke, they were gone.

Then I saw it. A golden glare drew my attention. Something was out in the middle of the river. It floated there in the deeper part of the flowing current. Sunlight glinted off of a golden hilt. *What was it?* I thought. It called to me. Like a magnet, it pulled all of my attention to itself. There in the deeper water, an engraved scroll was floating in the current. Fine intricately tooled decorations rose to the surface. It was beautiful. A still small voice whispered in my ear. It revealed the secret held within. Somehow, lucid in my dream, I knew I was looking at the scroll of the Law of Moses. This was God's Law. This one single scroll contained the entire Law. This was the Law that provided salvation for fallen humanity. This was the righteous Law that saves us. By obeying and keeping the Law perfectly, we earn our redemption and win God's acceptance.

I stepped forward toward the scroll. The rocks felt slick underfoot. I was careful as to not lose my footing and fall. The river deepened with each step. I soon found myself wading waist deep. The current was stronger there, but I pushed onward. The scroll continued to call to me, but it remained just out of my reach. It floated just beneath the surface waiting for me to find it.

I continued forward, stretching out my arms. I strained, but the elusive scroll remained just out of reach. Continuing forward, I found myself neck deep in the cool waters of the river. The round stones became dangerously slippery under my bare feet. The current moved much quicker. Reaching forward, my fingers touched the ornate handle. With one final effort, I lunged toward it. Success. I grabbed the beautiful scroll. I held on tightly, not daring to let go. The salvation of all mankind was in my grasp. Joy and jubilation filled my heart. But I found myself treading water. I could no longer touch the smooth rocks that ran along the bottom of the river. The swift current was strong, an invisible force. It carried me downstream. I fought the rushing waters but to no avail. I was quickly swept away.

I struggled to keep my head above water. The peaceful waterfall, the gentle stream, the weeping trees were all left behind as the violent river washed me downstream. I realized just how heavy the scroll was. It seemed to become heavier with each passing moment. I tried to swim but it was impossible. The scroll was a burden, a great weight. It was pulling me under. This beautiful and precious scroll was carrying me toward my watery grave. I kicked and fought just to keep my head above water. Inhaling a mouthful of the river, I coughed and spat. I panicked and cried out, "Is there no one who can save me?"

Refusing to let go for fear that I would lose God's salvation, the scroll slowly dragged me under. I found myself sinking down deep through the bitterly cold waters. A cold that penetrated into my very bones, sucking the life from me. A terrible and heavy silence fell upon me. Darkness swallowed me. My lungs burned. They desperately needed breath. Below, shadows moved in the deep darkness. Something unholy stirred there. Clutching the scroll, I continued to sink deeper into the dark depths below. I could sense a great abyss awaited there. My lungs burned like fire. They were starved for air. My ears ached from the increasing pressure. Darkness set in all around me. Black shadows circled me like great predators. Finally, I lost all hope. I surrendered. This was my end and I accepted it. I closed my eyes and accepted death.

Suddenly, I felt someone take the heavy scroll from my hands. All its weight was removed and miraculously set aside. As if all its demands were satisfied. It was the lifting of a curse from my heart. A curse that was so deeply embedded. A curse that was passed down from generation to generation. And life was breathed into me. Like a blind man receiving sight, instantly I beheld a brilliant column of light. Brighter than the sun. It was as bright as lightning. Something moved from within the pillar of fire. Shrouded in the burning brightness stood a figure of a man. Beyond belief, he was stunning. A magnificent creature. Strength radiated from him. Long flowing robes of fire surrounded him. They were as white as the snow and swayed in an invisible breeze that engulfed him. This angelic figure stood before me in all his grandeur. He had deep amber eyes that stared intently into mine. They were hauntingly familiar. Eyes of power, eyes of might. He stared into my eyes, peering into my very soul. Then he spoke. His voice was calm, just above a whisper. Yet it was filled with the strength and ferociousness of a lion, "Barabbas, do you want to live?"

"Yes," I answered.

"Barabbas, I will take away your burden. Son of thy father, you have a destiny to fulfill. You have a purpose. Go."

My body jerked, and I was startled awake. I found myself sitting high in the top of my old tree. But when I awoke, I was not alone. A dozen large black ravens were perched in the branches surrounding me. Shocked, I jumped in my seat. This caused me to lose my balance and I almost fell backwards. Reacting, I tried to catch myself. I grabbed at a small branch, but the limb was weak, a dead skeletal arm. As I grappled with it, it broke and gave way. A loud snap filled the air. I tumbled out of the tree and plunged toward the earth. For the briefest moment, I was weightless. An unkindness of ravens screeched and cawed as I plummeted toward the ground. Realizing that I was falling, I threw my bow and arrows as far away as I could to avoid impaling myself. They clattered through the branches as a dozen arrows spilled from my quiver. Luckily, I hit several larger limbs on the way down. They helped break my fall. My body tumbled as it hit another branch and then another and then another. I landed hard on my shadow and I lay just where I fell. Great flashes of light danced before my eyes. The wind was knocked from me, I gasped for air as a dull pain overtook me. Strange shapes formed high above me. The black wings of the ravens flapped in the highest branches. They faded into the dark. Just like my dream, the blackness took me.

CHAPTER 6

Slowly I came to. I became aware of my surroundings. My vision was blurred. My head ached. I'm not sure how long I lay there, but the sun was now high in the morning sky. Dried blood was caked onto my face across my forehead. Pain wracked my body. Struggling, I rolled onto my stomach. I managed to get to my knees. I tried to rise, but dizziness set in. It took several attempts before I could stand. My knees felt weak. My body was hurting all over. My ribs ached, but miraculously nothing felt severely injured or broken. *Thank God.*

I managed to collect my bow and all of my arrows, along with my broken pride. I slowly made my way home. Every step pained me. I ached as I traversed the thick underbrush. The trip back to Samuel and Ruth's house took considerably longer than I had expected. I made it home that evening.

Over the next several days, I rested. I was tender and sore. My ribs were swollen, and they turned a hideous black and blue color. Deep bruises ran up my entire body. Ruth attended to my needs and nursed me as if I were a sick child. Samuel simply scoffed at me, "That is what happens when you sleep in trees." He laughed out loud. "You'd think he was a squirrel looking for a nut. If you're not careful, next time you'll sleep with the angels." *If he only knew,* I thought to myself. *If he only knew.*

Samuel quoted from the wisdom of King Solomon, "And the dust returns to the earth as it was, and the breath returns to God who gave it."

He teasingly punched me on the shoulder. Agonizing pain shot through my arm like the bite of a serpent. I cried out with pain, "Ouch!" Samuel just smiled, winked and walked outside as my arm continued to throb.

More days passed. As I grew stronger, I dwelled on the strange dream of the scroll in the river and the angelic being. His haunting words were a constant reminder. They echoed through my mind, "Son of thy father, you have a destiny to fulfill. You have a purpose. Go."

After almost half a year, I was prompted to leave the comfort of what I called my home, my sanctuary. A dread and sadness filled my heart. The following Sabbath, I sat down with Samuel and Ruth and shared my decision. I loved these two so much; it grieved me to have to leave them. Tears filled Ruth's eyes. A strange fear arose in me. A fear of what lay ahead and a fear that I might never see them again. Samuel's words were supportive and encouraging as he spoke to his wife. His voice was soft and low, but there was strength in it. However, I could sense the sadness in his words, "Mother, he cannot stay here. The Lord is calling Barabbas. He has a purpose for our son. He is needed."

Samuel's words were perplexing as I had not shared my visions nor my dreams with him. He simply knew. It must have been revealed to him. He knew, which was mystifying to me.

I spent several days preparing for my departure. Ruth patched my clothing and prepared extra food for the journey. Samuel and I managed to make one more trip into our beloved woods together. We killed a yearling doe and shared the meat with neighbors in our village. I sat with the scribes one final time as we recorded the praises from the *Tehillium*, the scroll of Psalms. They filled my heart with encouragement and strength, as I prepared my mind for the passage.

The night before my departure, Samuel left the room for a moment. Ruth and I could hear him outside. And just as before, he returned with a quiver full of arrows, at least three dozen. Now, I have always made my own arrows, as Samuel had taught me. I considered myself a good arrow maker. But mine were crude compared to his. His were like pieces of Roman art. Each one was expertly handmade. They were exact, each weighing the same. The feathers of each were precisely cut and with a slight helical twist. Each arrow was tipped with a razor-sharp iron broadhead. Each one was crested having been dipped in a white paint and marked with three distinct red stripes, one for me, one for Melessa, and one for our child. They were perfect.

The following morning, we rose early. Ruth prepared breakfast and we prayed together. Samuel prayed for the Lord to provide protection over me. I gathered my belongings, including my sword, bow and arrows. Samuel and Ruth walked me to the edge of our little village. Several of the other villagers gathered to say goodbye. Many hugs and kisses were exchanged along with other prayers of protection.

Finally, it was time. The moment had come. The sun was now high in the morning sky. I embraced my stepparents one more time. Ruth was crying openly. The other women comforted her. Samuel turned his head to hide the tears that ran down his cheeks. A giant knot formed in my throat as I turned to head south toward Jerusalem. I was in search of the Sicarii.

CHAPTER 7

I moved through the ancient mountains heading toward the Jordan River. I loved this land of Naphtali. An apprehension came over me. I feared that I would never see this beautiful place again, this place that had become part of my very soul. Drawn toward my unknown destiny, my purpose, the travel was easy, as no rain had fallen on this trip. The creeks were not flowing as they had on my previous passage, and the rocks were not as slick as ice. Soon I found myself overlooking the Waters of Merom. It was teeming with wildlife. Thousands of birds swarmed and circled above the swampy lake. An eerie feeling crept into my mind as I was reminded of the terrible ravens that haunted me. Fortunately, none were here on this day, only every other kind of bird imaginable. The sky was filled with God's beautiful creation. It was awe-inspiring.

Setting camp where the river meets the marsh, I stayed at Lake Semechonitis for several days. I hunted and set fish traps. I managed to kill a young antelope, that had come to the water's edge to drink. I cooked and dried the meat for my travel. I moved on following the Jordan River south. I needed to go to Galilee and see Jarviss.

Traveling downstream, I found myself at Bethsaida, where the Jordan empties into the Sea of Galilee. The heavy smell of the lake hung in the air. It was a distinct fishy smell, a smell found no place else on Earth. It filled my nostrils. A cool breeze blew across the surface of the water. It felt good on my bare skin. The sound of lapping waves was music to my ears.

The last time I stood on the rocky shore at the port of Bethsaida, I had looked back one last time at the boat of Zebedee. Zebedee was the man who had aided my escape from Capernaum all those years ago. There I had witnessed a mass swarm of demons as they had encircled his boat. The sky had been full of them. His boat had been covered. I had watched in horror, as dozens of the hideous creatures ferociously ripped each other apart and devoured their brethren.

A cold chill ran down my spine at the memory. But today the sky was clear, filled only with white gulls and their laughing cries. Shaking off that cursed memory, I embraced the happier memories of happier times. Memories of a childhood spent on the Sea of Galilee. Memories of Papa and Mother. Memories of Papa's shop and the boats he built. After crossing the river, I rushed toward the west following the shoreline. I needed to make it to Capernaum by nightfall.

The shoreline was rocky and difficult in a few places, but overall it was an easy trek. I made it to Capernaum before nightfall without any difficulty. When I arrived, the sun was setting against the silhouetted mountains of the western skyline. It cast a magnificent golden orange glow across the lake. After arriving, I made my way through the streets of Capernaum. They were less crowded than I would have expected. It must have been the time of day.. I made my way to the walls of the pottery makers' compound. There I found Jarviss' family wrapping things up for the day and preparing for the evening. And just like before, it was a wonderful homecoming.

I was greeted by the entire family. They loved me like a brother. And I, them. All of Jarviss' family were present, including his brothers and nephews – Joanan, Jared, Josh, Jannai, and John. And of course, all of their children. Children were everywhere, even more children than just six or seven moons ago. Hearing of my arrival, Jarviss ran and greeted me. As I had come to expect, he wrapped his arms around me, pulled me to his large belly, and wept. I loved this man. And he loved me.

No great celebration was held that evening. That evening we had no great feast nor wine. We simply greeted one another and everyone retired to their homes. I retired to Jarviss' house where I would stay for the duration of my visit. Next door, my chuppah, the home that I had shared with my beloved Melessa, remained empty. It stood like a skeletal shrine in the moonlight. The long shadow cast by my father-in-law's house clung to it. It engulfed the chuppah, completely swallowing it.

The following morning, we rose early. That morning I spent with Jarviss. Just he and I. We visited and caught up in private. We both still deeply mourned the loss of our Melessa, his precious daughter and my beloved *bashert*, my soulmate. It was something intimate we shared. The great loss. A part of us both had died that terrible day. This was a grief that only he and I could share.

After breakfast, I spent the remainder of the day with Joanan and his brothers. I helped them cut firewood for the ovens and haul water for the clay. That night, the brothers and I stayed up late watching the stars and drinking spiced wine. We told stories, laughed, and drank well into the night until we were all good and drunk. Joanan and the brothers began to talk of the mysterious new rabbi that was teaching in the synagogues around the Galilee. According to Joanan, the new rabbi brought a new message, a message of hope to the people. I said nothing that night. I simply listened.

The following morning, I asked my father in law about this, "Jarviss, your nephews talked last night of a new rabbi teaching in the synagogue."

"Yes, he used to. He doesn't teach in the synagogue here anymore." Jarviss commented nonchalantly.

"Why not?"

"The leaders asked him not to. They claim he stirs up the people."

"Stirs up the people? How?" I asked, truly curious.

Jarviss thought about it for a moment before answering, "He teaches of the kingdom of Heaven and the will of God. He claims that the kingdom shall be obtained here on Earth, but not by following the Law."

"Not by following the Law? How?" I asked, now with a slight anger stirring, for those words were blasphemy.

Kind eyes peered through his shaggy eyebrows. His hair and beard were a wild mess that morning. Jarviss continued, still relaxed and calm. "He is threatening the Pharisees and their teachings. Mostly, he is threatening their power. He claims that by simply following the will of God, one shall inherit the kingdom of Heaven."

Curiosity rose up inside of me. "That's blasphemy," I interjected, "The kingdom of Heaven shall only be obtained by following the Law, God's Law, the righteous Law that saves us. That is the only way. God's acceptance can only be earned by obeying and keeping His Law perfectly."

The memory of my recent dream returned. The strange dream in the top of the tree reminded me of that single scroll. The scroll that contained the entire Law. The Law that provided salvation for God's children. The scroll that I had lost in the depths of the dark waters. *Had I lost it? Or rather, it was taken from me.* I paused a moment to ponder on this.

My thoughts were interrupted when Jarviss continued, "The teacher speaks with authority, Barabbas. He confuses and embarrasses the experts in the Law. They are perplexed at his teachings. He states that we must serve the will of God toward our fellow man. We must have compassion. We must show mercy and serve our fellow man. That is greater than serving the Law."

"Blasphemy," I shouted. This time raising my voice more than I intended.

"Son, he speaks with knowledge and authority the people have never heard before. He brings the people a message of hope. They are following him. His movement is gaining ground."

"The people are so easily misled," I stated emphatically.

"No," Jarviss opposed, "The teacher claims that we must put to work our faith. He claims that to serve our fellow man is an act of faith greater than the Law. He states that we should not practice good works for the sake of the Law or for the sake of the good works, but instead as an act of faith. An act of love for our Lord."

Listening to that disturbed me. It worried me that Jarviss might be losing his mind. "Don't tell me you are one of his followers, Jarviss?"

"Son, I simply listen to his words. The things he says are amazing. They are the words of God. Wisdom. He teaches that riches and treasures on Earth are corrupt. He teaches that to pursue these leads to death."

Smiling, I replied, "Let me remind you Jarviss, you are a wealthy man. You have worked so hard and for all these years."

He reminded me of a child, a young boy, as he continued. "Riches and treasures on Earth are corrupt in the hands of a man who has made them his goal on Earth. In their desire to gain wealth, men have lost their way. They have lost their direction. They have become selfish and greedy. Their wealth consumes them. It has become their idol. For a man who has made these things his idol, he will not find the kingdom of Heaven. He will only find death."

Still amazed at the words of my father in law, I stared at him in disbelief.

He continued smiling with joy, "Son, I am using my wealth to serve the poor and the widows. I am serving the will of God. Barabbas, the human heart belongs either to the treasures of this Earth or to the treasures in Heaven. We are the stewards of our wealth and desires. We get to choose which we pursue."

Dumbfounded, I stood before Jarviss. Suspicion filled my heart. Finally, I spoke, "So, you follow this man?"

"The people are following him in great crowds. They claim that he is a miracle worker."

"A miracle worker?" I laughed.

"Yes, he performs great feats. Unimaginable feats."

"Who is this man?" I asked incredulously.

Jarviss answered, "He comes from Nazareth. The rabbi is named Yeshua, but his followers call him by the Greek, Jesus."

CHAPTER 8

After my breakfast with Jarviss, I joined the brothers for the day's chores. Skeptical, I asked Joanan about the mysterious rabbi. I expressed my concern for my father-in-law's mental state. I told him I believed Jarviss was fragile and susceptible to being deceived.

To my surprise, Joanan vigorously defended Jarviss. "Oh no, brother. Our uncle is no fool. Jarviss is as sharp as a Roman spear. The man is brilliant. Trust me, he has not been deceived."

"You, too, are a follower?" I asked now, even more concerned.

Immediately, all of the brothers seemed to oppose me. They adamantly defended their uncle. Apparently, they had fallen under that charlatan's spell.

"Have you all lost your minds?"

The second to youngest brother, Jannai spoke up, "No Barabbas, it's not like that. You must see this man. You should hear the things he says and the way he says them. He is truly a man of God."

John spoke up, "He is a miracle worker. He performs great miracles. Great and amazing things that can only come from God."

Still incredulous, I injected, "Miracles? What kind of miracles?"

"I saw it with my own eyes, brother," Joanan said, "He heals the sick and the crippled."

"This Jesus does?" I asked still skeptical.

Jannai spoke again, "I witnessed it too. The first time I saw him heal a man whose right hand was shriveled. It was Amos, the beggar. I have known

53

that man all my life. He wanders the streets of Capernaum and sits at the city gates. Father always gives him money."

He turned to the other brothers, who all nodded in agreement, "His hand was deformed and withered since his birth. When Jesus was speaking at the synagogue, Amos came to listen to the teacher."

John interrupted, "And the scribes and Pharisees from Jerusalem were there, too. A group of them follow the teacher closely. They want to see if he strictly follows the Law. They asked him if it was lawful to heal on the Sabbath."

"But the teacher seemed to know their intentions." Jannai continued, "He called to Amos, telling him to come forward and stand before the crowd. When he did, the teacher let everyone see him and his shriveled hand. The teacher turned to the Pharisees and said to them, 'I ask you, is it lawful to do good or to do harm on the Sabbath? To save a life or to destroy it?'"

John laughed as he interrupted his brother once again, "They were fools. They had nothing to say in response to the teacher. They were silent before him. He made asses of them all."

Irritated at his brother's interruption, Jannai continued, "The teacher glared at the Pharisees with anger. He said to Amos, 'Stretch out your hand!' And when he did, his hand was restored."

Joanan interrupted this time, "You wouldn't believe it, Barabbas, his hand was so badly deformed. It stretched and grew into shape. You could hear the bones and tendons snap and pop inside. It sounded like a crackling fire within. Amos stared as his hand was completely restored right before his eyes. Amos praised God. In fact, the whole synagogue did."

"Everyone except the scribes and Pharisees," John added laughing. "They were humiliated and fled."

We kept the fires of the ovens burning hot all day as they fired the fresh-turned pottery. It was a long day. We continued to discuss this new teacher all day as we worked alongside each other. They continued to tell me of amazing miracles performed there around the Galilee. I noticed an excitement growing among the brothers. It had swept through the entire city. Everyone was talking of the mysterious teacher, Jesus. My curiosity was heightened but

I remained skeptical. Apparently, Jesus had healed ailments of every kind, including lepers. My brethren told several stories of the crippled and the paralyzed being healed and made whole. They told even more fantastic stories of blind men receiving sight. These tales all seemed impossible to me. How could all of the brothers along with Jarviss be deceived?

At the end of the day, the entire family ate together. Afterwards, the men gathered in the courtyard. We sat drinking spiced wine well into the night. This time, Jarviss joined us along with his brothers, Eliud and Eliakim. In an effort to convince me of this strange new rabbi, they all seemed to direct their stories at me. Jarviss was the most inspired that evening. "Barabbas, you just wouldn't believe the things that the teacher has done. The most amazing and wonderful things."

"You are probably right Jarviss," I said sarcastically.

Sensing my disbelief, he continued, "Son, you cannot doubt. I have seen it with my own eyes."

He turned toward his family with a great sweeping motion of his arms. "All of us have seen him. With our own eyes."

Joanan injected, "And the things he says. His words are like honey. They are the words of God."

My response was quick, "Brother, that could be considered blasphemy. You know the punishment."

Jarviss defended his nephew, "It's not blasphemy, Barabbas. It's the truth."

They began to tell of one day when the rabbi led a large group of his followers out of town and into the hills just west of Capernaum. According to them, a great multitude of followers had gathered to hear the teacher. He had not led them to the synagogue, but instead they had followed him out of town. He had gone up onto the side of a mountain. There he had addressed the crowd. And unlike the Pharisees or priests, he had not spoken from a chair of importance, but rather from the top of a rock. Sitting before the crowd, reminiscent of Moses on Mount Sinai, he had spoken ten blessings. My curiosity was piqued. According to Jarviss, the rabbi had described the character of a true disciple as one who glorifies God with his life. He had said, "They shall enter into His kingdom." He had instructed the crowd to seek true righteousness. He had informed them that their good works should be for the glory of God and not for the Law nor for merit or fame. According to this rabbi, Jesus, this righteousness is superior to the purely legal obedience taught by the scribes and Pharisees.

Jarviss began to detail the account of the ten blessings, "Blessed are the poor in spirit, for theirs is the kingdom of heaven. Blessed are those who mourn, for they will be comforted. Blessed are the meek, for they will inherit the earth." Jarviss paused for a moment, as if in thought. He ran his hands through his thick beard. He took a long drink of wine before continuing. I saw a tiny red drop spill down his beard. "Meaning those who are humble and have an attitude of conviction and trust in the Lord, they shall inherit His kingdom." The other men nodded in agreement. Jarviss continued, "Blessed are those who hunger and thirst for righteousness, for they will be filled. I love that one, Barabbas." He held his cup up for all to see before taking another long drink. This time he stared into the sky as if searching for something. Stars twinkled against the black sky. Lightning illuminated a mass of clouds in the far distance, but I heard no thunder. Searching for his words, Jarviss continued to stare into the heavens. A strange silence fell over us.

A lone voice, that of Eliakim, spoke up, "Blessed are the merciful, for they will receive mercy."

"That's it," Jarviss exclaimed, "Blessed are the merciful, for they will receive mercy."

He paused. Deep wrinkles cut across his forehead as he struggled to find the elusive words.

Eliakim spoke, "Blessed are the pure in heart."

That's it," Jarviss exclaimed, "Blessed are the pure in heart, for they will see God."

Without hesitation, Jarviss continued his dissertation, "Blessed are the peacemakers, for they will be called the children of God."

This time Jarviss was not without words. His face was stern, "Blessed are those who are persecuted for righteousness' sake, for theirs is the kingdom of heaven."

He let those words sink in as he turned, looking each of us directly in the eyes. Jarviss looked physically stronger to me at that moment than at any time in his life. After a few minutes, he continued, "Blessed are you when people insult you and persecute you, and falsely say all kinds of evil against you because of the teacher."

A strange silence came across us. We all sat there quietly for a few minutes before Jarviss quoted the final blessing. This time with a cheerful and joyous voice, "Rejoice and be glad, for your reward is great in Heaven, for in the same way they persecuted the prophets who were before you."

Joanan continued to describe how Jesus' true disciples are those who glorify God with their lives. He explained how the teacher went on to describe the character of his followers as light and as salt. He used these to illustrate one's character before the Lord. One gives brightness to life and the other preserves that life from the forces of decay.

I noticed that all of the cups went up in synchronized unison and everyone drank together. I joined them. The sound of distant thunder rumbled as low clouds gathered on the nearby mountain tops. Lightning illuminated them, filling the sky with fire.

CHAPTER 9

Like a lamp, my curiosity had been lit. It burned within me like wildfire. Although I remained skeptical, I wanted to see this teacher for myself. I wanted to see his miracles with my own eyes. Yet he never appeared. The days passed. Each day the brothers continued to tell of his miraculous exploits and of his teachings. Each day I listened, remaining skeptical. I waited patiently for more than three months, but he never arrived.

One night, I was haunted by my recurring nightmare. It had been so long since it had last visited me. This time my dream was more real and more vivid than ever before. My little lamb's cries were louder and more terrifying than ever. JoJo cried out desperately to me. His blood-curdling screams reached toward the heavens. The mighty roar of the lion filled the dark like thunder. More blood and gore spilled that night, along with more violence. The lion's words were raw and penetrating. The lion's teeth and claws were sharper than before, bitter and piercing. On this night, the mighty lion devoured me alive. Screaming out loud, I awoke in a pool of sweat. Chilled to the bone. I did not sleep the remainder of the night.

The next morning, I was tempted to share my vision with Jarviss and Joanan. For the first time ever, I was going to share my secrets. I was tempted to relieve this great burden upon me; but before I could, we were interrupted by an excited messenger. Word came to us that the teacher was returning.

The entire town was in an uproar as they prepared for his arrival. One could feel the excitement in the air. Anxious energy swept through the people.

Some rumored that he could be the promised messiah. A hint of intrigue filled my heart, but I remained doubtful. Finally, the teacher, the rabbi Jesus, arrived in Capernaum.

Jarviss was extremely excited as he gathered his family like a hen gathers her chicks. The pottery makers compound came to a grinding halt. Work came to a complete standstill as the entire family, including all the brothers along with their wives and children, abandoned their jobs. We all headed toward the shoreline to see the teacher.

As we approached, a crowd had already gathered –several hundred people. The crowd was like a wall surrounding the rabbi. I could not see him for the mass of followers. Joanan pulled me by the arm, leaving everyone else behind. We pushed forward trying to get a better vantage point from which to see. The people pushed back, resisting our efforts. Shouts filled the air. Many called out to the teacher seeking his attention. Apparently, he was healing the sick as he talked to the crowd. The people were awestruck. Great cheers and praises to God arose before us.

I strained to see over the heads of the gathered. I noticed the crowd was very diverse. The poor assembled with the rich. The beggars with tax collectors. Even some Roman soldiers were gathered, but they did not appear threatening. Rather they seemed enraptured by the words of the teacher. *How odd*, I thought. I also noticed several scribes and Pharisees in their rich clothing. It was obvious they had been sent from the High Priest and the Sanhedrin in Jerusalem to spy on the rabbi. However, I was still unable to see the teacher, so I stretched and stood on my tiptoes. But to no avail.

Avoiding the crushing throng of people, many gathered along the rooftops of the surrounding buildings. Several sat along the edges watching the teacher below. Their legs dangling above the crowd. Others stood behind them. I noticed something that made my heart stop. Despite the heat of the day, a terrible cold chill ran down my spine.

Along the rooftops, several large black ravens sat perched. A terrifying feeling came over me, stealing the excitement that I once felt. There must have been at least a dozen of them. Their malevolent presence filled my heart with dread. These minions of evil stared down upon the crowd. Several sat perched on the highest points of the tallest buildings. But a couple of these sinister phantoms sat atop several of the people watching. They appeared to be standing atop the gathered witnesses' heads or shoulders. The wicked talons digging deep into their scalps. These victims appeared unaware of their unwelcome guests. I stared in horror as their talons dug deeper into the flesh. But this time, something was different. The ravens were completely still, unmoving, like Greek statues. Not a single one even glanced my way. Instead, they were fixated on the teacher. It was as if they could not tear their stares away. Their vile eyes glared down at him with burning hatred.

The crowd of people became silent. They froze as their attention was drawn across the street. A loud cry rang out. Two men approached. Two unclean men. Their filthy clothes and their demeanor identified them immediately. A pair of lepers. They called out to the teacher, "Master! Master! Please help us!"

The crowd recoiled and turned hostile toward them. Loud shouting echoed off of the buildings and rose into the sky, "Unclean! Unclean! Unclean!"

The gathered crowd of people were enraged, as it is forbidden for a leper to come into the city at all.

According to the Law, they must remain outside of the city walls, as commanded by Moses. These are the impure. These men were considered utterly unclean, both physically and spiritually. In fact, anything they touch also becomes unclean, infected. For it is known that the leper suffers either from black magic or from his own sins. These are the vile. They are the walking dead. These impure souls are feared by the people. They are considered contaminated, filthy and unclean, second only to a dead body. The Law gives specific instructions as to the treatment of the lepers. Anyone suspected of having leprosy must approach a priest for examination. If the priest finds one defiled and deemed impure, he shall be forced to wear torn clothes and let the hair of his head hang loose and uncut. He must cover his upper lip and cry out a warning for all to hear, "Unclean! Unclean!" He shall live alone and dwell outside of the city walls.

Lepers are so repulsive and abhorrent that it is forbidden for one to come within 150 feet of a human being if the wind is blowing, even their own family. And these two vile wretches had the audacity to come crawling into the town. Into this large crowd of people. The banished bringing their infection with them. And they dared to disturb the teacher.

More angry shouts arose, "Unclean! Unclean! Unclean!"

The crowd moved as one living being. It shrank back retreating from these infected souls. Several men in the group began to pick up rocks and hurl them at the lepers. They screamed curses at them.

The two miserable sufferers called out to the teacher, "Master! Master! Please help us!" Several rocks struck them both. More rocks continued to fly. One man was hit hard in the face. It was a violent blow. He stumbled and fell to the ground. Desperate, he continued to crawl toward the crowd. He continued to call out to the teacher. "Master! Master!"

They were now just 10 or 12 steps away from Joanan and me. We both took a step backwards. I noticed how filthy they were. Their flesh was raw, and they stank. The smell of rotting meat followed them. It filled my nostrils. Their skin was white and scaly. It cracked like old dried and rotten leather. Several open sores oozed a sickening yellowish and brown pus. Their long stringy hair was matted and tangled. Bald spots appeared on their scalps where huge clumps of hair had fallen out.

The raw open sores covered their entire bodies. Tumor like growths appeared on their arms and legs. Their faces were grotesquely disfigured. Their earlobes were misshapen and they dangled hopelessly. One man's nose seemed absent as if it had collapsed and turned inward or just fallen off. The others nose was badly deformed and dripped streaming droplets of a thick yellow nasal secretion.

They both had disfigured limbs as the leprosy had not only rotted their flesh, but also twisted their bones. I noticed that one man had a hand that resembled a claw. Repulsed, it reminded me of the raven creatures perched above us watching this spectacle. I glanced upward and noticed that they continued to stare intently into the inner crowd and at the teacher within. They glared at him, ignoring these suffering men. The other man was missing several fingers and toes.

It is said that a leprosy sufferer loses the sense of touch and pain, thus unaware of his injuries and leading to the loss of body parts. I have even heard stories of lepers having their fingers and toes eaten off by rats while they slept, completely unaware of the horror until they awoke the next morning. I was reminded of the ravens perched above us.

The man on his knees continued to crawl forward. Another rock struck him. This one bounced off of his shoulder leaving a bloody bruise. He looked up at me pleading. His eyes were a sickly gray. His pupils had turned ashen white. Weak and desperate, he strained to get the words out, "Lord, please help me."

I wondered in my heart, *what were this man's sins? What had made this man suffer so?* For surely, he had sinned. That is what the rabbis taught. The rabbis teach the moral lesson of leprosy as one of the concepts of *mezora*, meaning "one being diseased." It comes from *mozi shem ra,* meaning "the person of guilt of slander or libel." The rabbis regard leprosy as divine punishment for the sin of slander. *Surely that must be their sins.*

Suddenly the crowd parted like a wave. A hushed silence fell across the entire group of people. A man was standing before the two lepers. He looked at the crowd but did not say a word. His stare was harsh. He knelt down and helped the fallen man to his feet. A hushed whisper spread through the people. A whisper of shock and disbelief. The crowd was stunned, for he had touched the unclean. He had touched the living dead.

The crowd of people moved back, stepping away from the lepers. The teacher now stood alone with the two men. He turned to the gathered people. He looked ashamedly upon them. Sadness filled his eyes. Disappointment. The compunctious crowd was silent. The teacher scanned the group of gatherers. He searched their eyes and their hearts. He stopped and made eye contact with me.

He stared at me for a long uncomfortable moment. His deep amber eyes were penetrating. A strange sensation came over me. One of recognition. One of familiarity. For some reason, I knew this man. But how? He was so familiar, incredibly familiar. It perplexed me. I stared on with curious amazement. Somehow, I knew this man. I knew those eyes.

It dawned on me. This was the rabbi I had seen over a year ago. This was the rabbi from the synagogue in Capernaum. Surely that was it. This must be the mysterious teacher, Jesus.

I recognized him now. He no longer appeared as clean and pure as when I had first encountered him. His clothes were dusty. His feet covered in sweat and dirt from a long travel. His face was darker from time spent under the sun. He stared at me for a long uncomfortable moment. A feeling of shame crept into my heart. He winked at me and turned toward the others. I let the rock slip from my hand. It fell to the ground with a quiet thud.

The two lepers both fell to their knees. They grasped at the teacher's cloak holding tightly and cried out beseeching him, "Master, have mercy on us!"

Their brazen action was shocking. The crowd was repulsed by such a blatant disregard for the teacher and the Law. However, Jesus was not angered at this, but rather he was filled with compassion for these two. He spoke to them in a gentle tone, "What is it that you want me to do?"

"Lord, you can make us clean," they both cried out, "if you are willing."

The teacher turned to the gathered followers and paused, making sure the entire crowd witnessed this. I saw him look up toward where the raven creatures were perched. I am not sure, but it appeared that he glared at them. They never moved but stared back at him. Their stare was vicious. Drawing the attention of the crowd, he said quietly but very boldly, "I am. I am willing." The teacher, this Jesus broke the Law. He reached out and freely touched the lepers. He placed his hands atop each man's head. He looked up toward Heaven in a silent prayer. I was reminded of Moses calling out to God on behalf of his sister, Miriam. She had been stricken with leprosy as punishment for speaking out against Moses. Moses prayed to the Lord and she was restored. Now Jesus called out loudly. "Be cleansed," he commanded.

A bright light formed around the two men. It seemed to radiate from within them. At first, the raw open sores seemed to immediately scab over. The dead skin began to fall off of them in great flakes, like fish scales falling to the ground. It turned into a fine powder that blew away like white and gray ashes left from a burned-out fire. It left behind soft pink healthy skin, the skin of a newborn babe. Their faces were bathed in a light leaving them with fully restored handsome features. Their hair also transformed, leaving thick dark manes that shone like eastern silk. Their eyes were filled with amazement as they glistened and turned a rich dark brown. After years of suffering, these dead men were now filled with life once more.

Their limbs restored as the crowd looked on in wonderment. A hushed gasp of amazement filled the air. Twisted and bent bones straightened themselves as new hands and feet formed. We could actually hear the bones and tendons snap and pop. The one man grew new fingers as we watched. The sound was like a distant crackling fire that burned within them.

As both men's bodies were restored, they fell on their faces and praised God. "Thank you, Jesus. Blessed is the Lord God Almighty, El Shaddai." In fact, the entire crowd began to praise the Lord.

Jesus turned to the followers and spoke. He spoke with such force and authority. "Leprosy is like sin. It starts out small but if unchecked, it can spread, consuming the entire body. This leads to other sins and can cause great damage to our relationship with our heavenly father."

He turned back to the two men still on their knees, "Stand up. Your faith has made you well."

They stood on strong legs, clean for the first time in years. Tears streamed down their faces. They raised their trembling hands toward Heaven and continued to thank and praise God. In the corner of my eye something caught my attention. I turned and looked up to see a lone white dove fly across the blue expanse of sky. The ravens were nowhere to be found. They had disappeared.

CHAPTER 10

The teacher remained in Capernaum for about a week. Every morning we went to listen to his teachings. Every day he healed more of the sick and lame. And every day the crowds grew larger. In fact, the crowds grew so large that on several occasions he was forced to climb into a boat and cast out away from the shore. From there he would stand on the bow and preach to the people. His voice carried across the water's surface. The soft lapping of the gentle waves licking the shoreline sounded in the background.

Each afternoon we returned to our chores at the compound. Each day we seemed to fall further behind with our work, yet Jarviss and the others did not seem to mind. They were content. Each evening we would sit around the fire, drink a skin of wine, and discuss what we had witnessed. We reviewed the day's activities and what the teacher had said. Jarviss was convinced along with his nephews that this rabbi, this Jesus, could be the messiah. I was still unsure. I questioned my own eyes. I remained very skeptical. This man was no messiah. Yes, I had witnessed miraculous healings and unexplainable events. The teacher also spoke with amazing understanding and clarity. Maybe he was a prophet, maybe a very knowledgeable rabbi, yet he was not a king. He was not a warrior like King David. This man alone could not defeat Rome and restore Israel to all its glory. And he spoke of peace and forgiveness, even to one's enemies. In fact, he instructed us to love our enemies and pray for those who persecute us. In my mind's eye, I could not imagine him fulfilling that role. No, he could not be the messiah.

Jarviss and the brothers argued adamantly that I was wrong. They claimed that the power to heal could only come from God. Jannai claimed that the teacher would soon rise to power, gather a mighty army and defeat our enemies. At that time, he was gathering his followers. Jannai stated that we needed to be patient and be ready for the moment. They all pledged that they would rise up and follow, when the time came.

Remaining incredulous, I continued to disagree with them. The brothers became frustrated with my unyielding stance. However, I agreed that yes, this man was a wise prophet. And yes, he possessed miraculous healing powers. I also agreed that surely those powers were a gift bestowed upon the teacher by the Lord and none other, unless they were a hoax. However, I went on to explain that other healers or miracle workers were found throughout Judea. I argued that these people were also filled with a gift bestowed upon them by God. I argued that yes, unexplained phenomenon existed in this world, but that still did not make him the messiah. I was tempted to share my visions with Jarviss, Joanan and his brothers, but I did not.

After about a week, the rabbi left Capernaum. No one saw him go. One day he was just gone. Most believed that he and his disciples sailed away in the night. A sad melancholy swept through the streets of the town. Everyone felt it. That man had cast a strange spell of enchantment over the entire town. However, afterwards work continued at the pottery makers compound. We had some catching up to do.

Each evening was the same. We drank well into the night. Joanan, Jared, Josh, Jannai, and John continued to try to persuade me. However, I stood my ground and remained a resolute skeptic. They were all convinced of this man's identity. They were his loyal followers, yet I remained true to the Lord and to his Law.

After about another week or so, I was visited by one of my strange recurring dreams. Startled, I awoke panting and in a pool of sweat. I had dreamed of the crystal-clear river and of the beautiful scroll that floated there. I had tried to retrieve it, but to no avail. My intent was to save the scroll, the holy Law of the Lord, but in turn, I realized that it was me who needed saving. And to my horror, I discovered that the scroll could not save me. It never had.

In fact, it was the scroll that pulled me down into the dark and icy depths of the river. This dream disturbed me to my very soul. It was blasphemy. I condemned myself. This enigma haunted me, as I was a devout and zealous follower of the Lord. After all, I was a scribe. I knew the Torah far better than most, even better than the rabbis. My arrogance swelled.

As I lay there alone in the dark confines of Jarviss' guest room, a gentle breeze moved through the corridor. Without warning, it was bitterly cold, as cold as the summit of Mount Hermon. Freezing breath escaped my lips with a thick cloud of steam. The air became thick. Tiny ice crystals formed and hung suspended in the vague light. The cold seeped into my bones. My hands were as cold as ice and my feet began to ache. I opened and closed my stiff hands feeling the blood circulate through my fingers.

The air stirred and swirled around me. Within the breeze was the faint smell of fresh flowers after a spring rain. A memory of a mountain meadow filled my mind. The hillside was covered with beautiful alpine flowers. A splash of color against a green background. A pleasant feeling of peace filled my soul. The cold breeze pushed through the room. Another scent filled my nostrils. It overwhelmed the fragrance of the flowers. The slight aroma of sweat. It was unmistakable – the distinct scent of my beloved. Her scent filled the room like a sweet perfume.

"Melessa?" I called out.

No answer came, only the frigid air.

I choked back tears as her memories filled my heart. "Is that you my love?"

No answer was forthcoming, but a fine cloud of mist formed at the foot of my bed. It slowly turned forming a swirling column of smoke. Like a lamp burning in the distance, it began to glow a faint azure light. The cloud was illuminated from within and cast a soft blue light that filled the room.

A tiny voice whispered in the darkness. It was barely audible. "Barabbas, son of thy father, my beloved."

It was Melessa. Her voice was as sweet as honey. Tears filled my eyes and a knot arose in my throat. I could hardly swallow, let alone speak.

"Barabbas, it is time."

"What time," I asked.

"You have a purpose, Barabbas."

"Wait! I'm not ready yet."

"Son of thy father, you have a destiny to fulfill. Your time has come. Go."

"And what is my destiny?" I asked. A lingering silence hung in the air. The spirit of my dead wife answered me, "Your destiny is a dark journey. It is filled with violence and death. Yet, it shall end with the light. Now go." With that final word, the freezing cold breeze pushed through the room. The glowing column of mist evaporated, and the blue light was extinguished. Hot tears ran down my cheeks and my eyes stung.

"I miss you so much, my love."

No answer came, only bitter silence. I knew she was gone. Memories of Melessa filled my heart, memories of her smile, her laughter, memories of a happier time. A fire of what could have been raged within me. It burned out of control. Her final words echoed in my mind. I looked forward to my destiny, and yet I feared it.

CHAPTER 11

The very next morning at breakfast, I informed Jarviss and all of the family that I would be leaving soon. As expected they were sad, yet none were surprised as they had been expecting such. Three days later, after the Sabbath, they gathered to see me off. They were generous with gifts to aid in my journey. Jarviss placed a leather pouch heavy with coins in my hand and squeezed my fingers shut around it. Their generosity and unwavering love filled my soul. These people, this family were the incarnation of Melessa and the embodiment of all the good that she stood for. With a heavy heart, I set out.

Gaining passage on a cargo ship, I set sail southward. We crossed the Galilee with calm waters and docked at Kerakh. It was a busy port side town surrounded by massive ancient walls. The walls were 25 feet thick and made of mud bricks. The people claim that the walls were originally built three thousand years ago. The town had been an important coastal community until it was destroyed and abandoned. It lay that way for ages until the Persians re-inhabited the region and the Canaanites rebuilt the city calling it *Beth Yerah*, which means "House of the Moon God." Hundreds of years later the town was renamed in Greek, *Philoteria*, by the Egyptian King Ptolemy II Philadelphus. He named the town after his sister. It remained that until the Romans conquered the land. They built a fortified citadel at Philoteria and renamed it *Kerakh*. *Kerakh* simply means "fortress" in Aramaic.

Kerakh was home to a garrison of Roman soldiers along with the citizens.

The Roman guard lived within the citadel. The town was peaceful and laid out in a very convenient and efficient way. The townspeople all lived in a complex of spacious town houses built within the confines of the fortifications. The houses were accessed through colonnaded courtyards filled with gardens. Decorated plaster covered stone and brick walls. The architecture shone perpendicular lines that reached toward Heaven with large proud archways. Several very large villas also set within the town. They were decorated with polished marble and beautifully arranged mosaics. Overall, this was a very impressive town that had seen years of prosperity.

From Kerakh, I headed south following the Jordan River. I stuck to the trails that ran along the river's edge. Some were made by the locals. Some were animal trails. There, the vegetation was thick, and the wildlife abounded. I traveled slowly, constantly on the hunt for wild game. Signs of deer and antelope were everywhere, however, I found none. I tried my best to avoid the villages and people, but I did see a few women and children who were gathering water along the river's edge.

I continued southward. On the third day, I came to the place where the Jabbok River joins the Jordan. Several years ago, I had camped here and hunted. This was the area I had encountered two Roman soldiers in an ungodly act. Later they came into my camp and assaulted me. That was the last thing that they ever did. Their blood shall be upon their heads.

Shaking that memory from my mind, I turned back toward the *Jabbok*, an extraordinary spot where the two rivers collide. Huge eddies churned around the rocks pushing the current upstream. The *Jabbok*, called the luxuriant river, whose name means "to drain or empty itself," was crystal clear. In fact, the water was so clear that it appeared blue in some places. That leads some people to call it *Nahr ez-Zerqa*, which means "river of blue." The bed of the river flows through a deep cut gorge with steep precipitous banks. The river is lined with lush vegetation of all kinds. Beautiful but poisonous oleander covers the banks for miles, painting the valley with clusters of brilliant colors in reds, whites and pinks. Although the banks of the river are steep, the river is fordable at several points. In fact, it was at one of these fords just to the East, where the patriarch Jacob had his mysterious encounter and was changed forever. After leaving Mahanaim, he was returning from Paddan-aram to meet his brother, Esau. They had not seen each other since Jacob's deceit and theft of his brother's blessed birthright many years before.

As I stood on the banks of the river, listening to the current cascade past, the waters spoke to me. The words of the Lord from the Torah filled my mind. *Now he arose that same night and took his two wives and his two maids and his eleven children, and crossed the ford of the Jabbok. He took them and sent them across the stream. And he sent across whatever he had. Jacob was left alone, and a man wrestled with him until daybreak.*

Following the serenity of the river, I continued to follow it to the East coming to the very ford called Peniel. A large rock stood erect on the bank of the Jabbok. Its foot was buried into the rich black soil indicating that it had stood there for ages. It rose as an unwavering monument commemorating the very spot where Jacob wrestled the angel. I ran my hand across the top of the giant stone. It felt polished, surely by hundreds of others who had also laid their hands atop the ancient stone. Tiny lichens covered the pink granite with a multitude of colors from grayish blue to yellow and green. I stood watching the crystal-clear waters gurgle and spill across the white river stones that filled the bed of the Jabbok. The sun sparkled off of the cascading waters. This place had a beauty of its own. It caused my mind to wander. It wandered back in time, to a place long long ago. To a place of ancient times. To a time when God still intervened with His people. I imagined Jacob standing alone on the banks of the river. He stood isolated and abandoned in this place of solitude. He was utterly alone as he had sent his family and his servants ahead along with all of his wealth and livestock. A dark cloud hung over him. Jacob had a heavy heart. His soul was so weary, and his heart was black with worry. He had received the news that his brother, Esau approached with an army of 400 fighting men. Maybe it was his guilt or maybe it was just the fear of his brother's revenge, but Jacob was a broken man. Forsaken, he was completely alone. He was devastated and exhausted, both mentally and physically. Jacob prepared for either his death or his ruin. He was now alone and in communion with God.

In my imagination, I could see Jacob before me. An older man now, yet still strong and proud. Years in the sun had turned his skin to leather. His clothes were drenched with sweat and dust. His hair was a wild mane. Shocks of gray streaked through his beard. Wild and bushy eyebrows framed his dark eyes. Although strong, his eyes were filled with a profound sadness. Deep wrinkles furrowed from the corners of his sorrowful eyes and broad lines ran across his forehead. At that moment, his soul was black. His proud shoulders were slumped. A look of dread wracked his entire body. After crossing at the ford on the Jabbok, exhausted, Jacob knelt down. He slept, for tomorrow he would meet Esau.

I imagined Jacob, preparing for a much-needed rest, removing his tunic. I imagined an unexpected wind swirled. A strong breeze howled down the canyon. Leaves were ripped from their branches and the grasses bowed in subjection. A strange sound, carried on the wind, filled the night's air. Without warning a man of great strength mysteriously appears. He is half naked and muscled like a bull. Unprovoked, he attacks Jacob with a savage ferociousness. The two men clash violently. They push and shove each other trying to knock the other to the ground. Jacob feels the muscles of his antagonist bulge across his shoulders.

He must have had to suppress a rising sense of fear and panic, for this was a fight to the death. Grappling for an advantage, Jacob holds tightly to the man. Pulling hard, Jacob tries to unbalance his opponent and sweep his legs out from under him. However, his attack did not work, as the stranger moves with the agility of a cat, but with the strength of a bear. Twisting his hips, the man flings Jacob to the ground. He lands hard on his back, knocking the breath from his lungs, yet Jacob holds on with all of his strength, all of his heart and all of his might. He drags the stranger to the ground with him. Their head to head combat grows more violent. They roll and tumble across the bank of the river. Rocks dig into his bare back. Their tangled bodies cast strange shadows that danced in the silver moonlight. Monstrous shadows crawl across the river rocks. They continue to wrestle all of the night. The stranger is incredibly strong, yet Jacob holds his own. They each maneuver for a position of power, yet they are each thwarted by the other's efforts.

Jacob can feel the man's skin against his. Sweat slickens their bodies. The physical confrontation continues. Head to head, Jacob can smell the man's minted breath and the man's scent, a faint musky sweat. This was an intimate battle.

I imagine the men fought like animals. They must have growled. Savage grunts and groans must have risen into the night's sky. Their muscles flexed and strained. Jacob fought against exhaustion and fatigue. Every fiber in his body hurt. His muscles were hard. They were bands of iron, yet they burned like glowing iron from a furnace. Jacob could feel the stranger's strength. He could feel the stranger's power, yet he would not be overcome. He would never surrender. Jacob knew in his heart that he would prevail. He must.

Scripture says the two fought through the night and into the early hours of the morning. I imagine the faint orange glow that began to fill the Eastern sky. A sliver of burning gold cut the horizon. When the stranger saw that he had not prevailed against Jacob, he reached out and with one finger, touched the socket of his thigh. Was it a soft and gentle touch, like that of a feather? Yet it filled Jacob with excruciating pain as his thigh was dislocated from his hip. I imagine a raging fire burned through Jacob's body. Fighting against the pain, he refused to let go of his hold on the stranger. Jacob had fought valiantly, with the heart of a lion, but his opponent was no ordinary man. This was a mighty and ancient warrior. This was the Angel of God.

The stranger said, "Let me go, for the dawn is breaking."

Holding firm, Jacob said, "I will not let you go unless you bless me."

So, the stranger said to him, "What is your name?"

And he answered, "Jacob. I am Jacob."

In a deep voice, a voice of authority the stranger spoke, "Your name shall no longer be Jacob, but Israel; for you have striven with God and with men and have prevailed."

Jacob asked him and said, "Please tell me your name."

But the stranger said, "Why is it that you ask my name?"

He did not answer Jacob, but he blessed him there on the bank of the ford on the Jabbok.

So, Jacob named the place Peniel, for he said, "I have seen God face to face, yet my life has been preserved."

I found myself standing alone on that very spot. My hand still rested on the marker stone. The rock still warm to the touch. The gurgling sounds of water crashing over the stones mixed with the songs of the passing birds. The sparkling waters passed before me. A small shiver ran down my spine. The hair on the back of my neck stood and goosebumps covered my arms, for I too have seen the face of God.

CHAPTER 12

I spent that night camped on the bank of the Jabbok River at the ford called Peniel. No mysterious strangers visited me in the night, nor was I forced to fight for my life. I slept very well. It was a deep, peaceful sleep, the sleep of the dead. I slept so heavily that the sun had risen high into the sky before I awoke the following morning. That was unusual for me. After my breakfast, I gathered my belongings and set out heading eastward. I would explore this part of Transjordan, a land called *be·êv·er hay·yar·dên miz·raḥ hash·shê·mesh*, which means "beyond the Jordan towards the sunrise."

Along the Jabbok, the banks of the river were much steeper than those of the Jordan. The river had cut a wild and deep canyon through the ancient mountains of Gilead, leaving a deep scar on the face of the Earth. The ravine flowed to the west before emptying into the Jordan River between Gennesaret and the Dead Sea. It was a beautiful and savage river. Wildlife flourished there. Large layers of rock outcroppings hung above the waters, gazing down on the river's surface. Thickets of tamarisk grew along the floodplains and river's edge. In some places, dark forests of oaks grew along the banks and even forests of pines grew closer to the top of the canyon walls. Along the shallows and the upstream banks, reeds and cattails stood guard. The river was deep and moved constantly downstream with a strong current. At some places, the current moved slower, with a lazy and relaxed attitude. There the waters were teeming with fish. Silver fins flashed in the sunlight as they darted through the stream. I watched two otters play and chase each other in a comical performance as they pursued the quick little fish. Other places, the river roared. The foaming white waters churned and crashed over the rocks and boulders that lined the banks.

At one point, the route became impassable as giant boulders blocked the way. They had fallen from the highest points along the canyon walls and shattered as they crashed down toward the valley floor, before coming to rest along the water's edge. Some were the size of houses. Realizing there was no other way upstream, I was forced to climb up the steep canyon walls. The loose talus made climbing the face extremely difficult at first. Having my sword and bow strapped across the pack on my back made the ascent cumbersome. I climbed slowly, carefully placing each foot and checking each handhold before placing my weight on it. Several times, my foot slipped, or the rock that was my handhold pulled away and fell back toward the waters.

Each time a rock fell, it started an avalanche of rocks that slid and grew as it pushed its way downward. Most of the rock slides died out, but some made it all the way to the valley floor and spilled into the river. I found myself very high and exposed to the danger of falling to my death. I found that it was more dangerous to try and climb back down than it was to continue upward.

At one precarious section, the broken scree field played out leading to a perpendicular sheet of solid stone. Thin air moved below me. I found myself perched on a thin ledge. Only my toes held me to the impossibly narrow ledge of rock. My fingers held to small imperfections in the rock face. I prayed that the Lord would protect me. At one point I was able to slide my fingers into a small thin crack that ran upward. It reminded me of a bolt of lightning that had split the face of this mountain. Jamming my fingers into the crack I managed to pull myself up, inching my way one hand at a time. My feet frantically searching for each perch. My heart raced. Fear gripped me. The palms of my hands were slick with sweat. My leg began to vibrate and shake uncontrollably. I could not stop myself. The shaking became so violent that it almost caused me to come off of the wall. My breathing became fast and shallow. Instinctively, I looked down into the infinite space and the canyon far below. Fear gripped me. Below, the river continued to rush past the strange rock outcroppings. Their jagged peaks awaiting my fall. Great anxiety swelled up inside of me.

I felt a swift breeze rise from the canyon floor. Two ravens rose from below. Riding air currents up the face of the cliff, they hovered past me. They were so close. The sun reflected off their black feathers. I could see their beady eyes as they swiveled around to look at me. One let out an angry screech of displeasure as he passed. The other simply glared. I watched as they sailed away, carried by the canyon's wind.

It took several minutes for me to calm myself. Finally, I found a solid perch for my foot and the shaking eased. My breathing slowed but sweat poured from my pores. My undergarment was drenched. I was scared out of my mind, yet I continued to ascend the precipitous canyon wall. Soon the climbing eased, as the canyon's steep face began to relax and open up. *Praise the Lord*, I thought. There, small ledges became more stable. Handholds became numerous. Vegetation and grasses covered more of the hillside. It was a welcomed sight. I felt a sense of relief wash over me. It was like a crashing wave.

As I continued to ascend, the climbing became easier. More childhood lessons from Samuel came crawling back into my mind. He had been a wealth of knowledge and introduced me to all things in nature. There before me, I found distinct layers of rock formations laid one upon each other. White crystalline limestone lay beneath layers of dark shale. They alternated, one formation laying atop another. The shale was blackish with hints of green scattered throughout. In some places the limestone cracked and crumbled, exposing marine sediments. At first, I began to notice small marine animals that had turned to stone. These were the same creatures one might find in the Mediterranean. Layers of limestone were embedded with clams. They were blackish in color surrounded by lighter sediments. Hundreds of these clams piled upon each other and were embedded in the stone. They were small round disks about the size of one's hand. They were perfectly preserved, as I could plainly see the grooves and patterns that ran through their shells. I even found several places where the white stone had broken apart revealing tiny fish imprints that were found within. These were fascinating to me as they were also perfectly preserved, yet they were stone.

As I climbed higher along the steep canyon wall, the layers of rock changed. Above the limestone and shale, a thick layer of gypsum could be seen. It was a light-colored rock formation that extended upward at least the height of four or five men. The weather had eroded and crumbled it away in spots leaving broken fissure and exposing the beauty of the stone. It was almost a pure white formed from layers of crystals. Some appeared translucent like glass. In a few rare spots, darker veins ran through the stone. From the broken edges, one could see the sharp crystalline projections lending to its name and why it is called "spear stone." I scratched it with my thumbnail revealing how soft the rock truly was. It scraped away with a fine white powder. That explained to me why all the artists from the ancient Egyptians, the Greeks and even the Romans used this stone for their sculptures. This fine gypsum stone was called alabaster. Jarviss would have loved it, as it makes fine alabaster jars and pottery. Thinking to myself, *I must tell Jarviss of this place and what I have found the next time I see him.*

I was now very high on the canyon wall looking back down upon the Jabbok River. The rock cliffs fell away leaving only thin air beneath me. That uncomfortable feeling of exposure and vulnerability returned, bridging the gap between thrill and death. My hands continued to sweat profusely. As I climbed past the gypsum, I found more limestone and shale. These were darker, and the rock located there seemed to have a rusty reddish tint. There I found more marine creatures frozen in stone. Small fish and a large seashell, a nautilus, were exposed where the rock had eroded away from the cliff. The nautilus was huge compared to those I had seen in several markets along the coastline of the Mediterranean. They were very common in Alexandria. But this one was different. It was much thicker. It was at least twice as big as the largest one I had ever seen, at least three hand widths across. Plus, it was solid stone. This one's shell twisted and turned away from the center in a perfect rhythmic spiral. In a way, it reminded me of a ram's horn. I ran my fingers over it, feeling the deep ridges as they spiraled outward. It was amazing.

This was such a mystery to me as I wondered how such marine dwelling creatures of antiquity could have been found this far inland and placed this high along a canyon wall. I know that the Earth was covered by water at least twice, once during the creation and once during Noah's great flood. Could there have been more? The Torah does not mention it. But still, it raised more questions in my heart. Yet, the Lord is not constrained by the human mind. The Lord is ancient and timeless and beyond approach.

I continued to climb upward through loose and broken rock toward the top of the canyon wall. Above the limestone and shale, at the very top of the canyon, a thick layer of sandstone awaited. It too was in layers. The sandstone was heavily eroded by years of exposure to the elements. Broken pieces lay scattered along narrow ledges. As they crumbled, smaller rocks shattered and had fallen downward back toward the valley floor. It was there that I found the most amazing discovery.

A large sandstone boulder lay alone on its side. It lay precariously balanced on a ledge, hundreds of feet above the river. It had broken away from its mother in some ancient past. Their common adjoining faces were very evident. They would have fit back together like a puzzle. Along the boulder's broken face something was revealed there. Embedded in the rock itself was a bone. I couldn't believe it. It was a very large bone, resembling maybe a leg, like a thigh bone. However, it was much larger than that of a man. It was longer than my arm and bigger around. The head of the bone was evident. You could plainly see where it would have fit into the socket. Although the bone itself was also stone, the bone differentiated itself from the sandstone in color and texture. It was a light color, like a dirty white with a yellow hue. Shadows of a rust color were scattered throughout the bone. Small cracks and flakes ran through it. The bone had a texture to it, that revealed tiny minute holes or pores. It was definitely a bone. No doubt remained.

At the base of the rock were small fragments of bone that had eroded and broken away. They had fallen and were scattered at the foot of the large boulder. I picked up one of the fragments. The shattered piece was about the size of a finger. It was sharp along one side with a dull broken corner on the other. I found the exact spot where it had broken away from the larger bone. With steady hands, I placed it back. It fit perfectly. I held the bone up, so I could see it plainly in the afternoon sunlight. Tiny holes covered the fragment. It reminded me of fibers of wood. I sniffed the bone fearing that it might smell of death, but it had no odor at all. I touched the small bone fragment to my tongue. To my astonishment, it stuck. Very aggressively, it stuck to the tip of my tongue. Surprised, I actually had to tear it away.

What is this? I thought to myself. *It is huge. Could this be the remains of the ancient Nephilim? Maybe it was the remains of one of the fallen Watchers, those who had made the terrible oath standing on the summit of Mount Hermon, their bones buried here since the time of antiquity.*

No apparent answers were evident. Moving along the narrow cliff, I continued to search along the broken rocks at the top of the ridge. There, trapped in the sandstone were more bones. Some were perfectly preserved while others were broken and badly eroded. I found what appeared to be ribs and several vertebrae. They were all huge in size. Several other pieces were hard to identify. However, it was obviously more bone, as it was distinctly different from the stone that surrounded it. I wanted to remove these from the rock but unfortunately, they were held captive within the stone. It frustrated me.

I found something else on the underside of a large boulder that had broken away from the upper ridge. It was hidden in the shadows. I noticed the bone. At first, It didn't make sense to me. It slowly took shape for my mind. There before me, was an eye socket. It was attached to a long snout. It was longer than my arm. Below was a jaw bone filled with terrible teeth. These were not the remains of the Nephilim. These were the bones of a dragon.

My heart raced as I stared at this new discovery. I ran my hand across the face of the rock and could feel the rough texture of the stone and the bones trapped within. But the teeth, they were smooth along the outer part, yet they still maintained a razor-sharp edge along one side. You could feel tiny serrations along the inner cutting edge. My mind was transported back in time, back to Egypt. I thought of my friend Nicolas and his brother Nereus. I thought of the storeroom in the back of the spice traders' warehouse. I thought of the dragon and the bones contained there. I thought of the teeth. And I shuddered.

I tried desperately to free the skull, but it was cemented into place. The skull was one with the stone and it refused to release its hold. Not one to give up easily, I persisted. Using my knife, I slowly carved away at the sandstone.

It took several hours, but I finally managed to free a single tooth. Although it was just one tooth, it was magnificent. The color was a dark rusty brown. It was as long as the tip of my longest finger to the palm of my hand. The edge was serrated and as sharp as a knife. It would have been devastating. I could imagine how deadly this would have been to its prey. Treasuring my find, I placed my trophy into my pack. I looked back down into the canyon far below. There the river was glistening in the evening sun and the strange rock outcroppings, appeared like tiny piles of pebbles. The mighty oak trees, now mere black dots. I turned and admired the magnificent dragon skull one more time before I climbed to the top of the canyon's ridge. There, I bivouacked on the ledge, under the stars and above a dragon.

CHAPTER 13

The following morning, the sun revealed a spectacular view of the valley and the river below. From my vantage point, I could see the lands that had been given to the two and a half tribes of Israel. According to the Book of Numbers, called *Bəmiḏbar*, which means "In the desert," the tribes of Reuben and Gad came to Moses and asked if they could settle there in the Transjordan, South of the Jabbok. At first, Moses was dubious, but he conceded as long as they agreed to join in the conquest of the promised land. Both tribes agreed, and this land became theirs. Later, the half-tribe of Manasseh, from the House of Joseph, settled the land to the North of the Jabbok. It was there that I explored.

I traveled eastward until the canyon eased its steep slopes and gave into gentle rolling hills. People began to appear. Trails and roads criss crossed the land. Herds of sheep and cattle grazed on farms. I realized that I was deep into the Province of Syria. To the North of the Jabbok River, high in the countryside sat the city of Gerasa. It had been founded by Alexander the Great about 300 years ago, when he left Egypt and went to Mesopotamia. As he crossed Syria, he stopped and established Gerasa as a place for aged and retired Macedonian soldiers. The town thrived. Later, the area was absorbed into the Roman Empire. The Romans claimed it to ensure security and peace. But it came at a high price, just as it does for my people. I stopped there, without entering the city as I had wandered far enough. I turned and headed back to the West, back to Judea.

I followed the Jabbok, staying higher on the canyon until the bank became easier to descend. It's always easier to climb up a steep wall than it is to climb down. Along the wooded thickets of the river, with my bow in hand, I hunted for game but found none. I thought of the dragon. I thought of those teeth. I imagined it stalking its prey along this very river bottom. A cold thrill of excitement ran down my spine.

Soon I came to the place where the Jabbok and the Jordan collided. A pleasant scent filled the air as a gentle breeze pushed down the valley. I continued down the Jordan River following it to the South. At a shallow ford, I crossed to the West side of the Jordan. I passed the village of Coreae and managed to avoid the desert fortress and prison of Alexandrium without incident. Finding a peaceful spot along the river's edge, I slept there for the night. The next morning, I continued South.

I was just outside of the town of Archelais, approximately 12 miles North of Jericho. There, vast date palm groves extended over the surrounding hills and along the banks of the river. The town had originally been built by Herod Archelaus, the son of Herod the Great, before he was removed from power by the Emperor Augustus. Archelaus had built the town as the center for his date palm plantations and to house the workers. He diverted the waters from the spring of Na'aran to irrigate the groves of trees. It was a perfect environment with rich sandy soil and they thrived. An impressive forest of palms rose and covered the hills. The trees were massive, standing 70 to 75 feet tall. Their crowns were 20 to 30 feet across.

Walking through this orchard that spilled onto the bank of the river, I stared upward toward the blue sky. The shaggy palm fronds cast strange shadows onto the Earth below. They danced in the gentle breeze that blew down the valley. I was reminded of the Holy Temple and my first visit with Papa as a child. Ornate palm leaves of solid gold were carved high upon the walls and doors throughout the entire temple, on both the inner and outer rooms. It was to remind one of the lost gardens of Eden and paradise found within the walls of the Holy Temple and the dwelling place of the Lord. The palm tree itself is one of the most distinguished and recognized symbols signifying goodness, well-being and victory. They are used by the Romans in a triumphal procession whenever a victorious leader returns from battle. The crowds will bring cut palm fronds and wave them in celebration before laying the branches on the ground before their leader's feet.

Staring upward, I admired these magnificent trees. My mind was filled with the word of God. It came from the Psalms, *"the righteous shall flourish like the palm tree."* As I meditated on this word, something caught my eye. It drew me to the waters behind me. Moving toward the river, I noticed several ducks floating in the gentle current. Quietly, I removed my pack and nocked an arrow. Crawling through the tall brush and grasses, I managed to creep to the edge of the river where the bulrushes were tall. Rising to my knees, I readied myself to draw my bow. Through a small opening in the vegetation, I could see the ducks in the middle of the river. They were a pretty gray. Their bodies speckled with white. Their heads were cinnamon brown. A luminescent green stripe painted their faces surrounding their eyes. The green crescent extended to the backs of their heads. The same brilliant green splashed across feathers on each of their wings, revealing a patch of color that changed from green to purplish blue in the sunlight. These ducks whistled to each other in a whistling chatter. Their black beaks reflected the sunlight that danced on the water. I admired their beauty.

Picking the closest one, I readied my shot. The string felt heavy as it bit into my fingers. I drew my bow, touching the arrow to the corner of my mouth. Inhaling, I held my breath. I released the arrow. It flew with the swiftness of a falcon. Unfortunately, the arrow flew just to the left of its intended mark. I believe that I nicked the ducks tail, as I did see a few feathers fly free. Instantly all of the ducks took to the air in a rush of wings and splashing water. Within the time of a single heartbeat, they rose into the sky and were gone.

My arrow floated alone in the middle of the Jordan. I could still see the white cresting and the three red lines. The feather fletching stood out of the water. I watched as it turned, and the current began to carry it downstream. I watched helplessly as it floated away. It moved quicker now, being carried by the faster waters toward the middle of the river. Disappointment set in as I watched my arrow slowly disappear. I noticed something along the river's edge. It was floating within the bulrushes and other tall water grasses. It was hidden well, and I could not make it out. Recognition set in. I realized that it was a person.

I rushed to the edge of the river. Slipping, my feet went out from under me. I stumbled and fell down the bank landing in the mud and water. Pain shot through my elbow as I landed on it, tearing the flesh. Gaining my feet, I waded into the shallows pushing aside the tall bulrushes. There before me, floating in the green water was a body. Silvery shapes darted away from underneath him. They left daft wakes through the calm waters. The fish had been feasting. I had interrupted their dinner.

Floating face down was a waterlogged corpse. It was in a hideous state of decomposition, but from the build, I could judge that it was that of a man. The cold dead skin was pitted and had a mottled pale color. Gases had bloated the body causing it to float to the surface, escaping his watery tomb. The body was tangled in the thick vegetation and rocks along the shoreline of the river. Part of him was stuck in the mud and weeds while the rest of him floated in the slow-moving current. Gentle eddies swirled and pushed the body trying to break it free. I stood transfixed, waist deep in the Jordan River.

My attention was torn away. The thunderous sound of a thousand beating wings filled the air and broke the silence. As I looked up, a swarm of starlings swoop through the tall palm trees. A swirling black cloud, they moved in unison as if of one mind. Their glossy iridescent wings were painted with brilliant orange patches that shined as the sunlight bounced from them. The twisting flight spun through the trees. They moved with the choreography of Greek dancers. The swarm rose and fell as it spun, a tornado of movement. The flock circled above me, before moving over the face of the water, then disappearing down the canyon, following the ducks.

My attention was drawn back to the dead man. The man's muddy and filthy cloak twisted and swirled around him, as if moved by magic. It swam in the slow-moving current, reminding me of giant bat wings. His hair and beard were matted and thick with mud. Little black water bugs crawled through his filthy mane. Pulling on his tunic, I managed to turn him over. I wanted to free him from his trap, so I could drag the man up on the shore.

As I tried to free the body, my own legs became entangled and snared in submerged branches and vegetation. One of my feet became stuck and I was not able to pull it free. As I struggled, something sharp dug in and stabbed my other foot. Wrenching in pain, I lost my balance. With my feet ensnared I could not move. I fell forward falling onto the rotting corpse. His arms wrapped around me pulling me under the cold water. Shocked, I drank in a huge mouthful of water. The very thought of it sickened me. Overwhelmed with disgust, I fought to free myself from this dead man's grasp.

As I gasped for a breath of air, I pushed the corpse away. However, it held on, twisting me under the water's surface. Fighting for my life, panic set in. The sounds of rushing water and of a million tiny bubbles filled my ears. Just as quickly as it had started, my feet came loose from their restraints. They were free. I was able to gain my feet and I stood rising from the water. I coughed violently and spit out the river water. Fresh air filled my lungs as relief washed over me. The bloated body floated there before me, a harmless cadaver.

Angered, I grabbed the dead man's tunic. I pulled and wrestled the body loose. It made a sickening slurping sound as it pulled loose from the mud. Preventing it from floating away, I managed to drag it part way onto the shore. My feet slipped in the slick mud and I fell several times. Gaining traction, I tried to brace myself by planting my feet on the rocks. Finally, I managed to pull the dead weight of the corpse onto the dry land. Immediately a terrific stench filled my nostrils. It was the stench of decomposition, the stench of death. I gagged as I fought back the urge to vomit.

I covered my face with my scarf to breathe better. I turned the man and managed to roll the corpse onto his back. His limbs sprawled awkwardly onto the dirt. Water drained from his clothes creating a shallow mud hole in the shape of a man. Immediately swarms of flies found the body. They buzzed as they lit and crawled wherever they liked, disrespecting the man's life and his humanity. The man's face was covered and unrecognizable. It was a mask of mud and filth. Scraping mud from his eye sockets and from his mouth and nose, I stared into that forsaken face. I noticed it slowly moved. It was alive with wriggling worms and larvae. Disgust raged through my veins. The urge to vomit rose up inside of me, but this time I could not repress it. The contents of my stomach emptied onto the shore of the Jordan River.

Repulsed by the repugnant scene before me, I was also filled with compassion. A compassion and feeling of sympathy toward this poor man. A compassion toward his family and loved ones. I don't know why this feeling had come over me, but it was strong. It was a feeling of unity. It rose up inside of me like a fire. Rather than a feeling of repulsion, I felt sympathy and kinship for this man that I could not explain.

I crawled over and began to search his body for any personal effects. Other than his clothes, he had a leather satchel. It was hung by a single thin shoulder strap that was wrapped around his body. Wrestling it free from his entangled clothing, I removed the bag. Opening it, I found it empty. Apparently, someone else had helped themselves to the contents before me, probably the thieves who had robbed this poor man and murdered him for the contents of this bag. Turning the satchel over in my hands, I examined it. I found that the bag itself was a treasure. It was made from shaved leather, probably calfskin, but had been worked to a fine soft material. It was now waterlogged and probably ruined, as it would never be the same. The leather was painstakingly and delicately tooled around the edges with a herringbone design. Ornate leaves were interlaced around the edges and up the entire shoulder strap. Across the face of the satchel were tooled the most sacred of words. The age-old prayer of the Jewish people, the Shema.

Hear, O Israel! The Lord is our God, the Lord is one! You shall love the Lord your God with all your heart and with all your soul and with all your might.

The last letter of the first and last words were written with larger print. The artist had meticulously tooled these into the leather canvas to emphasize their beauty. I noticed that these two letters formed the word "ED," meaning witness. It was designed that way to remind one of their duty to serve as a witness to the Lord's sovereignty. We do this by leading exemplary lives and bringing glory to the Lord.

I ran my hand over the surface of the satchel. The wet leather was smooth to the touch. I could feel the tooled letters and the decorations beneath my fingers. They were crisp and sharp. They felt magical. It was obvious that the creator of this piece of art had done so with the skill and love of a master craftsman. The diligent care and effort that was put into making this was second to none. His dedication to his skill was evident. I was impressed beyond words. It was beautifully done. This was a special piece, a treasure, and I'm sure that it meant a lot to the dead man. Immediately I knew that I must return the sacred heirloom to the poor man's family.

Turning the bag over, I could see that the back was also tooled with the ornate leaf pattern. I realized the decorative leaves were those of the palm tree. They resembled the palm fronds found carved in the Holy Temple and those that hung in the canopy above me. As I looked upward toward the trees, I saw several large ravens perched there. They stared down menacingly. Yellow eyes piercing me. *Had they come for me or had they come for the corpse?*

CHAPTER 14

Moving upstream, I bathed myself. I attempted to wash away the uncleanliness and impurity of the dead body. Gathering my belongings along with the dead man's satchel, I left the river. I headed West toward the town of Archelais. Passing through the forest of palm trees, I walked up and over the hill. Standing at the top of the hill stood a large stone tower. It was tall, providing a good view of the countryside and the river passage below. The bottom of the tower was built of stones that were cemented together forming a large archway. The upper story was built upon the arches. A very sturdy wooden ladder led up to the top of the tower.

Two men sat staring out across the country. They both saw me and nodded an acknowledgement as I waved to them. They appeared unconcerned as I passed. A very small community surrounded the tower. This was not Archelais. This was *Magdalsenna*, which means "Thorny." It was settled and named after some of the people of Israel who returned from captivity in Babylon along with Zerubbabel about 500 years ago. They claimed to be of the tribe of Benjamin.

I continued West across the gentle sloping hills until the town of Archelais came into view. Stone walls surrounded the town providing adequate protection. A large towered entrance with double gates welcomed the visitors. It was flanked by two other towers providing good observation of the surrounding plains and much of the palm groves. Built by Herod Archelaus, the son of Herod the Great, soon after taking control of this part of his father's kingdom. Archelaus began planting huge Date Palm Orchards that thrived. They stretched for miles. He built Archelais to house the workers for the plantation. It soon became a flourishing agricultural center, as it continues to be. Archelais was now one of the road stations on the road that led from Jericho up to Skythopolis. This provided a lot of traffic and an easy way to transport the massive amounts of dates that are produced each year.

As I entered into the town, I noticed tall bins and store houses surrounded me. More store houses rose than living quarters. Large baskets of dates filled the streets. Carts drawn by donkeys and oxen overflowed with dates. Dates were everywhere. I had never seen so many dates. Through the town square, tents stood shading the workers. Large clusters of dates hung from the houses as well as from the sides of the tents all the way around. Large tables were covered with dates. Some were poured into piles while others sat in baskets. So many different colors splashed across the market. Some dates were dried turning a deep dark wrinkled brown color, while others were still red, orange or yellow and some were still green and not ripe yet, as dates do not all mature at the same time requiring several harvests.

I walked through the town square and entered the market. The tents were those of vendors selling their wares. Tables were covered with all kinds of products for sale, yet they were all dates. Some offered dates ready to eat. Some were fresh, others were dried. Some were simply pitted, and others were pitted and stuffed with nuts or other types of fruit. Some had been finely chopped. Others were in breads and cakes made with dates and nuts. Jars of a thick spread called *ajwa* stood on one table. Jars of date syrup called *silan* which is used as an alternative to honey were stacked on another. Date sugar, which was finely ground powder made from dried dates or palm sap filled small jars. Its white residue lay strewn across several tables. Even bottles of wine and vinegar made from dates lined racks in the street.

I was amazed at all of the uses that these people had found for the date palm trees. One man had a thick viscous syrup made from crushing ripe dates. He claimed that the black syrupy paste was used as a waterproof coating for construction, leather, or for clay pipes to prevent leaking. Another sold soap made from the oil of pitted seeds. These people used every part of the tree, leaving nothing to waste. In addition to the fruit, they used the wood. They used the leaves. They made ropes and baskets that had been beautifully woven from the palm fronds. They even made beehives from the palm leaves. And it was all for sale. But the one thing that caught my eye the most was at the far end of the market. As I approached, I saw something large lying just beyond the last tent. It was a fishing boat. It appeared to be made from bundles of dried palm fronds that were tightly wrapping together. Each of these was bound to the next. Once they were all lashed together, they were drawn up forming the front and rear of the boat. These were drawn into long narrow points on each end of the boat, leaving the middle wide and open. Wooden planks were stretched across the boat providing seating for several men and an oarsman. The boat appeared lightweight but sturdy. The man claimed that it was sea worthy, but I personally would not take it out on the rough open waters. It was fascinating how they had built it. I would have loved for Papa to have seen that.

As I continued through the market and the town square, I began showing people the engraved satchel. I asked if they had ever seen it before. Several people dismissed me. Others simply shook their heads and returned to their chores. However, it didn't take long. I came to a vendor selling charcoal made from the seeds of the palm dates. Apparently, it burned exceedingly hot and made excellent fuel for the blacksmith's forge as well as the silversmith's. The man held a long copper scoop in one hand. It reminded me of a large spoon covered in a fine black soot. The man placed both hands on the table and leaned toward me. He squinted as he inspected the bag. Anger flashed in his eyes. He asked, "Where did you get that?"

"Do you know who it belongs to?" I asked.

"Of course, everyone in Archelais knows."

Not everyone, I thought to myself.

He was an average size man with thick black curly hair. His beard was neatly trimmed and oiled. His eyes were a deep brown. They were shifty and one of his eyes wandered as he looked at you while the other eye stayed fixed upon an object. It was quite distracting. He wore a dull linen cloak that had no distinct markings. His clothes were covered with a fine black soot and ash. A strong smell of smoke permeated his clothing. It was overwhelming but not unpleasant. His skin was very dark from years in the sun. In fact, it was beyond dark. It was black. He was the blackest man I had ever seen. He stared at me with his strange eyes.

"Where did you get it?" he asked again.

"You know who it belongs to?" I demanded. He was silent. The man just stared at me with those strange eyes. Anger began to rise up inside of me at this man's petulance. He waved the scoop as if he were wielding a sword.

"Fisel."

"Fisel?" I repeated.

"Yes, Fisel." He was standoffish. He stood erect and crossed his arms. The scoop left a black smeer across his cloak. The man continued to stare at me with his one good eye as the other eye wandered off looking at the crowds. "It belongs to Fisel. Now where did you get it?" he asked a final time.

"In the river. I pulled it from the river."

The man glared at me with disbelief in his eyes. His black skin glistened in the sunlight. A bead of sweat trickled down his face. He inhaled deeply through his nose. His nostrils flared as he exhaled. He stood there motionless and silent for several awkward moments. Neither of us moved. Finally, I broke the silence, "Where is his family?"

He thrust his scoop into the bucket of charcoal, flicking his wrist with irritation. Black rocks spilled from the bucket. His wandering eye floated across the row of tents behind me. He bolted from the tent. Charcoal lay strewn across the table. After shouting orders to his apprentices, who stood agape at his sudden departure, he turned to me and demanded, "Follow me."

I did as I was told and followed him through the streets of Archelais. The sounds of the bustling market faded behind me. The man walked fast, keeping a brisk pace. He never turned back to make sure I was following him. He just continued his quick pace. Rushing to keep up, I held the satchel under my arm. The feel of the leather was comforting to my touch. Passing numerous store houses, we twisted and turned through a maze of narrow streets. Clusters of yellow and red dates as long as a man's leg hung everywhere. With each tree throwing off between 150 to 200 pounds of dates a year, these people used any space that was available.

Ducking under a row of hanging date clusters, the man stopped. He turned back toward me. A menacing expression crossed his face. The irritation returned. His one good eye stared into my face. His other eye began to wander away. "He's dead, isn't he?"

Caught off guard, I gripped the satchel even tighter. It was almost dry now. I could feel the engraved letters beneath my fingers. I felt the oversized initials *ED* and I thought to myself, *Witness, now I am the witness.* The man's odd stare penetrated my very existence. He asked, "He's dead, isn't he?"

I gave him an imperceptible nod.

He inhaled and licked his lips. He squeezed his eyes shut for the briefest moment. When he opened them both eyes remained fixed on me. "Did you kill him?"

"No," I whispered.

"How did he die?"

"I don't know," I answered.

He glared at me for a long moment. His eye began to slowly drift away.

I continued, "I found him floating in the Jordan. He was already dead. He had been there for several days. I don't know who killed him, but I would guess it was robbers."

He closed both eyes, squeezing them tight. His head began to nod as he swayed for a moment. "He was my friend," was all he said as he turned and continued through the narrow street.

I followed until we came to a house in the next block. The front was a white washed stone. A small courtyard welcomed visitors to the door that was recessed from the street. A small palm tree stood alone in a clay pot. Its bushy fronds just reached the edge of the roof. Two young children played there. They were both boys. When they saw us approach, smiles gleamed across their faces. They both rushed to the black man and embraced him lovingly. They giggled and laughed as this man knelt and hugged them both. He messed up their hair as he asked for their mother. I now saw that the expression on this man's face was not that of irritation or anger, but one of dread and sorrow. My heart broke for them all, for I knew of the coming pain.

The front door swung open and a young woman appeared. She wore a simple linen dress and no shoes. I noticed she had small dainty feet. Her skin was fair. Her almond-shaped eyes glowed. Her mouth turned up in a friendly smile. I dreaded this moment. The scene before me tore at my heart. Her features left her with a fragile look. She smiled at the three kneeling before her. The children's laughter filled the air. Joy filled her deep brown eyes. Reaching up, she pushed a loose strand of hair back, tucking it behind her ear. I noticed how very pretty she was. No words were spoken between the two, as she and the kneeling man communicated a silent message. Time stood still. I felt sick. My mouth felt as dry as the desert. They both turned, their attention now focused toward me. A flush of heat ran up my neck. I wanted to turn and run. I wanted to save them from the terrible truth. *I wish I had never come here.* I noticed that the woman's eyes were drawn to the leather satchel. Instinctively, I pulled it tight against my chest. The smile vanished from her face. It was replaced with a look of horror and a terrible unthinkable fear.

The blood left her face and she turned as white as a ghost. Those almond eyes were those of a wild deer. Fear and panic washed over her. She quickly returned her gaze to the man kneeling before her. She was a statue as she stood motionless. For a moment I thought she would collapse. Rising, the man immediately caught the young woman under her arms and supported her as he escorted her inside. The laughter disappeared as the two young boys noticed the change in their mother. Their faces now ran deep with worry and confusion. They knew something was wrong. Children are more observant than people realize. They too retreated inside. I followed them all inside and shut the door.

Once inside the house, the woman became like a dead person. Her speech was mumbled and unintelligent. She stumbled and could hardly stand. She swayed momentarily. Her legs collapsed beneath her. Despite the help, she slumped to the floor in a heap of sadness. She began to cry a low mournful howl. Her body was wracked with pain and agony that pierced her heart like an arrow. I knew just how she felt. The memories of my lost Melessa and our child flooded my soul. The thoughts of Mother and Papa also rose to the surface of a deep dark pool of emotions. I sympathized with this woman. My heart ached for her.

The two little boys stood next to their grieving mother. Concern gripped them both. They were afraid and confused. Fear crawled through them both as they still were unsure as to the reason behind their mother's behavior. The woman did not speak. She couldn't. Pain and despair were tearing her apart. Finally, the man knelt down beside the boys. He embraced the two. I heard him very quietly speaking to the children. I could not hear what he said, but it was obvious. Both boys began to cry along with their mother. Their bitter wails rose to the heavens. The man pulled them closer. He embraced this whole family. They all wept tears of desperation. I watched helplessly. Guilt crawled up my spine. It was venomous. I was filled with regret as I had been the bearer of the terrible news, yet I had not spoken a word. The witness indeed. The man looked up at me. We made eye contact. Both of his eyes looked straight ahead. They were filled with tears. Yet, they were strong and firm, and they were also filled with a horrible sadness. Misery had come to visit this home. I tasted salt as hot tears ran down my own cheeks. *Welcome to a life of pain*, I thought.

CHAPTER 15

I sat on the hard-packed floor the rest of that evening and all night. It was a very dark and long night filled with death and despair. I was cold and uncomfortable. The family had wept their hearts out. After hours of tears, the four before me had finally grown silent. They were spent. The sound of troubled breathing was all that escaped them. I believe the little boys had drifted off to sleep. I sat quietly in the dark awaiting the morning. Finally, a single spear of sunlight pierced the darkness and welcomed the new day. No one moved, but I could now see the grieving family. They lay together, the man still embracing them all. Tiny dust particles floated through the beam of morning light. They danced and swirled in an invisible breeze that moved through the house. The silence was broken. A light knock was heard at the door behind me. It was so subtle that I wasn't sure if I actually heard it. *Knock, knock, knock.* It was louder this time. Still no one moved. The four continued to lay there before me. I noticed that the young mother's eyes were open. They were red and swollen. Tears still leaked from them. Her pretty cheeks were puffy and blotched. Snot ran down her nose. She did not move a muscle. At first, I feared that she might be dead. She stared at me unblinking, a blank emotionless stare. How long had she been watching me unnoticed? It was an uncomfortable feeling as she would not break eye contact or look away.

Knock, knock, knock. This time it was louder. The man before me, released his hold on the three mourners. He rose and made his way toward the door. Dragging his feet, he clumsily stepped over me. I heard a metal clasp release and the door groaned as it swung on leather hinges. Golden light cascaded in, flooding the house and surrounding the widowed mother and her two sons. She continued to stare at me with blank emotionless eyes. It was haunting.

Several people waited at the door, including the young men and women from the tent in the market square. An older middle-aged woman was also there. She embraced the older man and they held each other for a long while. They wept together. I assumed that this was his wife and children. The new guests entered the house and began tending to the broken family before me. Helping the boys and their mother to the next room, they reclined in more comfortable surroundings. The older woman began tending to their needs. The widow continued to stare at me. Her attention drawn to the satchel.

A dark shadow fell across my feet. The man stood before me. With outstretched arms he helped me to my feet. My legs and back ached. They were stiff from sitting on the hard, cold floor all night. I stretched feeling the tight muscles pull across my lower back. My legs began to feel like a thousand tiny needles, as the blood circulation began to return.

"I am John," he said. This time with a smile that was forced and sad.

"I am Barabbas."

"It is my honor," he said, "Thank you for coming."

I simply nodded.

"Thank you. It was very kind of you to bring this back to her," he said, as he gestured toward the other room where the young widow sat. Her eyes still staring at me. He reached out and took the satchel from my hands. For the briefest moment I resisted. I held onto it, afraid to let go. He gently pulled a little harder. A flush of embarrassment rushed through my veins. I released my hold. My fingers brushed across the inscribed surface feeling the letters one last time.

This man, John, held the satchel before us. His large black hands caressed the engraved letters. They ran across the palm leaves tracing them with his fingers.

"It's beautiful," I said.

"Yes, it truly is," he paused for a moment. Both eyes looked straight ahead. They were filled with tears. I could see that his emotions were rising, and he was choked up. He could not speak at that moment. An awkward silence surrounded us. He continued to touch the satchel. His hands caressed the leather and the inscription. I could see it in his eyes, his mind had wandered off. He was a thousand miles away. He squeezed the leather tightly as he did his eyes. "Fisel loved this," he whispered with a sad expression.

"I understand. I truly do."

"No one can. Fisel, he was like a son to me," he said, "He was a gift from God."

I simply nodded.

"That's what Fisel means, you know, it means Gift of God."

I nodded as he began to quietly cry. Huge tears streamed down his face. His shoulders slumped and heaved with each gasping breath. The man's heart was shattered. I imagined the blood that coursed through his veins ceased to flow. I didn't know what to do. Placing my hand on the man's shoulder, I tried to comfort him.

"John, I have to tell you something."

He clutched the satchel tighter and continued to cry. He struggled to take in gulps of air. He had lost control of his emotions. My heart went out to him.

"John, it is very important," I demanded.

Slowly he regained control. With his composure, he looked at me with steady eyes. They were red and bloodshot, but they were also strong.

"John, I pulled him from the river. His body is still laying on the bank of the Jordan."

Realization filled his eyes. Determination replaced sadness. "Oh, Heaven help us! We must go," he said without reservation. An anxious foreboding filled the room. Immediately he addressed the rest of the family. "Mother take care of Elizabeth and the boys. We shall return." He turned and headed toward the door. I followed. At the door, he paused. "Call the Chevra Kadisha together."

John stopped and returned to the little room with the mourning family. He embraced and kissed each one, including his wife, the young mother and the two little boys. He called out, "Michael, come with us." The young man from the market obeyed. At the door, John stopped, He returned to the family once more. This time he placed the satchel in the hands of the young mother. He placed his hand on top of hers. He leaned forward, and their foreheads met. She began to cry.

The three of us exited the house and began our walk toward the Jordan. Passing through the market square, John stopped and removed a large tarp from under the table in his own tent. It was a thick canvas that was rolled and neatly tied with a leather strap. It appeared to have been covered in a fine black soot. When he lifted it, a cloud of fine ash flew through the air. A gentle breeze carried it away. Carrying the tarp with us, we passed through the market and out the city gates. As we ventured on, we came to the small community and the stone tower at Magdalsenna. The same two men that I had seen the day before, sat atop watching. They said nothing as we marched past them. They simply nodded. After passing the arched tower, we continued through the vast groves of palm trees. We could hear the river, before we could see it. I also smelled it, that sweet pungent smell of wet and rotting vegetation. I wondered if it was the stench of the dead man awaiting us.

Approaching from the West, we walked down to the river. The swift current of the Jordan pushed past us. Panic gripped me. I could not find the body. The man was gone. It was no longer where I remembered it. John and the boy, both became very agitated at this turn of events. John's anger rose, and it was evident. However, after further investigation, I found that I had made a mistake as much of the river all looks the same. The larger clump of bulrushes and the slow-moving waters of the bend was another one hundred paces to the North. I recognized where the ducks had been sitting and I led them there.

The body of Fisel lay where I had left it. From a distance, he appeared to be sleeping. His arms lay peacefully at his side. His feet still pointing toward the water's edge. No wild beasts had devoured it in the night. Yet it was crawling with flies. The buzzing was a roar. Thousands of tiny black insects, their glassy wings flapping, crawled all over the body. They invaded every orifice and opening. Flies crawled from out of his mouth and nose. Several others exited his ears. Anger rose up in all of us, as we witnessed the man's violation.

John leapt forward swatting at the flying horde. A black cloud rose and swarmed around us. Yet those filthy creatures did not give up easily. They were an insidious enemy that relentlessly returned to the body. John continued to swat at them, but it was of no use. The flies continued their harassment. We worked as quickly as possible. We unrolled and laid out the tarp. A fine layer of soot covered it. The black ash had penetrated into the fibers of the cloth permanently discoloring it. John and his son, Michael, began moving the body. It was a dead weight that refused to cooperate. They tried rolling the corpse onto its side. His cloak was tangled and wrapped around his legs. Angry flies swarmed them. They continued to struggle. Seeing their plight, I unwrapped the tangled cloth. Once free, I helped as we rolled the body of Fisel onto the tarp. A swirling storm of flies encircled us. They attacked us with the same ferocity as they did the dead body. Flies buzzed our ears. They lit on our necks and faces, their legs tickling as they crawled across our flesh. They flew into our eyes and noses. I swatted at them constantly. They crawled through my hair, tickling my head. Several crawled down my tunic. Michael spat as one flew into his mouth. He cursed. They were awful disgusting little creatures. Working quickly, we wrapped the body inside the tarp. We tied the ends together with leather straps.

Each of us grabbed a handful of the tarp providing a poor handle. John and his son each picked the man up by the shoulders. I carried the feet. The body was heavy and awkward. We moved slowly. Clumsily, we managed to carry the body of Fisel up the hill and through the forest of palms. Several times we were forced to set it down to rest and to gain a better grip. It was a difficult task, but we prevailed. As we moved further away from the river, we were plagued with fewer flies, but some were always present. Flies continued to harass us. They followed us all the way back to Archelais.

Entering through the city gates, we were immediately met by several men. Concern was written on their faces. Two men dressed in all white linen, led the way. These people were the *Chevra Kadisha*, the holy group of community leaders that formed the burial society. Four men relieved us of the burden of carrying the body. Exhausted from our chore, we gladly relinquished.

They laid the dead man on a stretcher with four handles. These same men picked up the stretcher and turned down a street to the South. They instructed us to follow them. Turning down several narrow streets filled with hanging clusters of dates, we came to a small white stone building. It was set off to itself a short distance from any other buildings. No markings identifying the building could be seen. There, four men entered. Two were the men dressed in white. They were joined by two other men, also dressed in plain white linen cloaks. The others brought the body inside and carefully laid it on a wooden table that stood at waist height. They unwrapped the tarp and removed the soiled filthy clothing. Once the body was at rest, the four carriers retreated, leaving only the four men in white. John and I stayed as family observers. Michael chose to wait outside. The *Tahara*, or ritual purification of the body had begun.

The Tahara is made of three parts, the cleansing, the purification and the dressing. It is not only to comfort the living, but to show respect for the dead. It is to comfort the soul and care for the body. According to tradition, it is the greatest service that one can show to another human being. The Tahara is performed by the Chevra Kadisha and it is considered a great honor.

The four men of the Chevra Kadisha each washed their hands three times. From buckets, they poured clean water brought from the living mikvah. They started with their right and then the left. They each did this three times. The men gathered around the body of Fisel. Before the washing began, the oldest man raised his hands toward Heaven. He began to recite a prayer, "May it be your will, Lord our God and the God of our fathers, to bring a circle of angels of mercy before the deceased, for he is your servant son." The men began to wash Fisel. They started with his right side and then his left. Using sponges, they first washed his arms. Next, they washed his legs, saving the body and head for the last. They scrubbed all of the unclean filth away. They were extremely careful as to show great honor and respect to the body. The men were overly cautious. They dared not reach over the body, but instead would go around as a sign of respect. Very quietly, one man explained that the *Neshama,* or the soul is hovering above the body and in transition. The Neshama remains with the body. It is the essence of the person. It is his consciousness and totality, his thoughts, his deeds, his knowledge, his experiences and relationships. The body is simply its container while it lasted here on Earth. The Neshama refuses to leave until the body is laid at rest.

It took some time as they thoroughly cleaned the body of Fisel. While they performed this ritual cleansing, they recited prayers and Psalms. They rhymed and flowed like the songs of birds. They recited them together, their voices like angels. John was moved to tears while goosebumps crawled over my arms and neck. When they completed the spiritual cleansing, they began to pour buckets of water over the body. As required, it was 24 quarts of water from the mikvah. Once they began, it was required to be poured all at once. Water cascaded down and splashed across the body of Fisel, washing away all of the suffering of this life here on Earth.

Water spilled down. It splashed and pooled across the white cut stones that made up the floor. Tiny rivers ran down the cracks between the stones. I watched as one ran across the entire room and darted between my feet. The four men of the Chevra Kadisha all stood bare footed. Water swirled and squished between their toes.

The older man raised his hands heavenward before he sang out, "Tahara he, Tahara he, Tahara he, He is pure. He is pure. He is pure."

The men began to dry off the body. They used soft white towels, showing the utmost respect for the body before them. One man opened a jar and the men began to rub the body with a mixture of aloes and myrrh mixed with other spices. When he opened the jar, a strong aromatic scent filled the air. At first it was overwhelming. It was a sweet earthy aroma that filled my nostrils. Immediately a peaceful calming sense of spirituality fell across the room. For the first time, I realized that these men were preparing for this man to go before God; to stand before his maker. They continued to dress the body in white grave clothes. They were made of linen. The clothes were fashioned after garments similar to those worn in the temple by the High Priest on the day of Yom Kippur. They had unfinished hems and no pockets. This was to accentuate the fact that you take no worldly goods with you into the next life. The clothes were sewn with no knots, so they would disintegrate quickly and easily.

Once the dressing was completed, the men wrapped the body with a white shroud cloth. This provides a sense of protection as the person enters into the next world to come. One of the men reminded us that all are dressed and buried alike. No matter if one is rich or poor, their deeds will be weighed and judged on that last judgement day. The Neshama, if found worthy, will ask for the needs of his family on that final day of judgement.

After the body was bound in the shroud cloth, one of the men opened another jar. This one contained soil from outside the Holy Temple in Jerusalem. He began to sprinkle the soil onto the eyes of the body, the feet, and finally over the heart. A deep silence fell across the group. All four preparers gathered around the body. Their white tunics were now soiled and drenched. The older man spoke. He asked the Neshama for forgiveness for any errors or disrespect shown during the Tahara. He assured the man's soul that they had done everything within their power to do it correctly and in accordance to the customs and the Law.

"Fisel, we ask forgiveness of you if we did not treat you respectfully, but we did as is our custom. May you be a messenger for all of Israel. Go in peace, rest in peace, and arise in your turn at the end of the days. I wish you well my friend."

John had tears streaming down his dark face. As I watched this holy work, I too realized just what a powerful thing it was. It was a spiritual experience. I watched as these men, the Chevra Kadisha, served their fellow man, their friend. They were humble. Their hearts filled with honor, and respect, and love. From that moment forward, I would see the world through different eyes. I realized that these men knew not only death but what it meant to be alive. They knew what it meant to serve. They understood it far more than most, far more than me.

CHAPTER 16

It was six hours until the sun would set. According to the Law, the body must be buried before the last rays of light. It was only on rare occasions that a body was allowed to wait overnight for burial. As Fisel had already been dead for a few days, it was imperative that he be placed in the Earth before night fall. This was a close-knit community. Several friends of the family volunteered for the *Shmira*, which means "the guarding." They stayed with the body, never leaving its side as required. Shmira is the protection of the body and the accompaniment of the soul between the time of death and the time of burial.

The members of the Chevra Kadisha, along with John, his son Michael, and myself were all unclean as we had touched the body of the dead. Therefore, we all journeyed halfway across town to the Mikveh for a purification ceremony. The local rabbi met us there and performed the rites. Local townsfolk brought clean clothing for each of us. The families provided the garments, but as I had no family, John's provided me with a clean fresh tunic and shirt. They would wash my own and return it to me the following day.

That evening, about two hours before sunset I joined John and his family. By now, I had learned that his wife's name was Salome and his daughter's name was Shelamzion. We all gathered at the home of Fisel along with his widowed wife, Elizabeth and two young sons. A terrible sadness hung over the house. It was a dark cloak of grief and sorrow. It weighed upon us all and filled the air. The house felt cold. John's dark features helped hide the anguish he felt, but inside a silent strength raced through his veins. He had a good heart. I could sense it in this man. He was a man of character, a man of honor. Although, he struggled to keep his composure, he managed. He was strong. He gathered the grieving family together as we waited for the funeral procession to start. A cloud of apprehension covered the house. Time stood still as we waited an eternity.

When a light knock on the door came, the young widow, Elizabeth began to softly cry. John's wife put her arms around the grieving woman one last time and squeezed. The boys clung to their mother's dress as they exited the house into courtyard and the waiting street beyond. The whitewashed stones were a sorrowful reminder of the tomb to come. The single palm tree stood next to the door. It bent its branches in a mournful bow. The *levaya* had begun.

The Hebrew word for funeral is *levaya*, it means "accompanying." It appeared as if the entire town had come out to accompany the body of Fisel to his final resting place. The streets were lined with people, their friends and neighbors. They all came as an act of love and kindness toward this family. As this was a time of death, everyone covered their heads. Some tore their clothes and wore ashes as a sign of sorrow and repentance. An eerie silence fell over the entire town. I glanced upward into a cloudless sky. I noticed that the moon had risen early that day. It hung in the eastern heavens above us, a glowing orb set against an ocean of blue. I was reminded of Samuel's lesson concerning the tekhelet strings and the blue blood of the mysterious Hillazon. "This is the hem of the garment and the border between us and the Lord. It is to remind us of God. It reminds us of the sea, which reminds us of the sky, which reminds us of God's holy throne." I shuddered as goosebumps crawled up my arms.

Waiting in the street were the pallbearers. They carried the body of Fisel on a stretcher, two long wooden poles held on their shoulders. His body wrapped in the white linen shroud cloth. They awaited the family to begin the procession to the tomb. The young widow and her two boys followed behind the body. John, his wife, and family followed behind her. Several other people joined them. I assumed that they too were relatives or close friends. I followed these people as the pallbearers led the procession through the streets. Other mourners followed behind. It was a very large crowd. They sang out prayers and psalms. The entire crowd joined in, their voices rising into the blue sky.

The procession of gathered mourners marched through the narrow streets. The rock and brick houses lined the way. Young palms softened the hard edges of the surrounding buildings. I watched as the body was carried forward. With a steady rhythm, it rocked from side to side on the stretcher. Wails of sorrow rose from the crowd. The late afternoon sun cast strange red shadows across the town. Palm fronds and clusters of colorful dates hung everywhere. They added a strange paradoxical contradiction to the surroundings. They represented nature and the manifestation of life in this time of death and sadness. A dark melancholy gripped my spirit. I was filled with a terrible sadness and guilt. It was not just for this family, but for myself. I was struck with a savage realization, a realization of something that I had missed. I was not there for my wife's funeral, for my Melessa. I was not there for the family or for Jarviss. I was not there for her, my one true love. I had fled. I had fled like a coward. The thought sickened me. I hated myself. The burning hatred for Rome flared quietly within my heart. I prayed to God to damn them all.

Suddenly that strange sense of being watched crawled through me. It was an icy spider that crawled up my spine. It broke my daydreaming, bringing me back to the present. I looked around but saw no one in particular. I was standing in a crowd of people. I was moving with the mourners amongst hundreds of others. The menacing feeling continued to grow. How could I feel so paranoid? Yet, I did. The feeling was strong. It washed over me like a massive wave crashing against the rocky shoreline. The hairs on the back of my neck stood erect. I felt closed in. I felt surrounded. I so desperately wished that I was away from this place. I longed for the freedom of the hills, for the openness of the plains, and the solitude of the forest. Something squeezed my chest and breath escaped me. My heart raced wildly. Forcing myself to calm, I collected myself. I managed to control my breathing. Soon I was able to calm my feral spirit. A still peace, a sense of relief from my affliction came over me.

Now calm, I searched the surrounding crowd. I tried to examine each and every face. It was impossible. Turning, I scanned the people behind me. Something caught my eye. Standing beyond the awnings that overhung the buildings to our left stood a man. He stood behind several people gathered to watch the funeral procession. He was hidden in the shadows between two buildings, but I could see him as plain as day. His stare pierced the crowd. There was no mistaking it. He deliberately stared directly into my eyes. As the procession of mourners slowly passed he never looked away. Rudely, he never broke eye contact.

The parade of people followed as the pallbearers led us outside the city gates. We continued West into the hills. There, we found many caves and tombs that had been used for burials for ages. The hillside was covered with them. The crowd followed, ascending a steep rocky hill.

We came to an open tomb. Several men awaited us there. The large stone had been rolled away leaving a gaping hole in the side of the hill. It reminded me of a large mouth. The jagged rocks were its teeth. The black depths, its grisly throat. This was the tomb of Fisel and his family before him. The women within the group of mourners began to wail loudly. Their cries were those of animals. Their sorrowful songs rising up to the Lord. The pallbearers and the immediate family entered into the tomb. John followed as everyone else remained outside. Within the tomb, they laid the body to rest. His body facing East to West. Finally, his Neshama was at peace. Finally, his soul could rest. As they did this, the rabbi began to lead the gathered crowd in prayer. He delivered a short eulogy. It was a heartfelt tribute to the life of this deceased man, Fisel bar Alpheus, the husband of Elizabeth, and loving father of Timaeus and Matthias.

Waiting with the gathered crowd of people I was stricken with that strange feeling. Turning, I scanned the crowd. I searched the sea of faces. Across the hillside stood the strange man. It was the same man from earlier. Our eyes met. He was deliberately staring at me. His impolite behavior was uncommonly rude and bordered on threatening. I stared back. He never looked away. This time he was closer and not hidden within the shadows. I studied the stranger. He had beady eyes that had a sinister glint to them. He was a tall wiry man. Thin wispy hairs were brushed back exaggerating a receding hairline. He wore a thin scraggly beard. But one feature stood out beyond all others. He had a large hooked nose. It reminded me of the beak of a large raptor bird, like an eagle or a hawk. He was dressed in a black tunic that drug the ground. *How odd*, I thought, *and belligerently rude.* The man gave me an uncomfortable uneasiness that I couldn't explain. I turned away and moved closer to the cave entrance.

Soon the family exited the tomb. A hush fell across the crowd. Not even the scuffling of feet against the rocks could be heard. They paused before the entrance. The young widow bent down gathering a handful of earth. She tossed it into the dark opening. A swirl of dust danced in the gentle breeze. Both of the boys did the same. They stood motionless as several men began to roll the large cut stone into place before the entrance. The stone growled in protest before coming to rest sealing the tomb.

Outside of the tomb was a flat area where several ornately carved benches formed a semi-circle. This was the mourning enclosure where people came to lament and eulogize the deceased. The family sat there as the rabbi addressed the gathered crowd of mourners, "Only God knows the secrets of the heart. Only God is truly capable of fathoming such grief. And Only God is capable of providing comfort."

He quoted the Torah, "Thus says the Lord, the God of your father David, 'I have heard your prayer, I have seen your tears; behold, I will heal you.'"

He paused briefly, running his hand through his gray beard. He turned toward the family and continued, "Consolation is not in human nature. At times like this, when the heart grieves, neither the passage of time, nor the awkward but well-meaning gestures of others can remove your pain. That is why we ask God to comfort you, because we cannot."

The rabbi turned toward the gathered crowd. Tugging on his cloak, he straightened his shawl. His tzitzit tassels swayed gently. He cleared his throat and led the gathered in the ancient Jewish prayer, the Avinu Malkeinu. His voice was as clear and precise as a man half his age. It was a slow and repetitive chanting. The melody representing the pious pleading of God's chosen people.

"Our father our king, hear our voice
Our father our king, we have sinned before you
Our father our king, have compassion upon us
and upon our children

Our father our king
Bring an end to pestilence,
war, and famine around us
Our father our king,
Bring an end to all trouble
and oppression around us

Our father our king,
Our father our king,
Inscribe us in the book of life
Our father our king, renew upon us
Renew upon us a good year

Hear our voice
Hear our voice
Hear our voice

Our father our king."

At the conclusion, the crowd formed two parallel lines that followed the path back down the hillside. You could hear crying and sniffling from the gathered people. Fisel's widow and her two sons began their long walk back down the hill. They were followed by John and the other mourners. They passed through the two lines, a symbol of the community coming together to support the family. As they passed, the crowd recited the traditional Jewish blessing, the prayer of mourning, yet they spoke not in Aramaic or Greek, but rather in the ancient Hebrew of our forefathers. It is believed that the depth and beauty of the Torah's original language offers us a unique perspective into

God's consolation as we face our own mortality. As the family passed, the people spoke, *"HaMakom yenachem et'chem b'toch shar avay'lay Tzion vee'Yerushalayim,"* which means, "May the Omnipresent comfort you among the mourners of Zion and Jerusalem."

Darkness began to fall as the sun was now completely gone. Fading gold and orange streaks still burned across the western sky. The moon was now high above us. So was the Evening Star, called *Meleket ha-Shamayim* or "the Queen of Heaven" by the prophet Jeremiah. It now joined the moon shining brightly against the darkening canvas. It is now called Venus by the Romans, named for their goddess of love and beauty. The thought of Rome's influence sickened me.

At the bottom of the hill, stood several large pots of water. Women attended them silently. As the crowd dispersed, everyone stopped and dipped their hands into the water. When leaving a tomb, it is customary to wash your hands without drying them. This is a symbol of leaving this place of death and reentering the world of the living. As I approached the water and dipped my hands in, I was startled as another set of hands rudely pushed mine out of the way. It was the strange man with the hawk-billed nose. We stood eye to eye, measuring each other up. He stank. I could smell his foul breath, a mixture of sulfur and rotting meat. I was immediately repulsed. He glared at me for a long uncomfortable moment. His eyes were a sickly gray set within yellowish bloodshot pools. Anger flared up inside of me. He smiled a twisted grin before turning and walking away. I stood there speechless, water dripping from my fingers and blood boiling in my veins.

CHAPTER 17

Now begins the Shiva period. Just as Joseph mourned the death of his father, Jacob for seven days, so did we. I stayed with John and his family for that entire week. Their hospitality was gracious and warm. We visited Elizabeth and her boys daily. For the first seven days, the family remained at home in mourning as the Shiva tradition called for. If they left the house at all, it was to visit the tomb and return. Each day neighbors and friends would tend to their needs by taking them food and water and anything else that they needed. During this time, the family did not bathe and continued to wear their torn clothing from the funeral. They also did not wear leather shoes or jewelry, as it was also prohibited. They received visitors who wished to comfort them and lament the loss of Fisel. The two boys were having a very difficult time with it. John and I visited often. John's wife Salome was there every single day. She would return to her own home each evening and return the following morning.

During that week, I learned that John owned his business. His entire family worked for him. I also learned that Fisel had worked for John as well. He was a collier. He made and sold charcoal made from the leftover seeds of the palm dates. I would have never guessed just how lucrative charcoal could be.

Charcoal has been used since ancient times. It is used for a large range of purposes, including medicine and art. However, its most important use has been for fuel. Although used for cooking and heating, its primary purpose is for metallurgy. Charcoal is the traditional fuel of a blacksmith's forge. Both iron and silversmiths require an intense heat that cannot be obtained with a simple wood fire. Plus, it produces very little smoke.

Daily, we would journey to the South, just out of town where his charcoal operation was located. It was not far at all, just a short walk. A short stone wall enclosed several large bins and storehouses. A new storehouse was under construction. Its walls were as tall as two men. They climbed upward and halted in thin air uncomplete. A wooden scaffolding stood next to it, but no one was working on it at that time. Living quarters, where I learned that his son Michael lived, stood at the back. John employed several other townsfolk as well. Massive bins were filled with date seeds. Thousands of seeds were stored, as they were cheap and abundant at Archelais. Several large wheeled carts were parked along the outer wall. One was filled with date seeds. The others were empty. Located in the center were several large mounds of dried clay. They reminded me of a bowl that had been turned upside down.

On each visit, Michael would greet us warmly. Each day he would inform his father of the day's accomplishments. Apparently, the process of making charcoal is a delicate one and must be attended to constantly. On my very first visit, Michael was preparing to burn charcoal. We watched as he and several employees built the mound. A tall wooden log was buried in the earth leaving it standing the height of a man. Four other smaller logs were placed in a circle around the first. They all leaned inward and were tied together against the standing log. These created a support structure. Dried and seasoned palm date seeds were piled around the logs. They created a circular mound as tall as a man and twice as long. Once this was complete, they began covering the pile with wet mud. It was a reddish-brown mixture of mud, clay and straw. It also had a blackish tint to it, like the charcoal itself. They began at the bottom, working their way up. They continued this, until the entire structure was completely covered with a thick plaster like coating. This was done to seal the mound and to allow no air to enter. A round opening, or chimney was left at the very top around the standing log. Eight other small holes were opened around the bottom of the structure. Once this was complete, a fire was introduced into the chimney at the very top. Using a ladder, Michael built a small fire with hot coals and a tender bundle. As yellow flames licked upward, the fire burned down into the opening.

It was a very slow process. John and I returned often to check their progress. Later that day, the mound was rumbling. It roared as a brilliant red flame shot out of the chimney and reached into the sky. The mound breathed as it sucked air through the lower eight air holes. Once the flame was visible from inside the air holes, they were plugged. The chimney itself was sealed. Michael filled them all with a mixture of wet mud. He also continuously searched for cracks or breaks in the mound. If he found one, it was immediately sealed. He would walk around the mound placing his hands on it at different places. He felt it. He listened to it. He nursed it like a mother hen. Michael's goal was to burn the wood very slowly, controlling and managing the sufficient generation of heat. I realized that this was a true art and both John and his son were masters.

It took five full days of burning to complete the process. Once it was done and the mound had cooled, they broke it open. The mound was a great egg. The mud had hardened and broke apart in chunks. They opened the mound to find it filled with black carbonized wood. The palm date seeds were now shattered pieces of beautiful charcoal. Michael ran his hand into the kiln. He withdrew a handful of the finished product. He gave some to his father and some to me. A fine black soot covered seeds. They were amazingly lightweight. White and silver streaks shot through the black. The charcoal had a musical quality to it. It tinkled with a metallic sound. It reminded me of broken glass. I was very impressed.

"So, you'll sell all of this to the blacksmiths?" I asked.

"Oh no," Michael said, "Charcoal has many purposes."

His father interrupted, "Medicine. We sell a lot of it for medicine."

"Medicine?" I asked.

"Yes, doctors and alchemists use charcoal all the time."

"For what?"

"Charcoal counteracts poisons in the body. It can offset allergic reactions as well as kill and remove parasites"

"It is also used to alleviate stomach problems, like nausea and diarrhea along with gas and bloating," Michael added with a silly smirk. He patted his stomach with both hands.

"Do you eat it?" I asked.

John continued, "They grind it up into a fine powder and mix it in water."

"You can also mix a thick paste with it and apply it to relieve insect bites, burns and rashes. It can even help draw out the poison from a snake bite," Michael added.

"I knew that," I replied, "Samuel used charcoal for bug bites and rashes."

"Who's Samuel?" Michael asked.

After a brief pause of contemplation, I answered, "He's my father." After all, that was a short answer that explained a lot. I continued, "Samuel would also use it to filter contaminated water. He claimed that it removed any impurities."

"Oh, it does. It makes unclean water drinkable," Michael added enthusiastically.

"Your Samuel is a smart man," John said.

"He is. More than you'll ever know." I said with a lazy smile.

After a brief pause in the conversation, Michael continued. He drew his hands across his face in an exaggerated movement, rubbing his cheeks, "Women use it for skincare. It helps with smooth skin and a clear complexion. You can also scrub your teeth with it. It whitens them and kills bad breath," he said with that silly smirk.

John added, "It even helps with hangovers." He said this with a laugh as he pushed me back toward town.

That evening we visited Elizabeth and her sons. The family had now completed the Shiva period, their seven days of mourning. Salome and John's daughter, Shelamzion had attended to their needs daily. On the seventh day, they accompanied them to the mikvah for the spiritual purification. They were now clean and welcomed back to the world of the living. They wore fresh clothes and their bodies were clean, but I knew that in their hearts they would mourn forever.

Elizabeth was gracious and thankful. She cherished the leather satchel. She told me numerous times how much it meant to her. It reminded her of her lost husband. She would sit and run her hands over the leather. I watched her as she fingered the tooled letters, "Witness." Her mind wandered a million miles away. Her eyes filled with tears. She dreamed of happier days, days of yesterday. Her hopes and dreams had been ripped from her, as had mine. I was filled with sympathy for this young mother, a sympathy that only I could share. My heart broke for her. Yet a strange sense of envy secretly arose in my soul. She was fortunate as she was surrounded by people who loved her. My time of mourning had been spent running and hiding from Rome. I was alone. The hate within me continued to smolder. It was a hot ember burning within my heart.

CHAPTER 18

That night something awoke me, something familiar. The vivid dream of the lamb and lion had returned. It was the same as always, I stood alone on a grassy savannah. My pet lamb, JoJo returned. The hyenas appeared. They tore my lamb apart. His cries echoed through the night. The sounds still haunt me. Blood bathed the landscape. The coppery scent of death filled the air. The majestic lion rose. He devoured the beasts. His shaggy mane dripped with blood as he spoke my name. Terrified, I felt the agony and pain as the lion pounced. His massive fangs dug deep into my flesh. Expecting death, I was startled awake. My heart raced, and I was drenched in cold sweat. I was not sure if it was the dream or something else. I was wide awake, and sleep would not return. A sense of impending dread hung over me. It was a heavy darkness. Something terrible was coming. I could feel it.

The words of the Torah spoke to me. From the scroll of Vayikra, called Leviticus, *"For the life of the flesh is in the blood, and I have given it to you on the altar to make atonement for your souls; for it is the blood by reason of the life that makes atonement for the soul."*

I arose, dressed and exited John's house. I was careful as to not wake anyone. I gently pulled the door shut. It made a loud scraping sound that startled me. I tried to quieten it. Apparently, it woke no one, as the household remained asleep. I was not sure where I was going. I simply felt the need to walk, to get out. I pulled my cloak around me to fend off the night's chill. I had left my sword and bow within the house, leaving me with a strange sense of vulnerability, but I ventured on anyway. Although a dark night, I could see. Moonlight lit my way as I explored the streets of the quiet little town. I liked it there. I had been impressed with this community. Everyone embraced the widow of their fallen neighbor. They came together and supported her as if they were family. They were a loving bunch. Most of the town folks had also been welcoming to me, a stranger who brought terrible news to their town.

Twisting through the streets, I saw a different view at night. A forest of palm trees surrounded the town. Their black silhouettes shown against the night's sky. I could hear the wind blowing through their bushy leaves. They gently swayed. Clusters of dates hung everywhere. Colorless, they were black and white and cast strange shadows in the bright moonlight. An owl hooted, breaking the silence. Several dogs barked in the distance. The town remained at rest. A few lamps burned in the windows of those still awake. The buildings and tents were well cared for. The homes were well kept. Toys and signs of children were frequent. The people were clean and neat. I did not see junk and trash that was so common in other towns. These people had a sense of pride to them. They cared. They were happy and enjoyed their work. They genuinely liked each other. And they were a faithful people. Their synagogue stood on the highest point in town. It was simple but elegant. It glowed a blue hue in the moonlight giving it an ethereal quality.

My thoughts turned to John and his family. He was a good man, an honest man. He had a good family, a wife that loved him and two adoring and respectful children. He had a good business and he worked hard. His neighbors held him in the highest esteem. The Lord had blessed the man. He enjoyed the life that had been stolen from me. I admired him, and I coveted his life. I know the Law of Moses forbids it, yet envy was in me. It swam through my veins. A pang of guilt ran through me.

I continued to wander through the dark streets. I explored parts of the town that I had never seen before. All of these buildings grew to look alike. Somehow, I got turned around and found myself on a strange alley at the far end of town. I was stricken with a strange sense of misplaced direction. I was profoundly agitated. Other than the occasional owl, everything was quiet. I turned and sought my sense of direction. Looking to the sky, I found the constellation of the little bear. At his tail I found the star, Polaris. I headed North. A strange paranoia lifted its ugly head. Afraid that someone might mistake me for a thief, I decided to head back to John's. A strange sense of being watched returned. An icy feeling ran up my spine. It tingled the back of my neck. I turned and stared into the darkness. I saw no one. Always attentive to my surroundings, I could sense something was wrong. I could feel it in my bones. Someone was out there. Someone was watching. My instincts are rarely wrong.

Considering my options, I walked slowly with an air of indifference. The feeling did not go away. Someone was out there. *Trust your instincts*, I told myself. Out of habit, I casually patted my side feeling for my sword. It should be hidden under my cloak. I remembered, it was not there. *How foolish.* Casually I turned a corner. I hid and waited in the darkness. Nothing. Continuing, I strolled down the street and made another corner. I waited. Again, nothing. I backed into the darkest shadows. I pulled my cloak tight around me, drawing it near. There I knelt, quietly waiting. I watched the street closely. I sensed a presence, but saw none. Caution rose in me. But worse than that, I felt as if I was being stalked. An unfamiliar feeling arose. I had become the prey. With patience I studied each and every shadow. Never taking my eyes off the street before me, I waited. I expected someone to show themselves at any moment, but they never did. I expected the bastard to make a mistake. My adversary remained invisible. I steadily studied the roof tops, yet I saw no one. *Was it my imagination?* I thought. *Was it a sick sense of paranoia?* Confused, I refused to think so.

The night's air was cold. It crept into my bones. A chill ran through me. The crickets sang their night songs, calling to each other. I knelt in the darkness long enough to watch the moon move westward, beyond the visibility of the buildings. It was now very dark. Only the stars cast any light. I watched as the constellations slowly turned and journeyed across the sky as they moved out of sight. The little bear rhythmically turned around his tail. Hours passed. I was cold. My knees and joints were stiff and pained me. A surge of anger pushed aside my apprehension. It bore down on me as I retired from my task and headed back to John's house.

It was now very dark as the moon had completely set. Its shining light now hidden beyond the surrounding hills. A lone wolf howled in the distance. Walking quickly, I turned through the twisting streets and alleys. The strange feeling returned. I stopped in my tracks and studied the night. I stepped back into the darkest shadows. At the farthest end of a long narrow thoroughfare, I saw a glowing light. It was a lamp that illuminated a single window at the far end of the street. It was a warm and inviting glow. I watched as the yellow flame flickered. A silhouetted figure moved within the light. Curiosity pulled me forward. Moving from shadow to shadow, I crept closer. Gravel crunched under my feet. The dim light continued to glow, inviting me onward.

Soon I was close enough to make out some details. Hiding in the dark shadows, I knelt with my back against a stone wall. It was cold and unyielding. From there I observed the house. I watched for several minutes. It was across the street and stood perpendicular to where I hid. The light shone from a window on the stone house. It looked out from a single room. Mortar held the rocks together, creating in intricate pattern with the entangled lines. Black shadows crawled across the stone works. A pair of wooden shutters hung loosely. They stood open revealing the interior of the house. They were faded and weathered from years in the scorching afternoon sun. A soft glow was cast by the single lamp that rested on the window sill. The light chased the shadows from around the opening. No one moved within the house. I saw no silhouette moving within the light. It appeared as if the room was empty. I crept closer.

Peering into the house, I could see a single table next to the window. It appeared to be very old, almost ancient. The wood was aged and dark. It was almost black, stained from years of use. Nicks and scratches covered the table's surface. Splintered edges adhered to one corner. A sickeningly sweet aroma wafted through the air. It smelled of a burning perfume, the faint hint of smoke and burned flowers. Several strange items were strewn about. A small leather pouch lay in the middle of the table. The leather strap lay undone allowing some of the contents to spill out. A fine red powder spilled onto the surface. Next to it stood a small yellow candle. A flame danced and flickered wildly. Melted wax dripped down the side and pooled on the table. Around it, a large circle had been drawn from a white chalky powder. It covered the entire table top. Within the circle, a triangle lay. Several strange symbols were also drawn using the white powder. They made a stark impression compared to the dark wood and the red powder. I had never seen such images or writings before. They reminded me of the symbols of Egypt. Those found on their high places. The symbols rested at each of the three points of the triangle. Lying within the circle were several bones. They were faded white from age and large enough to be those of a human, but I could not be for sure. Several feathers also lay scattered around the table as if they had no particular order. A spiral of long thin loops encircled the leather pouch and candle. They were a bluish gray and glistened with a wet mucus in the candle light. Immediately I recognized them for what they were, the ropy entrails of an animal's guts.

Repulsed at this discovery, I stepped back. Curiosity was now raging through me. I heard a soft scraping sound. Footsteps approached. They were within the house. Someone was coming back into the room. A shadow danced across the door that led into this room. I ducked and darted back to the darkness on the other side of the street.

A man entered and knelt at the table. In the soft lamp light, I could make out some of the details. He wore a long black cloak with a hood that covered his head. Shadows hid his face. He carried a larger leather bag. It was slung over his shoulder. It looked like unshaven goat's skin. His hands were hidden behind the window sill and I could not see what he was doing. I did hear the distinct sound of metal. I guessed that it was coins clinking against each other. The man began to quietly chant. His voice was deep and raspy. At first it was more of a mumble. It was unrecognizable. His tone was low, almost a growl. His chant repeated itself. He found a tempo. The dark incantations grew. He spoke in an unknown tongue. This continued for some time. I watched in disbelief. The lamp light cast eerie shadows onto the opposing wall. His shadow was monstrous in appearance. He raised his hands into view. Long bony fingers, his knuckles covered in black hair. For the first time I saw what was hidden within the bag. It was a skull, a human skull. The hollow eyes stared into his shadowed face.

From my hiding place, I continued to watch the loosening of time as his chanting grew louder. The state of his trance enveloped him. His deep voice carried into the night. His chant haunting. His body moved in a slow macabre dance. He rocked back and forth with a slow rhythmic pace. His head keeping time. The hood fell from him. The shadows were erased revealing his smug arrogant face. Immediately I recognized the man. It was the hawk billed man from the funeral. I gasped at this recognition. Dark shadows were painted under his eyes making his high cheekbones and forehead appear more pronounced. His beard was ratty, and his thin hair was disheveled and unkempt. He stared into the dark eyes of the skull. A toothy grin smiled back at him. His chanting continued, the unknown tongue, the tongue of devils.

I realized what he was. This was a *necromancer*, called a "bone-conjurer." Samuel had talked about it once. The ancient Hebrew name was *doresh el ha-metim*, which means "one who questions corpses." They sought the hidden knowledge of the underworld. Through their black magic, they communicate with the dead, either by summoning their spirit or by raising the deceased. Through divination they gain the knowledge of the dead and can foretell the future. It is said that the most powerful doresh el ha-metim can bring someone back from the dead and use them as a weapon.

The necromancer lives in darkness. They hide in the shadows. They secretly surround themselves with the morbid aspects of death. Their lives symbolize lifelessness and decay. They are grave robbers. They will wear the clothes of the deceased and have been known to mutilate and consume corpses. Their macabre ceremonies can carry on for hours, if not days or even weeks. Their rituals eventually leading to the summoning of the spirits. The doresh el ha-metim sleep in cemeteries and tombs, fasting to the point of starvation in order to become possessed.

They are evil and wicked. The Law explicitly forbids this black magic. They are to be put to death. From the scroll of the Devārīm, also called Deuteronomy. *When you enter the land which the Lord your God gives you, you shall not learn to imitate the detestable things of those nations. There shall not be found among you anyone who makes his son or his daughter pass through the fire, one who uses divination, one who practices witchcraft, or one who interprets omens, or a sorcerer, or one who casts a spell, or a medium, or a spiritist, or one who calls up the dead. For whoever does these things is detestable to the Lord; and because of these detestable things the Lord your God will drive them out before you.*

His incantations rose into the night. I was mesmerized. He continued to chant, speaking to the skull held in his boney fingers. The pace of his rhythm grew quicker. More words from the Torah flowed through my mind. From Leviticus, *Now a man or a woman who is a medium or spiritist shall surely be put to death. They shall be stoned with stones; their blood guiltiness is upon them.*

A thought came to me. *Should I kill him?* After all, that was my purpose. I was God's Avenging Angel. Maybe that was the reason I was there. The reason the Lord had led me to that spot at that very moment. The reason I hid in the shadows. I contemplated this. I turned it over and over in my head. A plan began to form in my mind. I would do the Lord's will. I would kill the necromancer.

As I planned my attack, something strange happened. I paused. A black shadow crossed the sky above me. It blocked out the stars leaving the night blind. Large wings flapped across the open window, a violent wrenching of black on black. When the commotion stopped, a large raven stood on the window sill. He stared inside. The man with the hawkish nose continued his chant oblivious to the arrival. The skull stared at him blankly. The raven crawled through the opening. It clumsily flapped its wings. I could see it standing on the skull. No light reflected from its black feathers. Beady eyes burned with red hot coals. It cocked its head to the side. It glared at the hawk billed man. He still appeared unaware of the presence that had joined him. The creature turned toward me and stared straight into my eyes. I retreated farther into the shadows trying to conceal my presence. I dared not move a muscle. I held my breath for fear of being discovered.

The raven turned back to the hawk-nosed man. The bird swayed gently. It moved with the rhythmic flow of the cadence. The chant quickened. An intense and unrestrained excitation filled the man. The raven responded in kind. It was filled with a violent pleasure. The chant reached a climactic peak. The raven's wings spread wide. They shook violently with excitement. Its head slowly swiveled. With the quickness of a snake, the raven jabbed its head forward. Its beak cut into the man's lip. Instantly he recoiled, but it was too late. The raven's talons dug into the man's cheeks. The soft flesh tore. Wings flapped wildly. He screamed. The bird drew back its head and plunged it into the man's mouth. The scream stopped. Muffled noises erupted from him. The skull dropped to the table and rolled before crashing to the floor. It made a sick hollow sound, like an empty bucket. It was met by the man's choking gurgling sounds. His hands instinctively grabbed at his face. He clawed at his cheeks. He reached helplessly as the bird forced itself into his mouth. His lips pulled back revealing swollen purple gums and large crooked yellow teeth. Strings of spit and saliva flew. I watched in horror as the specter forced itself inside. The vile creature crawled down his throat. The man panicked. His gray eyes were wild and filled with fear. The table legs screeched violently across the packed floor. A loud crash rose, as more items fell to the ground. The dry bones clattered. His hands, now at his neck. Muffled cries tried to escape. The bird's tail and one foot protruded from the cavity. The raven's talon dug into cracked lips and pushed itself inside. An exhalation of snot and spit and blood. The wicked apparition was gone. The man flailed wildly. The lamp was knocked from the window sill. Hot oil splashed in the street below extinguishing the flame. It sizzled. Hawk nose stood briefly on weak knees before he tumbled to the ground. Only the flickering candle light remained. Dark shadows formed islands that drifted across the back wall. I could no longer see the man as he fell beyond the window. The night became unnaturally silent. Not a sound could be heard. It remained that way for a long time. I dared not move. I knelt there in the shadows waiting and filled with a sickening anxiety.

An eternity passed. Time stood still. The sweet aromatic perfume filled the air. It burned into my nostrils. Darkness filled the night. The brilliant stars were a beautiful contradiction to what I had just witnessed. The darker the night, the brighter they shine. I waited. In the darkness I thought I heard something move. Then silence. The candle flame still burned and flickered within the room. It threw off a weak light casting eerie shadows within the house. Still nothing moved. I continued to wait. I thought I heard it again, like the whisper of a ghost. A soft rustling sound stirred within the house. I remained vigilant. Silence continued.

Without warning and without a sound, the black silhouette of a man's shrouded head filled the window. Darkness obscured the details of his face. Two skeletal hands gripped the window sill. He leaned outward tucking his chin against his chest. He cocked his head to the left in a precarious position. It swiveled to the right. It remained there, cocked awkwardly on his shoulders. The cloaked hood concealed most of his face. Two burning coals filled his eyes, glowing embers set within jagged slits. A wicked grin twisted across his face. A growl disturbed the silence. It was an unsettling sound, that of a beast. A wet and tattered voice spoke. It was a deep guttural snarl, grinding his words. "Did you enjoy that, son of thy father?"

I was filled with a cold naked fear. For the first time, I was keenly aware that I was alone, utterly alone. I held my breath, afraid to make a sound. I desperately longed to stop the beating of my own heart.

"Come now, Barabbas, I know you are there. I have been watching you."

I refused to speak. I remained crouched in the darkness. The words of my dear grandmother rushed through my head, "Never look at them, Barabbas. Never!"

"I know who you are," he growled, "You are Barabbas, you are the seer."

His wicked eyes continued to glow red, piercing the night. "I can see you," he mocked with a twisted laugh. "Crouched in the darkness. Don't be a coward. I have been waiting for you."

I stood, stepping away from my hiding place. I trembled inside as fear wracked my bones.

His vicious stare never wavered. "I have been watching you, son of thy father."

I mustered up all the courage that I had, "What do you want?"

It was silent. A long uncomfortable silence filled the air.

"I want you, Barabbas," he said, "You have a purpose."

"And what is my purpose?"

Another long uncomfortable silence filled the night.

"Death."

I paused. "No," was all I could muster.

With the agility of a cat, he climbed out of the window. He clung to the side of the building, like a spider. He crawled across the wall. His limbs moved like an awkward insect, each one double jointed in the strangest way. He climbed to the edge of the roof line.

"My boy. I have always been with you. I have protected you from the one who would do you harm."

"The Lord protects me." I answered.

He leapt with the gracefulness of a leopard. His body arched and stretched across the open sky. He landed on all fours, like a cat. His black cloak billowed behind him. Shifting his weight to his hands, he crawled toward me. Stopping, he rose, ascending to his full height. He now seemed a head taller than me. He stood just steps away from me. A strange gray mist followed him. It settled across the entire thoroughfare.

"The Lord!" he said, bursting out with laughter. "The Lord hates you, Barabbas. Just look at your filthy miserable life."

An evil grin tore across his face, his lips impossibly wide. His cheeks twitched. Huge teeth protruded from swollen gums. "The Lord took everything from you." His grin faded.

I said nothing. I had to fight my instinct to turn and run. It was overwhelming, but I stood my ground.

"I was there when they took your mother. I watched as they treated her like a whore."

Rage swelled up inside of me. This creature, what was the hawk nosed man, began to circle me. With slow and malicious steps, he paced around me. "I watched as they butchered your Papa. What did the Lord do?"

He leaned toward me. His eyes were inches from mine. They burned a black fire. I could smell his foul breath. It stank of death and decay. "I'll tell you. He did nothing!"

I noticed other black shadows began to move all around me. They formed shapeless indistinct specters.

"God did nothing when the Romans bashed in your wife's pretty face. She was just like another whore to be thrown out with the garbage. And your son.

Yes, it was a son." He smiled that twisted grin. "You Barabbas, had to take vengeance into your own hands. God did nothing. He hates you, Barabbas."

More of the shadow creatures joined. The inhuman shapes surrounded me. They clung to the darkest recesses of the surrounding buildings. Like giant bats, they hung from the rooftops. The strange mist now formed a thick fog. It filled the streets. It slowly swirled around me. I started to back away. I took a step and another. The hawk-billed man extended his boney hand toward me, "Barabbas, I was there with you. I always have been. I am your father." I took another step. I turned and ran. I ran as fast as I ever had. Illuminated only by the light of the stars, I raced down the streets plowing through clusters of palm dates and hanging laundry. They spilled and shattered, but I never stopped. I ran. Behind me, I could hear wicked laughter and the sound of a thousand beating wings.

CHAPTER 19

My heart pounded, and my lungs burned. My legs were weak with fatigue. My entire body was wracked with pain. I had escaped back to John and Salome's house. I began packing my few belongings. A strange pang of guilt crept into me. Although I had arrived with mournful news, the townsfolk had embraced me. These were peaceful people, God fearing people. A joy lived among them. They were good and honest. The whole community was. I sincerely liked them. Yet, I had brought evil here. It had followed me. The ancient enemy now walked their streets seeking destruction. No place existed where I could escape its grasp, but I could lead it away from here. A sense of despondency held me in its grip. I desperately wanted to see Samuel. His strength and his courage were an inspiration. His wisdom and knowledge, a double-edged sword.

A spear of light cuts through the eastern window. The morning greeted the little town of Archelais. Golden sunlight broke the horizon and began to trickle in. It was a pleasant day despite the night. John and his family began to stir. I loaded my pack and secured my arrows to the outside. I had fewer than a dozen remaining. *I need to replenish*, I thought. I was checking my bow when John greeted me in the doorway. He grinned a sleepy smile. His one eye slowly drifted away.

"Sleep well?" he asked.

"No, not really,"

"Oh, I'm sorry," he said. I saw his eyes studying my pack.

"Stepped out in the middle of the night," he said, more as a statement rather than a question.

"I had to get some fresh air."

"I see," he said. His tone sounded unapproving.

"It's time. I must be going."

He simply nodded his head.

An hour later, John's entire family had gathered. Michael had also joined us. For the first time, I noticed that he was the spitting image of his father. It was more apparent than ever. His gestures were the same. Even the way he walked was the same as his father. His skin was lighter in complexion and his eyes did not wander, but the similar structure of his face was uncanny. His jaw bone was sharp and distinct. He had a proud forehead crowned with thick curly hair. He was an honorable and confident young man. I'm sure his father was proud of him. He was joined by Elizabeth and her two sons. They had all come to share the breakfast meal and to wish me well on my travels.

Afterwards, they all walked with me through the streets to the gates of the city. Several of the town's people greeted us and wished me well. I never saw the hawk-billed man, nor did I want to.

Leaving Archelais, I traveled toward the town of Phasaelis. It was only a few miles from Archelais. It lay in the Jordan Valley on the Wadi Ifjim. Great plantations of palm trees continued to spread out before me. Phasaelis had been founded by King Herod the Great. He had built a defensive tower there and had named it in dedication to his elder brother Phasael, who had died after being captured by the Parthians. After his death, Herod left Phasaelis to his sister Salome. She in turn gifted it to the wife of Caesar Augustus, Livia. At her death, she passed it on to her son, Caesar Tiberius, where it remains. It's offensive how quickly and easily these royals believe that they can give and sell pieces of the Promised Land and its people. A disgrace and a travesty. They are the enemies of God.

From Phasaelis, I headed West toward Jerusalem. It was time for me to return to the temple. I would seek out my Sicarii brothers. Passing beyond the great orchards of palms, I journeyed into the foothills. A well-established Roman road ran through Phasaelis and connected several important towns and villages. Their roads were impressive, formed with cut paving stones meticulously laid or with tarmac, which is stone chippings mixed with tar. Each road was exactly eight feet in width while straight, curved, they were twice that width. They were cambered and flanked by ditches for drainage. These roads were vital to Rome's infrastructure and power. They were an engineering marvel. They provided Rome with the means to move goods and commodities, such as palm dates, over great distances. Unfortunately, they also allowed Rome to efficiently move vast armies across long distances, thus crushing their enemies and ruling with an iron hand.

On this road, I found trouble once again. Traveling westward, the land became more arid and dry as I ascended from the Jordan River valley. This harsh and desolate land was filled with barren rock. The hills progressed as each ridgeline climbed higher. Steep cliffs reached high above the road in places. The road switched through the mountainous terrain. Along these roads, people feared to travel due to the thieves and bandits. People who found themselves victims of such attacks in this isolated and remote place often died. Usually, they were beaten, robbed, and stripped naked. No water or food, nor any shelter could be found. One was completely vulnerable and utterly exposed to the elements.

I found myself in this isolated terrain. I had seen very few people after I left Phasaelis, and now I saw none. I understood the traveler's fear along these roads. Ample hiding places and escape routes presented themselves for any evildoer. As I ascended into the hills, I felt a growing sense of vulnerability. I remained vigilant with each step. I searched out places where one might lay an ambush. I opened my cloak and tied it back, so I might reach my sword quicker. I had traveled several miles when I came around a sharp bend in the road. Out of the corner of my eye, I saw something dart across the sky. A shadow followed it across the rocks. When I looked it was gone, hidden by the rocky cliffs. *Was it a bird,* I thought, *or one of the ravens, the harbingers of death?* I stared into the cloudless sky for several minutes. The sun beat down. It was hot that day. A hot dry breeze pushed across the landscape. Swirls of dust danced across the road. Turning the corner, I found something lying in the road ahead.

A man was sprawled out across the road. One leg lay at an odd angle. It appeared that he had been beaten badly. Dried blood had turned black. It had cracked across his back and shoulders leaving spider webs across his flesh. His hair was caked and matted with dried sticky blood. He had been stripped of his outer garments, leaving him with only his breechcloth. I approached him with caution, scanning the surrounding hillside for the perpetrators. They could still be hiding in the shadows. I noticed that his bare back slowly rose and fell. The man still drew breath. He was alive. I called out to him. No reply. I stepped closer and called out again. Nothing. I nudged his foot with the toe of my sandal. He did not move.

A dark shadow darted across the rocks before me. As quickly as it appeared, it was gone. I searched the sky. No menacing ravens circled above. I cautiously knelt next to the man. His skin was hot and burned in the afternoon sun. He smelled of sweat and a thick musty body odor. His back rose as he inhaled a large breath. "Help me," he said. His voice barely a whisper.

Pulling him by the shoulder, I rolled him over. To my surprise, his body flopped over easily. I was met with a twisted toothy grin. Dark wicked eyes stared up into mine. Instantly I recognized evil in those eyes. The menacing face smiled. This was a trap. *Damn! How foolish I had been to so easily be deceived.* Blood rushed through my veins as I saw the flash of metal. It was a short dagger, similar to the ones the Sicarii prefer. He lashed out at me as quick as a viper. Immediately and without hesitation, I grabbed the man by his wrist. With all of my strength, I pushed the blade away. The point of the dagger missed my throat by a hair, but it cut across the back of my arm. I never even felt the hot blade as it made its mark across my flesh. Crimson blood began to smear across his naked chest as we struggled with each other. He was stronger than he appeared. His wiry frame was deceiving. We fought for control of the knife, a battle to the death. Suddenly out of the corner of my eye, I saw another movement. It was another bandit. He crawled from a small crevasse set within the rock facing on the opposite side of the road. He attacked from the rear. Realizing my predicament, I raised my head and smashed it into the man's face. Flashes of light filled my eyes. It hurt, temporarily stunning me. I raised my head and smashed into the man's face a second time, breaking his nose.

Turning from him, I gained my feet. I drew my sword and spun to meet my attacker. He was upon me. His dagger swinging downward. With the speed of a cat, I struck out at the man barely able to escape his blow. My sword struck the man's blade knocking it away. Unfortunately, his momentum brought him crashing into me. We stumbled backwards, tripping over his partner. We all fell and rolled down a steep embankment. Rocks and dust flew in a violent storm. Our bodies tangled. Arms and legs flailed in every direction. In the fall, I lost the grip on my sword. It clattered across the rocks and landed some distance away from us.

When we stopped tumbling, I found myself on top of the second bandit. Our faces a breath apart. He had reclaimed his dagger, gripping it in his right hand. Immediately, I grasped his wrist with my left. With such close contact, I was not able to swing or punch. I raised myself up and dropped with all of my weight. I hit him in the face with my elbow. I hit him again and again. Each time my elbow striking him harder. A fountain of blood burst forth covering him in a bright red flood.

Then pain and the flash of light. I was stuck from behind. It was the half-naked and bloody bandit with possessed eyes. The blow hurt and momentarily stunned me, but I did not yield my grasp on the limp man before me. Blood poured from a cut above his eye. Another blow struck me. This one glanced off of the side of my head. It hurt badly. I braced for another blow from the bandit behind me. Using my own weight, I rolled to the side, pulling the limp man's knife hand with me. The limp man offered little resistance. His blade slashed upward finding its mark in my attacker's thigh. He howled in pain as he fell to his knees. Blood spurted from his leg. The attacker knelt beside us, holding the knife still in his leg. He cried in agony. I felt no sympathy. Drawing my own leg up to my chest, I kicked out at the man. I struck with all of the force I could muster. It was a perfect kick, as hard as I could. The heel of my foot connected squarely with the center of his bare chest. He jolted backwards as if kicked by a mule.

I rose. Both men lay sprawled out before me. The half-naked man lay gasping for breath; his possessed eyes wild with the struggle. He choked and wheezed through his broken nose. The knife remained in his thigh. Its bloody hilt pointed up to the sky, blood pouring from his wound. The second bandit lay motionless. He groaned as if trying to speak. His words were unintelligible. His head swiveled and turned to the side. Wild eyes stared at me in disbelief. Blood ran into his eyes.

I retrieved my sword. It lay several steps beyond me, lower on the embankment. It had come to a rest on the rocky debris. The sword felt good in my hands. Its weight perfectly balanced. It was the decider of fates. I turned back to the two thieves. Rage burned within me. Vengeance was mine. As I approached, neither of them moved. They both lay there motionless. The possessed man continued to struggle for breath. His leg still bleeding badly, a shocking amount of blood spilled all around him in a crimson puddle that soaked into the rocky earth. The other man simply lay there and moaned. Both men sickened me. This was not revenge, this was justice. They both deserved death, but I could not kill them in this state. I could not kill two defenseless men in cold blood.

"Get up," I shouted, "Get up, so I can kill you!"

Neither one moved. They both lay there in their own misery and pain.

"Coward bastards," I spat.

I sheathed my sword and climbed the steep embankment to the road, leaving the men behind. My feet slipped on the loose rolling rocks. Pebbles and debris cascaded down the steep ridge. On top I crossed to the other side of the roadway. I found a large leather bag hidden within the cleft in the rocks where my attacker had laid in waiting. The bag felt heavy. Its contents were obviously metal. A musical clanking filled the air as I spilled its coins to the ground. Sunlight glistened off of silver, copper and bronze coins. The silver shined the brightest. Several small gold coins glinted through the confusion. This was a treasure and worth many years of a man's labors, possibly more than a lifetime. Several small daggers also spilled from the bag. I surmised these were their victim's defenses, apparently ineffective. These men, these dogs were ruthless cowards who lay in secret awaiting their unexpected victims. They pounced on their prey and stole any valuables before leaving their victims for dead.

As I continued to investigate the contents of the bag, I found several gold and silver rings. One was delicately small. It was a woman's ring. I removed the leather thong that wrapped around my neck, holding a similarly beautiful ring, Melessa's ring. It sparkled in the sun. A perfect match. Memories flooded my heart, memories of my beloved wife. I thought of the day that I had given her the ring. I thought of her delicate hands and how she wore the pretty little ring with grace and honor. I thought of the magical nights, when all she wore was the golden band. And for a brief moment, I felt as if she had been the victim of these wretched men. I hated them. I would kill them. Their deaths were not simply justified, they were deserved.

I tucked Melessa's ring back inside my shirt and dropped the other little ring onto the pile of coins. I stirred through the collection with bloody fingers. I noticed several more gold coins mixed within the copper, bronze and silver. A silver chain that would have been worn around someone's neck snaked through the treasure. I lifted it out of the pile. A small silver medallion hung from it. It was round and etched with a menorah symbol. The seven branches were meticulously etched with fine details. At the base of the menorah was a shofar and a Torah scroll. I realized that the medallion was more than likely an ornament for a Torah scroll rather than someone's jewelry. These men deserved more than death.

Something else caught my eye. It was a small leather purse. It was not much bigger than my hand. It was sewn around the edges with a silver clasp. But the thing that caught my attention was the markings. They were unique. The leather had been painstakingly tooled by a master craftsman. A delicate herringbone pattern adorned the edges. Raised letters crossed the surface of the little purse. They were the most sacred of words, the Shema. *Hear, O Israel! The Lord is our God, the Lord is one! You shall love the Lord your God with all your heart and with all your soul and with all your might.* I recognized the artist's signature work. The last letter of the first and last words were tooled with larger print. These two letters formed the word "ED." It was a reminder that we are God's witnesses. It is to remind us of our duty to serve as a witness to the Lord's sovereignty. I was God's witness. This was Fisel's money purse. It was the matching money purse to the satchel that I had found floating in the river. Floating alongside his murdered body. Without a doubt, these were the men who had killed him. These men had stolen his money. These men had stolen him from his wife and family.

With the purse in hand, I leapt down the side of the road. My feet slid down the steep embankment pushing loose dirt and broken rocks. I landed on my feet like a cat. Both men still prostrate on the ground, where I had left them. As I approached, I held out the leather purse for them to see. Anger flared within me. To my surprise, the half-naked man did not move. I approached and kicked him. He did not move a muscle. He lay perfectly still in a pool of blood. The knife still protruding from his leg. He was dead. The blade had cut through his femoral artery inside his thigh. That explained why there was so much blood. A punishment too humane for such a coward.

I turned toward his companion. The man rolled onto his hands and knees and was attempting to stand. Taking three swift steps, I kicked him in the side. My foot connected with his ribs. He gasped and fell back to the ground. The man grunted in pain. Rolling away from me, he fell against a large boulder. He lay there holding his ribs. The wretched man glared up at me with hatred in his eyes. His face was bruised and swollen. A large open wound ran across his forehead just above his left eye. The blood that ran down his face had started to dry in the intense heat, leaving him a gruesome sight.

I held out the purse. "Where did you get this?"

He remained silent, continuing to stare hatefully.

"Where did you get it?" I screamed. I wanted to hear him confess his deed. I unsheathed my sword.

"Where do you think?" he replied. His voice was a low mumble. It was wet and full of gravel. He smiled a wicked grin. I noticed teeth were missing. I wondered if I had knocked them out. For the first time, I realized that my elbow throbbed in pain. My whole body was sore and wracked with pain.

"This belongs to a friend of mine," I said, not admitting that I had never met the man.

"Good," this was his only response. He spat. A long string of blood and saliva hung from his lip. A bloody drool stuck to his beard.

Slowly, I sheathed my sword. The sound of dry metal grinding against the sheath rang through the hot air. I tucked the purse into my cloak securing it with my belt. I turned my back on the man. I searched the ground before me. It took me several minutes. I chose a large rock. I took my time as I stooped and picked it up. I wanted him to watch me. I wanted him to know what was coming. I wanted him to experience fear. I wanted him to share the same terror as all of his victims.

The rock was twice the size of a human skull. Its rough surface felt good in my hands. It was heavy. Its weight pulled against me. Turning back to the bandit, I raised the rock high above my head. He continued to glare at me with hatred in his eyes. But now there was something else, fear. It was there. I saw it. It swam through his entire being. He drew himself up placing his hands over his head.

"I am the Lord's witness and his hand. God damn you. You don't deserve a quick death." With that, I brought the rock down with a mighty force. It smashed against his leg just below the knee. The rock crushed his leg shattering the bones. The man howled like a wild animal. His cries filled the dry valley. He cursed me. I turned from him and climbed back up the embankment. From the roadway, I drank my fill from their water skins. I washed and dressed the cut on my arm.

I gathered all of my belongings including that leather bag filled with the stolen treasures. It weighed heavily against the leather straps as they dug into my shoulders. The man's cries continued to fill the air. From the road, I looked down at that despicable creature one last time. Another shadow darted across the road in front of me.

I looked to the sky, a brilliant blue cloudless sky. No ravens hovered overhead; instead, several vultures circled high above.

CHAPTER 20

Leaving that place, I headed back east. I carried more than just the treasure. I carried a paranoia and nervousness that I had not experienced in a long time. I constantly checked behind me to see if I was being followed. I was not. I watched the hills and the road ahead of me. I checked the sky, but no menacing adversary stalked me. I followed the trade road as I descended back toward the river valley. In the distance, I could see the vast forest of palms. A gentle breeze stirred the trees and the shade blocked the sun's heat, providing a welcome respite from the desert road.

As I approached Phasaelis, I chose to bivouac there for the evening. Setting camp under the trees, I lit no fire. I slept very little that night. Moonlight filtered through the shaggy canopy of palms. I continuously scanned the shadows searching for bandits and thieves. None came. The following morning, I continued the short distance to the little town of Archelais. Although I had been gone for two days, it felt like some sort of homecoming. I entered the city gates and was immediately met with friendly smiling faces. This truly was a good town.

Making my way to the market, I dodged clusters of dates that continued to hang from every corner. They seemed to have multiplied in the two days that I was gone. I wandered through the maze of tents and shops until I came to John's charcoal business. The canvas canopy shaded several figures within. Unfortunately, John was not there. Instead, I was greeted by his wife and daughter, Salome and Shelamzion. To my surprise, Elizabeth and her two young sons were also there. The boys giggled and played behind the tables. They were all covered with a fine black soot. As I approached, the women grew excited.

"Barabbas, are you well?" Salome blurted out. Her voice was shrill and panicked. Dread rose up inside her.

"Of course. I'm fine," I said.

Their eyes inspected my clothing and the bandage on my arm. I looked down and for the first time realized that there was a lot of blood stains across my cloak and undershirt. The bandage on my arm had bled through and a dried brown stain shone through the cloth. Concern covered their faces. Salome was immediately at my side attempting to care for my wounds. Worry burdened her. I assured her that the blood was not mine, but yes, she could clean and dress the wound across my arm, but first I must speak with John.

"He has gone to the collier pits and storehouses with Michael," Elizabeth said. Her pretty little mouth shaped and formed each word. She spoke with a distinct and proper tongue. Her accent was that of these people south of the Galilee. It made her more alluring. I so desperately wanted to share the news of Fisel's money purse with her, but I had made up my mind that I must tell John first. Assuring them all of my return, I hurried off to find John.

I did find him, along with Michael. They were both very dirty when I found them. They were building a mud mound around a large pile of date seed pits. Michael was on top of a ladder. His father steadied it from the ground as he gave instructions. Several other men helped and brought wheeled carts filled with wet mud to them. John was surprised to see me. He met me with a smile. His smile turned to worry. Their welcome was similar to that of the women. They were concerned as I was covered in blood. I assured them all that I was perfectly fine.

"I met some bandits along the road," I admitted.

"Are you alright? What happened?"

"I'm alright. They tried to rob me."

"Well you look terrible," Michael laughed.

"You should see the other guys," I replied with a smile.

They all laughed an uncomfortable laugh. No one spoke the obvious truth.

It remained unspoken at that moment. Michael broke the silence. "What happened?"

"Later," I said with a sweeping gesture of my hand, "John, I need to talk to you,".

He could read the urgency in my voice. Immediately, he barked orders. Michael and the other men continued the mud work. John urged me to follow him. I did, as he led me to a small building adjacent to the largest storehouse. This was a one-room building. Inside was a bunk and a tall wooden cabinet. A small table stood to one side. This was Michael's house.

As we were alone, I opened my pack and removed the leather bag. It was heavy and bulky. I let it drop to the table. It made a loud metallic thud. John watched with silent curiosity. I opened it and poured the contents onto the table. John's eyes sparkled as I began to tell him my tale. I explained how I was ambushed and how I fought back. I told him everything, including all of the details. I told him of the gruesome ending that they deserved. He agreed as he ran his hands through the pile of coins. He picked up several and examined them carefully before dropping them back into the pile. He also examined several of the pieces of jewelry. He noticed the money purse. I said nothing. He picked it up and slowly ran his fingers across the tooled leather. Tears formed in his eyes. I knew for sure. The purse had belonged to Fisel. There was no doubt, as if I had had any.

"You killed them?" he asked.

"Yes," I nodded.

"Good," was all he said.

"May God damn them to the fires of Sheol."

He nodded silently.

"I want you to give it to Elizabeth."

"The purse?" he asked.

"All of it."

Silence filled the room as a tear ran down his cheek.

That evening we gathered all of his family at his house. After we had gone to the mikvah, Salome cleaned and dressed my wound. They also provided me with fresh clothing. We shared a meal after John had blessed it. He announced that I had something important to share. I told my tale. This time I left out some of the more violent details. I did tell of their deaths and explained that one of the bandits was left alone in the desert with a broken leg. He had no water or shelter and surely died. I did not explain how it came to be broken. I left that part out.

"Well, they surely got what they deserved," Michael stated.

"They surely did," John added. He revealed the money purse. A loud gasp was heard throughout the room. Everyone immediately recognized it. "These were the men who murdered Fisel."

Elizabeth broke down in tears. Her cries filled the room. The scab over her heart had been ripped away. Salome went to her, wrapping her arms around the sweet girl. She cried for several minutes before regaining her composure. Her eyes shone with sorrow, yet they were filled with a sad satisfaction. She held her head high. She was a strong woman, a proud woman, and I felt for her. I wanted to rush to her and embrace her myself, but I dared not.

John motioned to me. I retrieved my pack from beside the door and removed the leather bag. They all watched with a puzzled curiosity. I emptied the bag's contents letting them spill onto the table. Everyone's eyes were filled with wonder as they watched the treasure scatter across the surface. The coins clanked and made a musical sound as they danced and fell against the wood.

"Oh my Lord," Salome exclaimed.

Michael reached out and ran his hands through the coins. He scooped up a double handful and let the coins fall back onto the pile. They sang loudly.

"It's blood money," Elizabeth added.

"No! It is not," John said with a loud voice.

I said nothing, as I listened to John explain. He was adamant. "This is the stolen treasures from those bandit's victims. All of them are dead, including Fisel." He reached over and squeezed her hand. "Elizabeth, some of this is your money."

"All of it," I said.

A shocked look came over her face. She raised her hands to her mouth, "No, I can't. It's too much."

"It's your money, Elizabeth."

"No, I can't," she pleaded.

"Elizabeth, listen to me. I know this money will not bring Fisel back to you and the boys, but there is no one else that it belongs to. You must keep it."

"I can't."

"Yes, you can."

"What about you?" she asked. "You are the one who found it. You were almost killed. It belongs to you."

I smiled. I reached into the pile of coins and removed a single handful of silver and copper. I placed them into my money bag. I removed the silver medallion with the menorah symbol etched on it. I held it by its silver chain. It dangled as everyone watched. Light reflected off of it. I placed it into my bag and said aloud, "This is reward enough."

She began to cry again. This time silent tears ran down her cheeks. Her face was solemn. I stirred the pile of coins two or three times before finding what I was looking for. It was the small golden ring. I held it between my fingers for a long moment. The gold sparkled. The memories returned. I reached for Elizabeth's hand. She withdrew it, pulling it to her breast. "You keep that too," she said. "You wear it. It will make you look like a gentleman."

"It's a little small plus, I'd rather be judged by my actions than my looks."

A faint crinkle formed at the corners of her eyes. Her cheeks flexed and flushed with color. The corners of her mouth slowly upturned. She smiled, a smile filled with genuineness and warmth. On the inside, she suffered from her pain and hurt, but on the outside, she pretended a sweet and pleasant glow. I took Elizabeth's hand. It was so soft, like a baby lamb.

"Fisel would have wanted you to have this." I placed the ring on her finger. A long awkward silence filled the room. Her smile spoke more than any words could say.

"Thank you," she whispered.

CHAPTER 21

The following morning, we all rose and ate together before we said our goodbyes. I headed toward Jerusalem. I followed the same road as before. It led out of Phasaelis, passed the vast palm plantations and ascended from the river valley up into the high desert country. The road heading West had very little traffic; a feeling of paranoia and caution rode on me. It dug its claws deep into my mind. Fortunately, I encountered no bandits on this trip. I did however, come to the spot in the road where the two had laid their ambush.

As I approached, I noticed a strange commotion ahead of me. Dozens of vultures gathered around the two bodies. Their black wings flapped as they hopped and pushed for a better position. Their bare featherless heads were filthy and covered with debris. Their heads were stained red and wrinkled like dried dates. A terrible foul odor wafted through the hot air. It was the smell of death, but the vultures themselves stank horribly. Several screeched and hissed at each other. As I got closer, the vultures became agitated. They opened their wings in a display of aggression. Several hissed. When I was just steps away, they all lifted into the air in a flapping frenzy of wings. They all flew upward and scattered. Several began to circle high above. Others found perch on the high rocks surrounding me. When I looked back down the embankment, the two bandit's bodies lay there. A cloud of flies swarmed around them. The sickening smell of death filled my nostrils. I almost gagged. They appeared as if they had been dead for weeks. Wild animals had already found them. Decay had set in and the meat had been stripped from the bones, leaving a gruesome scene. White bone and ligaments could be seen through torn tissues and muscle. Dried meat still clung to circular ribs that extended upward from vertebrae covered with partially eaten organs. Thick dried blood covered the ground around them. I could see maggots already squirming within their open cavities. They writhed within their glossy entrails. The bandits' eyeballs had been plucked from their sockets and the flesh around their faces had been eaten away. The stench was horrible. The desire to vomit grew within me, but I managed to suppress it.

Disgusted, I turned away. To my surprise, a very large raven stood on the road just behind me. It startled me. I jumped. He glared with wicked eyes. I stared back with anger and outrage.

"What do you want?" I said, fully expecting an answer.

The strange bird said nothing. He simply glared at me with those beady eyes. The bird stood about waist high. He was as black as midnight on a moonless and starless night. Slick black feathers absorbed the afternoon sun. Light glinted off of his glossy beak. His feet were the size of my hands. His scaly talons scratched the rocky surface of the roadway as he stood his ground.

"Move!" I ordered.

The raven did not. He gave a small hop toward me. He slowly cocked his head to one side, peering narrowly at me. He seemed to look me up and down as if measuring me. I stepped toward him. I motioned with my arms waving violently. It was a feeble gesture. He did not move. I took another step and another. He still did not budge. His head rolled and canted to the other side. He peered at me through curious eyes.

"Move, you son of a bitch," I said as I pushed past him.

I heard a dry garbled voice. "Barabbas." I stopped in my tracks. The sound was terrible, a voice straight out of Hell. My blood ran cold. I could feel my heart racing. It was trying to beat its way out of my chest. My mouth went dry and a ringing filled my ears. I slowly turned. I watched as my shadow mirrored my movements across the ground. To my surprise, no raven stood behind me. No raven stood anywhere. He was gone. He had disappeared, like the wind. I stood alone. I turned circles in the road searching. I searched high and low but saw no raven. He had vanished. After the briefest minute or two, I continued down the road.

"Barabbas."

This time it was louder. I turned. I realized that the voice was coming from below the road. The sound rose. It was coming from the bottom of the embankment.

"Son of thy father," the voice said.

It was one of the dead bandits, the one with the broken leg. His skull had almost been picked clean by the vultures. His nose and lips had been eaten off as well as one of his ears. Red meat stuck to the bone in several places. Ragged tendons and chunks of dried flesh still clung in some other places. Patches of black curly hair still held to his scalp. The sounds of bones popped and snapped as he began to move. It was the sound of harp strings breaking. I watched as his head slowly rolled to the side and empty hollow sockets stared up at me. His eye sockets were gaping black holes. Something moved from within. Bugs and maggots crawled inside the openings.

"Son of thy father," he said. His voice was a scary reminder of the darkness in this world. "I know who you are." His lower jaw grotesquely moved. It was unhinged on the left side, barely hanging by a piece of flesh. A dried pink tongue still remained within the cage of teeth. I noticed the missing teeth along the front of its wicked grin. Several yellowish white maggots spilled out.

"What do you want?" I shouted.

"Son of thy father, you have blood on your hands." With the hissing of a snake, he drew out the last word.

"It was justified. They deserved it. They all deserved it."

The gruesome skull rolled back and forth. A quiet popping sound was heard. The flesh tore from the side of his face and the lower jaw swung free, but he continued to speak. "Son of thy father, you have a purpose."

Hearing that, I turned from this apparition. I turned and walked away. Anger and fear both ran rampant through my heart. Hatred consumed me. The shadows of circling vultures darted across the road. They descended onto the bodies of the two bandits, and they feasted. Behind me, I could hear wicked laughter.

CHAPTER 22

Continuing on the rocky road, I ascended higher into the hills. It was hot and dry. Plant life became rarer and more desert like against the barren landscape. The road was good; however, the terrain became extreme with a deep precipitous canyon falling away to the south. This was the Wadi es-Suweinit.. The road led to a village that sat nestled high along a rocky saddle. The ridge was a precipice with three rounded knolls above a perpendicular crag. The saddle ended in a long, sharp tongue that ran to the east. The village sat on the western end of the ridge. It was surrounded by steep cliffs providing seemingly impenetrable protection. This natural fortress led to the name "the fort" by the locals. Beyond it lay the open valley. Far across it to the south, a crag of equal height and respect stood. Its sheer cliffs also impassable.

I recognized this place. This was *Michmash*, the site where Jonathan and his armor bearer attacked the Philistine garrison. The description of the Torah was evident, *"Between the passes by which Jonathan sought to cross over to the Philistines' garrison, there was a sharp rock on the one side and a sharp rock on the other side, and the name of the one was Bozez, and the name of the other Seneh."*

I stood on the very spot where the Philistines had camped over a thousand years ago. A sheer cliff fell away at my feet. I picked up a small stone and tossed it over the side. It dropped a hundred feet before crashing into the sloping rocks and the scree field below. I heard the sharp crack as it shattered causing a small rock slide that tumbled to the valley floor. Several rock wrens scattered from their holes in the rocks and flitted away. Removing my pack, I sat along the edge of the precipice. I let my feet dangle into the open abyss. A sharp breeze rose from the valley below. It carried the faint scent of acacia flowers. It was sweet. It reminded me of honey with a hint of jasmine. From my vantage point high atop the ridge, I looked out across the valley. It was an impressive sight. One could see for miles. I stared southward, toward Gibeah, where Saul's army would have lain.

Looking across the valley, I was impressed with the massive cliffs to the south. As described in the Torah, the southern cliff was called *Seneh*, which means "the acacia or the Thorny One." It carries that name due to the number of acacia trees that dotted the hillside and the valley floor. This valley runs due east, leaving the southern cliffs in the shade almost all day. The shadows bathed the cliffs with a cool light, painting them with dark vibrant colors. It stood in sharp contrast to the cliff to the north. The northern cliff fell away sharply beneath my feet. It was hundreds of feet to the valley floor. As I looked down from my perch, a swirling sensation of vertigo swept over me. A strange irrational compulsion to jump crept in. It was like being in a dream. I could have leapt into the open space at that very moment. I leaned forward. It was the call of the void. It was terrifying and it unnerved me, not because of the height, but because I could have done it. I could have jumped to my death. I withdrew my legs and leaned back away from the edge. I sat cross-legged on the solid rock. I ran my hand across the stone. It was worn smooth from eons of weather. Yellow and orange lichens grew sporadically along the white surface. It reminded me of moss, but it wasn't. They looked like tiny flowers formed in a leaf like crust clinging to the rocks.

The northern cliff was named *Bozez*, which means "Shining or the Gleaming One." It stood in the hot sun almost all day with no relief. This crag was a light-colored rock with ruddy or tawny tints painted throughout. The northern cliffs shone brightly as the sun glared off of the upper crown of white chalky rock. I could plainly see why this cliff was called Bozez. The scenery remained unchanged from the time when Jonathan first looked over the cliffs and saw the Philistines camped here high on the white rock. Bozez must have shone just as brightly then as it does now.

From below me, I heard the songs of the rock wrens. Small brown and gray birds, they made their homes along the cliff face. Their songs were a loud dry trill. The repeated series of sharp whistles was the music of the hills. Samuel always said to listen to the birds. He said to listen to the bird's language. He claimed that if you truly listen, you would know what they had to say. Suddenly the birds' songs grew silent. I listened, hearing nothing but the wind. It was an odd silence that lasted several minutes. I waited. The light breeze swirled around me. A silhouette cut across the sky. It was the dark gray wings of a sooty falcon. He appeared as gray as smoke, almost blue with black tipped wings. He was beautiful. It was amazingly graceful. It flew close to the white cliffs. I could have reached out and touched him. Black gemstones surrounded by yellow eyelids stared at me. His yellow beak was as fierce and deadly as any weapon. He hovered in the wind, momentarily standing still. He turned and glided away, disappearing around the cliffs. I was in awe as I observed such a magnificent bird. A sharp whistle rose from below. It was followed by another series as the wrens began to sing.

As I sat there, I contemplated the words of Samuel. He was a master storyteller and teacher. His knowledge and his wisdom still encourage me today. He taught me from the Torah, from the words of the prophet, Samuel. He explained to me how Jonathan, the son of the king had left his father's army without telling him. Saul had an army of 600 men. They were outnumbered and frightened. They hid in the caves along the Valley of Zeboim near Gibeah. Jonathan and his armor bearer had made their way across the plateau. They found themselves here at the sharp cliffs of Seneh and Bozez.

The Philistine army encamped at Michmash. It consisted of 3,000 infantry soldiers and 200 special *hamashhith* units. Each *hamashhith* was composed of a horse-drawn war chariot. Each carried 3 to 4 men with swords and spears. Each chariot was accompanied by three squads of 4-man infantry runners. The Philistines placed a small garrison atop the cliffs where they could monitor the valley and the surrounding hills. This allowed them to control the entire Jezreel Valley and the central mountain ridge.

Travel north and south is significantly restricted due to the deep canyons and the lay of the land. Here in the Wadi es-Suweinit, there is one exception called the "pass." It is a natural land bridge, a broad place in the canyon where passage is much easier. The Philistines controlled the pass preventing any attack from the south. Jonathan said to the young man who was carrying his armor, "*Come and let us cross over to the garrison of these uncircumcised; perhaps the Lord will work for us, for the Lord is not restrained to save by many or by few.*" Jonathan and his armor bearer chose to cross here at the steep crags, rather than at the pass to the west.

When the Philistines saw Jonathan and his armor bearer climbing up this impossibly steep cliff, they called down to them and taunted them, "*Behold, Hebrews are coming out of the holes where they have hidden themselves. Come up to us and we will teach you a lesson.*" Jonathan saw this as a sign from the Lord and he said to his armor bearer, "*Come up after me, for the Lord has given them into the hands of Israel.*" Jonathan climbed up the steep crag with his armor bearer behind him. They climbed until the darkness of night swallowed them. The two single-handedly scaled the ramparts and attacked the garrison.

In my mind's eye, I could see the battle ensue on this very spot where I sat. Jonathan and his companion were exhausted from their effort, yet they fought valiantly upon arriving at the top. They took the Philistine garrison by surprise. Panic spread among the Philistines when they realized their enemy was within their impregnable fortress. I could see Jonathan yielding his spear. He fought fiercely. His armor bearer following behind with a sword. They slaughtered twenty men sending fear and confusion throughout the remainder of the Philistine army. God intervened and the uncircumcised awoke and beat each other down in a frenzied panic. A miraculous earthquake threw the entire Philistine host into disarray.

Drawn by the sounds of combat, Saul roused his forces. The Israelite army approached Michmash only to find the Philistine camp in turmoil. By the time Saul and his men arrived, the Philistine army had already torn itself apart in fear. Many of the Philistines had slaughtered one another in the confusion. The survivors took flight and fled before Israel.

Samuel explained further. His knowledge of warfare and military tactic was impressive. He said that the Israelite army consisted of light infantry.

They were not as well armed, yet they were fast and agile. However, the retreating Philistines consisted of heavy infantry and the hamashhith chariots. Their methods were to form a phalanx, a group of armed infantries formed close together, joining their shields in an impenetrable wall with long spears overlapping. But within the confines of the canyons, they were unable to form their defensive phalanx. Their heavy armor slowed them down. Their chariots were also useless as they were unable to maneuver within the steep rocky terrain. The Israelite army swarmed and fell on them with a fury.

Samuel's teaching continued. Long lost words floated to the surface. I remembered he asked, "Do you think the sheer overhanging rocks disheartened Jonathan or his armor bearer?"

"I don't know," I answered.

"Or do you think they filled them with bravery and courage?"

"I'm not sure," I said.

"Jonathan faced impossible odds. It was Jonathan's faith and more importantly, God's faithfulness that revealed the truth of Jonathan's words, *'The Lord is not restrained to save by many or by few.'*"

He quoted from the Torah, "*There was a sharp rock on the one side and a sharp rock on the other side, and the name of the one was Bozez, and the name of the other Seneh.*"

I listened as he explained, "Through your life Barabbas, you will face trouble and obstacles. Impossible odds, they will seem overwhelming and impenetrable. They will be your Bozez and Seneh and you will find yourself standing between them. You will not overcome them with your own strength and natural determination. It is only with the help of the Lord that you will find the strength to prevail."

I thought about those words as I stood high atop the white rock, Bozez. "*There was a sharp rock on the one side and a sharp rock on the other side,*" I spoke out loud to myself as I prepared to bivouac there for the night.

CHAPTER 23

That night the stars were brilliant. They sparkled and pierced the black veil. I dreamed of scaling the precipice with Jonathan and his companion. The same stars shone above us. My hands ached and fatigued as I searched for the next handhold. My forearms burned. My feet held precariously to a tiny ledge. Hundreds of feet of open air fell away beneath me. The fear of falling was so real, even in my dream. The following morning, I awoke having successfully scaled the cliff. I rose and headed into the town Michmash. The town was an ancient one and settled in the time of the monarchy. It was mentioned in the Torah on several occasions. First by the prophet Samuel and later in a prophecy by Isaiah. Michmash lay near the border between Benjamin and Ephraim. It lay on the border between the northern kingdom of Israel and the southern kingdom of Judah. It belonged to Israel most of the time. Ancient rock walls and buildings stood on the western end of the ridge. These were Benjaminites. The descendants of a small group of 122 that returned here after the exile. They were proud people. People who honored their ancestors and their heritage. Their village was a stopover for people traveling north and south through the Jezreel Valley country.

I spent a good bit of the day in town. After purchasing some food, I continued on to the south. I followed the road that led across the Wadi es-Suweinit. This was the famed "pass," the broad watershed ridge that bridged the canyon. I thought of the words of the prophet Isaiah as he foretold of a coming Assyrian invasion that would move from Michmash through the pass and on to Geba, Ramah, Gibeah and Jerusalem. His words would ultimately come true. Following the pass, I myself came to the little town of *Geba*. *Geba,* which means "a hill," was an ancient town as well. A fortified wall surrounded the town. The wall had originally been built by King Asa after he had destroyed the idolatry found in Judah and defeated Baasha, the king of the northern kingdom of Israel. White rock buildings stood perpendicular to each other. They were laid out in neat orderly rows. Tents and awnings were also scattered about the town. The town was clean and attractive, a solemn and quiet little village. It sat on the southern lip of the canyon above the steep cliffs of Seneh. The town had originally been given to the Levites in the tribal territory of Benjamin. It stood at the northernmost frontier of the kingdom of Judah. The people had a proud history as it was near Geba that David finally defeated the Philistines.

Entering the gates of the town, I was surprised as to what I found. The people were downtrodden. I could see it in their faces. They were an oppressed and fearful lot. They refused to look at me. These were not the proud Benjaminites that I expected, but a cowardly and submissive group. I walked the streets with an inexplicable sense of curiosity. The town felt deserted, like a ghost town, but it was not. People darted away in the distance as they observed me. I made my way to the center of town and the market. Several women, all wearing veils were gathered there. As I approached, the women scurried away like rats retreating to the darkness. I found myself standing alone in the center of the market. In the distance, I could hear doors shut and low voices mumbling. I called out, but no one answered. I called out. Nothing. Strange.

I strolled the pathways between the tents and the tables. A few vegetables and melons sat in the open. Some tables had cloth and thread for sale. Large spools hung on racks. Others had leather goods. Everything was abandoned. I stopped at one table that had baskets of dried fruit laid out. Grapes, figs, dates and apricots were there for the taking. They were dried and preserved individually or strung into long chains that hung from the awning. Some were pressed into hard square-shaped cakes called *develah*. I called out again. No one answered. I picked up a fig and took a bite. It was sweet and chewy. Tiny seeds popped between my teeth. It had been so long since I had eaten a fig. It was delicious. I had forgotten how much I enjoyed them. I took another.

I was startled by a voice behind me. I spun to find an old man sitting on a carpet under an awning. He looked ancient. His long white beard touched the ground. A gray cloud filled his eyes. "Come here," he said.

I stepped toward him. "Come closer," he instructed. He gestured with bony fingers.

I did. I noticed that he squinted and appeared to be looking me up and down. "Who are you?" he asked.

"I am Barabbas."

"What do you want?"

I waited a moment before answering. "I was passing this way. I am on my way to Jerusalem."

"You best be on your way," he said bluntly.

I continued to eat the last of the fig. I wiped my sticky fingers on the bottom of my cloak. I removed my pack and my bow. I sat down next to the old man. I purposely allowed my cloak to open, exposing the hilt of my sword. He squinted sharply. We stared at each other for a long time. He licked his lips. I noticed that his white beard was stained down his chin.

"Where is everyone?" I asked.

"We don't like strangers."

"Why?" I asked.

"Are you a tax collector?"

I laughed at his question. "Do I look like a tax collector?"

For the briefest moment, I thought I saw a smile on that old man's face. I liked this man. There was something unusual about him. I noticed movement behind me. Several men made their way toward us. Neither the old man nor I rose to greet them. They entered into the tent and gathered around me.

"Who are you?" one ordered.

The old man intervened with a wave of his hand. "This is Barabbas and he's a good man."

Surprised at his response, I was taken aback. I looked at him. He had a glint in his eye that wasn't there before, a hint of mischief. He instructed the others to join us. I learned that this old man was Jethro. He was the town's elder and chieftain. I also learned about the town and its predicament. With continued expansion of the Empire, Rome found it ever more difficult to collect accurate census information and to collect their proper taxes. Therefore, to ease their strain, taxes were collected on entire communities. These taxes were assessed by local magistrates. The tax collectors or *Publicani* would bid on the right to collect taxes in a particular region. They would pay the state taxes in advance. The Publicani had the authority and responsibility to collect the taxes due. They get to keep any excess of what they bid. This made the tax collectors very wealthy men. The system is ripe with abuse and corruption.

According to these men, some of the townsfolk of Geba had angered the local magistrate. They were punished with excess taxes and fines. When they were unable to pay, the tax collector punished them even more. Several people had been taken away to serve in prison until the debt is paid. The government had disarmed the people, taking away any weapons within the town leaving them defenseless. They levied additional taxes on those that remained. Even travelers stopping at Geba had all but halted. This had crippled their economy. And to make matters worse, the tax collector visited weekly. On each visit, he would take their women and bed them. The men were afraid to resist for fear of retaliation.

Anger grew within me as I listened to them tell of their problems. The corruption and abuse were rampant. These poor people had nothing left. Their spirit was crushed. They felt as if God had abandoned them. They were desperate.

"Why don't you appeal to the Roman governor?" I asked.

One man laughed. He was a large man with thick black curly hair. His hands were huge, and I would learn that he was short to anger. He was outspoken and opinionated. He was also bitter. I would come to know him as Gestas.

"Barak ben Nekifi," he said.

The name meant nothing to me. "Why don't you appeal to the temple?" I asked.

"Are you a fool? The tax collector is a cousin to Caiaphas himself."

I was shocked at this revelation. That increased the offense seven-fold. God will forever damn the family of Annas for they have betrayed Israel. At that moment I so longed to join my Sicarii brothers and end their reign.

"You must stand up to them, for the sake of your daughters," I said.

Several men agreed. Others expressed concern that the tax collector, Barak ben Nekifi would bring destruction to their town. "They will bring retribution," one said.

"Retribution, retribution belongs to us," another man said angrily.

A heated argument broke out among the men. They were passionate with their concerns. Some were passivists. They wanted to appease the tax collector. They feared the destruction of their families and town. Others opposed him. In fact, many wanted to kill Barak ben Nekifi for his atrocities. The argument escalated. Tempers flared. This town, these people were afraid and frustrated. Finally, the old man, Jethro, rose. Clinching his robe in his fists, he shouted at the men, "Enough!"

A hushed silence fell across the group. It was obvious that this man demanded respect among his people. He stood in the middle of the group. They glared at each other. Tempers were still hot. Jethro spoke, "We cannot stand to the might of Rome. We are small, and we are weak. They have disarmed us leaving us vulnerable. There is nothing that we can do."

When he finished speaking, he turned and left the group. He looked tired. Some of the men mumbled as he walked away but none disputed his words.

The big man, Gestas, spoke, "How would we repel the Romans? How would we withstand…" He didn't finish his words. Quietly, the remaining men dispersed. Only Gestas and one other man remained. He was Dismas. He was different from Gestas. He was a mild-mannered man. He was thin with light brown hair. His eyes were kind. A sad melancholy hung around his shoulders. Gestas on the other hand had an intense frustration. He was hardened and filled with hatred. He reminded me of myself in a way. He carried a raging fire.

"Kill the tax collector," I said. I spoke quietly but plainly enough for both men to hear. Gestas nodded his head in agreement. I could see the flame within his eyes.

"It will bring destruction to our town and families," Dismas argued.

"Destruction has already befallen us," Gestas said.

"Don't do it here. You hunt him down. Kill him in his own house, in his own bed," I said.

"They'll only send another," Dismas said. He turned and spat.

"But maybe he won't be as wicked," Gestas said. His fists tightened in anger. I could sense a bitter fire that burned under his weathered skin. There was something more to this man.

I was invited to spend the evening with Dismas at his house. He introduced me to his wife, Eliana and children. He had two sons, both of them around ten years of age. His wife was kind and a good cook. She prepared a stew with the little food that they had. Guilt pained me as I had not realized that these people were so hungry. I did not want to take their food, but she insisted. The entire town had very little food. The town was on the edge of starvation. Yet, just across the canyon, the town of Michmash seemed overflowing and 6 miles away Jerusalem flourished. I decided that the following day I would go into the wilderness and bring back some meat for these people.

As we visited into the evening, I learned more of this town and its plight. The tax collector, Barak ben Nekifi was a wicked and twisted little man. No one could remember exactly why he had waged his war against Geba. Dismas believed that one man had insulted him about two years ago. That man had been hauled off to prison and had not been seen since. His family had been left behind. Starving, they were desperate and filled with hopelessness. Their neighbors had been kind and helped take care of them. This simple act of kindness had enraged Barak ben Nekifi. He had punished the entire town as he continued to do. The abuse of power was an abomination. The story infuriated me. The Publicani crushed these people with additional taxes and fines. He enforced them with a small regiment of Roman soldiers. But now he traveled with only two temple guards. His arrogance and overconfidence had grown.

I also learned that his devious acts grew with his growing arrogance. The tax collector now collected his tariffs in other ways. Accusing each family as being deficient with their taxes, he took the women. By this time, he had raped about 20 of the women in this one community. In fact, Dismas told me that Eliana had been spared so far, but Gestas' wife had not been as fortunate. The Publicani had taken his wife on at least four or five separate occasions. I imagined his rage as armed guards held him down outside his own home as Barak ben Nekifi collected his sinful tax.

CHAPTER 24

The following morning, I rose early and headed into the canyons and draws. I took only my bow and quiver of arrows. I watched the sunrise in the distance casting a golden glow across Bozez and Seneh. I traveled down the canyon branching off into several smaller wadis. A cool breeze pushed down the canyons. They were barren and rocky, forming dry creek beds. White rocks lay scattered down the draws. Some were small and broken, others were boulders, as large as a house. Occasionally broken tree branches were wedged between boulders. Some were very large. These were remnants of ancient flash floods that left an indelible mark on the landscape. A definite line was left high on the canyon walls indicating how high the water must have come. I could imagine the raw power of the rushing torrent. A massive wall of churning water mixed with swirling mud and debris would be devastating. You could see where boulders had been ripped from their resting places and pushed down the rushing river. It must be incredible to witness such an event. However, if one was unfortunate enough to be caught in such a flash flood, there would be no escape. Its mighty roar would mean certain death.

But there was no water to be found on that day, only dry rocks and sand. Layers of rocks lay upon each other and rose up the canyon walls. They lay one upon another as stacked wood. Some were incredibly steep rising high into the heavens. Small desert plants sprouted from precarious cracks. A fine dried silt cemented the stones together and filled parts of the path. I found goat and sheep tracks several places but no animals. Dried droppings lay along the trails, but they were obviously old. I continued to search down the wadis. In one draw I noticed more green vegetation. I followed this path noticing that the plants grew more numerous and larger. Thick brush gathered in the bottoms. I came across several clumps of trees indicating that water must be nearby.

I pressed on until coming to a small spring. Lush vegetation sprung forth. Clumps of trees miraculously flourished. This was truly an oasis in the desert. Crystal clear water bubbled up out of the ground. It formed a small stream that ran a short distance before opening into a watering hole. The water went no further as it must have been swallowed back into the earth at that spot. I knelt and dipped my hand into the water at the source of the spring. The water was sweet and cold. I drank until my thirst was quenched before filling my water skin. Although animals contaminate the water, it is usually safe to drink at the source of the spring. Animal tracks were everywhere. The place was overrun. They covered the soft earth and mud that was around the watering hole. Goat and sheep tracks, bird and hare tracks remained in the mud leaving clues of their visits. I even saw jackal tracks mixed with smaller rodent tracks. This place was teeming with wildlife. And this would be a perfect spot for an ambush.

I searched out a small shelf that hung just above the spring on the side of the canyon wall. A boulder sat precariously perched. It must have sat there for thousands of years. It was a perfect hiding spot. A dark shadow fell across the boulder. I could remain hidden, yet there was still room to draw my bow. The only concern was the wind, as it tended to swirl as it pushed through this canyon. I had two clear shooting lanes through the brushy vegetation running to the water's edge. I took up my position and covered my face. I lay my quiver next to me leaning against the rock. I nocked an arrow. The feathers were a little ruffled and split, but they would work. The red stripes beamed at me. Now all I had to do was wait.

After two or three hours, my patience paid off. In the distance, I heard the sharp crack of falling rocks. They bounced down causing others to cascade after them. They came from higher up on the canyon wall. I ever so slowly turned my head in the direction from where they came. I saw nothing. I watched patiently, daring not to move. I held my breath. A few more rocks spilled down from above. That's when I saw them. A dozen ibex, the wild goats of the desert, stood perched on dubious ledges high above me. I understood from where they get their name. It made perfect sense, for *ibex* means "to ascend." I recalled my encounter on Mount Hermon all those years before.

I watched as they slowly made their way down the steep craggy terrain. They gracefully leapt from one rocky ledge to another with the agility of a cat. They were remarkably sure footed. This provided them with an uncanny defense, as very few predators could follow these amazing animals. I continued to admire them as the herd made its way toward the water. Once they were below my line of sight, I was invisible to them. I watched as they gathered around the life-giving spring. Fortunately, the slight wind was in my face pushing my scent away from the herd. But, I could smell them. A strong musky odor drifted on the breeze. They were now just twenty steps away from me. My heart began to beat with anticipation as excitement rushed through my veins.

The big male buck led the way. The others yielded to his authority. He was huge and very impressive. His hair was short and a reddish brown in color. Hints of gray ran through it. It turned darker, almost black on his underside and along his legs. A thick black beard hung from his chin. It was almost comical. It reminded me of a few people I had met in my lifetime. I smiled to myself. Dark markings accentuated his face. His horns were impressive. They were black and massive. They swept backwards in a semicircular shape. Deep transverse ridges lay across the front surfaces. They reminded me of the khopesh, or the crescent shaped sickle swords of Egypt. A couple of younger bucks followed the herd. They kept their distance from the old patriarch.

Several does began drinking while others stood by cautiously watching. Their sharp eyes searching for danger. The females were smaller than the male. Their horns were also shorter and thinner. They seemed to curve more backwards toward their rumps. I watched as these ghosts of the desert quenched their thirst. The big buck joined the does and began to drink. From this distance, I could hear the distinct slurping sounds.

I raised my bow, the arrow at the ready. I waited for the right moment. Most of the ibex gathered around the water hole. A couple still stood back at a distance. They refused to join the others. They were acutely cautious. They watched for danger as the group drank. Their wild eyes insane with apprehension. I watched with nervous anticipation as another one joined those at the water. One of the watchers jerked her head in my direction. The doe looked right at me. I dared not move. She stared, refusing to break eye contact. Throwing her head high, her nostrils flared as she scrutinized the rocky ledge and me within it. Her ears stood erect. She raised the hackles on the back of her neck. I did not move a muscle. I remained a statue carved from marble, afraid to even breath. An eternity passed as she continued to stare for several more minutes. She stomped her foreleg, expecting me to flinch and reveal myself. I remained still. My heart beat wildly. I could hear the others splashing and stirring the water, but I dared not even chance a glance.

Finally, the doe dropped her head and looked away. A great sigh of relief came over me. Moving only my eyes, I inspected the herd and the situation at the water's edge. Four does stood on my side of the water. Their tails facing toward me. No shot opportunity presented itself. I waited. One turned slightly, offering a quartering away shot. Another stood next to her blocking my shot. I readied myself. I waited. She moved to the right. A small window opened. Ever so slowly, I raised my weapon. I prepared to draw my bow. The string felt heavy under my fingers. My heart was beating out of my chest. I watched and waited. Finally, she moved her front leg forward opening the path into her vitals. "Aim small, miss small. Pick out a single hair on your target," Samuel said. I drew my bow and held it at full draw. I rose in order to shoot through a cleft in the rock. The raw energy stored in the limbs of my bow fought to escape.

Suddenly a loud whistle rose through the canyon. It was the female lookout. She sounded the alarm as every head rose from the water's surface. Beads of water danced through the breeze. I released the arrow. A quiet thud reverberated. The arrow sped silently cutting through the air. It found its mark perfectly, plunging into the back of the ribs. It cut its way through to the opposite shoulder. She leapt kicking wildly. Twisting, she tried to bite the arrow. Panic seized the entire herd as they scattered and raced up the sheer walls escaping danger. She followed. Crimson blood sprayed across the white rocks. The doe ran twenty steps up the steep embankment before crashing back to the ground below. She kicked twice and was dead. Nature could never provide such a quick and humane death.

The remaining ibex watched from their rocky perch high on the canyon wall as I revealed myself and climbed down from my ledge. They watched with pure curiosity as I crossed the creek and made my way to the dead doe. I knelt down next to her. She was beautiful. I stroked the animals neck. Her hair was slick, and she felt hot. A sense of triumph mixed with a sense of sadness. Glassy brown eyes stared into space. I gently shut them. Admiration and respect filled my heart. She was a magnificent creature. I whispered a word of thanks to her for giving her life. I said a silent prayer of thanks to the Lord.

I drug her body down the creek bottom getting her some distance from the water hole. I gutted and bled her there on the rocks, removing the intestines, stomach and lungs. I kept the organ meats and placed them back inside the cavity for safe keeping. Placing a rope around her neck, I secured her. I managed to loop the rope over both of my shoulders and tie it off. This allowed me to drag her more easily. I headed back east toward the main canyon of the Wadi es-Suweinit. Travel across the rocky dry river beds was difficult. Several larger boulders impeded my path forcing me to go around or in between. Her dead weight grew heavier and heavier. My legs burned. I was exhausted, but I pushed on. After several hours, I managed to drag her up the land bridge to the plateau and to the town of Geba in the distance.

CHAPTER 25

As I entered the gates, I found the village a ghost town. It was eerie. I entered cautiously. No one was to be found. I left the ibex laying in the shade at the front gates before proceeding into town. Slowly I examined Geba. I wandered down the street toward Dismas' house. The town remained quiet. I saw no one. Approaching his house, I knocked several times. No one answered. I knocked. Still no one answered. I pushed. Surprisingly the door swung in.

The sun flooded into the room. Dust swirled as it floated in the beams of light. I stepped inside. Against the back wall, I found Dismas' wife and children huddled in the corner. They were startled and afraid. I assured them that it was me and I meant them no harm. After a brief interrogation, I learned that the tax collector was here in Geba. I also learned that he had accused Gestas of theft and was at that very moment at Gestas' house with his wife, partaking of her favors. Dismas and several men from town were there in protest, while all of the women were in hiding within their homes.

Acquiring directions, I hurriedly exited the house and began to make my way to the far side of the town. I noticed a single raven perched atop the neighbor's house. He glared down at me with menacing eyes. A cold chill ran up my spine. I began to walk quickly down the street. As I turned the corner, I noticed several more ravens sitting on the houses. I began to trot to the south. More of the wicked bird creatures began to show themselves perched on rooftops. My trot turned into a run. I began to sprint through the streets. In the distance, I could hear a man screaming in anger. Turning a corner, I found a crowd of men gathered. They were solemn and quiet. Grave expressions painted their faces. Low grumbles were the only sounds from the crowd. The men of this town were so intimidated and beaten down that they were now heartless cowards. Their fire had been all but extinguished. They all stood watching as two temple guards held Gestas on the ground. He struggled and called out for help. None came. He shouted curses at the guards. They simply laughed in response. My blood began to boil as a dozen ravens lit on the roof of Gestas' house. He screamed out for his wife, "Adina! Adina!"

I approached the group with an intense determination. Shock and confusion filled the faces of the crowd. Their expressions turned to fear as I raced past them toward the guards. Several shouted at me. The guards were busy holding the angry husband. He still struggled. They paid me no mind. With three quick steps, I was upon them. The timing was flawless allowing me to kick the guard on my left square in the face. My foot connected perfectly sending him sprawling. He fell back with a jolt landing hard on his back. His helmet rolled across the ground with a hollow sound. Several ravens began to flap their wings excitedly. Surprise gripped the second man. He began to rise, but Gestas held him fast. His big hands gripped the man's leather chest plate. His eyes filled with panic. I struck him with all of the strength that I could muster. The blow landed on the side of his head. He stumbled sideward as Gestas pulled him to the ground. Finding the advantage, Gestas began to beat him mercilessly. I noticed that the entire flock of the harbinger birds began to shake violently. Their wings were a black storm.

The first guard was back on his feet. He charged like a bull. I sidestepped, narrowly missing him. As he passed, I shoved him using his own momentum to send him crashing. He quickly recovered and turned to meet me, but this time he had a short sword in his hand. His entire demeanor changed. A twisted grin shown across his face. Noticing the guards' two spears leaning against the house, I grabbed one. A raven hopped from the spear tip to the other. The long wooden shaft was fire hardened and smooth in my hands. The iron spear-head provided needed weight to the end giving the spear a perfect balance. It felt good in my hands. I recalled the times spent sparring with Samuel. He loved a spear.

The guard turned cautious as I levied the spear at him. Now I had the advantage of reach. The spear is deceptively fast and strikes extremely hard. The guard slowly moved in a semi-circle toward his companion and Gestas. I stopped him cold in his tracks. I thrust the spear at him. He dodged and blocked the tip with his blade. I thrust the spear again. He blocked the attack with his sword and attempted to rush me. Immediately, I stepped back bringing the spear back for another attack. I held the spear level with his chest. I thrust, quickly retracting the spear tip. It was wickedly fast. He swung and missed. I thrust again, this time stabbing him in the upper arm. He wrenched in pain as blood began to spill. The guard ducked attempting to dodge my next blow. But this time I did not retract the spear. Instead, I brought it down on top of his head. The shaft struck his skull with a loud crack. He was momentarily dazed allowing me to raise the spear above him and deliver another blow with the side of the shaft. The man crumpled beneath it. Blood flowed from a gash across his head.

I turned to Gestas who was still beating the other guard. He was a raging animal. However, the guardsman continued to fight back and to defend himself. They rolled across the rocky courtyard. Gestas' blows fell on the man's face. The man continued to swing wildly. I rushed to him stopping the fury. Choking up on the spear, I swung it like a quarterstaff. It cracked across the guard's head, leaving him motionless. The violence of the ravens was worked up into a climactic frenzy.

"Your wife!" I said.

Instantly he was on his feet. He rushed the house knocking the door wide open. I followed. His house had two rooms. The first was empty. He charged through tearing open a curtain that led into a back room. There we found Barak ben Nekifi, the tax collector. He was naked. He was on the bed with Gestas' wife having his way with her. Immediately he turned at the invasion. Arrogance and anger ran across his face. It quickly disappeared as Gestas grabbed the man by a leg. Memories from my past crashed down on me. They momentarily paralyzed me. I was swept back in time. I found myself in Alexandria, Egypt. I had followed the man with a scarred face, the Roman soldier who had killed my Mother and Papa to the pagan temple. There I found him raping a temple prostitute. She lay naked across the couch, just like Gestas' wife before me. Both violated by sick sadistic monsters. I had attacked the scar-faced man, but he fought viciously. Ultimately, I prevailed. I cut his throat bringing an end to his terror. I remembered each blow as we fought to the death. I remembered his final act of defiance. And I remembered the arrogant look in his eyes as my blade sliced through his neck. My mind drifted to the High Priestess of Isis, Netikerty. It was due to her cunning and kindness that I escaped with my life that night.

The screams of the tax collector brought me back to the present. Gestas jerked the tax collector out of the bed and across the hard-packed floor. Gestas fell on the man with the ferociousness of a lion. He began beating him with a merciless frenzy. The tax collector screamed out for his guard, but none came.

I went to the woman. A blanket lay crumpled on the floor. I picked it up and held it out for her to cover her nakedness. Tears ran down her cheeks. I averted my eyes out of respect.

Turning toward Gestas, I saw pent-up rage unleashed. I watched him pummeling the fat bastard. Barak ben Nekifi lay curled into the fetal position. He whimpered like a dog. He attempted to cover his face, but Gestas' blows continued to land solidly. When his hands were able to cover his face, Gestas would hit or kick him in the body. I am sure that he broke several of the man's ribs as he stomped on him with all his might. The man was a bloody mess. He coughed and cried out with each blow. After several more minutes of this, I stopped the beating. The Publicani was on the edge of unconsciousness. Wrapping my arms around Gestas, I pulled him off of the tax collector. It was a difficult task, as Gestas intended death.

"Stop! Do not kill him," I said, looking him straight in the eyes. "I did this. Do you understand? This is my doing, not yours."

Gestas stood dumbfounded, saying nothing. A puzzled look fell upon him. He was still trembling with anger and rage. His body quivered. I grabbed the tax collector by the leg and I drug him through the house. He was heavy, but I managed. A swell of strength and determination rose up inside of me. After all, I had just drug an ibex several miles. She was a magnificent and honorable creature. This man was not. This man had no soul. He was a piece of garbage to be thrown into the fire. I pushed on, dragging him out into the sunlight of the street. Barak ben Nekifi's fat pink body left streaks of blood across the ground.

The gathered crowd gasped in shock as they saw my naked captive. A few cheered but the consensus was fear and worry. A loud grumble rose among them. Several men shouted at me. I dropped his leg hard on the street. He let out a quiet moan. To my left, lay the temple guardsmen. They too lay whimpering in pain. One was sitting erect. He held his head in his hands. Blood trickled down his face. The other still lay on the stone pavement. His breathing was heavy and labored. They were both badly bruised and still bled freely. Turning from them, I addressed the crowd. "Men of Geba, fear not, for I did this."

"Who are you to interfere in our affairs?" an angry voice railed.

"I am Barabbas, and this is my doing," I shouted.

Angry shouts returned to me, "What have you done?"

Another voice shouted, "You have brought destruction to our town."

I looked around studying the faces of the angry crowd. The ravens all sat perfectly still. They surrounded us on the rooftops and watched with a stoic demeanor. I inhaled deeply and waited a moment before speaking, "Are you not sons of Israel? Are you not the proud descendants of Benjamin? The descendants of Aaron? Is this not a devoted Levitical city set aside by Joshua himself? Are you not set apart? It was your ancestors who slaughtered the worshippers of the golden calf and cleansed the tribes at the foot of Mount Sinai. And it was your grandfathers who were almost wiped out at the Battle of Gibeah, but you survived. God found favor in you. He showed you mercy. Geba, you are men of Valor."

An angry man tried to shout me down, "You have brought death to Geba! Death!"

"Men of Geba." I shouted. "You are Benjamin. Our father, Jacob blessed you on his deathbed, calling you a ravenous wolf. Your ancestors were mighty warriors. They were skilled archers and brave warriors known to fight left handed in order to wrong foot their enemies." I paused for a moment and stared at the gathered crowd. They stood listening to my words. A single raven leapt off of the roof and flew down and landed before me. He turned and cocked his head to one side. Beady eyes stared at me with a strange curious look. No one else seemed to notice.

I continued, "Men of Geba. You are not cowards. You are brave. You are the sons of warriors. God has found favor in you. Stand with me against this injustice. Stand with me against this puppet of Rome."

I stepped toward Barak ben Nekifi. He still whimpered as he attempted to roll away from me. I grabbed him by his curly locks. His hair was oiled, and he was perfumed like a whore. It was obvious that this man thought highly of himself.

"Do you know who I am?" he said with a haughty tone.

Jerking his head up, I spoke directly to him, "I don't give a damn who you are."

"I am Barak ben Nekifi, the Publicani of this province. And you have made a grave mistake."

"I see an arrogant bureaucrat, who abuses his power and has betrayed his own people. You are a coward, and a traitor, and a piece of shit."

He sneered at me, "I am of the Hasmonean bloodline. I am cousin to the high priest himself." A quiet mumble arose in the gathered crowd. He brazenly smiled.

Sarcastically, I responded, "You are a cousin to Joseph Caiaphas, the High Priest and son in law of Annas?"

"I am, and you have made a terrible mistake," he paused for emphasis, "Barabbas." He spat in my face as he spoke my name.

"Good, tell him Barabbas did this. Barabbas. And tell him Barabbas is coming for him next."

With a handful of hair, I pressed his face into the street. "Men of Geba. Who has been violated by this man? Whose wife or daughter has been defiled by this animal?" Several men stepped forward. Others faded backwards. I withdrew my sicae from beneath my cloak. The razor-sharp edge glimmered in the sunlight. At the sight of the dagger, the men all stopped, all except for two, Gestas and Dismas. They helped me hold down Barak ben Nekifi. He struggled and he screamed. There in the street, the ravens watched as I castrated the tax collector of Geba.

There was surprisingly very little blood. The Publicani cried uncontrollably. The gathered crowd looked on with shock and amusement. The ravens looked on with a sinister approval. I walked to the end of the house where their horses and a mule were tied. I rubbed the mule's neck running my fingers through her thick mane. The molly's nose was as soft as the finest Egyptian cloth. She was a fine sorrel mule of about fourteen hands. I untied her and swung into the saddle.

I turned to the temple guards, who were still sitting on the ground. "I'm taking the molly," I stated. They made no gesture of recognition as they both climbed to their feet. "You are both traitors to your own people and you have betrayed God. Take him to the temple and tell them Barabbas did this."

I watched as they helped Barak ben Nekifi to his feet. He still cried in pain and he continued to hold himself. One of the guardsmen began to remove his own outer garment and place it over the Publicani.

"No!" I shouted. "He rides naked and exposed, for all of Jerusalem to see."

He glared up at me with a vile hatred born out of Hell. I watched as they helped him onto one of the horses. He wrenched in pain. The two guardsmen shared the other horse. The crowd had grown in numbers. The citizens of Geba now lined the streets and watched as the three departed. I followed them to the city gates where they rode past the ibex.

"I'll be on the summit of Mount Hermon waiting for them. Tell the high priest. Tell him Barabbas did this. Barabbas! Remember the name."

I rode the mule back through the town to Dismas' house. There I gathered my belongings and packed them on the molly. A crowd of people gathered in the street. Several shouts of anger were hurled at me, but to my surprise other voices defended my actions. An argument broke out among the men of Geba. Gestas and Dismas both thanked me and addressed the crowd. I turned the mule and headed toward the gate. From the corners of the houses, shouts of "Thank you," filled the air. It was the women of Geba. They lined the streets as I rode past. Their voices were a sweet song as they sang their appreciation for what I had done.

As I approached the gate, the old man, Jethro stood waiting for me. His long flowing robe reminded me of an ancient and wise sage. He stood next to the ibex. I halted the mule. "The ibex is for your people," I said. I tossed several silver coins onto the ground. "Send some men to Michmash for food."

He nodded, not saying a word. I ran my hand down the molly's neck and patted her. The reins felt good in my hands. They were a fine leather that had been polished smooth. I pulled on them turning her bridle and gently kicked the mule. I noticed a slight hint of approval on the old man's face. "Our women thank you, Barabbas. They will sing of your deeds for generations." Pausing, I contemplated those words. *I have either doomed Geba or set it free.*

CHAPTER 26

I figured that I had about a three to four-hour head start, before they came. I was not going to waste a single minute. I headed into the wilderness. Rather than going east toward the Jordan River and following it to the Galilee, I headed straight north into Samaria, following the road to Sychar. On the plain of Moreh at the foot of Mount Gerizim I came to a well. This was Jacob's well, said to have been dug by the great patriarch himself. The water was sweet and cold. I stopped and watered the mule there at the well.

Several Samaritan women were gathered there. I dared not speak to them, nor them to me. They chatted on like chickens. I ignored them as I drew water and allowed the mule to drink. One of the women was quite loud and animated. Her thick hair had an unusual fiery red tint. She was a moderate build and I would guess about ten years my senior. She was overbearing and controlled the conversation. I couldn't help but overhear her. She went on and on about the prophet she had met at this very well. "He told me all the things that I have ever done," she said. The other women were engaged in the conversation. Apparently, they had all seen this man. They recounted their story.

Another woman responded, "and whoever drinks of the water that he gives, shall never thirst again."

I laughed out loud at this silly comment. The women shot me a hard look and continued their conversation. They were a little quieter now.

The redheaded woman continued, "He is the Messiah, the savior, I tell you. He told me himself. He said that an hour is coming, and now is here, when we will no longer worship on the mountain nor in Jerusalem, but the true worshipers will worship the Father in spirit and truth; for such people the Father seeks to be His worshipers."

I scoffed at these crazy women and their ridiculous talk. I turned toward Mount Gerizim. The mountain was particularly steep along its north side. It was a dry rocky mount sparsely covered on the top with desert shrubs. A stone throw to the east lay Joseph's tomb. It was the resting place of Joseph's mummy after it was brought out of Egypt during the time of the Exodus. There is little doubt that his mummy still lies there today. The town of *Sychar* lay half a mile to the north. It is from this tomb that *Sychar* gets its name, for it means "the town of the sepulcher." After the mule had drank and I filled my water bags, I departed the foolish women and I headed into Sychar.

At Sychar, two main roads led out of town. One went straight north toward Megiddo and Nazareth. It led out into the Jezreel Valley called the Great Plain of *Esdraelon*, which means "May God make fruitful." The other road headed north east. It would be rougher traveling. It passed through the rocky hills. It went around Mount Gilboa and descended into the Jordan valley. It eventually led to Scythopolis and on to the Sea of Galilee. Both roads were well travelled and seemed to have a lot of horse tracks. I chose the one that went north east. It was almost 40 miles to Galilee.

I rode the mule hard to put as much distance as possible between myself and any pursuers, however I was careful as to not overly strain the beast. I liked the molly as she was an exceptional animal. She rode well and was very sure footed across the rocky terrain. She was strong and had a good disposition. We rode deep into the hills, until it was almost too dark to see. We descended into the Wadi Far'ah, an open valley that extended from Mount Ebal all the way to the Jordan River. Soon it became pitch black and too dark to safely travel. We bivouacked there for the night. Fortunately, the valley was full of springs providing plenty of water for the mule.

The following morning, I rose early and resumed my journey. The road followed the Wadi toward the Jordan. The countryside came to life. The hills became greener and plants flourished. I passed the small villages of Aenon and

Salim. There I joined the river road where we headed north. I followed it, coming to the city of Scythopolis. It had originally been known as Beit She'an. As I approached, I gazed upon the large stone walls that surrounded the city. They were ancient but still impressive. It was from these walls that the Philistines hung the bodies of King Saul and his son Jonathan after their defeat at the battle of Mount Gilboa. King David ultimately defeated the Philistines and recaptured the city. Later, the Greeks changed the name to Scythopolis, naming it after the Scythian mercenaries who settled there. Around 90 years ago, after the Roman general Pompey conquered Judea, his commander, Gabinius rebuilt the city. Scythopolis became the leading city and the largest of the league of cities, known as the Decapolis.

The city had prospered under Rome. The architecture was the trademarks of the Greeks and Romans. It was impressive as the buildings were magnificent. White carved columns lined the streets and porticos. An aqueduct brought fresh water to the town from the springs at Mount Gilboa. A massive Roman theatre stood in the middle of the town. A hippodrome rose for horse and chariot races. Its shadow fell across the city. In the past, I had always skirted around this place. This time I followed the paved road and passed at the city gates, before continuing north.

As I approached Philoteria, I could smell the great lake of Galilee. Its scent grew stronger. It brought back a flood of memories. I inhaled deeply. I love the Galilee. Massive walls rose and surrounded the city. I was reminded why the Aramaic name for the city is *Kerakh*, which means "fortress." Outside the gates, several poor families were gathered. The beggars waited for the generosity of passing travelers. I looked them all over thoroughly. Several men who were sickly or disabled sat in the dust. I noticed one blind man sat alone a short distance from the gate. My eyes were drawn to a woman and her three small children. They were all filthy dirty. I would guess all of them under six years of age. The children looked hungry. She looked worse. The mother was sad, and a hopeless expression covered her face. I approached her. She immediately fell to her knees and averted her eyes. "Please kind sir, anything that you can give."

"Woman, when did your children last eat?" I asked.

She looked up at me. Her face was dirty. Her hair was matted and tangled. The dress she wore was threadbare. However, I could tell that in some distant past, the dress had been a fine quality. Her eyes were sunken with dark rings formed under them. Desperation clung to her like a disease.

"Yesterday," she replied.

"And when did you last eat?"

She looked down and away from me. She did not answer. Her children played around her. The youngest clutched her dress.

"Woman," I said, "I'll be back."

I made my way through the city gates and into the streets. Philoteria was a busy and robust place. People crowded the streets. A lot of soldiers were present, which is exactly what I was looking for. Philoteria was home to a garrison of Roman soldiers along with its citizens. The Roman guard lived within the citadel. I made my way towards it. I passed several villas. Most were made of stucco. Some were beautifully decorated with mosaics adorning their walls. Their front doors accessed colonnaded courtyards. Spacious townhouses stood at the center of the city. They were built on a complex orthogonal plan. The community thrived within the confines of the fortress of Kerakh.

Finally, I came to the citadel. Horse stables stood beside it. This was the *Equites*, or the cavalry. The cavalry was the most prestigious unit in the Roman army. It was where the wealthier young men sought to be. It was here that they displayed their skills, prowess, and courage. It was from within the cavalry that many laid the foundation that would lead to an eventual political career within Roman society. Each cavalryman was required to purchase his own equipment, which included a round shield, his armor and helmet, his sword and lance. He was also required to provide his own mount.

Several soldiers were tending to the horses. I'm sure they saw to the animals for the higher-ranking officers. I approached them.

"Excuse me, I am looking to sell this mule."

"You'll have to see the commander," one of them said.

"Can you get him?"

"I'll fetch him," another man replied. He sat down a bucket of feed and went inside.

A few minutes later the young man returned with a rugged looking fellow. I assumed that he was the decurion, the cavalry officer in command of the squadron. He had a three days growth covering his face and chin. Short cropped black hair stood erect. It was shocked with streaks of gray at the temples. He had large broad shoulders and a barrel chest. Cold steel eyes revealed a hardened man. He carried an air of command. He wore only an undyed linen tunic with no armor. A thick leather belt was worn around his waist. A sheath holding a decorated dagger was tucked inside, the handle sticking out. Leather lappets, called *pteryges* hung from his waist. These were heavily studded with metal. There were also several tokens and discs attached to the leather strips. These were to signify the campaigns that he had fought in. This man had many.

"Thank you, centurion," he said as he dismissed the young man. "I am Cornelius, the squadron commander. What can I help you with?"

I was pleasantly surprised, as the man spoke. He seemed kind and sincere. He did not seem brutish and arrogant as I had expected. He even smiled, erasing my uneasiness.

"I must make passage on a ship across the Galilee and I no longer need the mule. I need to sell her."

"I might be able to help. One of my cavalrymen may be interested." He walked over and ran his hands across the mule's back. He felt her up and down, including her legs and belly. The mule was strong and muscular. Obviously, the tax collector had chosen well. The Roman commander lifted each of her feet and inspected the hooves. He ran his thumb down the grooves and around her sole.

"She needs to be reshod. Her back left foot is bruised. It feels a little feverish." He ran his hands up her face. Prying her lips open, he inspected her mouth. "How much?"

"500 denarii," I said.

"Seriously, man. I'll give you 300."

"Commander Cornelius, this is an excellent beast. Probably one of the finest mules that you have ever seen." He watched me with a curious look. I contemplated my answer. "I'll take 450."

One hand remained on the molly's face. I could tell he liked the mule and was thinking about it. He walked around her one more time. He continued to touch her as he circled. He admired the mule.

"She is a beautiful creature. I'll give you 400."

"And 50 for the saddle?" I asked.

"Do I look like I need a saddle?"

"Well, I don't where I'm going," I said, thinking about the deal, "I guess I'll take it."

"And the saddle?" he asked.

"Keep it," I said.

We visited for a few more minutes before he retreated into the citadel to retrieve his money. I learned more about this man. I learned that he was a seasoned veteran of the Roman army. He had served in the heavy cavalry of the Italian Regiment for twenty years and would retire in two more. He planned on returning to his home and his family in Caesarea. I also learned of one more important fact, the man was a God-Fearer, one of the gentiles who sincerely revered the God of Israel. They were known as the *yir'ei HaShem,* which means "Fearers of the Name." These people revered and worshipped the Lord, but were not practicing Jews, nor did they follow the Law.

When he returned with the money, I wrote out a bill of sale on a clean sheet of papyrus. I wrote, "Cornelius, the decurion of Philoteria, has bought my mule. She is six years old, fourteen hands and sorrel in color, for 400 denarii. She is warranted healthy and not lame." The cavalry commander watched as I wrote out the bill. He watched over my shoulder. I do not believe that he could read well. We looked at each other for a brief moment. He smiled. I added one more line before I signed my name, "The mule is named Barak."

He paid me and took the receipt. His rough hands folded it and tucked it inside his belt. I rubbed the molly on her nose one last time. I handed the reins to Cornelius. With a nod, he led the mule away. I disappeared into the crowd of people and made my way back to the front gates. There I found the beggar woman along with her children. I quietly motioned to her. She gathered her skirt folds around her and made her way over to me. Her children followed obediently. Another woman had been watching with curiosity. She was old and haggard. I motioned to her as well. She grinned exposing her one tooth. She limped as she made her way over to us.

I gave the old woman one hundred denarii. She fell to her knees and began weeping. She was a poor woman and I'm sure that she had never seen that much money in all of her life. I helped her to her feet.

"Woman," I said, "tell no one of this."

With tears streaming down her face, she nodded. She placed the money into a small leather purse that hung around her neck. It swung between her flat dried breasts that had probably never suckled a child. I thought to myself, *If she had only had a son to care for her in her old age.* With shaking hands, she tucked it away inside her cloak. Her crying continued, but she could not speak. She clung to my hand and continued to kiss it until I pulled away. "Not a word," I said as she turned and limped away.

The young widow woman watched this. Her eyes followed me. They darted from me to the old woman and back again. Curiosity filled her eyes. I could sense her desperation. It consumed her. Her three children watched us with the innocence of dove. They stared at me, hunger in their eyes. "Woman tell no one. Swear it," I commanded. I counted out two hundred denarii. I placed them into the palms of her hands. She too began to cry. Hot tears cut trails through her dirty stained cheeks.

Her cries came in waves, like those of a crashing beach. Each time she gathered her breath, she whispered, "May God bless you. God bless you sir." I squeezed her hands shut around the money.

"Tell no one. Hide it and spend it wisely," I said.

She squeezed her eyes shut, tears forced from the corners. "I will. I promise. Oh, thank you, kind sir."

She tucked the money away, hiding it inside her cloak as well. When I turned, I noticed that several of the other beggars were all staring. They watched me and the woman with envy. A brief memory filled my mind. I recalled my first trip to Capernaum with Papa and Tobias. Limiel and Andrew were there too. As we departed the city gates, we met several beggars. Papa's generosity overflowed. He blessed those people. And he set himself apart as an exemplary model for his young son and his employees. Pleasant memories of Papa swirled in my heart. My musings soon turned dark as I recalled that day when Rome stole my Papa and Mother away. Bitter resentment rose shattering my recollections. I gazed upon the beggars with the compassion of my Papa. I made my way toward each of them, men and women. To each and every one, I gave a small alms. To the blind man, I gave about forty. I gave away all that I had, except for about forty denarii, which I kept for myself. They all thanked me and were extremely grateful. My heart swelled with compassion for these people. They were all starving. I know the poor are always with us, but I laid the blame at the feet of Rome.

CHAPTER 27

It was now late in the afternoon. As we stood there, just outside of the city gates of Philoteria, the sound of beating horses' hooves thundered before us. The ground shook and a cloud of dust rose and swirled in the afternoon breeze. A dozen temple guards rode past the beggars. Several Roman soldiers rode with them. We watched. I stood among the sick and the disabled. I waited with the hungry and the blind as the guards rode past, ignoring the gathered onlookers.

Damn, I thought to myself, *they are fast.* They had made significant time. They were far faster than I had anticipated. I had underestimated their swiftness and resilience. As soon as they were through the gates, I followed. I made my way through the streets, trying to blend into the crowds. Avoiding them at every turn, I made my way to the harbor. No guards lingered other than the soldiers already stationed there. Calmly, I walked right past them with no incidents. I found passage on a fishing boat that was just setting sail late in the day. They were heading out for the evening's catch. It was drifting away from the docks, as the oarsmen prepared to depart. I managed to leap across the expanse of water and land on board. The boat bucked gently under my weight. The captain welcomed me with an open hand and demanded his payment up front. I gladly paid him as the oars cut through the water and the ship pulled away.

I watched the docks anxiously as the sails were raised. They hung limp, like rags in the setting sun. I looked back at the shore. Several of the temple guards rode through the crowd. They dismounted and began moving through the gathered people. I watched as they searched the crowds. Just then, a faint breath puffed across the waters, a promise that the breeze would come. The sails swelled to life. Without warning, they fell limp. The surface was as smooth as an Egyptian mirror reflecting the darkening blue sky above us. A disappointment filled the entire crew. Looking back, I noticed that several people were now pointing at us. They were pointing at our ship, and at me. A terrible anxiety washed over me. Another gentle breeze moved past us. The sails flapped weakly and fell limp. Two of the crewmen trimmed the sails. I heard shouting. I turned to look and saw that several more of the temple guards, along with Roman soldiers were now gathered along the docks. They were shouting at our boat. They ordered us to return. I would not. My black heart swelled. I would kill everyone onboard the ship and sail it myself before I would return to the shoreline and certain death. I placed my hand on the hilt of my sword. However, to my surprise, I noticed that the captain ignored the shouting. He refused to even look their direction. His entire crew did the same. Instead they talked among themselves. It was as if they could not hear the shouting guards. These were fellow patriots. They loved Israel and loathed Rome. I noticed a couple of the Romans soldiers getting into a small row boat. It rocked back and forth as three of them climbed aboard. They began to row out toward us. The entire crew grew agitated.

I watched them as they rowed across the water. One man rowed and the other two prepared to board our ship. They shouted as they approached. Each time the oars cut through the surface, it brought them closer. They quickly crossed the glassy water. Our sails continued to hang limp in the dead air. I prayed as my heart prepared to fight. The row boat came closer. They were within an arm's length of our boat. One drew his sword and smiled a menacing grin.

Without warning, a small line of ripples moved across the smooth surface of the water. It raced ahead of the coming wind. It was the breeze rushing toward us. All around us, the water was darkened with cat's paws. A sharp snap was heard as the sails swelled to life. They grew ten times bigger as they filled with the wind. Every fiber and every stitch strained under the stress. The ship gave a swift lurch as it began moving forward. It quickened its speed. The water gurgled as a white foam churned beneath the bow. A rainbow danced across a fine mist of spray. We headed out past the safety of the harbor. The row boat was left behind. It foundered in our wake as our ship sailed away. A brilliant orange sun was just touching the horizon.

"You must be hot cargo," the captain said as I paid him double his original asking price. We sailed to the port of Hippos on the eastern shore. When we arrived, the night had fallen. A river of blazing stars burned across the black veil. They reflected off of the dark waters. This was a fishing port and a trade port. The actual city of Hippos rested atop a flat top mountain that resembled a horse's back. It stood high above the great lake. The soft glow of oil lamps shone through the windows of the houses. Occasionally I would see the silhouette of a person passing the light, but other than that, Hippos was fast asleep. It was the central city of the Golan. Within its walls, a fortified enclosure housed a squadron of Roman soldiers who helped protect the mountain passage. This was used as one of the major trade routes up to the Golan Heights. I dared not waste any time. I sought passage on another ship, yet at this time of night the port was quiet. Only a few people wandered the streets or moved among the ships.

I nestled into a piled fishing net for the night. It was damp, and it stank. I slept off and on as I awaited the morning and the rebirth of the sun. Still with the darkness of the night, the eastern sky began to softly glow. Several men stirred among the moored ships. A couple of boats began to row out toward the open waters. I could hear the quiet splashing of their oars as they cut through the water. A few more people began to emerge from the night. Soon the sky began to burn orange. More people began to move along the docks. I managed to secure passage on a cargo ship. It was one heading westward toward Tiberias, on the other side of the lake.

The Galilee was calm that morning. It was pleasantly cool. I watched as the sun crawled heavenward. Its reflection casting golden slivers across the water's surface. A gentle breeze filled the sails and pushed us westward. We landed at Tiberias, the largest city on the great lake. It was built on the site of the ancient village of Rakkath by Herod Antipas, the son of Herod the Great.

He had made it his capital and named the city in honor of the Roman emperor, Tiberius. His palace stood high on the acropolis overlooking the city. Tiberias was built around the natural hot springs, known for their miraculous healing powers. It was originally a pagan city as Herod Antipas had populated his new capital with non-Jews from other parts of his domain. However, now a growing Jewish population lived within its walls. I wasted no time in Tiberias, and immediately began seeking another ship to carry me back east. It took me two hours before I was able to secure transportation. Finally, I secured passage on another cargo vessel. We departed and headed toward Gergesa.

Gergesa lay across the great lake back on the eastern shore. I was unsure if my strategy of zigzagging across the waters of Galilee was a good one. Rome has a vast network of communications and they ruthlessly pursue their enemies. And with the High Priests family goading them on, I must outsmart them at every turn. I intended to leave a confusing trail, making it difficult to track me. I planned on disappearing into the wilderness, like a wounded animal.

As we rowed into the port of Gergesa, I immediately recognized it as a pagan city. This was the home of the unclean heathens, the Gadarenes. I noticed large herds of swine grazing the steep hillsides that ran along the edge of the water. Hundreds fed there. They reminded me of the pigs that Samuel and I had encountered in the woods, but these were domesticated. They were fat and light colored. They were not as fierce, nor covered with thick black hair of the wild beasts. Behind Gergesa, an immense mountain rose above the city. I noticed ancient tombs, like earthworm holes, were scattered across its face. Several large ravens circled the town. Others came and went from the tombs. An eerie feeling came over me as I studied this place, a dark eerie feeling. Turning back toward the Galilee, I could see Capernaum sitting far across the waters on the opposite shore. This would be my next destination. I found passage on a small fishing boat and departed that place.

CHAPTER 28

The men in the fishing boat dropped me off just south of Capernaum along a rocky sandy beach area. I hopped out of their boat and waded to shore. The water was cold. Schools of silver minnows swarmed around my legs. I smiled at their playful dance. I noticed that the hills appeared greener this year than I remembered them. Dark lush vegetation covered the hills surrounding the city. A familiar scent filled the air. It was an old friend welcoming me home. My heart raced as I splashed onward fighting to keep my balance. Reaching the shoreline, an unsettling yet familiar feeling of belonging seized me. *Welcome home*, it said. I realized that I returned a changed man, but Capernaum remained. It was still what it was and what it always had been.

I intended to build a fire and dry my clothes, but very little firewood could be found. I scoured the shore for dry driftwood and debris. Broken pieces of lumber lay scattered along the rocks. The wood had faded in the sun to a pale white. I finally managed to gather enough for the evening. Carrying the wood along with my pack and all of my belongings, I moved inland toward a clump of dark trees. Several large stones lay piled beneath. I set my camp there for the evening, as the sun was now dropping behind the western horizon. The heavens faded from the ocean of blue to a blazing gold that melted beyond the abyss of darkness. I managed to build a small fire next to a large boulder where I stretched my cloak and undergarments. The rock continued to radiate the day's heat. That along with the fire, slowly dried my clothing. As the sun set and darkness rose, the temperature dropped. A cool breeze moved from across the water leaving a chill in the air.

It had been three days since I castrated Barak ben Nekifi, the publicani of Geba, and I was positive that word had already reached the entire Galilee. I was a wanted man. Therefore, I would hide within the darkness. I intended to sleep and rise in the darkest hours of the early morning. I would sneak into Capernaum and see Jarviss and the family before the Romans ever expected anything. I nestled into my bed roll and covered myself with my cloak. It was still slightly damp. The ground was hard and rocky making it uncomfortable. However, the heat from the fire was adequate to keep me warm. The fire snapped and crackled. Occasionally it hissed and popped as the damp wood was consumed by the flames. Burning fireflies floated skyward. The sweet smell of smoke drifted through the night's air. It was hypnotizing. Soon I was fast asleep. I was visited by the dream, the dream that had haunted me my entire life. This time it was more vivid and richer than ever before. It terrified me.

I found myself standing on the grassy plains. A breeze moved across the savannah. An ocean of lush grass swayed before me. Above, a million stars twinkled against the black veil casting an ethereal glow across the prairie. A strange sense of calmness fell over me. I had no apprehensions, no anxieties, just a sense of peace. A falling star streaked across the heavens, momentarily illuminating the night. I stood alone, waiting in the night. It was silent, except for the gentle swishing of the tall grasses that surrounded me. I heard it. In the distance, I heard the faint bleat of a lamb. Anxiously, I began looking toward the horizon. I searched until I spotted the white ball of wool that playfully bounced through the high grass. It hurriedly moved toward me.

Like a shepherd knows his sheep and the sheep know their shepherd, I knew my little lamb and he knew me. This was JoJo. I had no doubt. He frolicked and leapt into the air with the joy and the innocence of a child. His bleats sang as he ran toward me. My heart swelled with love for this little lamb. This was JoJo, my lamb, and my friend. Memories flooded my mind as he grew closer. His big brown gentle eyes stared into mine. I was a child running my hands through his soft wool. His soft pink nose tickled as he nuzzled against my neck. I remembered how warm he felt as he curled up next to me to sleep. I remembered the sweet smell of his breath. Love washed over me at that moment as I waited to greet him.

This was my JoJo. This was my precious lamb, mine. He loved me, and I loved him. This was the one I had raised from the smallest baby. This was the one who my father had sacrificed on the altar for the atonement of our family's sins. Guilt still clung to me. It ate at my very soul. I had helped lead him to his death. I betrayed him. I saw it in his big brown eyes. I watched and held him in my arms as the priests cut his throat spilling his precious blood. Tears streamed down my face and I could barely breathe. As a child, I did not fully grasp the meaning as his blood was spilled to take away my sins. It was so complicated. I did not understand. I was angry, angry at the world, angry at my father and angry at God. Blood was required. Blood made us clean, my lambs blood. My lamb died so that we could live. But, now he lived. He raced to me through the tall grass. It was a joyous reunion. My heart swelled as I ran to meet him.

Without warning, the terror began. JoJo was just steps away when the grasses tore apart. Several large black creatures rose from the shadows. They appeared like large hyenas. They were so quick. They pounced with a horrific fury onto my lamb dragging him to the ground. This night, the attack was more violent. JoJo's screams were more terrifying than ever before. JoJo kicked and fought but to no avail. There were so many of them. Their fierce teeth ripped and tore his soft flesh. They began to devour my little lamb before my very eyes. His beautiful white coat was instantly stained with his scarlet blood. JoJo's screams filled the night. He cried out desperately for my help. His eyes searched frantically for me. They were filled with pain and terror.

Immediately I leapt forward. I must save my lamb from these monsters. But before I could take another step, the grasses ensnared my legs. I found I could not move. They were alive. Thick blades of grass and roots entangled my legs as they quickly wrapped around my entire body. They bound my arms and chest. Like thick bands of leather, they dug into my flesh. The grass was a snake that squeezed the life out of me. I struggled to break free but could not. Helpless, I watched as these beasts of Hell tore my little lamb apart.

His blood sprayed across the tall prairie grasses. Droplets rained down across the prairie. Dark orbs splattered across my tunic and face. I could taste the salty essence on my lips. I watched as the one I loved was murdered before my very eyes. I screamed out in rage, "God damn you!"

Instantly, one of the demonic creatures turned toward me. He was huge. His black coat was wet and glistened with JoJo's blood. It dripped from his wicked snout. Hot steam rose from him, ghostly in the cool night air. Long ears lay pinned back against his head. The hackles along his back stood on end. A ragged tail curled between his hind legs. He stared at me with wicked eyes. They glowed with red embers. Evil exuded from the beast. He let out a low guttural growl, not the high-pitched cry of a hyena. It was a rough throaty growl. Black lips rolled back as he bared his vicious teeth. I struggled to break free. The beast took a step toward me. Then another. I continued to fight against my restraints, but to no avail. I was held fast. He took another. Panic began to race through my veins. The beast took another step. He opened his mouth wide as he bared huge razor-sharp teeth. He was so close. I could smell his vile breath. His throaty growl grew deeper and more menacing.

Without warning the beast was jerked backwards. He disappeared as the tall grass shuddered violently and closed in around him. He howled in pain. Hidden from my sight, the snarls of the wicked pack fell silent. A mighty and terrible roar shattered the night. It was like thunder. It shook the very foundations of the Earth. The sounds of death and dying filled the darkness. Horrible screams of pain and agony fell upon me. Haunting silence fell across the plains. The only sound was that of the whispering grasses. Droplets of blood clung to the blades of grass. The light from the twinkling stars reflected in the wet blood.

The ensnaring vegetation loosened its iron grip and retreated. The tangle of grass and roots fell from me. My shackles were removed. I was free. There I stood, eerily alone, among the slow-moving grasses of the plains. Daring myself to move, I took a step forward. Silence hung in the air. I took another. I tried to peer over the hedge of vegetation. The grasses were still too thick and tall for me to see. The brutal scene before me remained hidden. The snarling pack remained hidden in the shadows. JoJo was nowhere to be seen.

I took another step. Silence continued. Suspense wracked me with each step. Finally, I was able to see over the vegetation and into a small depression of crushed grass. I searched frantically for my JoJo. He was nowhere to be seen. Carnage was everywhere. Signs of a violent and bloody slaughter were scattered about. Ripped and torn flesh along with the broken bones of the demonic creatures lay strewn upon the earth. Their bones shattered into splinters. Blood bathed the landscape. Crimson blood was everywhere. So much blood. Oh my God, so much blood. It was hot and sticky. It slowly dripped and ran down the long blades of grass. It was like a river of blood had escaped the constraints of its banks. The putrid scent of death hung heavy in the night's air. It clung in my nostrils. A coppery taste filled the back of my throat and I had to suppress a strong urge to vomit.

Standing over this massacre, words from the Torah fell upon me. Words from the scroll of Vayikra, called Leviticus, whispered through my mind. *For the life of the flesh is in the blood; and I have given it to you for making atonement for your lives on the altar; for, as life, it is the blood that makes atonement.* I took another step toward where my lamb had last fallen. I searched frantically and called out his name. Warm sticky blood squished up between my toes. A

breeze moved the tall grass all around me. It blew the hair out of my face. Subtle movement caught my eye. A dark shadow rose from where JoJo had fallen. I was both terrified and amazed. Before me appeared the dark figure of a massive beast. I gasped for breath. It was a lion, a massive and mighty lion. We stood nose to nose. I could smell his hot bloody breath against my face. I was paralyzed with fear. Though he was terrifying, he was majestic. He was a beautiful dark golden color. A massive dark tipped mane encircled his head and muscular shoulders. Large tufted ears twitched as they sat prominently atop his head ever alert. His white chin was stained red with blood and it dripped from his shaggy mane. A long pink tongue darted out between powerful teeth. It licked his chin and nose, before disappearing back into his mouth. Terrible penetrating eyes stared longingly at me. His imposing eyes were familiar. I knew them in my heart. They were the eyes of JoJo but these eyes were also the eyes of a predator. They stared deeply into my very soul. They chilled me to the bone.

The lion snarled as his lips peeled back revealing terrible and vicious teeth. He let out a deep guttural growl. It started deep in his bowels and grew until it shook my bones. Opening his savage jaws wide and baring huge teeth, the lion let out a terrifying roar. It was as loud as thunder. I took a clumsy step backwards. The lion did not move. He watched with a strange curiosity. I took another step back before I tripped and fell. He did not move. He merely stared me down with those penetrating eyes. The fearsome beast took a step toward me with a bloody paw. He growled menacingly. His fierce growl strangely became clearer. In a deep and magical voice, he spoke, "Barabbas, son of thy father."

Quickly, I rose to my feet, turned, and ran for my life. Usually, at this point in the dream, the lion would attack me with explosive speed and devour me. However, this night was different. The lion did not pounce. He did not attack. He stood his ground. As I turned to run, I collided with an iron pillar. From out of the night a massive warrior appeared. The man was a giant. He was clad from head to toe with shining armor. It glistened like polished silver. He reflected a nonexistent light that illuminated the darkness. Intense blue eyes stared out from the slit in the helmet. That was the bluest blue one could imagine, as blue as the deepest oceans or the farthest reaches of the heavens.

Somehow, I instantly knew this was Gabriel, the archangel of the Lord. With the strength of ten thousand men, he slammed me to the ground like a child's doll. Knocking the air from my lungs, I gasped for breath. He pinned me there with an iron boot. I was completely helpless. I heard the singing of his sword as it cleared the scabbard and cut through the night's air. I felt the razor-sharp tip pierce the skin at my neck. "Shall I kill him?" I heard the angel say.

"No," the lion said as he approached, "I have a purpose for him." His massive paws stepped across me. I felt the ground quake beneath them.

The constraint of the mighty angel was lifted. Freed, I continued to gasp for breath. I rolled over to my knees. Gaining my balance, I stood to my feet. Immediately, the angel knocked my feet from me, buckling my knees. He slammed my face into the earth. "Where you stand is holy ground. You shall bow."

I lay prostrate in submission. "Forgive me. Forgive me," I said. I lay with my face to the ground. The smell of the earth and grass was sweet, like that right after a rain. I said nothing, biting my tongue, and I dared not look upon the lion or the mighty warrior. The entire prairie grew silent. A heavy anticipation hung in the air.

The lion spoke once more, "Jeshua-ben-Jeshua, son of thy father."

I dared not look. I remained in darkness. I kept my eyes to the ground averting them from his presence. I remained silent.

"I speak to you, child."

"Who are you Lord?"

"Barabbas, I am your father."

With that startling revelation, I jerked my head up gazing upon the mighty beast. I could not help myself. Curiosity and shock gripped me. With my reaction, the angel stiffened. His piercing blue eyes cut through me. Yet, he did not move. He remained at the side of the magnificent lion.

"No, that's impossible," I said.

"I am."

I lowered my head back to the earth. I stared into darkness. I contemplated his words. They sent my mind into a swirl of confusion. How could this be? My father was Jeshua-ben-Jehoiakim, the ship builder of Gennesaret. And I had been adopted by Samuel, the rabbi and weapons master. How could the words of this beast be true?

He spoke again. His voice was deep and boisterous, yet, it was gentle and filled with kindness. It gave me comfort. "Barabbas, rise. Come walk with me."

When I looked up, the lion and the angel were gone, but I was not alone. Before me stood a man. He was wrapped in a pillar of light. He was dressed in a long flowing robe. A hood covered his face, obscuring it from view, yet it shone like the sun. His clothing glowed, bathed in a brilliant light, as white as lightning. An outstretched hand reached out to me.

"Rise," he said.

I rose to my knees and began to stand. I was met with a strange feeling, like I was walking on the wings of a butterfly. I took his outstretched hand.

As soon as I touched him, a flash of light tore through me. It was like lightning. I was filled with a burning feeling of happiness. It rushed through me. This was something I had never experienced before. A sense of fulfillment and satisfaction flowed through my veins. It was an intense sense of joy and peace and hope. It was a sense of love, an eternal love. It flowed through my veins.

We turned and began walking together through the prairie of tall grass. I noticed the heavens were slowly moving. The procession of twinkling stars was crawling across the sky, moving from east to west. They proceeded across the dark canvass. The occasional shooting star raced across the expanse. The milky way was a flowing river of light. In the far distance, brilliant clouds of colored lights burst into existence. Other swirls of colored lights, spheres and orbs danced across the darkness. They were blue, purple and red. A million new stars lit in the distance. They were the color of molten gold. At first it seemed random and unpredictable, a state of utter confusion in the galaxy. I noticed that they all spun in an orderly fashion, moving in a ceremonious manner. I was amazed. In all my life, I had never seen the sky like this before. It was awe-inspiring as I watched the heavens swirl around me.

"What is this place," I asked.

"What lies before you is the great cosmos. From it, all life burst forth from the dark chaos, spoken into existence. All of creation lies before you, my son."

"When?" I asked, "When is this?"

The being of light chuckled. He actually laughed. "Child, do you truly believe that the Lord is ruled by the constraints of time?"

"Where am I?"

"You are here, and you are everywhere."

I thought about that for a moment. "That is impossible," I said.

"Nothing is impossible, my child. You are the dust of the cosmos."

At that moment I realized that my feet were crunching along a wet sandy beach. Before me, a river of crystalline water flowed past. When I looked back up, the swirling galaxies were gone. An incredibly blue sky hung in the firmament. Sunlight danced off of the sparkling surface of the rippling water. Its golden glow spilled over the mountain tops and filled the valley below.

Jagged peaks rose heavenward. Their reflections painted across the mirrored surface of the water. They were covered with the purity of snow. Lush green trees and vegetation descended to the water's edge. The scenery was breathtaking.

The tall figure robed in the brilliant light stood with me. He stepped toward the water. I followed. I found myself standing knee-deep in the gentle river. I could feel the current lazily flowing past me. It pulled at my bare legs. Small silver fish darted passed. The sound of the churning waters and passing current was calming. A familiarity hung in the air. It brought peace to my soul. As we stood there, a recognition fell over me. I turned and looked all around. I realized this was the beautiful river from my other dream, the life-giving river. The magnificent waterfall was there before me. It cascaded down a rocky cliff before spilling into the stream. A cloud of mist hung in the air at the violent intersection. Rainbows danced in the spray. Yes, I recognized this place. I recognized it all, the mountains and the trees, even the smooth river stones just below the water's surface.

The fragrance of cedar and pine mixed with the smell of fresh water. It filled the air with a sweet and pleasant aroma. I inhaled deeply and smelled the sweet pleasant scent of the mountains. As we stood in the waters admiring the beauty, the river came alive. It was teeming with life. Every kind of fish and sea creature darted through the crystal stream. I noticed the forest along the edge of the river was alive. I watched as trees grew and reached skyward. Vines and thick vegetation covered the shoreline. Brilliant flowers of every color imaginable burst forth. Their sweet scent, like perfume overwhelmed me. I watched as several creatures like lizards and salamanders crawled from the waters. They crawled through the mud and disappeared into the thick brush along the river's edge.

The forest itself moved. It was alive with wildlife. Every creature imaginable made their way through the thick trees and brush. Some scurried along quickly providing only the briefest glance. Others moved slowly giving me a better view. Strange and massive creatures, some as large as trees, lumbered along. They were elusive, providing only the briefest glimpses. Birds of every shape and color filled the canopy of trees. They darted from branch to branch as they swirled upward into the sky. Their songs rang out across the valley. Deer and rabbits and squirrels scampered alongside the smallest of mice and rodents, mixed with the strangest of insects. Horses and camels strolled alongside goats and sheep. Oxen and buffalo joined them. Every kind of antelope from the smallest Royal to the mighty Oryx galloped through the openings. Several cats stalked the undergrowth. Their beautiful coats blending into the shadows. The roar of a lion filled the air. Packs of wolves and jackals moved along the banks of the river. Other strange and exotic animals crawled through the foliage. Snakes and lizards darted from one hiding place to another. There were so many animals, the lifeblood of the Earth. Far too many to count, strange unnamed and wonderful animals. Some massive, like dragons, their heads reached into the tallest trees while others crawled on their bellies.

I looked to the robed man. The pillar of light obscured his features, but I could tell a sense of pride, a sense of love and caring surrounded him. I could not hold back the smile. I was filled with the happiness of a child awestruck with wonder as I admired the beauty of creation before me.

As we stood there, a large flock of birds swooped across the river. Their reflections danced across the surface of the water. The flock moved in unison, hundreds of wings moving as one. At first glance, they seemed black to me. As the sunlight reflected off of them, it was clear that they were a deep rich navy blue; blue against blue as they swirled across the canvas of the sky. Clear attentive eyes were painted yellow. The flock swirled as one and dove, skimming the surface of the water. Like a wisp of smoke, they swirled into the sky and they were gone.

"What do you see?" asked the hooded figure.

I looked at him but had no answer. I was still overcome with emotion by the beauty before me.

"What do you see?" he repeated.

"Life," I answered.

"Good. It is the blood of the Earth."

The figure motioned to the water beneath me. I looked down. My own reflection stared back at me.

"What do you see?"

"I see the water."

"What else?" he asked.

"Nothing, only the water."

"Look closer," he said, "what do you see?"

"I see me. I see myself," I answered.

"Is that who you really are?"

"I don't know what you mean."

"Your reflection, what you see. Is that who you really are?"

"Yes. No. Wait. I don't know," I answered, truly perplexed. I was confused, as I had never thought of such things before.

"You are seeking meaning, yet you are blind to your true identity. Open your eyes, son. This is only your earthen vessel. It will pass away. Is this who you really are?"

"I'm not sure."

The pillar of light seemed to glow brighter as he answered, "You are more than that, Barabbas."

"I am?" I answered.

"It's all about perception. Tell me, how can so many people look at the world and see one thing, and another see something completely different?"

"Tell me who I am," I asked.

"You are my child. You are the light. You must see with new eyes. Do not walk in the darkness. Open your eyes. You must see and awaken to the light. You must abandon the darkness and walk in the light. This is your journey, Barabbas, to walk in the light of true love. Only in true love shall you find peace during this life. Walk with me and you shall walk in the light."

"Walk in the light?" I repeated.

"In the light, shadows flee. In the light, no darkness can prevail. You are the light. Be the light."

Confusion and sorrow overwhelmed me. I questioned the Lord, "If this life is a journey, it has a beginning and an end. It's the transition that leads to the next life. Yet, this life is filled with darkness. How can I be the light?"

"Do not conform to this world. Do not walk in darkness, for you will stumble. Set yourself apart. Be the light."

The golden glare drew my attention toward the middle of the river. Something floated there in the deeper part of the flowing current. Sunlight glinted off of a golden hilt. It called to me. All of my attention was drawn to it. A beautifully engraved scroll floated in the current. I knew this scroll, for I had seen it before. This was the scroll of the Law of Moses. This was the Law that provided salvation for fallen humanity. This was God's Law, the entire Law, mysteriously wrapped into one single scroll. I watched as it slowly twisted in the current and began to sink into the deep waters. Panic overtook me. *I must save the scroll. I must save the Law.* I took several steps forward toward the scroll. The water splashed all around me as it deepened. It felt cold as it rose up my legs.

The Lord robed in the brilliant light stood with me. "What do you seek, child?"

"The righteous Law that saves us. By obeying and keeping the Law perfectly, we earn our redemption and win God's acceptance. I must save it."

The Lord laughed. "Barabbas, what you seek is impossible, for the heart of man is darkness."

"Lord, I've obeyed all these commandments since I was young."

"All?" he asked.

"I have been zealous for your Law."

"My son, your hands are covered in blood. Pride and unforgiveness harden your heart."

I stepped toward the scroll. The rocks felt slick underfoot. I was careful as to not lose my footing and fall. The river deepened with each step. I soon found myself wading waist deep. The cold water splashed as the current strengthened.

"My child, the more you try to follow the Law, the more you shall fail. And the more it will fail you. The Law must be fulfilled. Fulfillment is the new law, called grace. Grace is found only in the light that is true love. Grace is mercy. Grace is forgiveness. Grace is love, a love that holds no record of wrongs. Grace is atonement."

I continued forward, stretching out my arms. I strained, but the elusive scroll remained just out of my reach. Continuing forward, I found myself neck deep in the cold waters. The round stones became dangerously slippery under my bare feet and the current moved much quicker. It pulled at me.

"Barabbas, you must love as I love. Grace is the new Law. Seek love and forgiveness rather than the Law. Seek mercy rather than sacrifice. Be the light. Fulfill the Law."

Reaching forward, my fingers brushed against the ornate handle. It was so close. I stretched toward my goal. With one final desperate effort, I lunged toward it. Success. I managed to grab the beautiful scroll. I held on tightly, not daring to let go. The salvation of all mankind was in my grasp. Joy filled my heart, but it was short lived. I found myself alone, totally and completely alone. I called out but there was no answer. The Lord had gone.

I was treading water. I could no longer touch the smooth rocks that ran along the bottom of the river. An invisible force as swift as the current carried me downstream. I fought the rushing waters, but to no avail. I was quickly swept away. I struggled to keep my head above water. The peaceful waterfall, the gentle stream, the weeping trees and all the animals were all left behind as the violent river washed me downstream. Only jagged rocks lined the river's edge. I realized just how heavy the scroll was. It became heavier with each passing moment. I tried to swim but it was impossible. The scroll was a burden. It was a great weight. It pulled me under. This beautiful and precious scroll was carrying me toward my watery grave. I kicked and fought just to keep my head above water. I inhaled a mouthful of the river. I coughed and spat. I panicked and cried out, "Is there no one who can save me?"

A small voice inside my head whispered ever so quietly, "Let go." I refused, for fear that I would lose God's salvation. The scroll slowly dragged me under. I found myself sinking down through the bitterly cold waters, an icy cold that was sucking the life from me. A cold that penetrated into my very bones. A terrible and heavy silence fell upon me. Darkness grew all around. It began to swallow me. No light penetrated into these depths. My lungs began to burn. I desperately needed breath. Below, shadows moved in the deepest darkness. Something unholy stirred there.

Clutching the scroll to my chest, I continued to sink deeper into the dark depths below. A great abyss awaited there. My lungs burned like fire as they were starved for air. My ears ached from the increasing pressure. Pain and darkness began to set in all around me. Black shadows circled me like great predators, the leviathans of the deep. Finally, I lost all hope. I surrendered. This was my end and I accepted it. I closed my eyes and accepted death. I opened my mouth and I inhaled the darkness.

Someone took my heavy burden. Someone took the scroll from my hands. All its weight was removed and miraculously set aside. All its demands were satisfied. It was the lifting of a curse from my heart, a curse that was so deeply embedded, a curse that was passed down from generation to generation. Life was breathed into me once again. I inhaled deeply.

I found myself standing once more on the grassy prairie. A million stars brilliantly lit the night's sky. A beam of light fell all around me. Like a blind man receiving sight for the very first time, I saw a brilliant column of light. Brighter than the sun. It was as bright as lightning. Something moved from within the pillar of fire. Shrouded in the burning brightness stood a figure of a man. He was stunning beyond belief. A magnificent creature. Strength radiated from him. Long flowing robes of fire surrounded him. They were as white as virgin snow and swayed in an invisible breeze that embraced him. I now recognized this angelic figure as the Lord himself, the creator of the universe and all that is. He stood before me in all his grandeur. Tongues of fire engulfed him from within the column of light. A hood covered his face, obscuring it from view. From within the hood, a blinding light burned. I was forced to shield my eyes. His voice was calm, yet it was filled with the strength and ferociousness of a lion, "Barabbas, do you want to live?"

"Yes," I answered. "Yes, I do."

"Barabbas, I will take away your burden. I shall lift it from you. Son of thy father, you have a destiny to fulfill. You have a purpose. Be the light."

Without warning, both of his hands came up and removed his hood. Instantly, I was blinded by the intensity of the light. It radiated all around me. It was like staring into the heart of the sun. The heat was intense. It burned my skin. Like molten iron, it burned through my veins. It burned through my very soul. My body jerked, and I was startled awake. I had seen the face of God… and I had lived.

CHAPTER 29

The darkness gave up its hold as pink and orange slowly painted the eastern horizon. I pulled my cloak around me to ward off the heavy chill in the air. My fire had gone out during the night, leaving only a fine white ash. Beneath the powdery ash a few hot coals remained. I stoked them and added more tinder along with some small sticks. Blowing gently, I tried to coax the flames back to life. I watched as the coals glowed red. At first, they smoked profusely but refused to light. I continued to blow, trying to breathe life into the fire. The smoke burned my eyes, filling them with tears. The coals glowed red hot and smoked before they burst into flames. I continued to add larger sticks and pieces of wood until my fire was roaring. It felt good as it warmed my bones.

I sat there in the cool morning air contemplating my dream. This had been the most vivid dream that I had ever experienced. It was real. Its clarity was haunting. The meaning should have been evident, yet it escaped me. It left me with more questions. The words of the angelic being echoed through my thoughts, "My child, the more you try to follow the Law, the more you shall fail. And the more it will fail you. The Law must be fulfilled. Fulfillment is the new Law, called grace. Grace is found only in the light that is true love. Grace is mercy. Grace is forgiveness. Grace is love, a love that holds no record of wrong. Grace is atonement." Those words conflicted with my very existence. Those words challenged everything that I stood for. *Forgiveness and mercy were not within my power. I sought justice. I sought revenge. I sought the destruction of the Lord's enemies. Plus there is no new Law. How can that be?*

There is only God's Law. My own dream was blasphemous. My own dream condemned me. Yet there was still that lingering feeling of hope and joy, that intense eternal love that rushed through me when I first touched His hand. A remnant of that feeling remained. I wanted more. I longed for it. *Was it truly the Lord, or was I deceived by some darker forces?* Two great oxen pulled at me. They pulled in opposite directions. They were trying to tear me apart. *I so desperately wished that Samuel was here. His wisdom and knowledge were a gift and a treasure.* The dark waters of confusion swirled around me and a chaotic battle raged within my very soul.

In my small metal pot, I boiled water and made tea from the stem shaped leaves of the joint pine shrub, called *sharvitan* or ephedra. Its sharp taste is not unpleasant but gives one a boost of energy. Samuel claimed that it had many medicinal properties too. He claimed that it was used primarily as a remedy for colds and coughs. It is also used for congestion and allergies. I drank it but wished that I had some honey to sweeten the taste. After a breakfast of dried dates, I broke camp. The sun was now rising above the mountains across the lake. It was time to make my way toward the walls of Capernaum.

Approaching the city gates, I removed my pack and my outer garment. I hung them over the crook of my arm. My sword remained hidden under my tunic, but my bow was exposed strapped across my back. I had bathed in the cold waters of the lake and slicked back my hair and beard. I intended to appear as a man traveling for business on a day's journey rather than a wanted man on the run. Several other people were gathered at the gates. They all seemed relaxed. No one appeared alarmed. I kept my head down as I passed them. Entering the gates, I was met by a group of the Roman guard. A nervous fear hit me in the face. Ice water ran through my veins. I immediately prepared to fight or die. *Damn my luck*, I thought to myself. But, to my great relief, these soldiers just walked past paying me no mind. I let out a great sigh of deliverance. I turned and walked quickly in the opposite direction.

Making my way through the maze of city streets, I found myself just outside of the pottery mason's compound. I searched the street before me for any signs of trouble. I watched diligently for a trap or a guard stationed before the gates. After an hour, I convinced myself that there was none, and I proceeded toward the gate. The wall was too tall to peer over without drawing unwanted attention, so I listened. Within the walls, I could hear the joyous sounds of the women's laughter. They mixed with the music of the children at play. I listened closely. I could hear Lilliah's voice above all the others. Her nasally voice carried on the morning air. A brief memory flashed before me of the first time I met this one. She was only a child and I was only a boy. So much had happened over the past years. It was a lost lifetime ago. Now she was a grown woman, still living at home. And I was a wanted refuge running from the Roman Empire. I continued to listen. Lilliah was talking to her Aunt Martha, the mother of the five boys I now called my brothers. Beyond them I could briefly make out male voices. It sounded like Jared and maybe Jannai or John. I scrutinized the voices hoping to hear Jarviss or Joanan. I did not. After several more minutes, I proceeded toward the entrance. I glanced around the corner of the gate. The women were across the courtyard. Children played all around them.

Deciding that the way was clear, I stepped inside. Immediately I came face to face with a man carrying a large box filled with glassware. We startled each other as I had somehow not seen him, nor him me. He almost dropped the box and its fragile contents, but I grabbed it from him saving the disaster. This was my dearest friend, Joanan, whose name means "God is Gracious." Immediately a huge smile filled his face and he embraced me.

Within the time that it takes a butterfly to flap its wings, I was surrounded. This was a joyous homecoming. My friends, my family all gathered around providing the warmest welcome. Several of the older children darted away, only to return with two men close on their heels. It was Eliakim and Jarviss. They raced across the courtyard to greet me. Both men were older now. Jarviss followed. His belly slowing him only a step or two. He embraced me, a father greeting a long-lost son. Tears streamed down his rosy cheeks and he cried. "Oh, my boy, I am so happy that you are safe and alive."

The rest of the family all began speaking at once. Eliakim closed the gate, sealing us off from the street beyond. I couldn't understand them through the chaos. Everyone was excitedly talking at the same time. Finally, Joanan took control and managed to quieten everyone. He proceeded to tell me that they had feared that I was dead or in the hands of Rome. He said that two days prior, Roman soldiers accompanied by a man of the Temple Guard showed up in Capernaum. "They began questioning everyone as to your whereabouts. They were anxious to speak to anyone who may have known you or your location."

"They haven't caught me yet," I said with a smile.

"Yet?" Joanan said with true concern on his face.

"Don't get cocky," someone grumbled.

"We all swore that we had not seen you in years," Jared injected.

"They believed us and went away," John said, "but they instructed us to report to the authorities if you showed up."

"They may return," Joanan said, "we must be careful."

"Let's get out of the courtyard and go inside," Jarviss said as he directed us all toward Eliakim's house since it had the largest dining and living room.

We spent the rest of that day visiting. I shared the stories of my travels. The brothers and the older boys wanted to hear every story. They loved my tales and wanted all of the details. I told them of finding the body of Fisel and his leather pouch. I told them of John and his family. I told them of the bandits in the desert hills, and for the first time I shared with them the ghostly stories of the living dead. I told them of the hungry people of Geba and what I had done to the Publicani, Barak ben Nekifi. However, they were most impressed when I removed the dragon's tooth from my pack. I told them of scaling the steep walls of the canyon and finding the beast frozen in stone. They were all fascinated and each took turns holding the tooth as they passed it around. The women remained squeamish, but the young ones squealed with delight. Soon the day turned into evening. The women prepared a stew of goat, lintels and onions. We shared the meal together before retiring for the evening. I spent that night with Jarviss. It was a treasured moment. We visited and talked until the late hours of the night. We talked of the old days and of Melessa. We both still missed her gravely and shared our grief. We cried together. We laughed together. While we were alone, I decided to share my vision. I told him of my dream. I was nervous. It was the first time to share it with anyone.

Jarviss contemplated my vision. He did not dismiss it as I might have expected. Rather, he embraced it. He told me there must be some deep meaning hidden within. He stood and paced back and forth across the room. He mumbled some unintelligible words under his breath, as he began talking of that prophet. He ranted and raved about the teacher. He said, "You should ask him. Ask Jesus. He could tell you the meaning."

At first, I was taken aback. I still had my doubts concerning this teacher. This Jesus was surely a wise man, but he continued to speak blasphemy. He continued to lead the people astray. I remembered the lepers that were healed. I had seen it with my own eyes, but doubt continued to guide me. I questioned my own memory. I questioned everyone else's. *Did I really see what I thought I saw? Was it a trick, a clever deception? Had I and everyone else been fooled by this false prophet?* I quietly considered the possibility.

Jarviss continued, "If only the teacher were here. We haven't seen him in several weeks, maybe a month. He would know. His wisdom and understanding are from God. The man is amazingly gifted. His words are inspired."

"Yes, you have said that," I said sarcastically.

"Barabbas, your doubt has blinded you."

"Blinded me? Blinded me from what?" I asked.

"The truth, Barabbas. The teacher is sent by God himself."

"Jarviss, do you know what you are saying? You are saying that this man, a mere mortal, is from God."

"That is right. He is his messenger."

"Blasphemy!" I shouted. I did not intend to raise my voice, but I did. I yelled at him. My passion raged. I shouted at my very own father in law. He had been deceived. His foolish gullibility repulsed me. For the briefest moment, a contempt swam through my veins. My condescending words cut him to pieces. Immediately I regretted it, but it was too late. I could not take it back now. Words are like a sword. Once struck, the blow cannot be taken back. The damage has been done and it is irreversible. Shock filled Jarviss' face. Embarrassment crawled through his entire being. He shrank like a little child, like a wounded animal. I had treated him with disrespect. I regretted it with all my heart. I never meant to hurt this wonderful man.

Sadness filled his eyes. Thick bushy eyebrows partly concealed his gray tired eyes. He looked very old. Deep lines formed at the corners of his eyes. They reminded me of bird tracks left in the soft mud. He slowly turned toward me. He straightened his tunic adjusting his belt. Very quietly he spoke. The words were directed at me but spoken to no one. "Many years ago, there were two men just outside of Jerusalem. Both were stone masons laboring over stone in a quarry. They struggled, and their muscles strained as they cut away at the large stones. A rabbi passed them and asked the first man what he was doing. The man seemed unhappy. He looked toward the sun and wiped the sweat from his brow. He responded, 'I'm hammering away at this godforsaken rock.' The rabbi approached the second man. He was diligently hammering at his stone.

The rabbi asked the second man the same question, 'What are you doing?' The stone mason ran his hand across his work. He blew the dust from its surface. He looked up at the old rabbi and answered, 'I am building the temple.'"

I stared at my father in law. He was a wise man. At that moment, I realized how fortunate I was to have such a man in my life. "I am sorry, Jarviss. Please forgive me."

"You must change your perspective. You must see with new eyes, Barabbas. Do not walk in the darkness. Open your eyes. You must see and awaken to the light."

A sudden awareness filled me. "What did you say? Where did you hear that?"

Jarviss stood erect. He was taller now. "I pray that your eyes are opened, my son." With that, he departed from me and retired for the evening.

I remained alone downstairs, standing in the dim lamp light. It felt as if I had been punched in the gut. "I'm sorry," I whispered.

CHAPTER 30

The following morning, I rose early. Shame was still clinging to me. It hung around my neck. I regretted my harsh words. Very quietly I moved about and dressed. As I descended the stairs, I found that Jarviss was already up. He was dressed and reading from a scroll.

"Ah, Barabbas, good morning. Come join me."

He patted a spot next to him on the pillows. I expected a harsh rebuke or a moping old man, but to my surprise, he seemed cheery and happy this morning. I approached and sat next to him. Regret and embarrassment flowed through my veins. "Good morning," he said.

"Jarviss, I am truly sorry for last night," I said.

"Barabbas, I forgive you. That was yesterday. This is today. We cannot go back, only forward."

A huge weight was lifted from me. He held no grudges, as I might have. Those simple words, that simple act of forgiveness eased my burden. It erased my shame. Jarviss smiled. His eyes twinkled and were filled with joy. "I am proud of you, son."

He opened the scroll. His left hand unrolled it revealing the precious words. I recognized them immediately. This was the *Mishlei Shlomo*, or Proverbs. It was taken from the third book of the Tanakh, called the *Ketuvim*, or the Writings. Jarviss read out loud, "As iron sharpens iron, so one man sharpens another." He did not know but that was my favorite verse from all the scriptures. He did not know that it was burned into my heart. He did not know that he along with Papa and Samuel were the iron that had sharpened me. I smiled. When he finished, he let those words sink in before he stood and directed us outside to join the others for breakfast.

Most of the family was already in the courtyard. They had gathered for the morning meal. The sweet smell of smoke and baking bread filled the cool air. I found myself standing before my old one room house, Melessa and my old house, our home. It had remained empty for all these years, an abandoned hull. A cold chill ran down my back. I watched as more of the family appeared and gathered in the courtyard. All of these people, this family, my family were so happy. They were all filled with a gladness and a joy. They were all so kind and loving. I looked around and watched as they gathered together. Sounds of laughter and children playing rose. It was bittersweet. A strange melancholy crept into my heart. *What would my life have been like? What if Melessa had lived? What if my child would have lived?* I had so much I wanted to share with them, so much I wanted to show my son. A huge lump began to form in my throat and I fought back tears. Standing in the shadow of our Chuppah, memories rose to the surface from deep dark recesses. My thoughts were shattered as several of the children ran to me and hugged me around my legs. They laughed and smiled. "Tell us a story, Uncle Barabbas."

"Not this early, children. Let Uncle Barabbas eat his breakfast first," Joanan interrupted. He put his arm around me and pulled me away. The laughing children followed. We gathered for a breakfast that the women had prepared. We ate heartily. I did share a story or two for the children. The conversation turned to the rabbi, the one called Jesus.

"Did you tell him, Jarviss?" I heard one of the brothers ask.

"No, I haven't," Jarviss responded.

An uncomfortable silence fell upon us. I looked at each of the men before me. Their eyes were filled with a heavy anticipation. No one spoke. "Tell me what?" I asked.

Jarviss cleared his throat. "Barabbas, we have listened to the words. We have seen with open eyes. We have witnessed miracles and seen mysteries revealed. Jesus is the messiah."

My heart sank. All of them had been deceived. A sadness and disappointment burned in the place of anger. I now pitied my brothers. *They were fools. They were so simple minded, so easily misled by this charlatan. This fraud, this imposter must be stopped,* I thought, *for he is leading people astray.*

"No, Barabbas, he is the Messiah." Joanan said.

"What makes you say such a thing?"

I questioned their very sanity and their wisdom. My brothers became like ants to me. A feeling of superiority rose within me. *How could they be so easily deceived?*

"No one can perform the wonders and miracles of this man." Joanan said.

"There are other miracle workers. History is full of legendary holy men," I said.

"Not like Jesus!" John shouted.

"What makes him so special?" I asked.

"Barabbas, you have seen it yourself. He heals the blind. He cures the diseased," Joanan said.

"People claimed that Honi the circle drawer healed the sick, and he brought rain," I said.

"He offended the leaders and was stoned to death during Passover," Eliakim added.

"What about Honi's grandsons, Hilkiah the Hasid and Hanan ha-Nehba? They are both said to be miracle workers," I said.

"Not like Jesus. They bring rain. Jesus heals the impossible," Jarviss said.

"Hanina ben Dosa healed the sons of Gamaliel and Johanan ben Zakai."

"Those children simply had a fever," Jared added.

"Yes," I argued, "and when he prayed over them, the fever went away."

"Jesus heals the lame. He restores sight to the blind and hearing to the deaf. He makes the lepers clean and restores broken and twisted bodies," Joanan said.

I recalled the day that I watched Jesus and the lepers. I questioned my own memory. I questioned my own eyes. *Had I really seen what I thought I saw? Or had I been deceived as well? Had a clever hoax been perpetrated on all of these people including me?* My education far exceeded these simple men. I knew God's word, even better than the priests within the temple walls. I knew the scriptures concerning the messiah. They were imprinted on my heart. I longed for the messiah myself, but this man was not it. Of that, I was sure. The brothers rambled on. I listened to their arguments. They sounded like fools. They were all so passionate in their belief. They wanted so desperately to believe. They wanted me to believe.

"And Jesus drives out demons," John said.

With those words, the hair on the back of my neck stood on end. A cold chill ran down my spine. I instinctively looked to the shadows and to the sky in search of the black-winged creatures. None were to be found.

"He does. I've seen it," Jared said.

"You've seen him cast out demons?" I asked incredulously.

"Yes, we've all seen it. A man came to the synagogue one day. Everyone knew him. He was insane and out of his head. He lived in the caves along the hills outside of Capernaum. He had lived there for years. The man was filthy and stank like a wild animal. He wore almost nothing. He rummaged and ate from the garbage dump. He ate from dead rotting carcasses. The man was violent and filled with rage. Anyone who approached him was attacked and driven away." "That doesn't mean he is possessed by devils."

Joanan interrupted, "He spoke in strange voices, several of them. He talked to himself in a strange foreign tongue that was not of this world. And he was filled with incredible strength, as strong as three or four men."

I thought of the hawk-billed man and of the terror I had witnessed that night in Archelais. I knew of the supernatural world. Only me. I alone had glimpsed into the realm of the demons. Others may share the gift of sight, maybe even this Jesus. Yet, I still doubted the claims that this man was the messiah. That was impossible.

Jared continued, "On a Sabbath day, all the people were gathered. The rabbi from Arav, Yohanan ben Zakkai was speaking. He was reading from the Torah when a disturbance broke out at the back of the congregation. Shouting arose, and the crowd parted as the bedeviled man pushed his way through the people. He hit and punched several men as they tried to stop him. He screamed out profanity and blasphemy in the synagogue."

"Jesus approached him," John interrupted.

Jared cut him a sharp glance and continued, "Yes, Jesus approached him. As soon as he did, the possessed man fell to his knees. In a strange and wicked voice that sounded like many people, he shouted to Jesus. He said, 'Let us alone! What business do we have with each other, Jesus of Nazareth?' He spoke softer, just above a whisper, 'Have you come to destroy us? I know who you are … the Holy One of God!'"

Dead silence fell over the entire compound as Jared told his tale. The other brothers, the women, even the children hung on every word as Jared continued the story. "But Jesus rebuked him, commanding him to be quiet. He ordered the unclean spirits to 'come out of him!' The man leapt at the teacher with a savage ferociousness, but the demons immediately obeyed. The man collapsed harmlessly at the feet of Jesus."

"What did it look like? The devil I mean, what did it look like?" I asked.

No one said a word. They simply stared at each other and then me. "Nothing. We did not see the demon. It just wasn't there," John added.

Jarviss cleared his throat and stepped toward me. He held out his arms in a gesture. "The poor man collapsed into Jesus' arms. The Teacher caught him. With his hands under the man's arms, he lifted him and held him like a child as the man wept bitterly."

Jarviss stood in silence as he wrapped his own arms around himself. He continued, "We heard a single voice. 'Zachary is that you?' It was the man's own brother. He too joined in the hug as he wrapped a shawl around the man's naked shoulders. The man continued to weep. Several other men gathered with them and began to praise God. Jesus' face shown with compassion. He smiled and said, 'Go in peace.'"

"That doesn't mean it was a demon," I said.

"What else do you want, Barabbas?" Joanan argued, "You want to see the demons for yourself?"

"Trust me, that would help."

Eliakim added, "Jesus said, 'If I drive out demons by the finger of God, the kingdom of God has come to you.'"

"I don't even know what that means," I said.

Jared interjected, "Barabbas, Jesus cast out the demons. We know what we saw. Just because you didn't see it doesn't make it not true."

"What about Eleazar the exorcist? People claim that he casts out devils. And what about Simon the magus? And of course, there's Apollonius of Tyana? All of these are believed to be miracle workers. People claim that they cast out demons," I argued.

"But Jesus is different," several voices responded at the same time.

"Different from the other miracle workers?" I said. It was more like a statement rather than a question.

"Yes," they responded.

Jared grabbed the front of my cloak. He pulled me close. He stood inches from my face. I could smell his breath. It was sweet like fermenting melon and honey. He spoke very quietly but with a seriousness that I had never heard from him. "Barabbas, he raises the dead."

"You are out of your mind, man."

"No, it's true," Joanan said.

"It is true, Barabbas," John said.

"You are all out of your minds."

If I had any remaining doubt, it was gone. The brothers had either all gone insane or they were so misled by this fraud that they had lost their grip on reality. This man, this so-called teacher must be stopped for he was leading the people astray. He was an imposter blaspheming God. For a brief moment, a thought arose. *Maybe this was my purpose. Maybe this was my destiny, to stop this charlatan. To stop this purveyor of wickedness against the Lord.*

Jannai, who had remained silent all morning spoke up, "I saw it, too."

"It was Jairus' daughter," Eliakim said.

Jared continued the tale of the account, "The Teacher had been away for several weeks. It was during this time that the daughter of Jairus fell ill. She was twelve years old. Jairus is a good man. He sits on the board of elders with Jarviss at the synagogue. We all know him. As soon as the teacher returned, Jairus met him at the lakeside. He fell at Jesus' feet and begged him to heal his daughter. Jesus agreed and together they headed to Jairus' house. However, a large crowd gathered around them and they were delayed."

"I was there. We were all there," John interrupted.

"Jesus spoke to the crowd and he healed a woman," Jannai said.

"Servants of Jairus brought the devastating news. 'Your daughter has died. Why trouble the Teacher anymore?' they said. But Jesus wrapped his arm around Jairus and said, 'Do not be afraid, only believe.' They continued on to Jairus' house where they found a commotion. Mourners were already gathered and were weeping and wailing. Jesus dismissed them saying, 'The child has not died. She is only sleeping.' Well, the gathered crowd began to laugh at him. But Jesus put them all out and entered the house with only the child's parents and his own companions. A few minutes later, they all returned with the little girl at their side. It was a miracle Barabbas. He raised her from the dead."

I smiled at their gullibility. "Jesus himself said she was not dead; she was only sleeping."

"Oh my God, Barabbas! You are impossible," Jared said, and he turned and walked away.

Jarviss placed a gentle hand on my shoulder, "Unlike the other miracle workers, Jesus has power over sickness and death. You must see with new eyes, Barabbas. Do not walk in the darkness. Open your eyes."

CHAPTER 31

We spent the rest of that week with the labors of the pottery business. I helped the brothers just like the old times. It was hard work but satisfying. I loved it. Sweet memories flowed like a river. For a short time, I forgot about my troubles. I forgot about the Romans and the Temple Guard. I forgot about Barak ben Nekifi, the tax collector of Geba. I forgot about the life on the run. I forgot about the Sicarii. I forgot about my visions and the black ravens that haunted me. I even forgot about the fraudulent teacher and his deceptions. For that short time, I was free.

The work was tedious. Their inventory was at a surplus as they were preparing to ship the pottery across the great lake. I assumed Jarviss would soon be leaving to sell the goods. One day, we made several trips down to the docks with a hand drawn wagon carrying crates filled with pottery and glassware. Each was stuffed with dried straw to protect the fragile contents. I remember carrying the first load. As we walked around the market, the docks came into view. I was stopped dead in my tracks. There at the end of the pier, floated the Osprey, the finest ship to ever sail on the Sea of Galilee. Nostalgia crashed over me. It took my breath away. The ship's double masts stood erect and reached to the sky. They were naked as the white sails were tied and bundled on the deck. Through the years the wood had bleached in the Galilean sun. The red and white painted hull had faded and chipped against the blue waters. A crusty salt formed along the hull and a greenish line of algae marked the water level. But time had added character to the galley. The weather and wear had only strengthened the resolve of the old ship. Papa would still be proud as this was the finest boat that he ever did build. I watched as the bow swayed gently in agreement.

It took several trips from the compound to the docks. Each trip took longer than the last. It was slow and took longer than we anticipated. We filled the lower cargo area almost full. We would finish by the following day. As evening approached, we found ourselves standing alone on the dock. It had been a great day filled with hard work but also with laughter and companionship. These were my friends, these were my brothers, these were my family. I so longed for the days ago. I imagined what my life would have been like if things were different. *What if Melessa had survived? What if our children played alongside their cousins within the walls of the family compound?* A sad despondency rose inside of me. It fueled my hatred for those responsible for taking her from me. Each day was the same. Happiness lay just beyond my reach. My thirst for revenge was ever present, and yet the blood I had spilled brought no peace. I did not share this darkness with the brothers. I dared not speak of it. Rather, I suppressed it. I kept it to myself. It was hidden within my heart. And It was slowly eating me alive. I recalled that briefest of moments when I had touched the hand of the Lord. That overwhelming feeling of joy and happiness was beyond my understanding. It filled my heart. It filled my very soul. I desired it. I longed to experience it once more. *But how?* I wondered. My thoughts were shattered. One of Joanan's sons ran to us. He was excited and breathing hard. At first, we did not understand what he was saying. We saw Jarviss following him. He walked quickly down the alley behind the market street. He looked over his shoulder. I noticed that he was carrying something. It was a large bundle wrapped in a blanket under his arm. As he approached, I saw the limb of my bow sticking out from under the blanket. I saw the feather fletchings and the white dipped arrows protruding from my pack.

Jarviss motioned to us. We obeyed and met him at the dock entrance. Concern washed over me. He too was panting. His cheeks were blotchy and red. He struggled for a breath. "Barabbas, you must go," he said.

"What has happened?" Joanan asked.

I did not need to ask. I knew.

"The Roman soldiers, they are everywhere."

"At the compound? What about our families?" someone asked, panic in his voice.

Several of the brothers began to run back home, but Jarviss stopped them. "No. They have not come to the compound yet. They are just marching in the streets around our home."

"Is everyone safe?" Jared asked.

"Yes," Jarviss explained. "The children noticed them first. Lilly left the compound and walked to the market. She noticed an increase in the soldiers throughout the town. We observed more of them walking the streets surrounding our home."

The brothers were silent. Guilt flooded my veins. It was molten metal flowing through them, and soon it turned to ice. "Barabbas, you must go," Jarviss said as he opened his bundle revealing all of my belongings including my sword and bow.

"Yes," I agreed. It was just above a whisper. I threw my pack on my back and buckled the sword to my belt hiding it away under my cloak. Jarviss draped the blanket across my shoulders. It was a thick dark wool that had a faint musty smell that was somewhat familiar.

"It is from your house," Jarviss whispered in my ear. He forced a small leather pouch into my fist. It was heavy. I immediately knew what it was. "Now go," he said. Tears streamed down his face. Each of the brothers embraced me. Worry filled their eyes.

"God be with you," they said.

"And with you." My hatred flared as I turned and walked away.

God, why?

I drew the blanket over my head like a hood. Soon, I realized it would probably draw more attention than my uncovered head, so I removed it. Walking quickly, I blended into the crowds. I made my way toward the city gates. Unfortunately, I found several Roman guards stationed there. Turning away I walked through the side streets passing many houses. I did notice an increased Roman presence. Passing the synagogue, I cursed and asked God *why.* He did not answer. The Lord was silent. Rather than seeking His favor,

I laid the blame at His feet. Anger toward the Lord of Heaven rose inside of me. *Why me? Was I cursed? Maybe this was my purpose? Maybe this was my destiny, to live in misery and pain forever. To be damned,* I thought. I headed toward the western gate. It is smaller and has far less traffic, so I made my way toward it. Unfortunately, I found that it too was well guarded. *Damn!* I thought, *I am now trapped within the walls of the city.* I was a caged animal.

Turning, I made my way through the crowded marketplace. Pressing through, I came to the docks. Jarviss and the brothers were gone. Several seagulls stood in their place. Surprisingly no Roman soldiers gathered at the docks. I turned and made my way out toward the Osprey. It still stood majestically watching over the harbor. I reached out and ran my hand across its bow. It was like touching a piece of yesterday. The faded wood was rough and dry under my fingers. A sad melancholy ran through me. I noticed, a few boats down from the Osprey. Among them was a small rowboat that was tied alongside a medium sized fishing boat. Freedom called to me.

I tossed my pack into the rowboat along with my bow. I stepped inside removing the rope from the mooring pillar. The boat rocked back and forth protesting in a violent manner, almost causing me to lose my balance. Sitting in the middle, I lowered the oars into the water and began rowing away. I fully expected shouts from someone running down the dock screaming "stop that man," but it never came. I managed to row away and out into the deeper waters. I watched as the Osprey bid me farewell. In my mind, it granted me this safe escape. I headed southwest toward my hometown, Gennesaret.

The sun was setting beyond the western hills casting a fiery glow across the bottoms of thick billowing clouds. The sky was on fire. The clouds were ablaze with brilliant colors of orange and red. I rowed harder racing the setting sun. It became obvious that this was a race I was going to lose. The fire began to fade as darkness began to wrap its cloak around the Galilee. In the distance, I could see the lights of Capernaum peacefully glowing. I turned the little boat and headed toward the shore. The night was upon me. Cool air began to settle leaving a chill across the lake. Very few stars shone this evening as the clouds veiled the sky. The sound of waves breaking against the shoreline called me their direction. The water lapped at the oars as I rowed into the darkness.

CHAPTER 32

Making it to the shore, I pulled the boat onto the beach. I gathered my belongings and headed up toward the hills. I managed to find a flat clear area that would provide a good spot to bivouac for the night. A large boulder provided a wind block from the north if needed. The other three sides were open and would provide a good view of anyone attempting to follow me. A dead tree lay shattered against the rocks to the west. The tree had seasoned and dried in the Galilean sun making perfect firewood. I broke the branches into usable pieces. I gathered some small twigs and grass for kindling and managed to build a fire. Its warmth was a welcome friend.

I found that my pack had been stuffed with dried fish and lamb. Dried fruits and nuts were wrapped in a thin linen cloth. This was a pleasant surprise. Jarviss and the family were so kind. I continuously placed them in danger, yet they continued to love and support me. For a brief moment, I wondered *Why? Why would Jarviss constantly endanger himself and the family members for a man like me, a man who couldn't even protect his daughter?* Self-pity crept through my heart. I tried to push it aside, but it had roots. I ate sparingly that night, staring into the dancing flames and contemplating my life. After some fish and dried dates, I unrolled my bed roll. The chill grew colder and I placed a larger log onto the fire. I pulled the wool blanket around me and settled in for the evening. A few more stars began to reveal themselves in the night's sky as the clouds began to part. A lone owl called in the distance.

My sleep was restless. I tossed and turned. My back ached. My shoulder ached. Several times I awoke, my arm numb and tingling. I stoked and fed the fire, encouraging it back to life. Its warmth was comforting. Finally, I fell into a deep sleep. I don't recall any strange dreams or heavenly visions. I simply slept.

In the darkest hours of the night, something startled me awake. I lay there in the darkness fully aware of my surroundings. A strange feeling came over me. Something was there. Something hid in the blackness. I could feel its presence. I listened but heard nothing. Staring upward, I noticed that the clouds had dissipated revealing a million stars. Only a few wispy clouds remained like puffs of smoke. They were illuminated by the waxing moon which cast an eerie glow across the hillside. High above me in the southern sky, the constellation Orion the hunter stood guard. His bow was drawn, ready to release his arrow across the celestial heavens. Just above my wind block boulder, stood the great bear. Its front legs pointed directly toward the North Star, Polaris. The ever reliable and faithful Polaris stood alone at the tail end of the little bear. As Samuel had taught me, this star never wandered. It remained fixed in an ever-moving night's sky always providing directions marking the way due north.

As I stared into the night sky, I listened intently. Still nothing. Yet, I remained leery. Something was there. Something was hiding in the darkness. I sat up. My muscles twitched as I peered into the blackness. I could see nothing. Yet, something loomed just beyond the light of my fire. I could feel it. I could sense a presence lurking in the night. I held my breath listening for the slightest movement. Nothing. I dared not move. I heard something. It was subtle. The rustle of dried grass or leaves just beyond my sight. It was barely audible. I strained to listen. The sound of crunching rocks against the sandy floor. Something or someone moved in the night. It was behind me. It was to my right, toward the lake. With incredible speed, it moved to my left. What creature moved like this? What animal had that kind of speed? I slowly removed the dagger from its sheath. It remained hidden under the blanket. My grip tightened around the handle. A strong foul odor filled the air. It was putrid. It was the smell of death. I studied the darkness but saw no one. I waited.

I heard it again. This time it was back to my right. *Maybe there were more than one*, I thought. *Maybe there were many.* An uneasy feeling grew within me. My nerves were on edge. I continued to wait. The silence was shattered as a deep chuckle filled the night. It was a thick and wicked laughter that sent ice water through my veins. A face appeared hovering just beyond the firelight. The yellow flames illuminated a skeletal face that hung in the darkness. Black shadows filled the sunken eye sockets. The fire cast strange shadows revealing an eerie visage. Crooked and broken teeth grinned at me.

"Hello Barabbas," he said with a smile.

It was the hawk-billed man from Archelais. A sinister laugh spilled from him. "I have missed you, my boy," he said.

I said nothing. I remained silent.

"Oh, come now, Barabbas. I have come all this way just for you."

"What do you want?" I asked, just above a whisper.

"Oh, I think you know."

"I don't," I argued. "I haven't a clue."

"Come now, Barabbas, you are the seer. Tell me a prophecy. Tell me the future. Tell me why I'm here."

"I don't know," I shouted, "I just want to be left alone."

The flames erupted and grew into a raging fire. They licked upward into the night's sky. The hawk-billed man stood and with a strange unnatural movement, he rose to his full height. He reminded me of a praying mantis standing over its prey. In the flickering light of the fire he grew before my very eyes. He was larger than I remembered. He stood at least a head taller than me. His shoulders were wide, but he was thin and wiry. His beard was sickly. His wispy hair rose from a sharp widow's peak. Two black eyes stared down at me. There were no whites, only black pupils. They gleamed in the firelight.

"Good Lord of Heaven, protect me!"

He laughed, "The Lord cannot protect you. I already told you, the Lord hates you, Barabbas."

"No! It's not true," I shouted.

"It is true. Only I care for you, son."

"No! It's not true. And don't you call me that."

"I have been searching for you, Barabbas. I have been waiting for you. Only me."

Confusion and chaos filled my mind. I trembled uncontrollably as fear sank its teeth into my soul.

His vicious stare never wavered. He did not move. "I have been watching you your whole life, son of thy father."

"Why?" I asked, "Who are you?"

A long uncomfortable silence filled the air. Hollow black eyes stared through me. Finally, he spoke, "I want you, Barabbas," he said, "You have a purpose."

"And what is my purpose?"

A silence so thick that you could cut it with a knife filled the night. He chuckled, "I told you... death."

"Who are you?" I shouted.

The hawk-nosed man stepped forward into the light. The fire exaggerated his grotesque features. I tensed and prepared to defend myself. "My boy. I have always been with you. I have protected you from the one who would do you harm."

"And who is that?" I asked. He smiled his wicked smile. His head leaned over his left shoulder in an awkward position. He made a sucking sound as his tongue slid across his teeth. His mouth formed an abnormal grin as huge yellow teeth protruded from cracked lips.

"Why, God, of course."

"That's not true," I shouted.

"Barabbas, I was there with you. I always have been. I am your father. I made you who you are."

"No, it's not true!" I muttered.

"I made you who you are. Don't you understand?"

"No," I shouted.

"Don't you understand. I was there when you killed the Romans. I helped feed your hatred. I delivered them into your hands. And I was there when they butchered your Papa." He paused for a long moment and studied me. He motioned with his long bony fingers, "And I held the sword as it dripped with his blood." He smiled a menacing grin, "And I was the one who raped your mother. I treated her like the whore she was. I made you. I am your father, you filthy bastard. You have no other father but me."

"No!" I screamed.

A fury of rage burned through me. It was an eruption of hatred and anger. No fear, only the venom of my hostility. I cast my blanket aside as I sprang forward. I felt the heat of the fire as I leaped across its flames. They licked at my legs. Hawk nose did not move. I slammed into him driving him backwards a step or two. I drove my dagger into his belly. It sank to the hilt but resisted like driving the blade into a bag of sand. He smiled that pretentious smile. His head slowly rolled to the other side and his opposite shoulder. I twisted the knife with a cruelty that I had never known before. "Die! You son of a bitch!"

"That's my boy," he said. "Full of hatred." With the speed and agility of a wild animal, his hands shot out and grasped my arms. His grip was like iron. His fingers dug into my flesh crushing my bones. Agony screamed out to be released. I tried to twist and pull free from him, but his strength was not of this world. Like a child's rag doll, he threw me across the fire. I landed on the other side of my bedroll with a hard thud. My head hit hard. A loud crack echoed through my ears and a bright light flashed behind my eyes. I was momentarily stunned. The wind had been knocked out of me. A sharp pain ran through me as I felt several ribs break.

Before I had time to react, he was upon me. His grip was unnaturally strong. I fought to escape. With the strength of ten men, he picked me up and threw me. My body flew helplessly through the air. I landed on the fire. Hot coals scattered everywhere. A spray of red embers erupted into the night. It burned my hands and arms as I tried to brace my fall. Hot embers showered across my face. They sizzled as my flesh burned. Panicked, I tried to push myself up, but my left arm hung useless. I rolled across the fire and tried to gain my feet. My left leg did not work well. It did not want to cooperate. But it was to no avail as the demon man was upon me. His speed and agility were that of a fierce animal. He was a leopard in the darkness playing with his prey.

His hands closed around my neck and he lifted me high into the air. He squeezed my neck. I could feel my windpipe being crushed. My feet kicked wildly. I dug my fingers into his wrists trying to break his grip. I believe my left forearm was broken. It was a useless effort, as if I were prying at iron bars. He tightened his grip as I fought for a breath. *What would Samuel do?* I thought. *He would go down fighting. He would never give up. He would fight to the death.* Panicked, I found the knife handle protruding from his stomach. Gripping it, I pulled the blade free. It made a terrible sucking sound. A black sticky blood spurted forth. I kicked and flailed as I needed air desperately. Blindly I plunged the dagger into his chest over and over. The blade penetrated deep into his heart. Yet, the hawk billed man did not die, nor did he relinquish his grip. Instead, he laughed. He laughed a wicked laughter, the most evil laugh I had ever heard. A laugh straight out of Hell. I sucked hard trying to inhale. His fingers squeezed tighter, constricting life. He continued to laugh. I feared that that laugh would be the last thing I ever heard as darkness began to set in around me. I felt the world slipping away as I began to fall into unconsciousness.

"You are such a disappointment. I had such big plans for you. But now, I am going to eat your heart out, son of the father."

Blackness consumed me. My body betrayed me, and I fell into a dark dream. I was adrift in a slow-moving river. I lay in the bottom of a boat mindlessly following the dark current. The sound of lapping water echoed against the hull. In the distant world of the living, I heard a voice. It was a lone voice, calling in the night, but one of authority, one of power. "Release him! Let him go!"

Immediately I felt his grip loosen. My body fell weightlessly through space. I crashed into a heap on the ground. I gasped for breath as the air filled my lungs. I sucked in the sweet sweet air of the Galilee. I labored to inhale and exhale as life slowly crept back into me. The man with the hawk-billed nose cried out in agony, "What do you want of me, Nazarene?"

Silence filled the night as the hawk billed man stumbled and backed away. My world was slowly returning as I became more aware of my surroundings. Pain returned through the fog of unconsciousness. A dull ache shot through my ribs and forearm. I could feel the bone in my wrist bulging upward, trying to tear its way out of my skin. I could also feel pain in my left leg. Something was terribly wrong. My thigh felt tight, and the muscles bulged just above my knee, which was turned as if it were facing the wrong direction. It was more of a dull crushing ache than a sharp excruciating pain.

The hawk-billed man spoke, but this time he spoke softer and with an edge of anxiety, "I know who you are… the Holy One of God."

Pain continued to rise. Feeling returned to my broken body. I lay on the ground. It was hard and cold. Rocks stabbed me in the back. I felt sick. A wave of nausea washed over me. I wanted to vomit. Incapacitated by the pain, I strained my eyes to see through the darkness. Small flames still clung to life from several burning logs scattered with the coals. Two figures were visible beyond the remains of my fire. The cloaked stranger stood facing my adversary. The hawkish man towered over the other figure, yet he cowed before him. "Have you come to destroy me?" he asked.

Immediately, the other man responded. "Be quiet," he said sternly. He rebuked the demon. He spoke in Greek. He spoke with a power and an authority, like a teacher berating a disobedient child. "Come out of him!"

An eruption of savage force exploded into the darkness. The hawk-billed man shook violently. His body convulsed in a brutal seizure. He fell to his hands and knees. His body stretched unnaturally toward the sky and an ear-splitting shriek cut through the night. I watched in horror as the man's back ripped open, his skin tore apart. Bloody vertebrae shattered like broken glass. Ribs cracked and split open forming a gruesome flower of bone. Like a child leaving the womb, a grotesque creature rose from his bowels. It stood erect towering over the hooded man. It was black against the darkness of the night. Firelight reflected off of the glistening wetness of the creature's birth, revealing the demonic monster. It quivered as its gray lips retracted, revealing wicked teeth. Its eyes were black pools of oil. They began to glow with fiery red embers. Pointed ears lay pinned back against its head like a ferocious dog. His skin was wrinkled leather. Hatred exuded from its pores. This unclean creature of evil stood to its full height. It stepped out of the hooded man's body and kicked it aside. Giant talons dug into the earth. They clawed at rocks that shattered beneath their force. This was a formidable foe, a creature straight out of Hell. Huge bat like wings unfolded from its back. They spread across the night's sky, glossy raven wings blocking out any stars. The feathers quivered in a threatening manner. This devil was monstrous. The creature let out a great howl. It shook the earth. He spoke words in a strange forgotten tongue. It was a tongue not known by man. Baring his teeth, he turned toward me and hissed. I recognized both hatred and contempt. But I also recognized another emotion… fear.

The stranger spoke once more. In a soft but firm voice, he spoke in Greek. "*Na fygei,*" which means "Be gone!" Instantly, the creature melted and dissolved into a thick mist of fine ash that dissipated into the sudden breeze. It was calm once more. The cloaked stranger was left standing alone on the rock slab overlooking the great lake. I watched him kneel down next to the body of the hawk billed man. He placed his hands on the remains and stared into the heavens. A moment later, the hooded man's body twitched and began to move. He sat up. His features were concealed in the darkness, but it seemed that he was healthy and alive. It also appeared as if he were weeping. Soft sobs filled the night. The stranger knelt beside him and placed his arm around his shoulders. *How odd,* I thought.

A wave of pain gripped me. It took my breath away. It was followed by a brief moment of relief. Like waves crashing on the beach, another came. Each was worse than the last. I almost lost consciousness but managed to cling to my altered sense of awareness. I was aware of someone standing over me; his dark silhouette blocked out the stars above. He was kneeling beside me. It was the shrouded stranger. The sensation of falling came over me. I felt myself falling into blackness. I fought it. I desperately clung to consciousness. I urged myself to stay awake. The stranger placed his hand on my face. He touched my cheek. He swept the hair off of my bloodied forehead. I stared up trying to make out the obscure details of his face. He had a thick beard and strong eyes, but the veil of darkness hid the details. Yet, somehow something incredibly familiar surrounded him. It was those eyes. They were hauntingly familiar. *Who was this?*

He placed both hands on my head and began to pray quietly. In a louder voice he said, "Son of thy father, be healed." The darkness enveloped me. I felt myself slipping into unconsciousness. But before I did, I heard him speak one final word, "*Tha ton prosécho óli mou ti zoí*," which means, "I will watch over him for the rest of my life."

CHAPTER 33

The following morning, I awoke to the brilliant sun breaking over the eastern horizon. An orange glow reflected off of the lake as beams of light painted the sky. Its light was a welcome sight after the night's horrific events. Its warmth would soon chase away the chill. That night I had slept the sleep of the dead. Somehow, I found myself comfortably warm on my bedroll. The wool blanket was neatly tucked in around me keeping the chill away. I cautiously moved my hand and wiggled my fingers. To my surprise, there was no pain. Reaching down, I felt my left leg. No pain. It felt strong and healthy. I bent my knee and wiggled my toes. No pain. I inhaled, filling my lungs with the cool morning air of the Galilee. I pressed against my rib cage as I inhaled. To my surprise, there was no pain. My body felt rested and refreshed. I examined my hands. I opened and closed my fingers. They appeared perfectly healthy. The bones along my left wrist did not protrude. It was not swollen and bruised. In fact, they were healed, completely healed. Throwing the blanket off I leapt to my feet. I found that my whole body felt rejuvenated. I felt like a young man. Gone were the daily aches and pains that I had come to live with each day. My back was not tight nor my joints sore as they were each and every morning. I felt strong and energetic.

Confusion and disbelief hung over me. *What happened last night? Had I dreamed it? A horrific nightmare? Had I imagined it all?* It was impossible. I questioned my own sanity. I questioned my own existence. But no, that was impossible. It was too real, too perfect. That was no dream. It did happen.

The truth surrounded me. It screamed at the mountain tops. There was no doubt. *Last night was real. The hawk-nosed man was real. And the shrouded stranger was real. It had to be.* I examined my camp. Dead coals and the charcoaled remains of my fire lay scattered. They were everywhere. I hesitated. The contents of my pack lay strewn across the rocks. I picked up a wrapped bundle of dried dates and tossed them onto my bedroll. I stooped and picked up the dragon tooth. It felt cold and heavy in my hands. Its rust color shone in the morning sun. My thumb ran along the side feeling the serrated edge. *What had happened?* I thought. I noticed spots of red blood. I touched them. They had started to turn dark around the edges as they dried. Some were large drops. Others were only sprinkles. They were dispersed across my entire camp. In some places, blood was smeared across the rocks. Beyond my bed, lay a dark pool. I noticed my tunic. It too was covered with blood. Holes had been burned through it in several places leaving charred edges. There was no doubt at all. Last night was real, as real as the morning sun rising over the Galilee. As real as the breeze that exists, yet it remains invisible.

Something strange and fantastic had happened, but I couldn't explain it. It left a mystery embedded in my heart. A savage reluctance clung to me. What was it? I still questioned my own eyes. But I had seen it. There was no doubt. *The hawk-nosed man was here. He was a demon. He had tried to kill me. Somehow I had been spared.* I had escaped evil and the clutches of death. *But how?* I paused and examined the dragon tooth. *The shrouded man. He had saved me. But who was he? And why?* My mind raced as I searched for the answers. None came. I inhaled deeply, sucking in the Galilean air. I exhaled with a breath of frustration. *Who was this mysterious man?* There was something so familiar about him, but I could not put my finger on it. I knew this man. I knew those eyes. They haunted me. They haunted me still. There was an intimate feeling. But there was also something missing. I could feel it. The truth was there. It lay just beyond my recognition, hiding in the darkness. I recalled something else. A feeling of joy, a feeling of happiness. It chased away all of my sorrows. I remembered feeling that same euphoric feeling just as I faded into unconsciousness, as I lost my grip on this world. It was the same feeling that I had experienced when I touched the hand of God.

I climbed the small boulder that was my wind block. I stood on top of the rock and raised my hands toward Heaven. Exaltation filled my heart. I praised the Lord as I cried out a shout of admiration and cheer. Looking out across the vast body of water that lay before me, a golden fire reflected off of the surface of the Galilee. Two suns burned in the distance, one in the morning sky and one in the water. I stood awe-struck, praising God; but the mystery still churned within my heart. *Who was that man?*

With the energy of a child, I broke camp and prepared to leave. The feeling of jubilation and joy filled me. It wasn't as strong as the night before, but it remained. It also filled me with a new courage. My dark thoughts faded. Depression was gone. It was replaced with a sense of hope, a sense of purpose. I so desperately wanted to go to Samuel and Ruth. I wanted to share with them the story of this nightmarish night and my incredible morning. I wanted to see them with my own eyes. I wanted to embrace them. I wanted to hold them in my arms. I wanted to tell them of my appreciation for everything that they had done for me. I wanted to tell them how grateful I was. And I wanted to tell them how much they meant to me and how much I loved them. Yet, as I prepared to travel North, something pulled at my heart. A hundred voices whispered in my ear. They spoke as one. "Come," they called. It was the voices of many, speaking as one. The voice was pleading. It was filled with fear. It was filled with agony. I can't describe it, but something was calling me toward the people of Geba. I could not resist, nor could I turn my back on a plea for help. That is not within my soul. I desperately wanted to go to Samuel and Ruth, but there was an undeniable yearning on my heart. "Come," they called. I had to go. I had no choice. Like chains, it pulled me. No matter how I tried, I could not resist it. I turned and headed South.

Not wanting to return on the same route that brought me for fear that I was more likely to encounter Roman soldiers or the Temple Guard, I chose to first head toward Cana. It lay to the southwest climbing up from the Jordan valley. It was approximately a twenty-five mile stretch but the road was well established, and travel was easy. It was a good day's journey. Upon arriving at the city gates, I set out to purchase a mule for myself or possibly a horse. Unfortunately, none were to be found. The town of Cana was a small and unimpressive town, so I moved on. Turning due south, I traveled to Nazareth. There I found traders standing just outside of the city walls. However, no mules were to be found in Nazareth either. Plenty of sheep and goats were for sale but no mules or horses. A caravan chieftain offered to sell me a camel. I hate camels. They are awful beasts. They stink, and they're mean. My experience has always been bad, one of stubbornness and disobedience. I chose to continue on foot.

Just south of Nazareth, I bivouacked for the night. I bedded down in the darkness because there was no fuel for a fire. I was tired from my long journey and my feet ached, so I slept well. Fortunately, no strange visitors harassed me during the night, nor did I dream. The next morning, I awoke and after a small breakfast, I broke camp. I walked another ten miles coming to the town of Nain. It sat at the foot of Mount Tabor. I stopped for water and to inquire about a mule or horse for sale. I asked several people walking through the streets toward the market. There were none to be had; however, I did find Nain an interesting town. The people were lively and buzzing about. The entire town had an excitement to it. Its citizens were filled with a devout and ascetic attitude. An older man stopped me in the streets and asked me, "Have you heard the good news?" He had wild curly hair that was turning white. His beard was neatly trimmed. It also was shocked with streaks of white. He spoke with a high-pitched voice in a nasally tone.

"What good news?" I asked.

"A great prophet has arisen among us!"

"A great prophet?" I asked.

"Yes, God has visited His people!"

"What are you talking about?" I continued.

The man spoke with an excitement that made him hard to follow. Several other people stopped and joined us as he told his good news. "The Teacher came. As he entered the city gates, he encountered a funeral procession. A dead man was being carried out to be buried in the tombs. That young man was the only son of a widow woman. When he saw the dead man and his mourning mother, he felt compassion for her. He stopped the funeral procession and the crowd that followed. The teacher said to the widow, 'Do not weep.' He walked toward the bier and touched it. He said, 'young man, I say to you, arise!'"

The old man's enthusiasm was contagious. "Arise! Arise! Did you hear that? He said, Arise!" The crowd around him continued to grow as he told his tale. His voice grew louder. He became more animated. His arms flailed about. The crowd listened intently. Several nodded their heads acknowledging his story. They encouraged him to continue. Several men laid their hands on his shoulders and I noticed several of the women were crying. The old man continued, "The young man came alive, he sat up, and began to speak."

Several shouts of "Amen" and "Praise the Lord" rose from the crowd that had gathered around us. Immediately doubt rose within me. *These people have lost their minds*, I thought to myself, *the dead do not rise*. My doubt was a wall. It was a dam holding back the waters of a mighty river. It was strong and tall, but this time a tiny crack appeared in my doubt. I thought of the tale that the brothers had told, one of the man's daughter and one of the teacher.

"You know, that sounds impossible," I said.

The entire crowd descended on me with words of confirmation. They defended the old man and his story. "It is true!" they said as more words of affirmation fell on me.

"It is true," the old man argued, "It was Silas, Naomi's' only son. He walks the streets of Nain to this very day."

"And who is this Teacher?" I asked.

"Oh, he is the prophet... He is Jesus."

CHAPTER 34

Leaving that place, more confusion filled my mind. The tale was too fantastic. It conflicted with everything that I knew. It conflicted with nature and the very laws of the universe. This world was going mad. *Was I the only one still sane? But, what if these people were right? What if the brothers were telling the truth? What if it were true?* My head ached from the thought. Yet I had no time to contemplate such. A sense of urgency hung over me. I set out across the Jezreel Valley. It is a vast and open fertile plain. It is bordered on the west by Mount Carmel and a mountain range that runs all the way to the Mediterranean. Mount Gilboa rose to the east and, in the far-off distance, I could see the Samarian highlands to the south. That was where I was headed.

Crossing the valley took much longer than I anticipated. It is big country. It felt even larger than it really is as the mountains rose in the distance surrounding the flat open basin. I noticed the earth was a rich fertile soil. Lush grasses covered the valley floor. Large herds of sheep wandered the hills and the plain before me. The smell of sheep rose through the air. Their bleats and cries were carried on the gentle breeze. *Baa! Baa!* Shepherds watched over their flocks in the distance. Fleeting memories of Mount Hermon passed through me. Fields of crops that had been cultivated lay throughout the valley creating a mosaic of colors. Fields of green wheat stood as this was the time of the year when it began to grow tall and head out. The Jezreel Valley takes its name from the ancient city of Jezreel. It is a city located in the central part of the valley. It stands on a low hill overlooking the southern edge of the plains.

Looking at the rich lush grasses and the crops, I could see where it gets its name, the word *Jezreel* means "God sows".

I passed the city but did not enter. Its walls and gates stood in the distance. It was there at Jezreel that the treacherous King Ahab and his wicked Phoenician wife, Jezebel established a fortification and their royal palace. Parts of their castle remained built into the city walls. It was also there at Jezreel, that Ahab built the pillar of Baal and where Jezebel housed the priests of Baal and Asherah. Several windows stood open high on the palace walls. I wondered to myself if it was one of those windows from which Jezebel was thrown to her death.

In my mind's eye, I imagined the wicked queen's last act of defiance. She stood adorned in her royal dress, her face was painted, and she was crowned with a formal wig and her finest jewels. She stood in the window confronting her rebellious commander, Jehu. Jehu had just executed her son, the sitting king, Joram. He approached the palace mounted on his warhorse and ordered Jezebel's own servants to throw her from the window. They did as they were ordered. Jezebel's blood splashed on the walls and horses. Jehu's own horse trampled her broken corpse. Jehu entered the palace where he and his men ate and drank. Later, Jehu ordered Jezebel's body to be taken out for burial. However, when his servants went out, they discovered a gruesome sight. Only the queen's skull, her feet, and her hands remained. Jezebel's flesh had been eaten by a pack of wild dogs, just as the prophet Elijah had prophesied many years before. At that moment, I noticed several stray dogs wandering around the outer walls of the city and I smiled at the striking coincidence.

From there, I continued southward across the open valley. This place was rich with the history of God's people. Before me was the scene of the victory by Israel over the Children of the East. It was there that the reluctant leader Gideon led the army of 300 Israelites into battle against the mighty armies of the Midianites and the Amalekites. God delivered them into Israel's hands. I embraced this history and the rich heritage of this land… and I longed for God to free his people from the tyrannical invaders once again.

Pushing on, I was blessed to discover several springs that flowed from Gilboa. With the summit of Mount Gilboa now behind me and its smaller mountains pushing south, I felt the valley begin to constrict as the mountain range of Carmel stretched toward the southeast. This portion of the plains was known as the "valley of Megiddo". It is named after the city of Tel Megiddo which is located there. The area is also known as the Plain of Esdraelon.

Before me, I could see the Tel Megiddo. It is an ancient city that stands on a large hill overlooking the valley. The city is so old and ancient and has been built and rebuilt upon the same site for thousands of years. Each generation building upon the last. This created a large archeological mound known as a Tel. It is from this mound that it gets its name. Tel Megiddo was known for its historical and geographical importance due to its strategic location at the Wadi Ara, a narrow pass through the Carmel Ridge. This route connected the Israeli coastal plains of the Mediterranean with the Jezreel Valley. It remains an important trade route and whoever controls Megiddo controlled the route. Due to this location, it has been the site of countless bloody battles and wars, the most famous of which was the Battle of Megiddo where the Egyptian King Thutmose III defeated the Canaanite king of Kadesh. Of course, today the Romans control the trade route. It is also known by its Greek name, *Armageddon*, which means "Mountain of Assembly."

I headed toward the Tel and the city that stood on top of it. As I approached, I noticed that men worked the fields across the plains. They worked vigorously. I also noticed vast fields of wheat stood surrounding the city. Large orchards of olive and pomegranate trees stretched away from the city. A large ramp climbed the incline to the city walls. A stone gate stood at the top that some say was built by Solomon. I doubted it, but it made a good story. Entering the gates, I found Megiddo a bustling place. It was alive with excitement. Merchants were everywhere selling their wares. The city was crowded. People of all nationalities pushed through the streets. The smells of cooking food mixed with sweat of the people. Megiddo was a very impressive city that appeared quite self-sufficient. In the market, I purchased a bowl of a beef stew. It was delicious. I had not realized just how hungry I was. I returned for a second bowl before wandering through the city streets. I noticed several Roman guards but there were fewer than I expected.

Several large grain silos stored vast amounts of grain. One street near the silos was lined with flour mills. Awnings provided shade for the workers. Women sat at each and turned a large stone crushing the wheat into a fine powder. Some were so large that they required two people to turn. White flour dust floated through the air and covered everything on that street. I also noticed that the influence of the Canaanites was still very present as the remains of their ancient altars were found scattered throughout the city. Beyond the flour mills, I came to the water system. It was an elaborate system of tunnels carved deep into the ground. Years of work must have been put into these tunnels as each step was perfectly carved into the rock. These steps led deep into the earth where springs fed sweet water into a cistern system. Several guards were stationed there. I avoided their eyes as I passed by. They lazily watched over the crowds.

I found what I had come looking for, a large stable boarding horses. In fact, Megiddo had two large stables, one on the north side of the city and one on the south. The one on the north side was closest to the main city gates. I discovered it was occupied by a garrison of Roman soldiers and their horses. I avoided that one at all costs. However, the southern stables housed horses of common citizens. It was much more inviting. These stables were huge, able to board hundreds of horses. They were made from cut limestone. Even the feed troughs and the water troughs were made from the cut stone. I was impressed. Several boys carried shocks of hay inside before returning for more. Other servants led horse drawn carts filled with manure out and down the streets. The smell floated in the air. This was the place I had been looking for. I inquired about a mule. Unfortunately, no mules were for sale. However, there were several horses that I could acquire for the right price.

I began to negotiate with the stable master. He did not move quickly. He moved at an exceptionally slow pace. It irritated me as my sense of urgency loomed. He was a short plump man who was bald on top, but his beard was as thick as a goat's. In fact, it reminded me of a goat's beard. It was black with a few gray whiskers scattered throughout. The man's dried lips formed a crooked smile that never stopped moving. The man chewed constantly as a cow chews her cud. His constant chewing irritated me and became a distraction as I watched his crooked mouth move nonstop. His servants brought several horses for me to look at. All of them appeared old and poor to me. Some looked lame. Some looked poor. After my rejections, they brought a few more. He was wasting my time. My anger started to rise. The voices of Geba still called.

"Is this all you've got?" I asked with irritation.

"These are desert horses," he said, "they may not look like much, but they are hardy."

I pointed at a corral that held several fine horses. "What about those?" I asked.

"Oh. Well, they are not for sale," he said.

I felt my hands clench tightly. My fingernails dug into my palms. I inhaled and fought to suppress my annoyance. This man was a fool, a shyster. He was wasting my time.

"Show me something else or I'm leaving."

The stable master could sense that I was feeling provoked. He stood there chewing his cud and studied me for a moment. The bald man and one of his servants, a dark-complexioned young man looked at each other. Through their eye contact, they silently communicated with each other. The young man hesitated for just a moment until the bald man nodded his head. *They take me for a fool,* I thought. My exasperation was showing. The young man led the horses away. He was gone for a few minutes before he and another servant returned with four more horses. These were much better specimens. These horses looked healthy and fleshed out. Their backs were straight, and they were strong. They brought three mares and a gelding. I examined each of them.

They were all about the same height. Two were dark, almost black. One was a sorrel color and the other was completely white. The gelding was relaxed, but he was toned and muscled up. The mares were toned but had a feminine disposition to them. I examined each of their heads and their throats. I looked at the eyes and their mouths. I inspected their feet and their leg positions. One stood pigeon toed. Two needed to be reshod. I studied each horses' overall build and their bone structure. One of the mares was long bodied. Samuel always claimed that made for a weak back. I narrowed my decision down to two, the gelding and the sorrel mare.

"I want to ride these two," I told the stable master. He agreed. I mounted the gelding riding him around an empty corral. I rode with only a bridle and no saddle. He was a fine animal. He was strong and powerful. He seemed level headed, a good horse but there was something about the mare. She appealed to me. Her back was straight and she was muscled up. She held her head high, her ears at attention. Her soft brown eyes were filled with intelligence. She seemed quiet and calm. I mounted her and rode around the corral. Both horses seemed calm and good natured, but the mare moved with grace. I gently kicked her. She trotted with an easy balanced gait. It was comfortable. She moved with a fluid feminine motion. The mare was calm and self assured. Nothing seemed to rattle her, even the commotions outside of the fence or the other horses in the next corral. I really liked her. Bringing her to a walk, I intentionally dropped one of the reins. She slowed but proceeded waiting for my command. I squeezed her with my legs and softly spoke, "Whoa." The mare stopped.

"How much?" I asked.

"500 denarii," the bald man shouted.

"I'll give you 350," I said.

"350 won't buy you one of the first horses," he shouted back. My irritation grew. I really did not like this man.

I rode the mare around the corral one more time coming to a stop next to the bald man.

"Look, I'll give you 400 for her, if you reshod her and throw in a saddle and bridle."

He smirked at the offer. "A saddle too? Maybe I should throw in one of my slaves also? Maybe my wife or daughter?"

Maybe you should, I thought sarcastically. "425. That's my final offer," I said as I dismounted. I handed him the reins, but he did not take them. He stood there motionless. He chewed his cud for a long uneasy moment. He didn't speak. However, he never broke eye contact creating an uncomfortable feeling. He just chewed his cud. *You're wasting my time*, I thought. My sense of urgency grew.

Finally, he turned toward the horse and rubbed her neck. "It's an old used saddle."

"That's fine," I said.

With that, we closed our agreement. Still annoyed, I fished 200 denarii in silver coin from the small leather purse that Jarviss had given me. I paid the stable master. One of his servants retrieved the mare and they disappeared into the stables. Another brought out the old saddle. It truly was an old saddle. In fact, it was an old retired Roman war saddle. The leather was dried and needed oiled. It had faded with age and curled up on the edges. A few places the leather appeared cracked. Several metal studs and copper medallions hung from the edges indicating campaigns and battles that the previous owner must have fought in. *He was well decorated*, I thought, *Probably the campaigns to crush and enslave God's people.* It was also decorated with amulets of thinly sliced deer antlers as was common among the Roman cavalry.

The bald man smiled, "I told you it was old."

"It's fine," I said.

"She'll be ready in the morning," he said. His voice carried too much cheer.

This man continued to annoy me. I needed to be on my way. I needed to get to Geba. Did he not understand that? I inhaled and let it out slowly, "I'll be back in the morning for my horse. I'll pay you the rest of the money."

"She'll be ready. I'll have her brushed and shod and we'll oil your new saddle," he said with a sarcastic grin. I turned to leave, but stopped.

"Thanks… And cut that shit off the saddle would you."

The bald man simply grinned.

CHAPTER 35

The last several days had been very long and hard. I needed a good night's rest, but I was anxious to be on the road. I found an inn where a family took in boarders for the night. They lived in a typical four room house that was common in that town. However, their house had extra rooms built on upstairs. They allowed guests to sleep in an upstairs room for a small fee. I joined them for the evening meal and I retired early. The house was comfortable, and I slept very well. The following morning, I joined them for breakfast before I returned to the stables.

I anticipated further delays, but the bald man was true to his word. The mare was ready. She was clean. She had been brushed and she wore new shoes. They also had cleaned up the saddle. It was oiled giving it a fresh leather look. All of the Roman insignias and amulets were gone. The old saddle looked surprisingly good, considering the shape it was in the previous day. I examined the mare one final time. She was a dark copper chestnut. Her mane and tail were a lighter color. It reminded me of a reddish gold. A dark narrow line ran down the center of her back. The mare was well proportioned and strong. She was a fine animal. I admired her. Intelligent eyes stared into mine. *I wonder what you're thinking*, I thought. Rubbing her forehead, she gave a little nicker. She nuzzled me with her nose. It was as soft as eastern silk. She nuzzled me with a playful snort. I could smell her breath. She had just eaten. It smelled of wet hay.

The bald man interrupted the moment, "She likes you. That's good. She doesn't like many people." My annoyance with this man returned. However, it was repressed by the horse. She nuzzled my neck. I rubbed her nose. "Let's get this over with," I said, "I must be going."

"Don't be in such a hurry. Life is too short," he said.

My irritation grew. He could sense my displeasure. "I have a long journey ahead."

Ignoring me, he turned and patted the horse on the neck. "Are you pleased?" he asked.

I inhaled and let it out slowly. I thought about his question for a minute. "Yes. Yes I am."

"I wasn't talking to you. I was asking the horse," the man said with a sheepish grin. He chewed his cud. I found no humor in his comment.

Anxious to be done, I opened the leather pouch and counted out the remainder of his money. I paid him in silver coins. The stable master began to write out a receipt of sale. He stopped and turned toward me. "And what is your name?"

A long pause hung in the air. An uneasy apprehension began to rise in me. I noticed he began to chew his cud. *That is so irritating*, I thought. His servants stood by staring dumbly at me. I thought about it for a long uncomfortable moment. I answered, "Barabbas. I am Barabbas." I watched each of their faces as I answered. I studied their eyes. I searched their souls. There was no reaction, no frantic response, not even a hint of recognition. The bald man simply filled out the receipt and signed it. I watched him as he rolled up the small parchments and tied a leather string around it. He handed it to me with a smile.

I let out a sigh. It was a sigh of relief, but it was wrapped in frustration. I needed to be moving. I had wasted enough time. As we settled our business, his servants began to saddle my horse. They first threw a saddle blanket across her back. It was an old red blanket with dirty gold trim. It was very thin. They sat the saddle in place. It was a typical four horned saddle commonly used by mounted Roman cavalry. I watched as one of the servants examined the poor shape of the padding. They briefly discussed something among themselves before one servant disappeared inside the tack barn. He reappeared a few moments later with an unshaven sheepskin. He positioned it in place under the saddle giving a good padding and making the saddle more comfortable for the horse. They fastened both girth straps in place. The servants also took my pack and my belongings and secured them into saddle bags that were lain across the horse's rear and fastened to the saddle. I hesitated before giving them my sword and scabbard from under my cloak. They did not act surprised. They simply attached it to the saddle as a cavalryman would. The servants also attached an extra water bag to the saddle. The mare did not resist and stood patiently. The stable master gave a command to the horse, "Down!" he said as he slapped her on the rump and pulled back on the reins. The horse clumsily altered her steps two or three times. She rocked back and forth before she knelt down on her knees, coming to rest on the ground. The bald man turned toward me and motioned to the saddle with his hand. "She is all yours, Barabbas."

Free of my pack and other belongings, I slung my bow across my back. My quiver now rode in one of the saddle bags. The feathers of the fletched arrows were exposed making them easily available. I approached the mare and threw one leg over the saddle. The bald man handed me the reins and stepped away. He made a clicking sound with his mouth. Immediately the mare stood, rising to her full height with me in the saddle. Although I knew what was coming, it still caught me a little off guard. I squeezed my legs and held onto the saddle. I managed to maintain my balance. The horse stood strong and proud. I was glad that I had chosen this mare. I turned the reins and began to ride away. The bald man stood watching and chewing his cud.

CHAPTER 36

On my new horse, I left Tel Megiddo and rode across the Valley of Armageddon. I followed it south where the mountains of Carmel ended. I headed toward the village of Ginae and the Samaritan highlands. This was before Ginae was massacred and the village was burned to the ground. I passed the village and rode deep into Samaria. We followed the road to Bemesilis. I could see Mount Ebal looming in the distance. Rather than seeking shelter for the evening in a village filled with filthy and unclean Samaritans, I chose to spend the night in the foothills to the west of Bemesilis. These hills are dangerous and known to shelter thieves and robbers who will cut one's throat for a single mite. It was a dry and arid place with no water and very little to eat for my horse. Yet, I refused to defile myself with such filthy people. I would rather sleep under the stars. We bivouacked there in the hills that night. I unrolled my bed roll with my sword and my dagger at my side. I hobbled my horse near to me and slept next to a clump of sage that offered no protection from the elements. I slept very little that night, but fortunately, the evening was uneventful. However, the voices continued to call to me, "Come."

The following morning, I saddled my horse and rode to the southeast until intersecting the road that led to Sychar. Passing Mount Ebal and the town of Sychar itself, I followed the road coming to the plain of Moreh that lay at the foot of Mount Gerizim. There, just beyond the town, I came to Jacob's well. Several women were gathered there filling their water jugs. Others made the walk back to town with their water jugs balanced atop their heads. I did not speak to them, nor them to me. We simply went about our business without regard for each other. I watered my horse and myself before filling the water bags. As I remembered, the water was sweet and cold.

Leaving that place I continued south, passing Tirathana and Mahnayim. This land became more rugged and hilly the further I traveled. However, the road was good allowing for easy passage. I was still pleased that I had purchased the mare as it made my travel so much easier. The horse and I worked well together. She was gentle and easy to ride. Her stride was comfortable. She moved with an elegance and grace that was different than a mule. We rode with a shared rhythm. And I found that she was very smart. She seemed to anticipate my every command. I grew to cherish that horse. I also came to enjoy my journey as we traveled the winding road. We met many travelers on the road that day. I assumed that most were traveling to or from Jerusalem, which still lay more than 30 miles to the south. Following the road, I passed Accrabbein, which is considered the boundary of holy soil between Samaria and Judea. Immediately I felt a sense of relief. Even the air tasted sweeter. The horse could sense it too.

Geba still called to me. "Come." The chain pulled me onward. It drove me. Fear and concern for what lay ahead churned inside of me. It stirred within my guts. Ahead of us, lay *Tel Shiloh*, which means "Hill of Tranquility." It was an ancient city built on a mound. It lay in the hill country of Ephraim. Shiloh had been the major center of worship before the great Temple of Solomon was built. It was in Shiloh that the Israelites, led by Joshua, set up the *Ohel-Mo'ed*, or the Tabernacle called the "Tent of Meeting." There, they housed the Ark of the Covenant. It remained in Shiloh for 369 years until it was captured by the Philistines at the Battle of Aphek. Later, the Ark was moved to Gibeon before it was moved to Jerusalem by King David. By virtue of the presence of the Tabernacle and the Ark of the Covenant, Shiloh became the center of Israelite worship. It became the destination as people made pilgrimages to worship. And now it was my own pilgrimage that brought me to Shiloh.

The city lay to the east of the main highway perched on the hill. It was surrounded by a massive wall of stone and reinforced with a large sloping earthen glacis. The wall had stood for two thousand years. It was as tall as four men and completely surrounded the entire city. Within its walls were a wine press and an oil press to serve all of the vineyards and olive groves that lay in the hills that surrounded the Tel. A market and a semi bustling economy flourished, but Shiloh was only a shadow of its former self. But I had not come to visit the city. I had no time, Geba was waiting. There are five major springs and a well outside the city walls. I stopped at the well and watered my horse before filling my water bags.

As I watered my horse, the ghosts of Shiloh called out to me. The story of Jeremiah crept into my heart. The prophet spoke of Shiloh as he warned the inhabitants of Judah and Jerusalem to repent from their evil ways or suffer the divine judgement. Speaking at the temple gates in Jerusalem, he said, *But go now to My place which was in Shiloh, where I made My name dwell at the first, and see what I did to it because of the wickedness of My people Israel. And now, because you have done all these things,' declares the Lord, 'and I spoke to you, rising up early and speaking, but you did not hear, and I called you but you did not answer, therefore, I will do to the house which is called by My name, in which you trust, and to the place which I gave you and your fathers, as I did to Shiloh. I will cast you out of My sight, as I have cast out all your brothers, all the offspring of Ephraim.*

From Shiloh, I headed into the heart of the hills of Ephraim and into the canyon country that lay to the south. Geba was close. I could sense it. It called. Yet, with that came the restless uncertainty of what lay ahead. I bivouacked there for the evening. A small meadow was irrigated by springs that seeped from a gravel bed that lay along a hillside. Grass grew knee high and a small pool provided plenty of water for my horse. I noticed several varieties of flowers covered the meadow as well. The sweet fragrance filled the air. I inhaled deeply enjoying the peaceful scent. The mare seemed to like them too as she ate all that she could within our camp. We rested there for the evening under a cloudy sky that hid the stars for most of the night. It was only on a few occasions that a star or two would peek through the veil of clouds. I ate dried beef and bread. I found that the bread had dried and was now hard and brittle. Digging through my pack for something else to eat I came across the dragon tooth resting in the bottom. It was wrapped in a threadbare cloth. I had forgotten it was there. I examined it in the light of my fire. It was huge and glowed red reflecting the flames. It was fascinating. The tooth was harder than stone and felt as cold as ice. I ran my thumb up and down the edge. It was as sharp as a knife. *What a terrifying creature this must have been during its life. Why and when did God create such a beast?* A quick chill ran down my spine. I recalled the day that I had freed it from the rock.

I slept very little that night. An uneasy nervousness lay just beneath the surface. Like the dragon stalking its prey, it troubled my mind all evening. The following morning, I rode my mare up into a deep canyon terrain that ran to the west. Steep precipitous cliffs rose on my left and my right. They grew taller reaching upward toward the sky. They created massive impenetrable walls that surrounded me on both sides. A great valley lay before me, but a rising feeling of being boxed in began to raise its head. It added to the anxiety of my journey. Several springs fed a small stream that cut down the middle of the canyon floor. Thick vegetation grew along the edge of the stream. I noticed thorny acacia trees grew throughout the canyon. They grew more plentiful. I heard several sharp whistles as tiny birds darted across the cliff face. This was the song of the rock wrens.

Looking upward I found a village nestled high on the northern cliffs. The morning sun painted the crag a brilliant gold. It shone like a gem. This cliff was the Gleaming One, Bozez. The village was surrounded by steep impenetrable cliffs. Immediately I recognized this place. This was the village known as "the fort." This was Michmash.

Turning to the south, I peered across the open valley. Far across stood a crag of equal height. It stood in sharp contrast with the cliffs to the north. Shadows veiled the entire wall as the sunlight broke over the upper lip of the canyon. Beams of light struck far beyond, casting shadows that reached well onto the valley floor.

There was a sharp rock on the one side and a sharp rock on the other side, and the name of the one was Bozez, and the name of the other Seneh. I recognized where I was, this was the Wadi es-Suweinit or the valley of the little thorn tree. Beyond the southern rim and just out of sight, lay my destination. There lay Geba.

I continued down the gorge to the west. I came to a gentle sloping ramp that ran from north to south and joined the two sides of the massive canyon together. This was the famed "pass," the broad watershed ridge that bridged the canyon. Although steep in a few places, my horse climbed it easily. Once obtaining the top of the ridge, we cut the road that followed the pass across the Wadi es-Suweinit. My apprehension grew. Butterflies fluttered in my gut. My mouth felt as dry as the desert. My heart beat wildly and I began to sweat. I prepared myself for what lay ahead. Trouble loomed beyond the canyon. In the distance stood Geba. Its fortified walls and white rock buildings shined in the early sunlight. Yet a dark cloud brought shadows across the land.

CHAPTER 37

We followed the pass across the canyon and to the gates of the village of Geba. My horse and I entered cautiously. It seemed that the town was different. I expected trouble. I expected destruction. I was wrong. Geba was thriving. Unlike my first visit, the streets were filled with people as they went about their daily lives. Their market was vibrant. People traded their goods. Women walked openly through the streets. Children played in the shade of the houses. This was not the same town that I had left just a short time ago. This town was alive. A great relief washed over me. The voices had led me to believe that death and destruction awaited me. *Had I misunderstood?* The massive burden was lifted. A flicker of the joy I had experienced when I touched the Lord's hand returned. It was a light chasing away the darkness.

As I rode past the place where I had left the ibex, a lone man stood.

"I have been waiting for you to return," he said.

An old man with a long white beard stood in the shadow of an awning. He wore a long flowing robe and appeared as a wise sage. This was Jethro, the town's elder and chieftain. He stared up at me through gray smoky eyes. A simple smile could be seen hiding behind his whiskers.

"Jethro, it is good to see you," I said.

"And you," he replied.

I nodded.

"I see that they have not caught up with you," he said.

"No, not yet."

He grinned sheepishly.

"Where is Gestas?" I asked.

"He is at his home. He has not left his wife's side."

An awkward silence hung in the air between us.

"And Dismas?" I asked.

Jethro motioned with his head toward the market. "Third tent to the south."

I nodded a thanks and walked my horse down the street. The sounds of people gathered and children's laughter filled the air. The town prospered. It even smelled better. Sweet aromas of cooking pots mixed with spices swirled through the air. There was a familiarity in them. They triggered precious memories from my childhood. This was not what I was expecting. Relief chased away my apprehension. A pleasant happiness began to grow. But I remained cautious.

At the market, I dismounted and tied the mare to a post. I went in search of Dismas. I found him just where the old man had promised. He was standing behind a table under a colored awning. I watched from a distance. He was selling woolen fabric. Rolls of undyed fabric lay on the table. Several large spools of woolen yarn sat throughout the tent. A weaver's loom stood behind him. His wife was hard at work sitting at the loom. Two other women were fulling fabric in a large vat. Dismas was helping. The vat of water sat over an open fire. Steam and smoke rose into the air. The women immersed the cloth into the steaming water. The fire sizzled and spat as water spilled over the edge and fell onto the hot coals. Using large wooden rods, they removed the cloth from the water and began beating it with hammers. This was done to thicken the fabric as it made the fibers of the hair mat together tighter.

I watched for a few more minutes before approaching. At first, Dismas had a look of shock on his face. It turned into a smile as he greeted me. "Barabbas, you are alive."

His wife, Eliana and the other women greeted me as well. They all seemed genuinely happy to see me and pleased that I had returned. A few other people also gathered around and greeted me.

Dismas invited me to stay with them. I accepted their hospitality and stayed with his family for several days. That very evening we all went to Gestas' house for a visit. Eliana had prepared a simple soup and bread that we took. Gestas' house remained under a dark cloud. His wife, Adina, was in a dark place. Since the dreaded day with the tax collector, she remained unstable. She was still beautiful, yet she was as fragile as glass. Her moods changed by the hour. The poor girl was an emotional shipwreck. One minute she would smile and be filled with laughter, the next, she would cry uncontrollably. Other days, she simply slept, dead to this world. Gestas was filled with frustration. He helplessly looked on as an outside observer peering through a tiny window. He watched the slow ruin of her soul.

For the last few weeks, friends and neighbors had continued to bring them meals and tend to their needs. Other neighbor women sat with Adina, but Gestas never left her side. For such a strong man, he too was teetering on collapse. He was at his wits end and sick with worry. He looked exhausted. His eyes were tired, and his fire was slowly dwindling. They were the only two people not filled with the new life found in Geba.

Each day we would visit Gestas and Adina. And each day I noticed no improvements. They lived in darkness. I felt sad for both of them, but I knew not what to do. The voice from my vision whispered to me, "Be the light." I tried to give Gestas a few silver coins, but he refused to accept them. His pride got in his way. So, I gave Dismas the coins with the instructions to help pay for some of their needs. I stayed with Dismas' family during this time. I enjoyed their company but I didn't want to be a burden. I tried to pay him for my room and board, but he refused. These people had a strong sense of pride. "That's an insult to me," he would say, "You have done enough." To earn my keep, I helped with his wool business. Each day I joined Dismas and his family at the market. They were weavers and had been for generations. They were successful until the Publicani Barak ben Nekifi had terrorized the town. His business along with the rest of the community had all but dried up. Over the last few weeks trade had slowly picked back up and Geba was now thriving. Travelers stopped, and people came to buy needed goods, including woolen fabric. They brought their own imports with them along with money and most importantly, food.

His family had an efficient system in place. I tried to help when I could. Much of the time, I just stood around as I was in their way. Their family was too kind to say anything but I could tell. I felt useless and bored. After about a week, I realized I could better serve Dismas and all the people of Geba by providing meat. That was my gift and I was good at it. That would be a much better way to serve them. Plus, I needed a break from the city life. I felt like a domesticated wild beast. I needed some time alone. I needed answers. Time in the wild allowed me to think and thoughtfully contemplate on the future. I still searched for my purpose. Yet, it eluded me. I had obeyed. I had listened to the voices and I had returned as it commanded. Uncertainty had been my companion. I had feared the worst. But, I found Geba far better than I hoped. *Why had I been summoned? Why had I returned?* The answers escaped me. I decided that I would head into the canyon lands to hunt far more than the wild game. I would hunt for answers.

I walked to the south end of town where I had boarded my horse at the small stable. I retrieved the mare and rode her back to Dismas' house. There I packed and told Dismas and Eliana goodbye. I assured them that I would return within the week. Eliana gave me a new wool blanket to fight off the cool evenings. It was thick and soft to the touch. The blanket had different colored stripes that ran across it, reminding me of the rainbow. It was beautiful, a work of art. I tried to pay her, but she and Dismas both refused. We embraced and I departed. I assured them that I would see them soon.

CHAPTER 38

I headed into the deep canyons that I had explored once before. I rode the mare gently not wanting to push her across some of the rocky dry creek beds. In fact, at several places, I dismounted and walked leading her over several spots where rocks had piled into large obstacles. She managed to navigate over most of the places. She was an excellent horse, but not as sure footed as a mule. When we did come to a dam of rocks that was impassable, we were forced to climb out of the canyon. No trails existed, forcing us to find our own way. I led the horse up an extremely steep embankment. That was a mistake. By the time I realized that it was a terrible idea, we were at a point where there was no turning back. Loose rocks and soft soil broke free and fell into the canyon below. Footing was almost impossible. I managed to find handholds and plants to aid my climb, but for the horse there were none. We continued up the steep ascent. The unthinkable happened. The horse slipped. Several rocks rolled under her and the side of the hill gave way. An avalanche of earth and rocks began to slide and fall away. My horse fell onto her side. She screamed out in terror. The horse swam across the rolling rockslide, but miraculously somehow, she regained her footing and began to climb wildly. I managed to escape her panicked hooves as she climbed past me. I released the reins and allowed her to go on. She ascended the last thirty feet in a wild frenzied clamber sending more rocks cascading down the steep incline. I managed to avoid the barrage. A few minutes later I too reached the top of the slope. A peaceful breeze met us there. It blew the mares mane across her neck and her sweat soaked back. The horse and I were both relieved to have escaped unharmed, but a wild panic still flickered in her eyes.

After resting, I mounted her, and we rode toward the northwest. We continued over gentle rolling hills. I noticed several animal trails that we followed. Some disappeared while others dropped into steep canyons along the way. Finally, we came to a gentle sloping ridge that descended into another canyon. A heavy animal trail followed it. Although the grade of the incline was steep, the trail switched back providing an easy path to the bottom. Along the way, I noticed several seeps where water was dripping out of the side of the rocky slope. Green plants painted each of these marking them plainly. At the bottom of the draw a small creek formed from the springs that ran along the hillside. Lush vegetation, clusters of brush and trees gathered along the edges. This was an oasis abundant with life.

I watered my mare before following the creek down the narrow canyon. We came to a small clearing that looked perfect. Lush grasses grew along the water's edge which would provide for the horse. A stand of trees provided some shelter along with the steep walls of the canyon. I decided to set camp there. I tied my horse close by within the stand of trees. That evening was cool, but I slept well. The new blanket added to the comfortable night. It was a thick soft wool that was warm. I thought about the love and care that must have gone into making it. I thought about Dismas and his wife, Eliana. I thought about Gestas and his poor troubled bride, Adina. She was still a striking woman, but she was dying on the inside. I could tell. She felt no hope. She was in a dark place. Joy had been stolen from her. It was replaced with shame. I had been there. I empathized with her. Adina was like a finely polished alabaster jar that was beautiful on the outside but no one knew how dirty and unclean she felt on the inside. I pitied her. My thoughts drifted off to my own love. It was the last thing I thought about. I could see Melessa's face as I drifted off to sleep.

I awoke early the next morning. It was still pitch black. The stars gleamed in the heavens. There were a million tiny pinpricks of light spilled across black marble. My view of the sky was limited by the steep canyon walls, but what I could see was spectacular. These were the same stars that had greeted the ancients. Now, these constellations watched over me. The wandering stars, the planets, shone brightly. Venus glowed the brightest. The red star, Mars glowed below it and to the left. *How rare to see those two so close together,* I thought. Another thought occurred, *What was their purpose? Was it to wander aimlessly across the great expanse of the heavens or was it perfectly guided by divine hands?* The answer eluded me, as did the answer to my own question. *What was my purpose?* I was filled with an uneasy dread. I shuddered with a chill. I rose and pulled my cloak around me to ward off the cold. I wrapped my head scarf around my head and pulled up my hood. I bent my bow beneath my knee. The energy and strength that was bound up inside of the limbs struggled to escape. I managed to harness its power and string it properly. I plucked the string with cold fingers. It made a low thud that reverberated into the canyon. I flexed my hands. They felt stiff. The knuckles stubbornly opened and closed. It felt exceptionally cold that morning. I slipped the leather shooting tab onto my hand. I slung the quiver of arrows across my back. As I started to depart, the mare uttered a short nicker. Stopping, I turned and reassured her. I ran my hands down her face and through her thick mane. She nuzzled against my cheek and neck. Checking her ties, I drew the knots tighter. I headed into the darkness.

I traveled down the draw following the small creek. The running water tinkled with a musical sound. I moved very slowly as there was almost no light at all. Several places I stumbled across rocks or brush that remained hidden in the darkness. I proceeded with caution not wanting to break an ankle or leg. It was excruciatingly slow. Several times I spooked animals from their hiding places. Each time it was a surprise as they erupted in a flurry shattering the quiet. And each time my heart raced as they scampered away into the blackness. After about an hour, the sky began to lighten allowing me to see my way through the thick brush along the creek's edge. This was a relief. I continued to move slowly, but now with efficiency and stealth.

I cautiously moved down the creek. In places it was no wider than a man's foot, other places it was too wide to jump across. Springs fed it in several places where water trickled out of the hillside. Usually, it was a gravel bed that seeped out of the ground. I knelt and drank from these. The water was as sweet as honey and as cold as the springs of Mount Hermon. Lush grasses and brush followed the waters. Animal trails followed the little stream and crossed from every direction. I could plainly see where the walls of the canyon funneled the animals into certain areas as they came to drink. Fresh tracks were everywhere. This was an oasis in the desert and a life-giving refuge.

I stalked onward and followed the creek to its headwaters. It took the better part of the day. Tracks and signs were everywhere, but I found no prey, only frustration. With disappointment in my heart, I returned to my camp and the horse. That evening, I built a fire. I warmed myself as the temperature dropped. The mare also stood closer to the fire, enjoying the warmth. Later she lay down next to my bedroll, which I thought was unusual for a horse. I came to like that horse more and more each day.

That night a cold front moved through. I could hear the winds howling above me, but the canyon walls protected us from its fury. The stars were absent as dark clouds filled the heavens erasing any sign of light. Thunder rolled in the distance. It became bitterly cold as the night progressed. I was thankful to have the extra blanket as the temperature continued to drop. The winds raged on in a violent torrent. The horse stirred nervously. She whinnied. I spoke to her gently to keep her calm. Finally, sometime in the middle of the night, the winds set. A quiet calm fell across the canyon. Exhausted, I fell into a peaceful sleep.

I slept so well that I failed to wake early. When I did, it was already light. I was greeted with a pleasant surprise. The earth was white. It was covered in a fine blanket of snow. It covered everything including myself. The world was washed anew, filled with a pure innocence. The snow transformed the canyon. It was familiar, yet different. I awoke in a new world, a world of beauty and wonder. Ornate snowflakes continued to fall. They tickled my face. It wasn't a heavy snow, but it fell continuously. It fell to earth with a grace and subtle tenderness like great feathers. It collected in the boughs of the brush and the trees. It collected on the rocks and boulders. The rocks appeared as fat snowballs. The canyon walls formed lines as snow collected on shelves high above me. White snow caps clung to the tops of the trees, which stood holding offerings up to the Lord. The little creek continued to run, cutting a sparkling line through the pure white canvas. I sat up and took in my new surroundings. The loving hand of the creator shown in the magic of nature. The raging storm of the night before had unveiled the engrained beauty of the world around me. The landscape was transformed along with my soul. I saw the truth. Creation reveals God's glory.

CHAPTER 39

I lay there for some time admiring my surroundings. I coughed several times and felt a slight tickle in my throat. I coughed. Inhaling the frigid air, I decided to brave the cold. I crawled out of my bed roll. My feet sank into the snow. Instantly they stung with an icy burn. I dug through the snow finding my sandals. Dusting them off, I tied them on. They provided little protection. My feet continued to pain with the icy sting. I dug into my pack in search of something, anything to help protect my feet. I found nothing. Frustrated, I searched my camp. The horse stood in the small cluster of trees a few steps from my bedroll. She was covered with a thin layer of snow that ran down her back and neck. My gaze fell upon the horse's saddle and the unshaven sheep skin. I retrieved it. It was perfect. I shook the snow from the hide and split it down the middle with my dagger. With strips of leather, I bound each piece around my feet. It provided immediate relief. I was reminded of my time spent on the slopes of Mount Hermon, so long ago.

Walking to the horse, I dusted the snow from her back. I draped the multicolored blanket across her. I ran my hands through her mane and rubbed her face. She turned and nuzzled against my neck. Her nose felt surprisingly warm. I laughed as we stood together and watched giant flakes softly fall to the ground. For the first time in a long time, I felt a feeling of peace. It was unfamiliar to me. I was reminded of that briefest of moments when I touched the hand of the Lord. *Was that real?* I thought. The intense feeling of peace and joy and love had felt real. Tiny slivers of that night continued to echo through my heart. I wanted to experience it again. *But how?* I searched my mind but found no answers.

The snow continued to fall, providing me a glimpse of peace. My hands soon grew cold. I needed a fire. It was difficult to relight my fire as most of the wood and kindling was wet, but after some time, I managed. Soon I had a roaring fire that warmed me to the bones. The horse also stood closer enjoying some of the heat. For breakfast, I heated some of the dried meat and ate it along with some bread. I took a handful of the acacia leaves and crushed them into a pulp. I placed the ground pulp into my pot of boiling water and let it steep for a good half hour. I drank the hot tea. It was bitter, but it warmed me from the inside. Samuel had taught me the ways of the wild. He said the acacia plant had many medicinal properties. It was good for the gut. The tea settled an uneasy stomach and was used to treat dysentery as well as malaria. It was also used to treat a sore throat or a cough. Plus, the pulp was used to stay blood flow from a wound and relieve pain. I finished the tea and immediately felt better.

Soon the sun was climbing into the heavens. Its light spilled over the canyon walls. The snow had stopped and the clouds disappeared leaving a spectacular blue sky. It was a stark contrast against the white surroundings. Leaving my horse tied near the trees, I ventured into the canyon following the little stream. I stalked slowly moving with as much stealth as possible. The snow both helped and hindered. It was wet and slick against the rocks causing me to slip several times. It also camouflaged obstacles that lay hidden beneath. However, it provided a soft cushion making my steps as quiet as a mouse. On occasion, it crunched, but for the most part, it was silent. It also provided the greatest benefit. In the fresh snow, I could easily see the tracks of the animals as they moved up or down the canyon.

I had traveled a good way before I crossed the first tracks. They appeared to be those of a hare. He had followed the water before crossing the creek and scurried up onto the steep rocky scree that lay beyond the snow. As I ventured further, I began to notice more tracks. Tiny birds left little imprints in the snow beneath low hanging branches. They dug in the snow in search of something to eat. Several different birds darted from the trees and up into the canyon walls. Their songs filled the cool air. I also found what looked to me like the tracks of jackals. It appeared to be a pair. I never saw them, but the tracks were headed in the direction of the hare. A short distance further I was moving slowly to cross a large rock. It was slick and I crawled across it cautiously. A sharp whistle cut through the peaceful morning. I froze. I studied the canyon before me. I saw nothing. A shrill whistle echoed. Not moving a muscle, I searched for the source. After a few moments, I found the culprit. A tiny head, the size of my fist was staring over a large rock surrounded by snow covered brush. He stared at me with an alert eye. As I moved toward him, the little face vanished behind the rock.

Closing the distance, I peered over the boulder. Immediately I was hit with a strong musky smell. Beyond lay a family of *shalan sela*, called rock hyraxes or rock badgers. They were short, no longer than a man's arm. Their fat little bodies were covered in a thick brown and gray fur. They had pointed heads attached to short squatty necks. Small round ears rode high on their heads. Their muzzles were darker and bled into a mask around their eyes. They had cute little noses and long black whiskers that twitched nervously. They each had an unusual set of upper incisors that protruded from their mouths. They also had large rear ends with no noticeable tails which added to their funny look.

About a dozen of them played in the snow. Although they appeared clumsy, their squatty and heavily built bodies moved surprisingly fast. Several scurried about playfully as others lay basking in the sunshine. Two stood guard acting as sentries. They stood erect on their hind legs. They both immediately stared at me. They watched for any sign of danger. I smiled at the funny scene. Other hyraxes continued to scamper from one rock to another. Two collided and tumbled through the snow. They wrestled with each other making loud grunting sounds. One leapt to his feet and scurried away with a scolding chatter. Others grunted. I watched with genuine pleasure and curiosity. There was no other way to describe them, they were cute. I had seen rock hyraxes on the high slopes of Mount Hermon but never in the lowcountry, although colonies are known to live near the Dead Sea. They were fascinating and to be this close was a true gift.

I did not move quickly as I did not want to scare them. I simply stood and watched them from the boulder. The two sentries never took their eyes off of me, but the rest apparently did not consider me a threat. I watched them for some time. They were funny and a delight. Several of them chased each other. They bound effortlessly from one rock to another. Several loud whistles rose from the sentries. Immediately, every single one stood erect. They were statues, alert to any danger. Their attention focused on the open sky above us rather than on me. They waited. A dark shadow fell across the snow-covered canyon. I looked skyward. At first, only the open blue gulf rose above the canyon walls. The silhouette of an eagle soared across the divide. He was black and mighty. The hairs on the back of my neck stood on end. Another whistle rose. Instantly, the hyraxes darted for the rocks. In the blink of an eye, they were gone, buried in their subterranean fortress.

Although they are unclean creatures, the Lord admired and compliments them in His Word. The words from the Torah spilled through my mind, words from the Proverbs.

Four things are small on the earth,
But they are exceedingly wise:
The ants are not a strong people,
But they prepare their food in the summer;
The hyraxes are not mighty people,
Yet they make their houses in the rocks.

I looked one last time as I passed their lair. Small openings in the snow revealed their tunnels into the rocks. I searched, but no tiny faces exposed themselves. They were gone.

I pressed on, following the little stream up the deep draw. The snow was beautiful. The sun reflected off of it like millions of tiny mirrors. At times, it even hurt my eyes and I was forced to squint. My eyes watered in the cold along with my nose that dripped constantly. I was comfortable despite the frigid temperature. Fortunately, my feet felt warm. My hands were the only thing that really hurt. They stung from the cold that penetrated deep into my bones. Even my fingernails ached. I tried to warm them by alternately sticking them into my outer cloak. I had to swap hands each time in order to carry my bow. Despite my aching hands, I continued. However, soon I found what I was looking for. Several cloven tracks began to appear in the fresh snow. A new sense of excitement rose inside my heart. I followed them, cautiously stalking ahead.

Following the tracks for about a quarter of a mile, I came across several more tracks. These came from the broken scree field that lay at the bottom of the steep canyon walls. They gathered around some brush and an open place in the stream. A short distance later, they returned to the scree. This told me that those belonged to the ibex, for only they could ascend the steep incline. The other set of tracks continued. I followed.

Ahead of me, just beyond some brush, I saw movement. Quickly I dropped to a knee. On instinct, I drew an arrow from my quiver. Without looking, I nocked the arrow. I held it at the ready. Remaining low, I peered through the branches. I waited but saw nothing. Testing my patience, I slowly crawled forward. When I reached a bushy tree that was completely covered in snow, I dared to peek over. About fifty paces ahead stood several of the small antelopes, the gazelle. They were hidden by snow-covered obstacles. I examined my surroundings and devised a plan.

On the south side of the creek, on which I stood, several small boulders had fallen from the canyon's rim in some ancient days. Brush and a few small trees had grown up around them. They were now all covered in snow, leaving a white fluffy blanket. This created the illusion that the rocks and brush were one single ball of ice, forming a bridge that ran toward the canyon wall. It formed a barrier that blocked their view of me. However, it was at least 20 paces across a flat open area that was an exposed white canvas. The gazelle lay beyond that. If I could get to the boulders without being seen, I would have a chance at a shot. I would have to crawl the distance remaining on my hands and knees. I would need to stay as low as a mouse if I wanted to avoid being detected.

Making my decision, I removed the arrow and placed it back into the quiver. I slowly left the cover of the brush. My hands sank into the bitter cold.

It burned like fire. In my left hand, I carried the bow. I tried to keep the limbs of my bow above the snow as much as I could. However, with each movement forward, it sank deeper. I crawled as slow as the movement of the moon and stars. Each step was a deliberate and precise placement. I dared not make a sound or a sudden move. Each hand or knee made a hushed whisper as it sank into the snow. I cringed with each step, praying that my quarry did not hear. My hands sank several inches into the snow. The cold bit into my flesh with a burning pain. After several minutes my knees dulled to the pain. However, my hands never did. They burned with an intensity.

I pressed on, dropping to my belly for the last several yards. My outer cloak became matted with snow. The snow found its way into every opening possible, up my sleeves and down my neck. A wet cold seeped into my undergarments and penetrated to my bones. I began to shiver. My hands screamed out for me to stop, for me to return to the fire and plunge them into the warm flames. However, I was so close. I would not turn back. Finally, I reached the cover of the boulders. The gazelle had not spooked. In fact, they remained completely unaware of my presence. They remained where I had last seen them, now just 25 paces away. They stood under a couple of larger acacia trees that were crowned in white. The gazelle pawed and picked through the snow in search of their morning breakfast.

Under the protection of the snow-covered boulder, I gathered myself. I attempted to warm my hands by placing them inside my cloak and in my armpits and by breathing hot air on them. They were still stiff and burned, but the pain slowly subsided. After a few moments of this, I removed an arrow. I nocked it. It snapped securely onto the string. I slowly rose from the crouching position. Where the rock and the brush intersected, a notch formed. The snow had settled in the branches above creating a window for me to peer through. I watched the gazelle and devised my plan.

Four of them browsed through the snow. These were Mountain Gazelles. They are small members of the antelope family. Their black horns spiraled upward. Although both sexes have horns, all four of these were males that traveled together in a bachelor herd. Each had unique characteristics, yet they all shared similarities. These gazelles were slender built. They had long narrow necks with long speedy legs. In fact, they are incredibly fast. Their coats were a light tannish brown on their heads, neck and back. It spilled down their legs. Their bellies and rump along with the inside of their legs were a pure white that blended into the snow. These two tones were separated down their flanks by a dark narrow band. A short black tail wagged vigorously as they ate. They were not sleek and glossy as I had seen gazelle before. These still wore their winter coats, which were dense and shaggy from the wet snow. A light steam rose from their backs.

Their faces were beautiful. Across the tan faces, two conspicuous white lines ran from their eyes toward their noses. Dark brown lines followed and accentuated their features around their cheeks and muzzle. Large ears stood erect and alert to any sound that might betray a predator. They were tufted with white fur that trimmed the edges. Black spiraling horns rose above their dark eyes. Their horns were long with a slight curve. They were grooved with prominent rings that spiraled the entire length.

Mountain gazelle typically live in the lower mountains and avoid steep rocky areas where one might find ibex. They prefer the foothills and valleys and the open plateaus where they rely on their speed to survive. I'm sure these came into the draw to avoid the weather. I watched them for several minutes. They were handsome and noble creatures. Plumes of smoke exhaled from their mouths. They pawed at the snow and nibbled on their findings. Their diet is usually comprised of grasses, forbs and shrubs. However, I watched a couple of these stand on their hind legs and reach high into the low hanging branches of the acacia trees. I watched with fascination as they danced through the snow. It was quite entertaining.

The moment of truth had arrived. I was 25 paces away and they were unaware of my presence. At any moment the wary gazelle could spook and dash away or they could simply finish eating, turn and walk away. Either way, I would have lost the opportunity. I prepared to stand. Unfortunately, the small window through the snow was filled with brush and limbs which obstructed the shot path. I would have to stand tall enough that I had a clear shooting lane. However, this would expose me to my prey. I would need to be stealthy yet quick.

I peeked one last time through the small opening. All four stood close together. One faced away from me and another turned toward me, providing no shot opportunity. However, the two in the middle both stood broadside offering me a perfect shot into their vitals. Placing my feet directly under me, I squatted. My heart began to race. My muscles quivered. Slowly, I rose. I rose in one fluid motion. I rose with my bow in hand and the string taut. I began to draw. Rising to an almost full standing position, I drew the arrow backwards. The string was heavy, and it bit into my tabbed fingers. The limbs resisted as they bent under the weight. I felt the feather vanes touch my cheek as my fingers came to rest at the corner of my mouth. At full draw I had already picked my prey. The second from the left stood broadside. His head was down with his nose in the snow. He was slightly quartering away from me. His front leg was forward moving his shoulder bone out of the way. I picked the spot. I aimed at the crease where the dark line ran down his flank separating the tan from the white. As Samuel had taught me, I did not aim at the target. I did not aim at his vitals. I aimed at a spot. I aimed for not just the spot, I aimed at the smallest of spots. I aimed for a single hair. I released the arrow. A soft thud reverberated. The razor-sharp broadhead gleamed as the arrow cut through the cold air.

Instantly the four gazelles jumped and scattered. They turned and raced away rushing up the canyon. They disappeared beyond my sight. A path of scarlet red followed them. The blood trail stood out as a stark contrast against the white dunes. I knew I had made a fatal shot, but I waited. I had to restrain myself from going after the gazelle. I wrestled with my impatience. As Samuel had taught me, one never goes after a wounded animal immediately. It is always wise to wait. Allow the animal to run ahead un-chased. It will typically stop and lay down realizing he is hurt. Hopefully, he will close his eyes to sleep and bleed out right there allowing the hunter to find him easily. However, if the wounded animal is pushed, he will run blindly and continue to run feeling he is pursued. That animal may be lost forever. That would dishonor and disrespect his death. I sat back down next to the big rock and waited.

As I sat there, I took in my surroundings. The blue sky shone overhead.

Tiny birds darted about. Their songs echoed from the canyon walls. The little stream trickled past me with a musical melody. Elaborately detailed crystals of ice decorated the edges of the stream. Snow covered everything in a thick blanket of white. The skeletal shapes of trees were capped in white. The outlines of trees, rocks, and brush vanished, swallowed in the white. This place was pure and it was peaceful. The only place that I ever found peace was in nature and I had changed that. It was bittersweet. I was the one. I had brought chaos to the peaceful order of the valley. Yet, I also brought peace in a strange way.

I pulled my cloak tighter around me. I brushed the snow from my sleeves. Patiently I waited. Memories from my dream crept through my mind. That strange feeling of love haunted me. Its shadow persisted. I longed for it. That internal joy that I sought taunted me, as it remained just beyond my grasp. *Why should God grant such to me?* I asked. I was cursed. My life had been filled with tragedy and disappointments. A thought came to me. It was an understanding of the Lord's words. It was a revelation. Each day is a gift. Each day we must realize that the past is gone, never to return. Each day is something new. It is a stepping stone into the future. It is a path toward our destination, a path toward our destiny. Behind me, lay my own footprints in the snow. They stretched down the labyrinth of the canyon and disappeared beyond my sight. Looking ahead of me, I could see the blood trail. Its crimson path led into the unknown.

CHAPTER 40

I stood and dusted the snow from my clothes. Crystals of ice sparkled as they swirled in the sunlight and fell to the ground. I turned and headed up the canyon following the red. A distinct and unmistakable trail led into the unknown. I followed it. Bright red blood glistened against the virgin snow. It spilled across the whiteness. The purity forever changed by the life-giving blood.

The gazelle ran less than a quarter of a mile up the canyon before he died. A continuous blood trail in the snow made it the easiest tracking job that I had ever followed. I spotted him from a distance. The gazelle lay peacefully on his side under an acacia tree that created a canopy with its snow-covered branches. I admired him. He was a magnificent creature. I was faced with the dual emotions. I was happy and filled with a great sense of accomplishment, a sense of humble triumph over a very worthy opponent. He was not my adversary. Rather, he was my respected rival in the struggle of life. He was to be honored and revered. An emotion washed over me. It was a feeling that most people will never experience. It was something that only one who hunts could possibly understand. Joy and sadness both shared a space inside my heart. Joy for my victory, sadness for I had spilled his blood. I had brought chaos to the peaceful order of the valley, yet I also brought peace in a strange way. I had taken this majestic beast's life, yet I had also given him peace. I had given him the quickest and most humane death possible. No animal ever dies of old age in nature. It does not happen. In the wild, the sick and aged are simply torn apart by the predators. They are eaten alive as they struggle to escape. Nature is a fierce and violent place. I brought peace.

I knelt in the snow next to the gazelle. I placed my hands on him. He was still warm to the touch. I stroked his neck and ran my hands down his body. I raised my head toward the sky, and I prayed to the Lord, thanking him for providing this gift. His flesh was my sustenance and I would share it with the people of Geba.

With a deep veneration, I rolled the gazelle onto his back and began the process of gutting and cleaning him. It did not take long. I removed my outer garment and rolled up my sleeves. Soon I had prepared him for the journey back to my camp. Although my hands had found relief in the warmth of his body, I scrubbed them clean with handfuls of snow. The pain of the cold returned, but not to the extent of earlier. The snow made it easy to clean up afterward plus the meat remained clean as there was no dirt or grass to contend with. I replaced my clothing and placed a short leather cord around his neck. I began to drag him down the canyon. I looked back one final time and saw the pile of innards. Blood stained the snow in a circle around the pile. A couple of birds lit in the trees and around the entrails. The jackals would eat good tonight.

Continuing down the canyon from where I had come, I drug the gazelle. He was lighter than a deer or an Ibex. The snow also made my chore easier. The animal slid over the snow easily, plus the meat remained clean. Crossing over difficult terrain slowed my progress but it went smoothly. Yet after some time, it began to warm up and I worked up a sweat. At first, I felt a single bead of sweat twist down my spine. My whole body began to perspire. Heat rose up my neck. I removed the scarf from my face and head, and I opened my outer cloak to allow some body heat to escape. It is always best not to overheat and sweat in a cold environment, because that can lead to frostbite or worse. Samuel always explained that in a cold environment, one should avoid getting wet at all costs for fear of death.

I slowed my progress and I did manage to cool my body back down. However, my hands remained cold and stiff. I also noticed that the valley was gradually warming. Sunlight poured down between the canyon walls. The light brought a welcomed warmth. I also noticed that the snow was slowly melting. The wonder and beauty of the snow storm was fading away. Water began to drip from the trees and brush. Occasionally, large clumps of snow fell with a thud. Each time, clouds of ice crystals swirled in the daggers of sunlight. As the day progressed, the melting snow became like rain and the bare branches began to expose themselves. The tops of wet rocks became visible revealing colored lichens and the beauty of the stone. Broken branches and leaves became visible. The snow at my feet became slushy. It was deceivingly slippery, so I proceeded with caution across the slick rocks. The sheep skin around my feet became wet. For the first time all day, my feet became cold, but not unbearable.

Dragging the gazelle, I continued toward my camp. I was almost there when I happened upon one more unexpected encounter. At a place where the canyon narrowed and the walls steepened, I noticed a movement. It was across the creek and along the far wall of the canyon. A large boulder clung to the side of the wall about the height of two men. Through the branches of an acacia tree, something dark moved just beyond my vision. Leaving the gazelle there along the stream, I investigated further. I approached keeping the brush in front of me to disguise my movement. Peering through the branches I witnessed something sinister awaiting me. Perched atop the rock stood a dark figure. Cold chills ran up my spine. I shuddered.

However, that was brief, as I recognized what stood before me. Fascination replaced fear, for this was no malevolent phantom but rather it was a massive bird of prey. He was huge. His keen eyes were focused on me as he had already seen me from a distance. This was the *eit tzfarde'im*, or the great spotted eagle. He stood as tall as a man's thigh. He was covered with a medium brown plumage, but his head and upper wings were considerably darker. Small white crescent moons were scattered across his wings forming an irregular pattern. His beak and feet were a yellow color. They were both deadly sharp. Dark glassy eyes stared at me as I pushed my way through the thorny brush and emerged on the other side.

I was now just ten or fifteen steps away. My heart raced. The eagle did not appear nervous. He opened his beak and let out a sharp barking yelp. I stood in awe of this magnificent creature. He was beautiful and I recognized him for what he was. He was majestic and powerful. He was brave and fearless. He was the perfect hunter. At his feet lay a dead rock hyrax. His bloody fur had been ripped by razor like talons from his back hind-quarter. The raw flesh was exposed, and several bites had been torn away. The eagle never took his eyes off of me, but he reached down and tore another piece away. Raising his head toward the sky, he choked it down in one bite. He continued to stare intently. I could see intelligence in those eyes. I could also see the bond that we shared. This great eagle survived alone. He was a fearsome predator, filled with courage and a relentless tenacity.

We continued to stare at each other for a long time. I admired this amazing creature. He studied me in return. Without removing his eyes from me, he leaned down and pecked at another piece of the raw flesh. He bit into it. He pulled and strained with a piece about the size of a man's thumb. Jerking at it violently, it tore loose. A long string of sinew hung freely. He threw his head up and choked it down. Witnessing this incredible encounter, my mind drifted off to Samuel. *He would have loved to have seen this, to have experienced this,* I thought. I remembered his teachings, the lessons of the weapons master.

He reminded me that eagles are often used as symbols of strength and power by many people, including the Romans and the Egyptians. It is easy to see why this comparison is made. He also reminded me that the Torah oftentimes referred to eagles. At first in the context of God's holy judgements. Often the nations used by the Lord to punish Israel for their disobedience are described as being like eagles. They were fierce and swift in their attacks as described by the prophets Jeremiah and Ezekiel. However, unlike the other people, the Word of the Lord also describes eagles as nurturing and loving parents. They will fiercely defend their young while nurturing and providing for them. When young birds are ready to take their first flight, the parents are there to encourage them from the nest. And eagles will continue to feed and vigilantly protect their young until they are capable of caring for themselves. The scroll of Deuteronomy compares the Lord to that nurturing eagle.

The mighty bird bent and plucked another piece of the raw meat from the hyrax. He swallowed it down in a single gulp. I smiled as I enjoyed the encounter. I had never been this close to such a bird as this before. I thought of my favorite reference of eagles from the Torah. The words of the prophet Isaiah spilled through my mind.

Yet those who wait for the Lord
Will gain new strength;
They will soar with wings like eagles,
They will run and not get tired,
They will walk and not become weary.

Samuel's voice continued to haunt my mind. His lessons forever burned into my memory. His wisdom and knowledge were unsurpassed. Samuel's understanding was unrivaled. He went on to explain that we, God's chosen people are the eagles. The wings of the eagles represent our faith and belief. Faith for the believer is like flight for an eagle. It is essential to one's survival in this world. And finally, the rising wind currents represent God's Holy Spirit. These wind thermals ever lifting the eagle to new heights. Isaiah teaches us that those who have hope in the Lord will soar on wings like eagles. Samuel continued, "This is more than a promise of strength and perseverance, it is a testament to the compassion and love of our Heavenly Father. He is a mighty God, yet a nurturing God who will never abandon nor forsake those who follow in his ways." For the first time in my life, I questioned Samuel. *Had I not been abandoned by God? Had I not been forsaken?* Yet, I remained zealous for His word. I remained zealous for His Law. It wasn't Samuel's voice that filled my head. It was an ancient voice, the voice of the heavenly being from my dream. It was the voice of the Lord.

"My child, the more you try to follow the Law, the more you shall fail. And the more it will fail you. The Law must be fulfilled. Fulfillment is the new law, called grace. Grace is found only in the light that is true love. Grace is mercy. Grace is forgiveness. Grace is love, a love that holds no record of wrongs. Grace is atonement." Once again, I could feel the cold water splash as I reached for the sacred scroll that floated just beyond my grasp.

"Barabbas, you must love as I love. Grace is the new Law. Seek love and forgiveness rather than the Law. Seek mercy rather than sacrifice. Be the light. Fulfill the Law."

I frowned at this memory as the eagle and I continued to stare at each other. Without warning, the eagle let out a deafening screech. He spread his wings and leapt off of the rock. At first, he plummeted toward me. At the last moment, he soared upward. His mighty wings lifting him toward the heavens. A dark shadow passed over me as he blocked out the sun. I watched as the great spotted eagle flew away carrying his prey in his talons. *They will soar with wings like eagles.*

CHAPTER 41

I continued to drag the gazelle toward my camp. By now much of the snow was gone. It had come quickly and now it departed quickly. By the time I reached camp, snow could only be found in the shadows under the trees and rocks and along the canyon walls that saw little sunlight. It left the ground a wet and sticky mud. Fortunately, I had made it back to camp before it was such a mess. I found my camp site in good order. The horse stood grazing in the little meadow still tied under the trees. She snickered as I approached. She appeared truly happy to see me. The air was still cool and as the end of the day approached it quickly became much colder. I had a terrible time relighting my fire as most of the wood was damp. I managed to pull old dead branches and sticks out of the standing trees which was considerably dryer than anything on the ground. After some effort, I had a roaring fire. Its warmth was welcomed and greatly appreciated. I warmed my hands and feet as I sat next to it. The horse nuzzled at my neck as she stepped closer.

That night I cooked the tenderloins taken from inside the gazelle's belly. The smell wafted through the canyon. My mouth watered in anticipation of the evening meal. I was not disappointed. The meat was juicy and tender. The fire added a sweet smoky taste. It was delicious. After the meal, I rolled out my bed roll and the new blanket. I undressed and hung my wet clothes near the fire in hopes that they might dry out by morning. I removed several hot stones from around the fire ring and placed them around my bed roll. At first, they were too hot, but they continued to radiate heat well into the night.

I held a smooth rock against my belly to warm my core and my hands. I fell asleep quickly and slept through most of the night.

Sometime in the darkest hours of the morning, I awoke. My heart was beating fast. A terrible heaviness fell over me. I couldn't explain it, but I was filled with anxiety and dread. I sat up but found no one there. I was alone, just me and the horse. I shivered as the cold penetrated to my bones. I placed several broken branches onto the coals and managed to coax the fire back to life. Its warmth was comforting. I lay awake, unable to go back to sleep. Time crawled. I stared up into the heavens that were visible between the canyon walls. I watched the slow progression of the night's sky. The constellation of the hunter, Kesil hung in the heavens high above me. The three stars of his belt shone brightly. He stood, his bow aiming an arrow across the great expanse. The Greeks and the Romans refer to the constellation as Orion. Their myth stories tell of their false gods and their adulterated lives. They claim Orion was a supernatural hunter, born of the sexual union between a Gorgon and Poseidon, the Greek god of the sea. The Amorite people of Syria call the constellation *Nephîlă'*, or the Nephilim. They claim Orion was the father of the Nephilim before the great deluge. I wondered if he was one of the Watchers. Had he stood on the peak of Mount Hermon and been part of their rebellious pact?

The Torah speaks of the constellation several times. It was mentioned in Amos and when the Lord questioned Job.

Can you bind the chains of the Pleiades?
Can you loosen Orion's belt?
Can you bring forth the constellations in their seasons or lead out the Bear with its cubs?
Do you know the laws of the heavens?

The three stars of his belt twinkled the brightest against the black veil. I thought of the lessons of Samuel and of all the nights spent out under the dark heavens. In the Greek myths, they recount the story of Orion in Crete. He hunted wild game with the goddess Artemis and her mother, Leto. In the course of their hunt, he boasted that he could kill every animal on earth. This enraged the mother earth goddess, Gaia. The story claims that Gaia sent a giant scorpion to kill Orion. After his death, Artemis asked Zeus to place Orion among the constellations. Zeus agreed, and as a memorial to the huntsman's death, he added the scorpion to the heavens as well. This story explains why the constellations of Orion and Scorpius are never in the night's sky at the same time. Samuel had taught me the stories of the night sky. As a child, we lay out under the stars. He used the Greek and Roman myths to help me identify the constellations and to navigate by them. He also taught me the difference between the myths of the unclean and the truth of God's word. I thought of all of those stories. I thought of the Greek name Orion and its meaning, the Light of Heaven, but I prefer the Hebrew *Kesil*, which derives from the word hope. I wondered at that moment, if maybe this was a sign, a sign from God, a message of hope; a hope for peace in my life or just maybe, a hope that God would soon deliver his children from the hands of their enemies.

I lay there for some time before sleep returned. Finally, I dozed off and fell into a deep sleep. I do not recall a dream, but something startled me awake just before dawn. I sat up and recognized a sweet smell. It was carried on a gentle breeze that swirled around me. The sound of rustling leaves filled the air. I recognized the faint smell of fresh flowers after a rain. The memory of a mountain meadow filled my mind. I was briefly taken back to Mount Hermon. In my mind, I walked the hillsides in the late springtime as the alpine flowers began to bloom. I could see them before me as they painted the meadow with splashes of yellow, purple, and blue. The pleasant feeling of contentment and peace fell upon me. It filled my soul. Bitter cold filled the air. It was considerably colder than the night's chill and the warmth of my fire was overcome. A smoky cloud of steam escaped from my lips as my breath froze. Another scent filled my nostrils. I expected it this time. I looked forward to it. The aura overwhelmed the fragrance of the flowers. It was a pleasant but musky smell. It was the sweet aroma of sweat against her naked body. It was the essence of a sweet perfume. All of my senses were aroused. It had a familiar and intimate characteristic. No doubt existed in my mind. It was the distinct scent of my beloved.

"Melessa?" I called out.

There was no answer. A strange preternatural silence fell across the little valley. The sounds of the night fell silent. Not a creature stirred. No crickets, no birds or owls, no wolves or jackals howled in the distance. Only the frigid air and the stars shone above. The mare stirred at the unsettling disturbance.

"Is that you my love?"

No answer. I lay there motionless, waiting for the inevitable. Nothing happened. The chill grew colder. "My love," I called out, but this time barely above a whisper, "Melessa."

In the rising smoke of the fire, a thick cloud formed. It slowly turned forming a swirling column of smoke. It drew hot embers upward. They burned with tiny flames and swarmed like glowing fireflies. Tiny trails of fire followed each. Faint azure light began to glow. The cloud was illuminated from within and cast a soft blue light. Strange shadows crawled. The burning embers swam slowly. In the farthest reaches of my mind's eye, I saw my beloved Melessa standing within the smoke. She was as beautiful as ever. My heart was filled with a burning desire to hold her once more. With the voice of an angel she whispered, "Barabbas, son of thy father, my beloved."

Her voice was as sweet as honey. It echoed through my heart as tears filled my eyes. A lump arose in my throat. I could hardly swallow. My mouth was as dry as the desert sand. I tried to speak but the words stuck in my throat. I forced the words from me. "My love."

"Barabbas, it is time."

"I don't want to go," I said. Panic began to rise. A fear of the unknown, a fear of impending danger began to crush me.

"You have a purpose. You have been chosen, Barabbas. You are the light."

"What if I refuse? What if I refuse to be your purpose?" Surprising even myself, an anger flared up inside of me. An anger at the unfairness of it all, an anger at the world, an anger at Melessa, and an anger at the Lord.

"Son of thy father, it is inevitable. You have a destiny to fulfill. Your time has come."

"No!" I shouted. The words echoed off of the canyon walls.

I lept to my feet and stood facing the apparition of my dead wife. My fists were clenched tight in anger. The fingernails bit into the palms. Fire raged inside of me consuming my very soul. The cloud of smoke continued to turn and emit its strange blue light. It grew brighter and the image of Melessa became clearer. She stood within the fire. She was stunning. I gazed upon her perfect naked form. Her soft curves were obscured, yet her skin glistened with a sensual sweat. Her wild curly hair moved in a nonexistent breeze. Light ringlets danced across her face. My eyes were drawn to a single lock that gently caressed its way down her long slender neck and across her breasts. She held her head high and proud. Sharp cheekbones softened her other features. She was as lovely as ever. Something sacred radiated from within. An inner beauty lit her eyes. It shined. Her eyes revealed her soul. They were deep pools of a captivating green, the color of polished jade. They were an ocean of endless joy. As I looked into those eyes I knew, all the beauty of the universe could not compare with the love and joy that filled her soul. It was an everlasting hope.

I was overcome with emotion. The anger and fury that had fueled my hatred for so many years faded away. I regretted my bitterness. I longed for the days gone by. I longed to be with her. I began to weep. Hot tears stung my eyes. My beloved stepped out of the fire. The swirling cloud of smoke followed her. She stepped toward me. She stood naked revealing all of her beauty. A strange ethereal glow surrounded her. She was so provocative and tempting that it ached. Desire burned within me. She reached out and touched my face. The touch was so delicate. The soft caress of her fingers was surprisingly warm. I burned with a hunger. She smiled. The slight curve of her full plump lips was seductive. I wanted to reach out and touch them. I wanted to taste them. I wanted to fall into them. I was spellbound. Something so magically alluring radiated from Melessa. Even in death, I wanted to be with her. I wanted to join her. I would have gladly given up my own life at that very moment to spend eternity with her. She pressed hard against me. The curves of her body firm and warm. She was deliciously inviting. Her breath was of lilac with a hint of cinnamon. Our lips met. She kissed me. Her lips were hot and wet. It was a hungry kiss filled with passion and desire. She pulled me closer. An ecstasy crashed over me. It was magic and it took my breath away.

Without warning, my beloved wife melted into me. The glowing cloud evaporated, and the blue light was extinguished. I felt her essence pass through my very soul. It burned through my veins and spread like a raging wildfire. I was filled with every kind of emotion imaginable but love prevailed. An overwhelming sense of love, a sense of joy and hope filled my heart. My wife was love.

A musical voice whispered in my ear, "My love, you have a purpose. You are the light."

With that final word, a bitterly cold breeze pushed through my camp. The flames of my fire danced violently and she was gone. I stood alone. Only the scent of flowers remained. Hot tears streamed down my cheeks.

CHAPTER 42

I did not sleep the rest of the night. I sat next to the fire mesmerized as to the events of the evening. The yellow tongues of the fire danced where my wife had once stood. Smoke rose into the night's sky, but without further incident. The haunting occurrence played over and over in my mind. Each time was sweeter than the last. I was obsessed with the moment and I feared losing it. I held on tightly. I could still taste my beloved's sweet lips. They dripped with honey and exotic spices. Her memory was a fire reborn within my heart. I thought of her words, "You have a purpose. You have been chosen, Barabbas. You are the light." I contemplated those words and their meaning. A sense of dread and fear surrounded those words. Yet it conflicted with the feeling of joy and happiness that had invaded my soul with her kiss, that feeling of hope. All of my sadness, all of my worries had disappeared. All of my anger and hate. This was the same experience I had when I touched the hand of the Lord. It was an eternal love. It washed away all of the darkness, all of the sadness from my heart. For that one moment, all of the troubles of this world evaporated. I had been given a gift, a second chance and a change of heart…and I would cherish it for eternity.

I sat and watched as the night was chased away by the encroaching light. The eastern sky began to glow as spears of orange painted the horizon. They grew into massive golden columns that reached across the heavens. The darkness faded away. The great sphere of molten gold soon followed. Its brilliance too bright to look upon. I prepared a breakfast of dried dates and acacia tea. I also ate a little more of the gazelle before I broke camp. The mare and I were soon on our journey back toward Geba. I had tied the antelope across the back of her rump laying across the saddle bags. I was concerned that the horse might protest carrying a dead animal, but she accepted it with grace. We followed a similar trail back but managed to find an easier ascent out of the steep draw. Escaping the canyon, the travel was considerably easier as we crossed the rolling hills and the plains. Very little evidence of snow remained anywhere. A few shaded areas still held small drifts, but for the most part it was as if it had never happened. Yet this dry and arid land drank it up with an intense eagerness. It was thankful. The hill country seemed to come alive. The wilderness was transformed, if only for a short time.

I continued to ride for most of the day. I traveled Southeast. I began to recognize more and more of the hills and ravines. Approaching the town, a strange smell was carried on the southern wind. It was that of a fire, yet not of a grass fire. It was strangely different. I noticed the smell seemed to intensify the further I traveled. In the distance, lay the broad place in the Wadi Suwenit, the Pass. Geba lay just beyond. Yet, something was wrong. A sick feeling befell me. It was a heaviness that weighed on my very soul. I can't explain it, but a terrible feeling of dread burdened me. It conflicted with the hope and joy that I had found the night before. I became ever so vigilant and alert to any danger. I scanned the hills for any enemy but saw none. I continued onward, but subconsciously I feared what lay ahead. I noticed the smell of smoke became stronger. It was an intense acrid smell. A terrible omen revealed itself. Two large ravens flew over me. Two more. They were huge. Their feathers as black as midnight. They made no sound as they passed just inches above my head. They flew toward the south, toward Geba. They disappeared over the hills that lay just in front of me. The smoke grew stronger. I kicked the horse and she began to trot at a quicker pace.

Avoiding the Pass, I crossed the Wadi Suwenit further to the west. It was steep and rough, but the mare managed to ascend a gentle slope that climbed out of the draw. From there a ridge and hills obscured the view of the town. When I reached the last of the hills that provided a protected view, I dismounted and tied my horse near a large boulder. Quickly I buckled my sword around my waist, and I slung my quiver across my back. I climbed to the top of the hill careful not to expose my silhouette against the setting sun. There I found several large white boulders. They stood like misshapen guardians overlooking the valley below. They glowed orange in the setting sunlight. A single black raven sat atop one of the stones. It stared onto the plains below. From my vantage point, I got my first sight of Geba in days. I was horrified at what I saw. Several buildings burned. Smoke rose into the evening sky. The sounds of panicked cries rose with it. The village was filled with Roman soldiers. The final rays of sunlight glinted off of their weapons. A feeling of nausea rose inside of my bowels. I fought back the urge to vomit. I stared into the darkening skies above the village. A hundred ravens eerily circled the chaos below.

Oh my God, I thought, s*ave your people. Damn your enemies. Damn them to Hell.* But the Lord did not answer. He was silent. I watched as Rome flexed its might and crushed the weak. They inflicted pain upon the innocent. Rage overflowed within me, but sorrow crushed me. I remained helpless. There was nothing I could do. I slumped to the ground next to one of the boulders and I wept. I wept for the women and children. I wept for the families. I wept for the old and the young. I wept for the fathers. And I wept for myself.

I sat there for hours and watched the ruin of Geba. Darkness brought the cold. I pulled my cloak tight and longed for the blanket still on the horse. The night enveloped the land. The quarter moon rose in the Eastern sky as the stars burned against a black curtain. A brilliant sky filled the heavens while death and destruction lay below it. *How had I arrived here? What had brought me to this place?* I found myself perched in a cleft in the rocks set above the small village. *Was this my purpose? Was this my destiny?*

Next to me sat the massive raven. It had not moved since I had arrived. It was a statue, a pillar of concentration. It was larger than an eagle. Its black feathers darker than the surrounding night. It sat perched on the rock and was fixated on the village. We both stared into the ruined Geba below. Roman soldiers ravaged the poor people of this country village. Women screamed and wailed as their men were savagely beaten. The cries of the little children rose up the canyon walls and echoed through the hill country of Ephraim. I watched in horror. The raven watched with no emotion at all. It simply stared. From time to time it turned toward me. It cocked its head and its yellow eyes locked with mine. The raven acknowledged my presence. The wicked creature nodded as if we shared a common thread, as if we were brothers both aware of a secret knowledge hidden to all mankind and shared with no one else alive.

Several buildings burned. The flames illuminated the night providing me a glimpse into the travesty below. The people stood huddled together in groups near the city's entrance. Soldiers surrounded them. Torches wandered through the streets, I assumed searching for other people. Screams and shouts of terror had subsided, but the wails of women and children still could be heard. The soldiers controlled everything. They brought terror and fear to the poor people of Geba. This was an added insult after their treatment under the Publicani, Barak ben Nekifi. *This was my fault. I should have killed the Publicani when I had the chance. I should have killed him and his guards. I should have drug them into the wilderness for the jackals and wolves to eat. The maggots would have feasted. But instead, my pride misled me. My misjudgment doomed the town.*

I continued to watch, sickened by my decisions. Guilt crushed me. It rushed through my veins, like ice water. Standing outside of a burning home, the commanding officer was silhouetted before the flames. He stared up into the dark hills where I lay hiding like a coward. He searched the hills for any sign of movement. Once, his eyes fell upon the rocks where I lay. He stared for several minutes. I dared not move. I could feel his eyes searching the darkness. He looked away. I watched as this man walked to the city gates. He stood in the open and began to call out. Shouting to the surrounding ridges, he screamed into the night. One single word echoed through the darkness. One word that would change my life forever. He screamed out, "Barabbas!"

I remained silent. The raven turned to me, cocked its head and nodded. I heard it again. The commander shouted, "Barabbas! I shall spare the town if you will surrender."

Both fear and hatred returned within me. I remained in the dark. The darkness hid me. It protected me. The night surrounded me and kept me safe. A small voice, one of reason urged me to remain, to remain in the darkness.

It urged me to survive, to live another day. I would seek vengeance on these Romans. And not only on the Romans, but on the traitors to God. Retribution would be mine. I would make them pay. I vowed at that moment that I would hunt down the Publicani, Barak ben Nekifi and I would find the High Priest himself. I would cut his heart out. Both fear and hatred burned within me, yet it was trampled by my guilt.

Something more bizarre happened. Another voice spoke quietly in my ear. Startled, I turned to find that it was the raven. Its yellow eyes stared into mine. They blinked once. Its black beak reflected the glow of the fires from the town below. To my surprise, the raven spoke, "Barabbas, Son of thy Father, you are the light. Be the light." It took my breath away, for it was the voice of my beloved wife.

The raven spread its wings and flew off into the night. I was left alone. The commander shouted into the darkness, "Barabbas! I shall spare the town if you will surrender."

I hesitated for a moment. Time stopped. The earth stood still. That one moment lasted an eternity. Overcoming my fear, courage rose within me. I returned his call, "How do I know?"

Almost immediately he replied, "You have my word."

"Spare the people of Geba," I shouted.

"My word has been given. No harm will come to them"

I stood from my hiding place behind the rocks. I scrambled to the top of the hill and retrieved my horse from the other side. I did not ride her, rather I walked beside the mare as if we were old friends, old friends who would never see each other again. A bitter sadness filled my heart. I rubbed her neck as we walked. We descended the gentle slope that brought us to the town. The Romans stood with the commander waiting at the city gates. They did not move. My legs became wooden and a lump rose in my throat. For the first time in my life, I felt completely alone. A fear rose up inside of me, a fear of the unknown, a fear that my life would soon come to an end. I was filled with regret.

The commanding officer stepped forward. He wore a richly ornamented metal cuirass. It was the color of gold and it reflected the fire of the torches.

He removed his helmet. He carefully ran his hand down the red crest. "You are Barabbas?"

"I am," I answered.

Without any emotion, he replied, "You are under arrest for rebellion and insurrection against the Empire."

And with those words, several soldiers pounced on me. They knocked me to the ground and disarmed me. One took my sword and dagger, while another tried to remove my quiver. The strap became entangled around my shoulder and neck. It dug into my throat as they pulled at it. They punched and kicked me until it tore free. I did not resist. It would be futile, but the soldiers beat me anyway. One punched me in the face. A bright light flashed behind my eyes. Pain seared through me. I struggled to remain conscious as several more blows fell to my head.

Blackness began to overtake me. The flap of a raven's wing brushed across my face. Momentarily, I escaped. I was not in my body. I felt no pain. I was floating in an ethereal cloud. I found myself sitting on a bolder, along the edge of a mountain lake. The image of the snow capped peak of Mount Hermon lay perfectly reflected in the water below. My entire life flashed across the water's surface. I was a child. Mother and Papa were there. They smiled at me. The Romans came. A black raven flew past. Samuel and Ruth crossed quickly. Samuel held a scroll. It immediately turned to a sword. They both bowed before Melessa. She was beautiful. She wore her wedding dress. Jarviss was kneeling beside her dead body. Tears streamed down his face. Ravens scattered. My rage exploded as I watched myself beat the soldiers to their deaths. Their blood spilled across the summit of Mount Hermon. Snow and ice pelted me. It blinded me. I stood among Jair and the Sicarii. Their daggers dripped with blood. Mine, more than any other. I found myself standing at the foot of the Great Pyramid in Egypt. Nicolas was there with a camel. It was laden with bags of spices. The scent of cinnamon wafted through the air. Someone called my name. As I turned, I was greeted by Netikerty. She was radiant. She handed me my dagger. She watched as I cut the scar-faced man's throat. His blood spilled across the lake turning the waters red. It formed a river. Several ravens emerged from it, like birds bathing in a pool.

They immediately flew away. The body of Fisel floated to the surface. John stood next to me as we pulled him from the river. The hawkish man also emerged from the river. His demon shadowed him. They towered above me. I felt myself being lifted and thrown to the ground. Pain racked my body. Without warning, the hooded stranger knelt over me. Peace fell upon me. That familiar haunting returned. *Who was he?* A lion roared as loud as thunder. It stood behind him. The beast stood next to the hooded man. It was the lion from my dream. He was the hooded man. He called to me, "Son of thy father, you have a purpose. You are the light." Feelings of hope and joy returned. They erased the fear, the anguish, the hatred that I felt. It was love.

Another blow struck the back of my head. Pain brought me back to Geba. One soldier stood with a knee in my back as another pressed my face into the ground. Rocks and gravel dug into my cheeks. They wrenched my arms behind me. Pain shot through both shoulders, but I did not cry out. My hands were bound behind my back. The ropes tied wickedly tight. My hands numbed and my fingers turned cold. A noose slipped over my neck.

The Romans led me away into the darkness of the night. The cries of the women sang out. With the rope around my neck, I was led like an animal to the altar. We marched through the night toward Jerusalem and toward my destiny. I had become the sacrifice. Geba was safe. The people of Geba had been spared.

This was my purpose. For this, I was born. Yet, little did I know the horror awaiting ahead.

EPILOGUE

Professor Hershel D. Moussaieff stood and stretched his back. It was tight and stiff. He twisted. Several pops escaped his spine. Hershel realized that he had not been home to his apartment in three days. But what was there to go home to? Just an empty two room apartment. He hated it anyway. It was sad and lonely. No one came to visit. They hated it too. He hadn't seen his grandson in a month. A pang of sadness washed over him. He was filled with self-loathing. *I must remedy that,* he thought.

Turning, he noticed the family picture that stood on his desk. The whole family stared into the camera's lens and smiled. It was a scene from happier days. He thought of Deborah. It had been 6 months since the divorce was final. Bitter resentment rose up inside of him. He could taste it like bile in the back of his throat. After all, he had done everything for her. That was why he worked so hard. She was the reason he got up every morning. His resentment faded. It was replaced with sadness and a feeling of failure. His wonderful life had turned into a disappointment. Hershel let out a deep sigh. He was exhausted. Now all he had left were the scrolls.

Hershel removed his white cotton gloves. He laid them on the corner of the table. Stretched out before him was an ancient scroll. It was darkened from age. He admired it. It was beautiful. In fact, it was precious. It lay against a white sterile background. The ancient symbols rose to the surface revealing their long-hidden secret. The animal skin parchment was brittle and as fragile as glass. The ragged edges of broken and shattered pieces lay together like a jigsaw puzzle. It had taken months, in fact, almost a year to unroll the scrolls. Hershel and his team at the Hebrew University had used mechanical techniques to unroll the delicate pieces of ancient history. Working away in a climate controlled environment providing a relatively high humidity rate, they treated the parchment scrolls and fragments with various methods in order to not only soften the skin but to preserve them as well. They were physically unrolled. It was a slow and tedious process. One that demanded patience and perseverance. Once unrolled, it was compared to the original sampling of the database that had been established earlier through the use of infrared spectroscopy and particle induced X-ray emissions. After that, began the stoic process of translating the text. Hershel was old school. He preferred the paper and pencil method. Being an expert in both Greek and Aramaic, he translated each and every word, each and every sentence in its context. He knew about the newer computerized methods. He just didn't trust computers. He also refused to delegate such an important task to a grad student or even a colleague. He had seen too many mistakes, too many mistranslations in his time. Hershel would complete this task himself.

At first, he had questioned the scrolls. He questioned the validity. He questioned their authenticity. We wondered if they were a hoax. Yet, sophisticated dating methods placed them in the middle of the first century right at the time they claimed. He flipped through several pages of his notebook. The story that it revealed was beyond belief. He continued to be astonished. Each and every day the story became more fantastic. Each day it led him down another rabbit hole and into another world. Surely these were the lunatic rantings of a man who had lost his grip on reality? The writings of a delusional and sick mind? The writings of a twisted imagination? All of the symptoms were there. Surely, this was a man who suffered from a personality disorder.

Hershel flipped through several pages of his notebook. He read of the ravens and the demons that haunted Barabbas. He read of his dreams and his struggles. He was not schizophrenic as Barabbas showed no symptoms. He also showed no signs of Multiple Personality Disorder. He did however, experience the paranormal. Hershel thought to himself, *We all live in our own stories. We each live in our own construct of this world. We each see the world through our own eyes, as we expect to see it , as we want to see it.* He ran his fingers through his hair. He rubbed his chin. He had not shaved in a week. Studying his book, Hershel noted the attention to detail that the author had given. The professor was filled with intrigue. He was filled with a fascination along with a million questions. He contemplated this mystery but sought the answer to just one question. *Was it true?* A natural born skeptic and a man of science, at first, he doubted the words that he read. Yet, the details and the historical truth was crying out to him. It shouted! Now he doubted his doubt.

He asked himself if this was a man suffering from a mental illness. Could it be the terrifying struggle of a paranoid mind? It had all the indications of a personality disorder. The professor was empathetic, as he too struggled with his own feelings of paranoia, his own demons. He thought of his own plight. He considered his own mind. He thought of the large black ravens that constantly stalked him and that strange feeling of being watched from the dark shadows. He thought of the nightmares that plagued him each night. It had progressively grown worse over the last several years. He thought of Deborah. He thought of his failed marriage. Had his paranoia caused the rift? Had his obsessive personality caused their break up? *Maybe*, he thought. He had noticed her distancing herself, but in fact, it had all started with the discovery of the scrolls, those damn scrolls.

Hershel looked at his watch. It was 2:38 a.m. He yawned. He glanced toward the window. Nothing but the night lay beyond. Something moved. It caught his eye. Hershel approached cautiously. Black against black. More movement. Outside of the window stood a massive raven. It was magnificent. It stood on stiff legs. Talons like razors gripped the window sill. Moonlight reflected an ethereal glow off of glossy black feathers; its monstrous head was proud. It cut a regal profile against the illuminated clouds of the moonlit sky. Hershel noticed a glint reflecting from its beady eyes. They shined as they darted back and forth with malice. There was no doubt that this creature was watching him. It opened its mouth and emitted a high pitch screech. Hershel stumbled backwards alarmed. Thankful for the double glazed pane of security glass, he reached out and touched the window. The glass had been designed to provide maximum protection against attacks and to protect the priceless artifacts stored within. The raven became silent. It slowly swiveled its neck from left to right. The raven now stared directly at the professor. Their eyes met. He expected another shriek; but instead, it closed its mouth. Its jaws coming together to form a sharp black beak. It was wickedly pointed, a nasty weapon. Mindful that he was safe inside, Hershel gave the glass a playful little tap. The creature hissed and struck the glass with a mighty blow. *Whack!* A crack spider-webbed from that spot. The raven turned its back. With a fluid motion, it pushed its taloned feet off of the sill. Enormous wings extended outward as it leaped into the night's breeze. Rattled, Hershel caught his breath. He stared in amazement as he lost sight of it. *Oh my God!* he thought. Revelation and disbelief wrestled within his mind. Still shaken from the strange experience, he peered out the window. The distinctive crack pattern remained. Its diced fragmentation impossible, but it was there. Hershel touched the glass, running his finger along the fracture. He didn't see the other eyes that watched him from the darkness. A cold chill ran down his spine. Hershel breathed. He slid his cotton gloves back on. He sat down and began translating the text once more.

For there was more to be revealed. This was not the end.

MESSAGE FROM THE AUTHOR

Thank you for allowing me to share my story with you. I truly hope that you enjoyed it. The fourth part of this tale should be forthcoming soon. If you did enjoy the story, please do me a favor. Tell your family and friends about it. I would also love to hear your feedback. Please leave reviews at Amazon, Barnes and Noble, and Good Reads.

Thank you,
Kevin L. Brooks

https://www.thelostgospelofbarabbas.com/

Made in the USA
Coppell, TX
30 November 2021

66778632R00164